"Fans of historical fiction romance novels will be delighted to read the arch of Sophie and Joe's love."

The Book Life Prize

"Deeply moving and emotionally intoxicating, Dare Not Tell is a tale of love, loss, and redemption, a story of one man's struggle to leave the past behind. The writing is replete with vivid descriptions and the kind of drama that keeps readers turning the pages. It is skillful, balanced, and emotionally rich."

Ruffina Oserio for Readers Favorite, Five Star Review

"I adored the way Elaine Schroller explores the protagonist's inner world, allowing Joe's anguish and pain to come across in the writing with unusual vividness. In Dare Not Tell, Elaine Schroller unfurls a gripping, emotionally and psychologically rich narrative that explores trauma from a unique perspective."

Christian Sia for Readers Favorite, Five Star Review

"The characters are deeply flawed, believable, and elaborately written; they instantly pull the reader in and it is easy to feel a strong connection with them. The author writes brilliantly about the experience of war, love, loss, and the quest for redemption. Dare Not Tell is an affecting tale, deftly plotted and expertly executed."

Romuald Dzemo for Readers Favorite, Five Star Review

"Dare Not Tell by Elaine Schroller is a wonderfully written piece that exposed me to the true horrors of the Great War and the two decades that followed it. The empathy and sorrow that Schroller created within Joe's life were beautifully described and portrayed the terror of war."

Joanne Ang for Readers Favorite, Five Star Review

"Author Elaine Schroller tells an engaging tale about a couple of star-crossed lovers who find comfort and solace in each other's company at some of their lowest points in life. I had a wonderful time reading Dare Not Tell, and I would highly recommend it to other readers who enjoy historical fiction and romance novels."

Pikasho Deka for Readers Favorite, Five Star Review

DARE

Not

TELL

ELAINE AUCOIN SCHROLLER

"The Things We Dare Not Tell" by Henry Lawson was originally published in 1905 and is now in the public domain. See http://gutenberg.net.au/ebooks20/2000801h.html#TheThingsWeDareNotTell

ISBN 979-8-9852616-0-8: eBook
ISBN 979-8-9852616-1-5: Paperback

Cover design: Jenny Quinlan, Historical Fiction Book Covers

Cover images: © Mark Owen/Arcangel (soldier); @huseyintunser/iStock (poppy field)

eBook and paperback formatting: Suzanne Minae

DEDICATION

To Gary, who I'll always want to go forward, and home, with.
To Cass, who set me on the path that started it all.
To Lyn, who held my hand through every step and stumble.

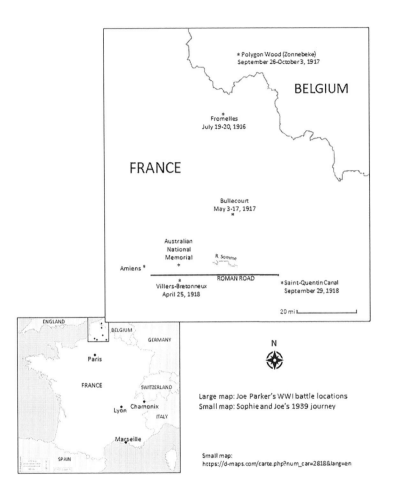

* Polygon Wood (Zonnebeke)
September 26-October 3, 1917

BELGIUM

*
Fromelles
July 19-20, 1916

FRANCE

Bullecourt
May 3-17, 1917
*

Australian
National
Memorial
+

R. Somme

Amiens *

ROMAN ROAD

*
Villers-Bretonneux
April 25, 1918

* Saint-Quentin Canal
September 29, 1918

20 mi ।

ENGLAND

BELGIUM

GERMANY

Paris

FRANCE

SWITZERLAND

Lyon Chamonix

ITALY

Marseille

SPAIN

N

Large map: Joe Parker's WWI battle locations
Small map: Sophie and Joe's 1939 journey

Small map:
https://d-maps.com/carte.php?num_car=2818&lang=en

EPIGRAPH

More than kisses, letters mingle souls.

John Donne

PART ONE

The fields are fair in autumn yet, and the sun's still shining there,
But we bow our heads and we brood and fret, because of the masks we wear;
Or we nod and smile the social while, and we say we're doing well,
But we break our hearts, oh, we break our hearts! for the things we must not tell.

Henry Lawson, "The Things We Dare Not Tell"

ONE

THE INVITATION

Sophie Parker needed a stiff drink and a long, hot bath. Her day had been challenging: constant London drizzle, overcrowded taxi stands, tedious errands taking longer than they should have. Then there was the letter that had been delivered while she was out. Envelopes bearing the return address of the Australian War Graves Commission weren't typical for their daily post. It must be something about Joe's brother. Please, please, let it say they'd found Robbie's remains. Finally. After twenty-two years.

She sank into the bathtub, hot water easing the minor aches from carrying too many parcels while wearing heels that were an inch too high. A deep breath, and then another, and fragrant bubbles cleared the soot and petrol fumes she had breathed all day. Bliss. She reached for the little tub-side table, knowing the first sip of whiskey and soda was going to be marvelous....

Darn it. Her drink was still in the bedroom.

With any luck, Joe would arrive soon. He could bring her drink and they would uncover the mystery of whatever was in that envelope.

Her husband's voice sounded outside the bathroom door sooner than she expected. "I'm back."

"Come in, darling. Have you finished at Scotland Yard?"

Joe loosened his tie and unbuttoned his collar as he strode to the tub to greet her properly. "Yes, I have. And you must have just started. I'll leave you to it." He kissed her lips lightly and lifted a finger of lavender-scented bubbles to her nose.

She reached out and tugged his hand. "Don't leave," she said, brushing the bubbles off her nose with her other hand. "Get undressed and join me."

He cocked a brow as if pretending to consider her offer. The first time she suggested he join her in the bath, he blushed and admitted he had never bathed with anyone before. "Shall I bring you a drink?"

"You brilliant man. I knew there was a reason I love you. I was in such a rush to get the day's grime off that I left my glass on the dressing table. There's a letter there for you, too."

She heard paper tearing, presumably the envelope being opened, and then hangers sliding in the wardrobe as Joe undressed. When he reappeared with her drink, she fluttered her eyelashes at him and hummed appreciatively as he shrugged off his dressing gown.

"Move up." He gave her the glass to hold while he maneuvered his lean frame into the tub behind her. She leaned back against him, and they shared the drink and soaked in silence for a few minutes until she couldn't bear the suspense any longer.

She wanted to see his reaction to her question, so she turned in the big tub to face him. "What was in the letter? Have they found your brother?"

"No…. It's an invitation to visit the Australian war memorial at Villers-Bretonneux. It's the one-year anniversary of the dedication."

"Oh." Joe's jaw had tightened as he spoke. They hadn't been able to travel from their home in Sydney to France for the dedication of the memorial last year. The names of the missing,

Robbie's included, were carved on the memorial's walls. She did a quick calculation. "We could leave Paris a day earlier than planned."

"Villers-Bret isn't a place I thought I'd ever go back to."

Joe took a sip of their drink, but his jaw stayed tight after he swallowed. He fought there in 1918. He had written to her afterward, a brief note about being promoted to captain and going to England for training, but he had never spoken to her about the battle. All she knew for certain was he was more tense on the anniversary of that battle than any of the others he had fought in, even the one where he'd been wounded.

"We don't have to go if you don't want to."

Joe was staring at a point over her shoulder. Was he even listening? Perhaps visiting the memorial was a bad idea.

To give him time to let the idea of going back sink in, she turned her attention to the two healed bullet wounds on his shoulder. In twenty-five years of police work in Australia, Joe had avoided serious injury until a drug raid in February. His men were unharmed, but he had been shot twice in the left shoulder. She ran her fingers over the scars, grateful she hadn't lost him when the gunman panicked and fired three shots.

She shifted to the smaller, finer scar from the third bullet that had grazed his temple, running her fingers through his hair to see it better.

Joe pulled back and eyed her warily. "Do I pass inspection, nurse? Or have I sprouted more grey hairs?"

She rolled her eyes at him. He was almost forty-seven years old, so a little grey mixed with the brown was to be expected. She thought it made him look dashing, and she'd told him so many times. Still, it wouldn't do to let him fret about it. She combed his hair back into place with her fingers. "I pronounce you fully healed, and able to assume the duties of a man on a much-needed holiday."

For several moments, Joe seemed fascinated by swirling the whiskey in their glass, but he was matter of fact when he came back to the present. "What do you reckon?" he asked. "Three hours from Paris to Villers-Bret, and spend the night in Amiens? Then what? Drive back to Paris and then to Lyon?"

That was interesting. Was Joe agreeing just to humor her or had his desire to honor his brother's memory overruled any hesitation he felt about returning to Villers-Bretonneux? "Probably. We need to check the map. There may be a better route than back-tracking to Paris."

"Right. Let's make that one change and keep everything else from Lyon the same. We can stick with our plan to visit the Roman ruins in Provence on our way to Marseille." He seemed perfectly calm as he smoothed the bubbles from her shoulders. "You still haven't told me what you did today."

Joe wasn't acting like he had any reservations about the itinerary change, so she forged ahead. "I finalized our travel arrangements. We sail from Marseille to Sydney on August 4th. Tomorrow evening we'll board the Night Ferry at Victoria Station. It's a sleeper train that goes to Dover. The cars go straight onto the ferry and *voilà,* on Wednesday morning we'll step off the train at the Gare du Nord in Paris. We'll finally have our honeymoon in Paris."

Paris, Joe thought as he leaned back in the tub. The first stop on our journey home. God, they'd been away a long time.

He had enjoyed their round the world trip and the opportunity to advance his professional interests immensely, but they'd been traveling for several months now, and the longer they were gone, the more he felt like he was losing track of time and days. He hadn't been away from work so long since the war. London had been a chance to reset his frame of mind. He had a place to go every morning that felt like work. English customs and colleagues felt almost like home. If he was honest, he had enjoyed the work parts of this trip at least as much as the traveling and sightseeing.

As much as he enjoyed being in new places, he didn't really like traveling, at least not as much as they'd done on this trip. Being constantly on the move—living out of suitcases and sleeping in unfamiliar rooms—was grueling. He missed reading in his study, puttering in their garden, rowing on Sunday mornings. He missed watching boats from their verandah overlooking Sydney Harbour and waking up to lorikeets chattering in the tree outside their bedroom window.

He even missed being able to buy a pie for lunch from the cart outside the police station if he wanted one.

He stifled a snort at that idea. He was an idiot if he'd rather have a gristly pie than the trip of a lifetime with a woman he adored and who, for some unknown reason, professed to adore him. They'd seen and done things in parts of the world he only dreamed of as a lad—islands created from volcanoes in the Pacific Ocean. Crossing the great plains of North America. Ancient redwoods on one side of the continent, Niagara Falls on the other side.

His childhood dreams of travel had come true with Sophie, and now his dream of being in Paris again with her was finally going to come true as well.

Villers-Bret, though.

He'd been a good soldier, and a good officer. He'd done what he needed to do to win the battle there, fighting savagely and mercilessly, with no fear of losing his own life and no guilt for the lives he took.

When the war was over, he had pushed that part of himself away, told himself he'd done his duty for his country, for the men under his command, even for his brother Robbie, but he would not be that ruthless man again.

He had never wanted to return to any battlefield, and despite all the letters he and Sophie had exchanged during the war, he hadn't told her what had happened at Villers-Bret. The usual sense of guilt over that omission rose, and he shoved it down. She had been a wartime nurse and had seen the devastation men could visit on each other. Surely she understood some memories were better left buried, and some things were better left unsaid.

Sophie stood and said something about dinner in or out—he didn't catch all her words—transfixed as he was by the last of the bubbles slipping down her thigh. At forty-two, her breasts were a little fuller and her hips were a little rounder than when they first married seven years ago, but she was still the most glorious thing he'd ever seen.

He could do this. He could go back to Villers-Bretonneux. Then they could go home. Finally. But first, Paris.

TWO
BY THE EIFFEL TOWER
AUGUST 11, 1916, PARIS

Second Lieutenant Joe Parker jumped to the platform as the troop train shuddered to a stop at the Gare du Nord in Paris.

The four men under his command who accompanied him were determined to find feminine companionship. Davy and Sid strutted and leered at every woman who passed. Frankie's appraisal of the female form was more subtle. The three of them had promised Geordie he would not die a virgin and the poor lad was shaky with anticipation at the prospect of finally becoming a man.

Joe fervently hoped Geordie lived long enough to understand that being a man meant far more than a quick tumble. He clapped a hand on Geordie's thin shoulder. "Come with me instead if you want to," he muttered so only Geordie could hear. The boy flushed but shook his head, so Joe turned to the others. "Go on without me. I'll meet you back here tonight."

Davy eyed him in disbelief. "Are you sure, mate? You might never have the chance to enjoy the company of a Parisian mam'oelle again."

"I'm sure." Annie and Sam were twelve thousand miles away, and he missed them so much his chest hurt, but being unfaithful wouldn't ease that pain. "I might never have the chance to see Paris again."

Armed with his travel pass and map instead of his rifle and grenades, Joe set out to explore the city. Never in his wildest dreams had he ever imagined he would be in Paris. When he reached the River Seine, he slowed his steps from a rapid march to an amble. He spied the Eiffel Tower in the distance and followed the river to reach it, walking in the shade of trees that were whole and healthy and dozens of feet tall. The air smelled clean. Clear. Fresh. The scent of the river, not cordite and smoke, wafted on the warm breeze.

No explosions echoed in his ears either, only the babel of soldiers from around the world revolving around him. The tower, in use as a radio transmitter, was ringed by barbed wire and guards, but that hadn't deterred every soldier in Paris flocking to the surrounding park. Frenchmen in blue wool. Scotsmen in kilts. English and Canadians in uniforms very much like his. North Africans in flowing robes. Turbaned, bearded Sikhs. Japanese sailors with pom-pom hats. Two Māoris in their New Zealand uniforms nodded at him.

Animated young women hurried past him, chatting in rapid, fluid French. An ancient couple shuffled towards him, a string shopping bag holding their daily baguette and whatever cheese and produce they could afford at the market.

Children skipped and chased while their mothers chatted. Sam would have fit in this scene perfectly—some things were the same all over the world—and Joe smiled despite a pang of home-sickness.

Every so often, a little one tripped and fell and the inevitable cry of surprise, pain, and *Maman* rang out. When one particularly insistent cry produced no immediate sign of a mother, he helped a little lad to his feet and brushed the dirt off his knees. "*Ça va?*" he asked, feeling helpless because he knew so little French.

The boy's eyes widened at the big stranger crouched in front of him. His chin quivered. Joe removed his hat and wiggled his ears. The trick usually worked to distract Sam from tears or a tantrum. To his relief, tiny French boys found wiggling ears just as funny as little Australian boys did. The toddler's lips stopped trembling. He giggled.

A woman's panic-edged call sounded above their heads. She stood twenty feet away, twisting to the right and then to the left, the hem of her skirt brushing the parcels on the pavement next to her feet.

The little boy toddled toward her. Joe rose from his crouch and followed. He couldn't explain what had happened—his limited French vocabulary didn't include the words for '*He fell, and I found him crying,*'—but he could at least reunite a mother and her son.

She rushed to them, scolding and comforting the boy at the same time. "*Merci, monsieur,*" she said, smothering a giggle as he stumbled through, "*Je vous en prie, madame.*"

Holding the boy's hand to keep him close, she rose and studied the insignia—rays of sun extending from an imperial crown—pinned to his hat and lapels. "You're Australian!"

Still trying to retrieve every French word he knew, he blurted, "*Oui, je suis Australien,*" hoping he wasn't mangling the words. Opportunities to speak the phrases he'd learned during training had been rare.

She looked up at him, a sprinkling of freckles across her nose and stray tendrils of dark hair peeking from a small-brimmed hat. Merriment sparkled in the deepest brown eyes he'd ever seen. "Thank you for rescuing my runaway!"

His brain finally registered her words were in English and he returned to that language. "He reminds me of my boy." Sam started running only days after he took his first steps. His smile, a barely there lift of lips and left brow, transformed into a full grin at the memory. "He'll take off running every chance he gets."

The young woman stuck out her hand. "I'm Sophie Holt and this little man is Jean-Luc."

He was still so surprised by her perfect English that his manners failed him. "You're not French. You're…."

"American, with an English mother," she offered. "I was born in Australia, and I grew up all over. Now I live in Paris. I'm a nurse at the American Hospital here."

He absorbed the onslaught of information, analyzing as he listened. He had never spoken with an American before. Were all American women so forward and forthcoming? She was too young to be a nurse, and a mother, wasn't she? "And your husband is…?" He cast about for the most likely nationality. The boy's name was French, but her surname wasn't. Perhaps she hadn't taken her husband's name. "French?"

"Good heavens, no. I'm not married."

"But Jean-Luc looks just like you. Isn't he your son?"

"He's a darling boy," Sophie said, "but I'm only his godmother. His mother is my dear friend. She's a nurse, too. Her husband is French. While he's off fighting, I share their flat and help to look after Jean-Luc."

Sophie studied the man standing before her. He wasn't heart-breakingly young like most soldiers she'd met. A tiny nick marred his clean-shaven chin. His uniform was neat. His boots were clean and bore only a light coating of dust. He was present and correct, but there was something about his bearing that intrigued her. He was still, as if he was watching and waiting, not for the next shell to fall, but for whatever she would say next.

If the faint crease between his blue eyes was a clue, he was studying her, too. He had an ordinary face, serious and sober, but his wide smile earlier had transformed it to boyish. Trying to coax smiles from her patients had become second nature. She wondered if she could convince this man to smile again.

"When do you have to be at the train station?"

The crease deepened. "Why do you think I have to be at the train station?"

"It's an easy deduction. Soldiers are always going somewhere, aren't they?"

He nodded. "Too right."

Hmm. No smile yet. His Australian accent was lovely, though. She hadn't heard one since her family moved back to the States when she was a child. "Where have you come from?"

"Vignacourt. It's three hours east of here if the trains are running and you don't get sidetracked delivering troops and materiel."

Oh, Lord. Three hours east of here was Somme country. She'd heard there were a staggering fifty thousand Commonwealth casualties on the first day of the campaign last month. No wonder this man's smiles were few and far between. "Where are your friends? You didn't come to Paris alone, did you?"

"No, they're...well...let's say sightseeing wasn't on their minds when we arrived."

Aha! The corners of his eyes crinkled. Perhaps he would smile again after all. "You didn't want to go with them?"

"I'm married. They aren't."

Good. She enjoyed meeting new people, but she didn't have the patience to fend off advances from lonely young men who thought they were the answer to all her dreams. "If you have time before you have to meet them, come home with Jean-Luc and me and have a meal with us. It won't be much, but I can promise you it will be better than most places."

"That's…that's very kind of you, but I couldn't."

"Nonsense. Jean-Luc's mother Natalie and I often feed visiting soldiers. She'll want to thank you for helping her son."

"But you don't even know me. Should you be so trusting?"

"You helped a lost two-year-old boy. Aren't you trustworthy?"

"Well, yes, I am, but…."

The crease between the man's brows reappeared, deeper this time. To be fair, she'd offered a lot of information at once. She stuck out her hand again. "Let's start over, shall we? I'm Sophie Holt. And you are…?" She peered at the shoulders of his uniform jacket: one pip on each shoulder. "Second Lieutenant…?"

"Parker," he said, remembering his manners, and shaking her hand. "Joe Parker. Australian father, Australian mother, born in Australia. I spent all my life in Melbourne and now I live wherever the army tells me I live. I'm afraid I have a much less interesting life than yours, Miss Holt."

She glanced at the healing scrapes and cuts marking the back of Joe's hand. "You've been in battle recently, haven't you?"

His gaze dropped to his hand, and the crease deepened again. "How did you know?"

"I've seen many men come into the hospital only days, hours even, after battles." She resisted the urge to brush her gloved thumb over his hand before she released it. He was battered and bruised, but he wasn't bleeding. She didn't need to do a thorough inspection. "Their hands look rough, that's all."

"It was late last month, at a place called Fromelles. My first taste of action," he admitted. "I have no idea how I made it through. Was it just luck? I don't see how anyone's luck can hold out for long. How am I supposed to tell my wife—?" He stopped short, as if horrified he had admitted his feelings to a stranger. "Sorry. I didn't mean to rabbit on. Seems I'm not used to it all yet. My battalion only arrived in France two months ago."

Sophie watched Joe's expressions flicker from guarded to dismayed and back to guarded in only a few seconds. That's all it took for her to know he hadn't yet made the leap from thinking it was morally wrong to kill, to believing it was his duty to do so. Soldiers had to make that leap, or they wouldn't survive. Joe would make it soon enough, assuming he lasted that long.

"I don't know what a battle is like," she said, "but I understand your dilemma. I can't explain to my parents the awful things I see and do. They have no frame of reference for bullet and shrapnel wounds or shattered limbs or…. The best I can do is describe inconsequential things happening around me. I complain about the weather. I ask them to send me new slippers and more of my favorite toffees. I tell them about the bossy head nurse."

Joe was still so subdued that she redoubled her efforts to make him smile again. "I know! You could tell your wife about rescuing a little French boy, couldn't you?"

He flashed her an amused look with a hint of a smile.

"What do you do when you're not being ordered around by the army, Lieutenant Parker?"

"I'm ordered around by the Victoria Constabulary. I'm a police officer in Melbourne. As soon as I get home, I plan to study for the detective sergeant exams."

"A detective? I was right, wasn't I? You are trustworthy." The crinkles reappeared at the corners of his eyes, spurring her on. "Since I can't convince you to let me feed you a meal, can I convince you to join us for ice cream?"

He hesitated until she said, "Ice cream is Jean-Luc's favorite treat. Watch the little dance he does when I tell him we're going to have a *glace*."

Jean-Luc bounced excitedly on the balls of his little feet, waving his arms, and sing-songing, "*Glace, glace, glace!*"

A broad grin bloomed across Joe's features. She was so pleased she could have clapped.

"I reckon I have to say yes to a dancing kiddie, don't I?"

Sophie laughed, and Joe was glad of it. He couldn't remember the last time he'd heard a woman laugh. Annie, probably, and that was eight months ago.

While they waited their turn at the ice cream kiosk, Sophie answered his questions. Her father was an engineer; the family business was construction, mostly bridges and railways.

"Father likes the challenge of making things work," she said, "and Mother has an adventurous streak a mile wide. She told him she wasn't going to stay behind while he had fun building things around the world. My older brother and I were both born in Australia—Ben in Sydney, me in Ballarat. We had a marvelous time traveling and living in different places. California, Panama, London, and finally back to the States. Last year, Ben left university with a lot of other students to come over here and drive ambulances for the French."

Joe puzzled through that statement as they searched for an empty bench. "But America isn't in the war."

"Legally, Americans aren't supposed to fight for France because the US is neutral, but we can volunteer, and many of us are doing everything we can to help. Driving ambulances, trucks, even flying with the French. The American Hospital has been treating wounded French soldiers for two years already."

They found a bench in the shade, thankful for a respite from the heat, and settled Jean-Luc between them.

"Do you think there's a chance America will join the war?"

"We have to!"

Until now, Sophie had been so cheerful that the vehemence of her response surprised him. She had a wonderfully expressive face—first annoyed, then thoughtful, then resolute—as she worked through whatever she was going to say next. "Look what Germany has done to Europe in just two years! Belgium is in ruins. France is being crushed."

Her expression changed again, pride tinged with sadness, or sadness tinged with pride. He didn't know which. "Thousands of young men, including my brother, have already left American colleges and universities to volunteer for the French. We can't let the Allies do this by themselves," she declared, her lips setting into a determined line.

He hadn't known there were Americans who had volunteered. "You should be proud of what you and your brother are doing."

"I'm very proud of Ben, but I couldn't stay at home and let everyone else do all the work. I wanted to do my part, too. That's more than enough about me. Tell me about you and your family."

He blew out a breath. He'd been right earlier. His life wasn't nearly as exciting as hers was. "There isn't much to say. I have a brother too. Robbie. He's two years younger than I am." He shook his head, trying to figure out how to describe his often careless, occasionally cruel, brother. They'd fought constantly when they were younger.

"Robbie has guts, but sometimes he forgets to use his brains. I tried to look out for him after our father died when we were still just kids. Our mum runs a small brewery in Melbourne that her dad started when he came over from England. He signed up at the very beginning of the war, got sent to Turkey, and made it through Gallipoli."

Sophie cocked her head at him. "The French were there, too."

"Right. It's where the Australians and New Zealanders fought their first big battle. April 25th, last year. We call it Anzac Day now."

Recognition dawned on her face. "I've heard Anzac before. It means Australia New Zealand something. Sorry, I can't remember."

He glanced over at Sophie. The more he talked with her, the more impressed he was with the breadth of her interests. "Australian and New Zealand Army Corps. Anyhow, Robbie's in Belgium now."

"And what about your wife? Are you the sort of husband who insists the man should make all the money and decisions and…?"

He huffed a laugh before she could finish. "Annie would never let me get away with that. She and I decided we both had to do our bit. I'm here and she's volunteering wherever she's needed at home. Except I can't tell her what a waste it is. She's already lost one brother. I don't want her to be afraid all the time that something will happen to me, that she'll be left on her own."

He was still pondering his own mortality when Sophie asked, "When did you enlist?"

He normally didn't volunteer much personal information, but it was surprisingly easy to open up to this young woman. "I wanted to sign up in 1914 with Robbie and my friends. But police are a reserved occupation, and my superiors insisted the war would be over by Christmas. It was a letter from Robbie that convinced me. He wrote that things were getting worse and worse, so I decided to go." The letter from Robbie was without his usual *we're showing Johnny Turk what Aussies are made of* bravado. *We need your help, Joey. Bring your copper friends. Bring the crims too. There's no bloody way this thing will be over by this Christmas or the next.*

Sophie finished the last bite of her ice cream and patted her lips with a hanky she had tucked in her cuff. Jean-Luc chose that moment to wriggle down and chase a pigeon, and Joe paused to chase after Jean-Luc and resettle the boy on their bench. "Since I'm a copper, I had more skills than most of the others who enlisted with me. The recruiting officer mustered me in as a lance corporal instead of a private. That meant I had responsibility for nine men but no authority to get anything done."

Sophie glanced at the shoulders of his uniform. "You've been promoted to second lieutenant already."

He leaned forward on the bench. "My battalion was supposed to stay behind the front lines to study the terrain and practice the skills we'd learned at training camp. Then someone at headquarters had the bright idea to ask for a handful of junior officers and lance corporals to get a bit of fighting experience. I like to know what I'm up against, so I volunteered."

He fell silent. The minute he scrambled over the parapet he knew the battle was going to be a slaughter. Bloody hell, they were attacking over open ground in broad daylight. All the Germans had to do was shoot. They didn't even need to use the sights on their weapons.

He'd been certain he would be buried alive by massive chunks of dirt raining down from the artillery bombardments or riddled with bullets trying to get past the barbed wire and shell holes separating his trench and the German trench. Between the fifth and fiftieth time he dove into the dirt to avoid becoming yet another casualty, he had tamped down his terror and concentrated on a rhythm of slithering forward, aiming, and firing that kept him alive until someone had the good sense to sound the retreat.

Twenty-four hours later, they hadn't gained an inch of ground and over five thousand five hundred diggers were dead, missing, or injured. More than Gallipoli, from what he'd heard.

But he didn't want to tell Sophie any of that. "Most of the second lieutenants didn't survive. I was promoted right after the battle."

Jean-Luc chose that moment to wiggle off the bench again, only this time, he fussed when Joe cleaned his sticky fingers. Sophie pronounced it was time to get him home, fed a proper meal, and tucked into his cot for the day.

Sophie held out her hand to shake his. "Take good care of yourself, Lieutenant Parker. Do your best to come back to Paris someday. There's a lot more to it than just the Eiffel Tower."

"If I can manage it, will you promise me another ice cream and this dancing nipper?"

THREE
WARTIME CORRESPONDENCE
SEPTEMBER 1916 - JUNE 1917, FRANCE

September 10, 1916

Dear Miss Holt,

It was a pleasure to spend time with you and Jean-Luc the other day. It was a treat to do something so thoroughly, unexpectedly, normal. I took your advice and wrote to my wife about finding Jean-Luc. I hope she'll take some comfort from that and won't worry too much about me staying safe.

Thank you for listening to me ramble on. I hadn't realised how much I needed to talk with someone who isn't a fellow soldier.

If we have the good luck to meet again, it will be my turn to buy the ice cream.

Yours very truly,
Joe Parker, 2Lt, 57th Btn, AIF

His note felt stilted and formal, but his mother had drilled good manners into him, and Joe figured she would approve of his effort. He sent the letter in care of the American Hospital in Paris and trusted it would find its way to Sophie.

September 20, 1916

Dear Joe,

What a lovely surprise to receive your note this morning! You must call me Sophie, please. Miss Holt is far too formal, especially since you rescued Jean-Luc and helped me clean all of his sticky fingers after ice cream!

My offer of a meal next time you're in Paris was absolutely serious. If you're worried about propriety or something equally silly, don't be. Natalie and Jean-Luc would be here, and there's nearly a constant stream of people between the flats on our floor because our neighbor has set for himself the goal of producing portraits of personnel from every country involved in the war. He's a marvelous artist. Usually, he does landscapes and religious stuff in oils, but for these portraits, he works in pastels. He meets people on his strolls around Paris and asks them to sit for him. Last week's subject was a Polish captain, very gallant and chivalrous, who kissed Natalie's and my hands when he left after dinner and insisted Prague is just as sophisticated as Paris.

Yesterday we had an Australian sergeant. He was from Canberra, and I told him about meeting one of his fellow citizens —that's you, by the way—by the Eiffel Tower. When I mentioned I'd spent the first five years of my life in Australia, he dug around in his pockets and produced a eucalyptus leaf, which he gave to me to remind me of "my friends from home!" It was a lovely gesture, and the smell of the leaf reminded me of my childhood. It's funny, I've lived in so many places, I've always considered wherever I am as home, but the idea of Australia being my true home has stuck in my mind. I have an aunt in Sydney. Maybe one day I could visit her, then go to Melbourne, and you can introduce me to Annie and Sam.

I need to close for now but write to me again if you have the time. I'd love to hear how things are going for you.

Your friend in Paris,
Sophie

P.S. I asked around to see if anyone here heard about what happened in Fromelles. The Australian sergeant filled me in on more of the details. It sounded awful. Please be careful, Joe, if not for your own sake, then for Annie and Sam.

October 15, 1916

Dear Sophie,

I never imagined I'd have the chance to clean a kiddie's hands during my time here in France. Training didn't prepare me for that, but I have a lot of experience with Sam, so I think I managed well enough.

Someone found a copy of Pride and Prejudice in a dugout, said it was only for sheilas (that's girls, in Australian slang), and tossed it over their shoulder. Luckily, I caught it before it fell in the mud because I'm starved for reading material. I've never had the chance to read Jane Austen. It's nonsense to say blokes can't enjoy this book, too. There's as much satire and commentary about the role of women as there is romance. Maybe even more.

Speaking of books, at home we often use long, thin gum leaves for bookmarks. My mum used to place them between a few pieces of newspaper and weigh them down until they dried flat. I should ask her to send me some. The scent would help mask us not getting as many washes as we need!

One of my lads, Geordie, has taken to carrying a kitten around in his uniform tunic. It's a tiny thing with claws like needles, and it climbs over his chest and shoulders. I've no idea how I'm going to get him to leave it behind when it's time for us to move on. It will probably be as hard as trying to convince Sam to put down his favourite toy.

January 3, 1917

Dear Joe,

The Germans shelled the ambulance Ben was driving, and he was badly injured. I managed to wrangle his return to the hospital in Paris, but he died during surgery. He lost so much blood en route that he was in dire condition when he finally arrived. At first, the doctors thought they might save him if they amputated his leg, but he couldn't pull through surgery.

What's the use of putting huge red crosses on ambulances? The Germans don't look through the sights before they fire and say, 'no we can't shoot there. We might hit that ambulance. We might kill someone's brother or their father or their best friend.'

I'm sorry. I shouldn't lay my burdens at your feet. Mother, Father, and I are heartbroken, but they're in England and everyone here in Paris is so busy that I can't ask anyone to take time to comfort me.

I feel so guilty for insisting that he be sent all the way back to Paris. All I can think is that Ben's dead because of me.

January 7, 1917

Dear Sophie,

I'm so sorry about your brother. I can't imagine what it must be like for you trying to care for wounded patients right now.

There's no need to apologise for needing the comfort of someone to talk to. Since it only takes a few days for letters within France to be delivered, write to me whenever you need to. I'll always be willing to listen.

February 1, 1917

Dear Joe,

I don't know what to do. It's so hard to work in this hospital since Ben died here.

Some amputees think they're going mad because their missing limbs itch. They can't understand why their brains are still sending messages to a leg or a foot that isn't there anymore. Telling them it will stop eventually doesn't do much good.

Then there are the shell-shocked boys who scream and shout in their sleep. It's heartbreaking to hold them when they wake from their nightmares. They've just relived whatever horrific thing happened to them. They're so shaken and fragile that I wonder if they'll ever be able to go back to their old lives when this war is finally over.

I've often wondered if I should volunteer to move to a hospital closer to the front, like the one in Rouen where Natalie is posted now, or even a casualty clearing station. But these boys need me here, don't they? If I stay in Paris, I'm able to look after Jean-Luc so Natalie can stay in Rouen. Her French is fluent, not like mine, so she's needed there more than I am, isn't she?

Sorry. Enough of that. I'll wait until Natalie is back for a break and discuss it with her. How are you? Settling into your new rank?

April 23, 1917

Dear Sophie,

I think your decision to talk it over with your friend is the best course. Let me know what you decide to do.

I've learnt a thing or two about being in charge of thirty men. It's harder than looking after the nine I had when I was a lance corporal. First off, I have to make sure their equipment is in proper order, and they have sufficient supplies. It's freezing now, so I have to make sure their feet are in decent shape too. Inspecting their toes for frostbite is not my favourite thing to do.

Then there's finding ways to let them work off steam or boredom when they need to. It's amazing how far impromptu football games will go when we're behind the lines or pulling out a draughts board or a deck of cards when our orders are to wait until it's time to attack in the early morning hours. I don't smoke, but most of these blokes do —like chimneys—so I started carrying a pack of cigarettes to divvy out when their supply runs low. It's the same with chocolate. Annie sends big packets of it when she writes, so I have plenty to share.

Most of the privates are just boys, only 18 or 19 years old. How many of them will I have to send over the top? If I think about it too much, I feel like the angel of death.

The only bright spot has been reading Pride and Prejudice, despite the blood splattered on the pages, and ignoring the ragging I get from some of the men. I suggested they might learn a thing or two if they read it themselves. Now they're badgering me to hurry and finish.

Until he began corresponding with Sophie, Joe hadn't ever considered having a woman as the kind of friend with whom he could share battlefield stories, but their similar shared experiences forged a completely different sort of connection than the one he had with Annie.

He was also thankful for having someone to talk to about his plummeting faith in the army's professional, institutional leadership after Fromelles. The more experienced men in his unit taught him that Australian soldiers were notoriously bad at respecting authority but were fearless in battle and famously good at looking after each other.

Joe was good at bottling up issues bothering him, but even he could see he needed to relieve the pressure. He couldn't risk losing the respect of those under his command by sharing his concerns, and he had to maintain the confidence of his superiors. He needed a confidant and there was no one he felt he could talk to. The men under his command had their own mates. The men who commanded him had theirs. Only someone who was close to the war could understand that his life, if he could call it that, had been reduced to kill or be killed with long bouts of interminable waiting in between the two. Sophie was his someone, and it felt completely natural to keep the two parts of his life—home and war—separate.

May 13, 1917

Dear Sophie,

Geordie didn't leave the kitten behind when we moved positions. It jumped from his shoulder to the top of the trench wall. He knew better than to raise his head above the parapet, but he did. All he was trying to do was catch the kitten. The sniper would have seen that through his scope, but the bastard took the shot, anyway. I should have checked before we set off. I should have made him empty everything out of his tunic so I could be certain he didn't have the cat anymore. I should have ordered him to leave it.

God, what a bloody awful waste. I can't shake the feeling that it's my fault he's dead. What am I supposed to tell his family when I write to them?

FOUR
NURSE SOPHIE
JULY 1917, PARIS

Joe asked for Sophie at the reception desk at the American Hospital in Paris, shoved his hands in his pockets, and paced nervously while he waited.

He hoped he hadn't made a mistake showing up unannounced, but he was desperate to forget where he'd been for a little while. Even though the Australians had been victorious, the battle at Bullecourt last month had been bloody and costly. Like Fromelles, he'd lived through it. Like Fromelles, he couldn't believe he'd been so lucky.

His heart skipped a beat when he saw Sophie racing down the stairs, holding her nurse's cap in place, her white uniform skirts billowing behind her. She came to a halt just in front of him, grinning.

A stern-looking woman with medals decorating her left breast stalked past and glared at Sophie. All she said was, "Miss Holt," in a commanding voice, and Sophie settled her cap, smoothed her skirts, and snapped to attention until the woman passed.

His lips twitched when Sophie rolled her eyes at the departing woman's back. He offered his hand. "Miss Holt."

She raised a brow and played along. "Second Lieu…." She

checked his shoulders. "*First* Lieutenant Parker. When did that happen?"

"About a week ago."

"What a wonderful surprise to see you!" She gave up the pretense of formality, stood on her toes, and graced him with the French greeting of a kiss on each cheek. "What are you doing here?"

Sophie beamed at him, and he felt better immediately. How could he not? She appeared to be as happy to see him as he was to see her. "I've come to invite you to lunch, as a thank you, for…." They'd shared so much on paper, but now that they were face-to-face again, he wasn't sure how to say he hadn't been able to stop thinking about her, that she had become his lifeline. "For being such an excellent correspondent," he finished.

"Where are your friends this time? The usual haunts?"

Despite his somber mood, he huffed a laugh. He had forgotten how straightforward she was in person—even more so than in her letters. "They still haven't found anyone else who's willing to have them."

She chuckled at his response, and then asked, "Where have you come from? Vignacourt again?"

He nodded, but his smile had already faded. Sophie took his hands in hers and examined the healing cuts and scrapes.

"Where were you before you went on rest?"

"Bullecourt." God, he'd never seen so much barbed wire. And the German artillery bombardment had been unrelenting. He was beginning to believe someone was playing a massive cosmic joke on him. How the hell was he still alive? Davy, Frankie, and Sid had come through it too, and with their innate sense of cockiness, they were beginning to believe they were bulletproof. Their run of luck couldn't possibly continue.

"It's a few miles southeast of Arras. But…."

"But what? What happened?"

"I haven't had the chance to write to tell you. My brother Robbie went missing at the same place in April, a month before I was there. I only found out a few days ago."

"Oh, Joe. I'm so sorry. What did they say? Are you all right?"

He struggled to answer—glancing around the foyer, then down at his hands—before he looked at her. "Missing in action. Presumed killed. My mother will have received the telegram by now, but it could be months before we know for certain." He couldn't stand not knowing, what must it be doing to his mother? "I've done everything I can to get word about him. All I can do now is wait."

She was still holding his hands and, unthinking, he twined his fingers with hers. "What about you? After Ben?"

Sophie's shoulders drooped. "I'm better than I was." She blinked a few times and scrunched her nose to control the tears that glistened. "The cemetery is close. I can go over and put flowers on his grave whenever I want to so that helps."

She took a deep breath. "I'm going to take you home instead of us going out for lunch." He demurred, but she insisted. "We've already established you're an upright citizen and I can trust you, remember?"

When he nodded and managed something close to a smile, Sophie said, "Good. That's settled then. It's quiet today so I can ask someone to look after my patients. I need to change out of this uniform and collect Jean-Luc from the nursery. It won't take long. You can wait for us here or go across the street to the gardens."

As lovely as the gardens looked, he only gave them a cursory glance and opted to wait outside the gates so he could watch the hospital entrance. A steady stream of doctors, nurses, and visitors moved through the doors, including four exuberant Americans wearing French flying corps insignia who doffed their hats and greeted Sophie when she emerged from the hospital. The Germans had what seemed like an endless supply of men to send to France. The British army was down to scrawny youngsters scraped off the streets of England. The French were just as desperate, and the Australians were tired and stretched too thin. These Yanks looked rested and well fed, and he wondered when the American army would join the effort. They would have to learn how to fight, and quickly, if they ever arrived.

Dressed in street clothes, Sophie hurried to him, Jean-Luc clutched in one hand and several bags and parcels in her other hand.

"Friends of yours?" he asked, lifting his chin at the Americans. "I can be on my way if you need to…."

She was breathless from rushing, and the tiny pearls on her earrings bobbled as she spoke. "No, no. They're here to visit one of their own. A lot of boys who came over to drive ambulances became pilots."

"Your brother didn't want to fly too?"

"Heavens no. Ben was terrified of heights." She released Jean Luc's hand. "We live near to here. If you'll carry Jean-Luc, we'll get there faster."

Joe stooped to the boy's height. Jean-Luc grinned at his wiggling ears, so he scooped the boy up with one arm and held out his other hand to carry some of Sophie's parcels.

As they climbed the stairs to the flat she shared with Jean-Luc's mother, all the reasons he shouldn't have accepted her offer niggled at his conscience, despite the assurances in her first letter. She was a single woman. He was a married man. Her neighbors might talk. They could make things difficult for her.

His misgivings evaporated when Sophie flung open the front door. The sense of coming home was so welcome and comforting that he stopped worrying about propriety. Pillows were piled on the sofa and armchairs. Framed photographs crowded the fireplace mantel. Hints of beeswax and clean laundry hung in the still air.

The billets in Bullecourt had been dugouts in a sunken road with graves scattered over the surrounding fields. He felt transported being in a proper home again after so many months of living rough.

Jean-Luc tried to wriggle out of his arms. Joe lowered him to the rug and the child headed straight for a basket of toys tucked under an end table.

Sophie pulled off her hat and a cloud of tresses tumbled down. "Oh bother," she muttered. "I've lost my hairpins again. They never stay put right after I've washed my hair."

Without thinking, Joe stepped behind her to help. Strands of bronze and copper glinted in the mass of dark waves reaching to her waist. "I found them," he said after a few moments. "They're tangled underneath." He worked carefully to extract the pins, increasingly aware of the scents of soap and clean, warm woman curling around him.

Sophie smiled at him over her shoulder. "I'm going to cut it all off. It's far too much trouble." She twisted her hair back up to its proper place and pinned the ends.

She was too close. He was too close. It was all he could do to keep from pulling the pins out again and wrapping a tendril around his...Christ! Where had that urge come from? He took a deep breath and stepped away from her.

Sophie gave the hairpins another hard push and bustled around the flat, opening the tall windows and fixing the latches so they would stay open in the breeze.

"You can hang your things on the hooks by the door," she called across the room.

She had already pushed up her long sleeves and was unbut-toning the top buttons of her high-collared blouse as she spoke.

Joe was still standing by the door. Poor man. He seemed so uncomfortable.

To put Joe at ease, she asked to see the latest photographs of Annie and Sam she assumed he had tucked safely in a pocket. Then she showed him the framed photographs of Jean-Luc with his parents. Except for the uniforms and photographer's stamps, there were few differences between the two families.

"I'm not sure what they were thinking with this one," she said, handing Joe a photo of Jean-Luc dressed as a miniature French soldier, complete with a realistic looking wooden rifle. "It's equal parts adorable and disturbing."

"I have one of Sam saluting me," Joe said. "At the time, it seemed so innocent. Now that I think about it, it just doesn't feel right he did it or that I saluted back." He flipped through his packet of letters and produced another photo.

Joe, clad in a pristine Australian army uniform, was saluting a very young Sam. The toddler's little body was soft and plump compared to the straight, slim lines of his father's. The arm Sam held up to salute Joe hid his face, but Joe's smile for his son showed the depth of their bond.

She turned away from Joe, blinking furiously. The chances that little boy would never see his father again were far too high. "You must be roasting in that wool uniform jacket," she said, fanning herself with an envelope she picked up from a table. "Unbutton a bit while I get lunch started."

Joe roamed around the room, reading book titles and examining photographs while she unpacked her shopping bags. He held up an unframed pastel portrait. "This is you. Did your artist neighbor do this?"

"Yes," she called from the tiny kitchen. "He's away this week or I would take you next door and ask him to do one of you."

She glanced over and saw Joe had relented and removed his uniform jacket. He had also rolled up his sleeves and loosened his tie and the topmost button of his shirt. The taut lines of his jaw and Adam's apple were even sharper against his open collar. She went to the larder and retrieved the potatoes and the crock of vegetable soup.

Next time she looked, he was sitting on the floor with Jean-Luc, trying to understand the boy's mix of English and French demands that Joe place a block *là* or a toy horse *ici*.

When their meal was ready, Joe devoured slices of crusty bread, two bowls of soup, and a glass of wine that was infinitely better than the cheap stuff he'd shared with his mates yesterday. He took his time with the roasted chicken, savoring every bite. "That was delicious," he said, laying his knife and fork down. "You're a wonderful cook."

"I have to confess." Sophie was smiling, and he didn't hear a trace of guilt in her voice. "I bought the chicken from the butcher already prepared. It's too hot to use the oven, and anyway, I don't have a lot of time to cook. I make a very good omelet though. I'll make one for you next time you're in Paris."

He crashed back to reality after the easy domesticity of their meal. As much as he'd needed this respite, he shouldn't come back to this flat alone with Sophie, not after the moment of insanity he had experienced earlier when he found her hairpins. He felt his ears getting warm; Annie had told him they turned pink when he was flustered.

Jean-Luc proved to be his savior from further embarrassment. The boy reached for him and babbled something in excited French.

Being with a little boy reminded Joe so much of Sam that he automatically wiped the remnants of chicken and potatoes from the child's hands and face. "What is he saying?"

"He wants to play horse."

He glanced at the toys scattered on the rug. "Isn't that what we were doing earlier?"

She laughed. "Now he wants *you* to be the horse."

"Oh." He pushed the toys out of the way and got on his hands and knees. "C'mon, lad, your steed awaits."

Sophie lifted Jean-Luc onto his back. He shifted to accommodate the boy's wiggling weight, flinching when Jean-Luc grabbed handfuls of his shirt. "Ouch!"

"What's wrong?"

"Dunno," he grunted. "Something sharp is sticking into my back."

Rising and wincing after Sophie lifted a protesting Jean-Luc off, he rolled his shoulders and stretched. "Ah! It's just to the right of my shoulder blade."

She smoothed her fingers across the back of his shirt. "It could be a splinter from one of Jean-Luc's wooden blocks, but I don't feel anything."

He stretched and winced again.

"Right. Take off your shirt and tie."

He stopped squirming and went still. She couldn't mean that. "Erm, I, erm…."

"We need to see if whatever it is has worked its way inside your shirt."

She was serious. Now what? "I….Here?"

"Go in the bathroom then. It's just down the hall."

Sophie called through the bathroom door a few minutes later. "Did you find anything?"

"No. Nothing." She heard the brush of heavy cotton and then a muffled, "Ow!"

"That's it, I'm coming in." She opened the door, took Joe's shirt from him, and hung it on a hook before he had a chance to protest. She pulled a bench from against the wall and placed it in the center of the room. "Sit down, please. Facing away from me."

She pulled the neck of his undershirt away from his back. Shrapnel wounds, fairly recent from the looks of them, marred his shoulders and back, down to his waist.

"You should have told me you'd been wounded before you agreed to be a horse," she scolded. "I suspect you have a sliver of metal working its way out. If that's the case, I can probably get it, but you have to undress so I can get to your back."

"It can wait until I get back to Vignacourt. No need for you to…."

She pressed her lips together to hide her smile. The poor man must be blushing if the color of his ears was anything to go by. "Joe. I'm a nurse. You have a simple problem and three options to solve it. You can be in pain for however long it takes to get back and find a doctor. We can return to the hospital and have one of my colleagues look at you. Or you can let me try to fix it now and get it all over with. What do you say?"

He turned to her, the corners of his lips tightening to form the smile she now knew preceded a wry comment. "Is your bedside manner always this bossy, nurse?"

She grinned at him. "Most of my patients don't give me nearly as much trouble as you. It'll be nice to have a patient who's whole and relatively undamaged. All you need to do is take off your undershirt. Leave your braces off, too." She turned and walked out of the bathroom, calling from the hallway, "I'll put Jean-Luc in his cot and get my kit. I'll be right back."

She returned a few minutes later, ready to catalog her observations, just as she did for every patient in her care. "Don't worry, there isn't anything you have that I haven't already seen at least a hundred times." She stepped through the doorway, cast an eye over Joe's torso, and stopped short.

Joe was lean, too lean, and she was inordinately pleased she had given him a good meal, but God, he was beautiful. He was fit, in the ways of someone who looked after his body, trained it and used it. Broad shoulders tapered to a slim waist. Biceps, triceps, and extensors flexed as he fidgeted under her gaze.

Thank goodness Joe's eyes had dropped to his boots because she felt herself swaying toward him. This was not supposed to happen.

"Sit," she blurted, placing her hands on the tops of Joe's arms to nudge him forward so she could see his back. The warmth of his skin and the sturdy rounds of his shoulders hummed under her palms. She jerked her hands away, stunned by the unbidden instinct to stroke his arms in a caress. That wasn't supposed to happen either.

She took a deep breath, pushed the forbidden out of her mind, and took refuge in her professional persona. "Lean forward and put your elbows on your knees, please. I'm going to check everything."

She lifted the cord that held Joe's identity disks so she could see the tiny wound below the close-cropped hair at the base of his skull, then moved across his shoulders, and down the length of his back, running gentle fingers around each wound. The routine settled her nerves until she could speak normally again. "Did you get these at Bullecourt last month? What happened?"

"The usual. Whistle everyone over the top and run like hell. Dive into a shell hole when Fritz fires. Fall flat and catch some shrapnel."

When he didn't elaborate, she ventured a guess. She had heard dozens of similar stories from her patients, after all. "Repeat until you gain the objective, or try to turn back if you fail?"

"Something like that. And hope it isn't your turn to cop it. We gained the objective this time. We took over the Boche trenches, and the Tommies pushed them the rest of the way out of the town. Done and dusted."

There was no bravado in his voice, but his blunt answer marked a shift from the first time they met when he could barely say anything about the battle he'd fought in. Joe had become battle-hardened, prepared to kill so he wouldn't be killed, but she was thankful. He might stay alive because of it.

"Well, I'm very glad you didn't. Cop it, I mean. And I'm sure there are lots of other people who feel the same way. As for your back, it's not too bad. You're healing nicely. Annie must have been glad when you told her how lucky you were."

"I...erm...I sort of glossed over it. I haven't told her every-thing yet."

Her fingers stopped moving. "What? You need to tell her, Joe."

"I don't want to worry her. She has enough on her plate dealing with Sam, and her mum, and my mum because of Robbie."

She blinked back a sting of tears. At least she knew where Ben's body lay. Missing usually meant killed, but since the family couldn't be certain, they kept hoping when there was no hope. Joe would have said something if he'd seen a prisoner's list, so Robbie hadn't been captured. She couldn't think of anything else to say about Annie or Robbie that wouldn't seem too personal, so she changed the subject. "When did you get that scar on your ribs? It doesn't look recent."

"I was a young, not very careful constable," he admitted. "I panicked and forgot everything they taught us about how to subdue someone with a knife. Luckily, our uniforms were such thick wool that the knife barely scratched me. It cut through my tunic though, and I had to decide whether to ask my mum to mend it or risk a bollocking from my sergeant for not being in proper uniform."

"What did you decide?"

"I went with the mum choice. For the record, her reaction was worse than the sergeant's would have been."

She snickered, despite still being far too flustered by the half-naked man in her bathroom. "I'd have liked to have heard that."

Joe grinned at the memory of his petite mother ordering him out of his tunic and then giving him a good talking to while she mended the slice through his union suit, too. "She gave me the full treatment. I should have gone to university. Or become a foreman at the brewery. Anything but a copper. I could get myself killed. What was I thinking? But she couldn't assign me to two weeks of the midnight shift like my sergeant would have. For what it's worth, I still don't like knives."

"I've never had to subdue anyone with a knife," Sophie said. "It could happen, I suppose. Soldiers often have weapons hidden in their uniforms. You should tell me what to do. How old were you when you were a not very careful constable?"

"I'd only been out of the academy for a couple of months, so 20? Almost 21?"

"So, you were about the same age as I am now. How old are you?"

"I'll be twenty-five in Sep—" He twisted to face her. "You're only 20? How on earth are you already a nurse?"

She met his astonished gaze with a steady one of her own. "Turn around, please. How am I supposed to see what I'm doing?" When he complied, she continued. "I turned 21 earlier this year. I convinced my mother to stretch the truth about my age so I could begin training when I was 19. I'm doing the rest of my training on the job."

He felt very old-fashioned, but he had to ask. "Didn't your father have a say in the matter?"

"Hmm. Mother convinced him after I convinced her. I can be very persuasive."

Yes, I can believe that he thought while she chattered on about convincing her parents to let her go to university before the war started. You convinced me to come home with you, and take off half my clothes, and now you're…why are you touching my arm?

Sophie crowed, "Got it!" before he could finish wondering what she was doing. "Put out your hand," she commanded.

He shifted, and she dropped a sliver of metal from her tweezers onto his open palm.

"There it is."

He let the tiny thing roll from side to side in his hand. "It's hard to believe something so small could hurt so much."

"Well, skin is our most sensitive organ. It doesn't like being pierced with sharp pieces of metal. I'll put antiseptic on this spot and a bandage on another spot that's looking a little irritated. Then you can get dressed again."

Sophie looked so pleased with herself that he couldn't help smiling at her. "I didn't even know you'd found it."

"That's because I am an expert at distracting my patients."

That's why you touched my arm, he thought, to distract me, that's all.

FIVE

GOOD INTENTIONS

When he finished dressing, Joe found Sophie leaning over Jean-Luc's cot, tucking a light blanket around the sleeping boy. He walked over to her, and they stood side-by-side, watching Jean-Luc sleep.

"Thank you," he whispered. "You're a wonderful nurse."

"I wasn't at first," Sophie admitted. "I was so nervous."

"What did you do when you started?"

"All the jobs the experienced nurses and the orderlies were too busy to do. I made beds and boiled bandages. Yes, we washed bandages so we could reuse them," she said in response to his look of disbelief. "I scrubbed bedpans. I helped to undress and wash the wounded when they arrived at the hospital. Some older nurses gave new nurses the rotten jobs to weed out anyone who was just playing at helping. Some thought we were more trouble than we were worth, that we were running away from home or looking for a man to entice."

"Were they?"

"I don't know anyone who was. We don't have the time or the energy for...," she rolled her eyes and imitated the stern woman from the hospital lobby, "romantic entanglements." She lifted a hand to her head and pushed a pin back in place. "I really am going to cut my hair short, so I don't have to spend so much time dealing with it."

He would never forget seeing Sophie's hair massed on her shoulders, framing her face like a halo. An unutterable feeling of tenderness for her washed over him, followed by admiration. She had already been through so much and had emerged strong, like tempered steel. "God, you're so young."

"I'm older than many of the men who're fighting," she reminded him. "Most of them are just boys."

"How did you cope when you started? Was it all horrible?"

"Yes. And no. How could it be when you're so needed? When it's quiet, we read to the men, from books, or their letters if they can't hold them. We often write their letters for them, too."

So many of the wounded men he'd carried out of No Man's Land after Fromelles had such horrific injuries they couldn't possibly have survived. "What do you do when…when you know someone is dying and there's nothing anyone can do?"

"If the man is lucid, I ask about his home or his wife and children or sweetheart. I want them to go with a loving thought in their mind." Sophie's eyes welled up. He patted his pockets for his handkerchief, but she shook her head and blinked the tears away. "Sometimes I just sit with them and hold their hand, so they know they aren't alone."

Tears pricked his eyes too. "What happened to your brother when he died?"

"I was with Ben just before he went under the anesthesia, so I had a chance to tell him I loved him. We knew there was a good chance he wouldn't survive it. The operating theater nurses are tough, but very compassionate. And the doctors take it very hard when they lose a patient."

A vision of all those wooden crosses scattered close—too close—to their dugouts in Bullecourt loomed in his memory. He had helped to bury so many men he no longer felt like he was intruding when he removed personal items from bodies to send home to families. "What happens when a patient dies?"

Sophie was looking at him as though she couldn't quite believe he didn't know. "We wash the man's body and wrap him in a clean sheet. They're given a proper burial in the hospital cemetery. The hospital chaplain conducts a service. It's all very reverent and lots of people attend. We want to, you see. We treat the dead the way we would want to be treated."

He stared at nothing while she spoke. Ashes to ashes, dust to dust. All those men who died at Fromelles and Bullecourt.

"What happens in the field, Joe?"

He shook his head. "You don't want to know."

"I do." She nodded, and he searched her face, wanting to know she was certain. She nodded again. "Tell me. Please."

"It depends. Sometimes we are able to dig a hole and recite a quick prayer. Other times, we can only pull the bodies into shell craters and toss in some lime and a few shovelfuls of dirt. We mark the graves with wooden crosses carved with the men's names. Then we record the names and locations in the battalion diary.

"Burying body parts…legs, arms, bits and pieces barely identifiable as human is worse, but we record those too." He suppressed the bile rising in his throat as the images flashed in his mind. Sophie flinched, but she didn't look away from him. "The crosses on those graves are etched with 'An Unknown Australian Soldier.' If Robbie's really gone, I hope he's whole when someone finds him. 'Missing in action presumed killed' means there aren't enough recognizable body parts to make an identification."

"Oh my God, Joe. Does your mother know that?"

He shook his head. "No. And I'll never tell her if I can avoid it. Do you write to the families?"

"Yes. Even when we're pressed for time. We try to write letters that are as personal as possible."

He had already written too many letters like that. Fighting, and living, side-by-side with his men, he knew what their dreams were, whether they loved someone, who was waiting for them to come home. "How do you find the time or the energy to write to me?"

Sophie smiled, wistfully, he thought. "Writing to you helps me write the sad letters. Besides, I always hoped you need me as much as I need you."

That possibility hadn't occurred to him. "You need me? Why?"

"Of course, I do." Her smile was less wistful, and the timbre of her voice was lighter. "It's a relief to have an intelligent, articulate correspondent. We can talk about anything."

Jean-Luc's eyelashes fluttered. Sophie murmured something soothing in French.

Joe smoothed a damp strand of dark hair from the boy's forehead. "I hope he never has to wear a grown-up version of that uniform."

Sophie's whisper turned somber again. "I hope your Sam never has to salute anyone."

She cupped his cheek and he teetered on the precipice of raw, crushing need for emotional and physical comfort. If Jean-Luc hadn't snuffled in his sleep, he couldn't have stopped himself from doing what his gut was screaming at him to do: to lift Sophie in his arms, carry her to bed, and make love with her until the guns stopped and the blood disappeared from the fields and streams.

But he was in a home that wasn't his, with a woman who wasn't his, with a child who wasn't his. He closed his eyes and sent his love to the woman and child who were.

He stepped back from the brink. "I should go. The last train back…."

Sophie nodded, but she didn't touch him again. "Please be careful, Joe."

$$\sim$$

Joe made it to the train station just as the departure whistle blew. He pushed through the crush of sweaty soldiers crowding the door of the last carriage, his eyes and nose assaulted by cigarette smoke and winy breath.

He found a seat between a sergeant and a private, both of whom were already snoring. He prodded the sleeping sergeant to move to the middle space and lowered the compartment window. The night was still hot, and he'd sweated through his undershirt and shirt on the quick march from Sophie's flat to the station.

Lifting his face to the breeze, he tried to settle his thoughts.

All the memories of the times he'd been filthy and scared, waiting to get into a trench, or out of one, disappeared when he was with Sophie. At home, it was his job to carry Sam in one arm and a handful of shopping in the other. Holding Jean-Luc's solid little body, and a few of Sophie's parcels, on their walk from the hospital felt completely natural. He felt like a husband again with a woman by his side. He remembered how to sit in a real armchair and how to eat a meal like someone whose mother had taught him good table manners. He remembered how to laugh and how to play with a child. He forgot he was wearing khaki wool and remembered he was a man and not just a soldier.

Sometime in the course of remembering he was a man, he'd also imagined Sophie, smiling as she looked over her shoulder at him, not Annie, in his arms.

He could almost justify that to himself—it had been nearly two years since he'd seen Annie after all—but how could he want and need a woman he barely knew compared to the long history he had with Annie?

He loved Annie. They had plans—promotions and a bigger cottage and a brother or sister for Sam. His memory of Annie's face was fading—fair hair and bright blue eyes, just like Sam's—he would study her photograph so he could summon her image at will again. He would re-read Annie's letters until he knew them by heart again. He would write home more often. He wouldn't go back to Paris. He wouldn't allow himself to have feelings for Sophie.

His sleeping mind betrayed him, though. He dreamed of the barely-there brush of Sophie's cheeks on his when she kissed him hello. The pale column of her throat as she fanned herself. Her sharp gasp when she opened the bathroom door and raked her eyes over his chest. The flush spreading across her cheeks as she looked away. Her hands on his skin and her breath on his back. He dreamed of unbuttoning all the tiny white buttons running down the front of her blouse and nuzzling her neck until she melted against him.

The train shunting over the tracks outside Vignacourt jostled him awake. Thank God his seatmates were still asleep, or he would have been mortified. He nudged the sleeping man beside him, causing his head and rank breath to roll to the other side, and willed his body back to a state befitting an officer and a gentleman.

After Joe left for the train station, Sophie clasped a sofa pillow to her breast and sank into the cushions, shaken and unsteady.

She had asked him about Annie and Sam in between bites of roast chicken and salad and keeping track of where Jean-Luc had smashed his potatoes. Joe had described their home in Melbourne for her, the vegetables and flowers they grew, their daily routine. How he came home from the police station after his shift, changing out of his uniform and into old clothes so he could spend a few minutes in their back garden, dead-heading roses, picking the ripest tomatoes, and playing with Sam, until Annie called them to come in and wash up before dinner.

She'd heard the longing in Joe's voice when he spoke of home and his little family. She hadn't envisioned that kind of life for herself, not after she'd chosen university classes and training to become a nurse instead of marriage.

But to be married to a good man like Joe, who loved her and their children the way he loved Annie and Sam? What had she given up? Why shouldn't she have a career and family, too?

And that moment in her bathroom after Joe took his shirt off. Had she actually gone weak in the knees at the sight of him half-dressed? She couldn't begin to count the number of nearly naked men she'd seen in her nursing career. All of them, regardless of whether they were handsome or ugly, skinny or chubby, mostly whole or badly broken, needed her skills and her care. After two years of nursing, she thought she'd become immune to the charms of the male body. Apparently not, at least not where Joe was concerned. Good Lord. He embodied her ideal of the male physique and she hadn't even known she had one.

She was twenty-one years old. A young man in America whom she'd enjoyed kissing very much had kissed her. But something momentous had happened when she cupped Joe's cheek. She had only meant to comfort him, but she'd been certain he was going to kiss her, and she would kiss him back and when they came up for air, she would lead him to her bedroom and…. She had never felt anything like that for the young man she'd left behind.

And the look on Joe's face before he stepped away from her? Grief, guilt, and desire had been distilled in those blue eyes of his.

It had taken all her willpower to let him go, and now she wanted to run after him, bring him back to the flat, and never let him leave again.

But Joe wasn't hers to keep. He was a good man who was very far from home. They were both hurting and vulnerable after the deaths of their brothers. The most precious thing they could offer each other was friendship.

SIX

HOPE AMID DESPAIR

AUGUST 1917 - MARCH 1918, FRANCE

August 15, 1917

Dear Joe,

Jean-Luc's father died in action. Natalie is devastated but can't get a transfer to Paris until next month, so I'm on my own caring for this poor boy. It's so unfair! Since he's so young, he never really knew his father and now he never will. I've cried so much I don't think I'll ever stop. Or if I stop, I don't think I'll ever be able to cry again.

Joe, please come back to Paris as soon as you can. We'll take Jean-Luc for ice cream, and I'll make you that omelet. I need you to help me forget this damned war for a while. I need something to look forward to.

Joe didn't reply as quickly as he usually did, and Sophie began imagining he'd been wounded and was so injured he couldn't write. Weeks passed, and she feared the worst might have happened, that he'd been killed or taken prisoner. She checked the post constantly. She had trouble sleeping. Her work colleagues asked what was bothering her. She became so absentminded that the head nurse spoke sharply to her several times.

When she finally spied Joe's handwriting on an envelope, she ripped it open, but his news was as heartbreaking as hers had been.

September 1, 1917

Dear Sophie,

I'm sorry for not writing sooner, but things are heating up here and I don't know when we'll be back on rest. I have bad news too. Davy, one of the lads who came to Paris the first time I was there, is dead. We were on a night patrol, four of us. Everything was going fine; we were moving quietly from tree to tree in a little thicket. We got so close to a Boche patrol that we could hear them whispering to each other. We were all set to ambush them when someone stepped on a twig. A tiny snapping noise and they knew we were there. They rushed us. Davy didn't get down fast enough. We killed all the Germans, but not before one of them caught Davy in the back with his trench knife.

We carried him back to our lines, and I stayed with him as far as the battalion aid station, but he died before we arrived. What am I supposed to tell his mother? I can't tell her that one little twig led to her son's death.

Her first thought, thank God it was Davy and not Joe, left her reeling. How could she be so crass about yet another mother losing a son? She couldn't tell Joe she'd been worried sick about him or how relieved she was that he was alive. She forced herself to keep her response as light-hearted as possible. She had a ruse— Joe's birthday was approaching.

September 7, 1917

Dear Joe,

I was so sorry to hear about Davy. What did you write to his family?

I was glad to hear from you, though. I was wondering if you'd run off, although I can't imagine there are that many places you could run to at this point. You'd have to practice your French a lot more to get by.

Natalie came back to Paris for a few days. She couldn't believe how much Jean-Luc had grown. I told her all about how you played with him, and she sends her thanks.

Paris has been unbearably hot this August, so much hotter than when you were here in July. We're living on bread, cheese, and fruit, plus the occasional chicken roasted by the butcher. It's too hot to even think about cooking anything.

Last, but not least, happy birthday. You never told me the date, only that it's in September, so I'll get my greeting in early and you can save it until the proper day.

She began to feel as if she were holding her breath during the long periods between Joe's letters. To fill the time, she wrote to Natalie and her parents more often. She redoubled her efforts at the hospital to help patients write their letters.

October 14, 1917

Dear Sophie,

I told Davy's parents the usual—he didn't feel any pain, he died doing his duty, he was a credit to our battalion—the same thing I write to every family. It's true for all the dead lads, except the pain part. But no one wants to know their boy was in agony and I'm not about to tell them. Their grief must be hard enough without that.

Thank you for the birthday wishes. I turned 25 on 3 September. Thank Christ we're off the front lines now after a hellish fight that began late last month and carried through the start of this one. Luck was on our side again and we sent Kaiser Bill's men packing. Now we're billeted in a tiny Belgian village whose name I can't spell—Zonn something—much less pronounce. If you think my French is bad, my Flemish is even worse. Your hot-weather rations sound like haute cuisine *(I have picked up some French!). Baking bread was the first thing we smelt when we arrived in this village, and we nearly went wild. I'd almost forgotten freshly baked bread existed. There's a tiny café here, and the lads surprised me with a late birthday meal— eggs and fresh bread. It was truly a feast. I have no idea how they knew the date, but they're a resourceful lot.*

Belgium is even flatter than the Somme valley. All the canals are destroyed, so when it rains everything floods. The only good thing about being knee deep in mucky water is the rats prefer the sandbags at the top of the trench. The lads put a bit of food on the tip of their bayonets and shoot the rats when they get close enough to take the food. It's disgusting, I know, but they make a competition of it and it's a way to pass the time.

October 30, 1917

Dear Joe,

It sounds like you had quite the birthday celebration!
We've had a slew of influenza cases. I don't know much about

the illness, since I'm not on that ward, but it's horrible how quickly patients die when they're infected. No one knows why it affects healthy young adults and not the aged, the infirm, or the very young. The doctors say the symptoms are not unlike cholera or typhoid. The course of the disease is awful, especially the bleeding, and death occurs within just a few days. It's utterly baffling. And frightening.

*An English surgeon came to visit the hospital. His specialty is fixing maimed faces—*gueules cassées *the French call them. I attended a lecture he gave describing his work with a group of doctors in London who graft skin from one part of a patient's body to another part. They've been able to grow new skin and do some amazing reconstructive work of men's faces. I found it fascinating to learn about the surgical advances they're making every day.*

She folded her letter and addressed the envelope. Joe seemed to be coping well with life as a soldier, far better than he had when he first arrived in France. That was good. It might keep him safe. It might keep him alive.

SEVEN

THINGS HE MUST NOT TELL

On the 25th of April 1918, in the earliest minutes of the day, after hours of tugging and straining at the leash of orders to wait, and wait, and wait some more, First Lieutenant Joe Parker and three thousand other Australians rose from their positions.

Several miles south of them, Villers-Bretonneux burned. Beyond the town, Australian and British tanks waged war against German tanks. The smoky air shook with percussions.

The order to move out was whispered.

Three thousand Australians silently advanced toward the town, their bayonets wrapped in hessian so they wouldn't flash in the moonlight.

A single thought rippled through the ranks: it's Anzac Day. Three years ago, our diggers were slaughtered at Gallipoli. This is our chance to avenge them and everyone else we lost at Fromelles and Pozières and Passchendaele and all the battles between and since.

The next order was shouted.

Unleashed, they charged, legs pumping, hearts pounding, blood running hot with the spontaneous roar on their lips.

In that instant, when his voice joined with three thousand

others, Joe knew how every warrior since the dawn of history felt. He wasn't here to think or justify what he was doing or wonder about the future. He was here to fight, to give this effort every ounce of his strength. The fate of France, Europe, the world as he knew it, was hanging in the balance. He must emerge victorious or die trying. Nothing else mattered.

The first rounds of German machine gun fire flew high, a sure sign the attack surprised them. The Australians dropped to the ground for safety. Then they rose and roared and charged again and again until they were face-to-face with Germans who couldn't believe these Australians were mad enough to keep coming despite being outnumbered and outgunned.

Those Germans who could, turned and ran.

The Australians began a brutal rhythm: cracking skulls with rifle butts, thrusting bayonets into bellies, barely pausing their ruthless dance to swipe sweat and blood from their faces, cracking and thrusting, thrusting and cracking, until there were no more Germans between them and the burning town.

Joe lifted his face to the night sky. His shout was primal. Savage. Victorious.

EIGHT

THINGS HE DARES NOT TELL

"Parker!"

"Sir?"

"Take some of your men and get into the town. Round up any of the enemy you find."

"Yes, sir! Stanley, Frankie, Sid, Peters, Billy, Thommo! You're with me!"

A series of shells exploded where the Australians and British were finishing off the enemy south of Villers-Bret. Each new explosion illuminated the ravaged town for a few moments and laid down another layer in the haze of smoke hanging in the air.

Joe flipped the cover off his wristwatch and checked the time. Their orders were to stay in the town and round up Boche for another couple of hours. So far, they'd slipped through the shadows unharmed and checked three houses but had found no one. He signaled for the men following him to enter the next house.

They crept into a large, dark, low-ceilinged room, watchful and wary, keeping close to the walls.

The stairs creaked. Joe sensed rather than saw the grenade lobbed from the staircase.

Instinctively, he grabbed the top of his head to make sure his helmet was on securely. "Grenade!" he yelled at the top of his lungs. "Get down, get down!"

His order was drowned out by shrapnel and plaster showering onto their heads and shoulders.

He took one second to check the far end of the room. "Stay dow—" Why was Stanley standing? He was frozen in place in front of a shattered window, a look of sheer terror on his face. Bloody fucking hell. He'd kept Stanley close all night, had managed to get him through the bloodbath out in the fields, and *now* the kid was scared? He scrambled over, shielded Stanley's body with his, and pulled him to a dark corner.

"What the hell are you doing?" he hissed in Stanley's ear. "Stay down and don't move until they come downstairs!"

Heavy boots thumped down wooden stairs, and Joe braced himself for the inevitable attack. Within seconds, several Germans swarmed into their midst, some with knives and pistols drawn, others with clubs studded with spikes.

His men had their own knives and weapons designed to do maximum damage in close quarters.

Joe leapt up and joined in. Fighting raged around him—a battle on a small scale but the sounds were the same—shouting, swearing, grunting as weapons crunched bone and knives sliced flesh. A litany of ripe curses. A gunshot, and another.

Then quiet, broken only by groans and heaving breaths.

With adrenaline still coursing through his limbs and blood pounding in his ears, Joe squinted around the dark room and took stock. Acrid cordite in close quarters stung his eyes and nose. Billy was grimacing as Peters wrapped a field dressing around his arm. Thommo was panting and standing guard over a fallen enemy soldier.

He pushed his way to them. "Thommo! You know the drill. Tie up the survivors. Then search all of them, wounded and dead.

Take everything of importance. Weapons, papers, maps. No souveniring! Peters! Go find the stretcher bearers when you finish with Billy. Sid? Frankie? Where are you?"

"Copper!" Joe froze. Only Sid and Frankie, who had been with him since training camp in Melbourne, ever called him by that nickname, and only under the direst circumstances. "Come quick! It's Stanley."

Joe pushed his way back to the direction of the shout, skidding now and then on the wooden floor, slippery with blood. Sid and Frankie were pulling a big German away from a corner, trying to hold on to the soldier as he struggled.

Stanley sat slumped against the wall, blood blooming and entrails spilling. The German had thrust his trench knife into Stanley's belly and then slashed across his body to inflict maximum damage. Joe dropped to his knees and pressed his fingers against the boy's neck, desperate to feel a pulse. It faded to nothing beneath his touch.

Joe muttered the foulest curse he could muster and bowed his head in grief.

In the second that Sid and Frankie grieved with him, the German wrested himself free of his captors and yanked the knife from Stanley's body. Then he launched himself at Joe, knocking him over and landing half on top of him.

A wave of stale breath and ripe sweat flooded Joe's nostrils. Stanley's blood dripped from the knife onto his cheek.

They grappled for control of the knife, twisting and grinding into the mess of blood and guts on the floor.

"Take the shot, Frankie! Take the fuckin' shot!"

"They're moving too much, Sid! I can't see a bloody thing!"

Thommo loomed, and he whacked the German from behind with his rifle butt. "Take that, ya Boche bastard!"

In the instant the soldier reacted from the blow, Joe knocked the knife from the German's grasp. It clattered on the floor.

He felt the German being pulled off his body but didn't trust him to stay down. He twisted up and over, pinned the soldier's chest under his knees, and wrapped his hands around the man's throat.

He squeezed, for Stanley, the baby of their unit, the lad who wasn't all there, with his constantly snotty nose and his big stinky feet, who would never again drive them bonkers with his stupid jokes that didn't make sense. He squeezed for Geordie, who had clutched a tiny kitten to his chest as the back of his skull exploded from a sniper's bullet, and for Davy, who had arched and then fallen to his knees as a trench knife pierced his back, his kidney, his liver. He squeezed for his brother Robbie, who had gone over the top at Bullecourt and disappeared. Missing, presumed dead, his body in so many pieces he could never be identified.

He squeezed, muscles shaking with effort, while the German's legs scrabbled on the floor and hands tore at his wrists. The whites of his eyes flashing in the darkness, the German rasped a sound that could have been a guttural gasp for breath or the beginning of *Kamerade*, the word the enemy used when they surrendered.

First Lieutenant Joe Parker squeezed harder than he thought possible, no longer caring he shouldn't, not seeing Sid, Frankie, and Thommo's grim satisfaction, or Billy watching on slack-jawed. He put his hate for every German ever born into his squeeze, until the soldier beneath him stopped struggling and lay still.

NINE

BEGINNING OF THE END

MAY 1918 - JANUARY 1919, FRANCE

May 1, 1918

Dear Sophie,

Well, it has finally happened. I've become the killing machine the army has always wanted me to be.

Joe held the edge of the letter to the flame, staring, unfocused, as the paper burned.

You can't tell her about Villers-Bret or the German soldier, not even by mocking yourself. How can you tell her it took only a few heads to perfect cracking skulls with the butt of your rifle? Or that it took surprisingly little effort to thrust a well-honed bayonet blade through wool uniform tunics and slash so that blood wells up and guts spill out? And afterwards, when the red fog obliterated every rational thought, and you forced the life out of a man with your bare hands?

It's bad enough you can't look yourself in the eye. She'll never look at you the same way again. She'll never want to speak to you again.

Christ, she's your lifeline. What the hell are you going to do without her?

He flexed his hands, certain the warp and weft of the German's uniform would always be imprinted on his fingertips.

The candle sputtered. Joe drained off the melted wax and relit the wick with trembling fingers, then tossed the spent match to the earthen dugout floor and stared into the flame again.

May 6, 1918

Dear Joe,

Is everything all right? I haven't heard from you in ages.

May 15, 1918

Dear Joe,

Please, if you can, let me know you're safe. I'm getting worried.

May 20, 1918

Dear Sophie,

Don't worry, I'm fine. On Anzac Day we took a town called Villers-Bretonneux that the Boche captured from the Tommies the day before. I was in the Australian group that fought through to the town centre from the north. Another battalion of Aussies and Tommies fought through from the south.

They want to promote me again, to captain this time. I'd have to go to England for training. Cambridge, I think, I'm not sure when. At least I'll have a chance to see Big Ben when I pass through London.

Sophie tore open the envelope, reading through quickly, as usual, to make sure Joe was unhurt, then slower to digest his news. On the surface it was bland, perfunctory, even, and he hadn't explained why he had taken so long to write, but he was safe. That's all that mattered. And London? She loved London!

May 25, 1918

Dear Joe,

I could meet you in London! I have a week of leave that's long overdue. We could wander St. James' Park, feed the swans, and then walk to the Houses of Parliament and listen to Big Ben chiming the hour. We could go to Sung Evensong at Westminster Abbey. I have to warn you, I'll tear up! I always do when I hear the heavenly sounds of the choir echoing through that ancient, sacred building, and

And Joe would hold her hand. Then they….

What was she thinking? She crumpled the sheet of paper and started over.

May 25, 1918

Dear Joe,

I wish I could go to London too, but we're hunkering down

here. The air raid sirens are a regular occurrence now, and the German planes have been dropping bombs all over the city. They are getting closer and closer to a place on the Marne River called Château-Thierry about an hour southeast of here. They have something called the Paris gun that can reach the far suburbs of Paris. I'm told the guns are 77-millimeter cannons and they have a range of at least 50 miles. Even though the hospital is on the western side of the city, we can hear the explosions. They feel like minor earthquakes we experienced in California when I was a child. The rumor is the French are begging General Pershing to send American troops to fight there because the French army has been decimated. We've treated so many civilian casualties, and the city is crawling with people trying to escape. We're holding our breath and hoping and praying the German advance can be halted.

Nightmarish images of German troops fanning out through Paris invaded Joe's dreams. While on rest, some of his men sought the comforts of a willing woman's bed. Invaders, though? They didn't ask—they snatched, they seized, they plundered—whatever they wanted.

June 1, 1918

Dear Sophie,

Please tell me you can get out of Paris somehow. I know you think you've experienced some of the worst effects of this bloody war, and you have, I know you have, but you cannot be there if the Germans invade Paris. You cannot. Promise me you'll leave. Please.

June 15, 1918

Dear Joe,

Whatever happens, we would never abandon the hospital and our patients. I appreciate your concern, truly I do, but would you abandon your men because the people who care about you worry about your safety? I would rather be a prisoner than forsake my duty here. And anyhow, the American Marines are proving their mettle on the Marne, so there's hope.

Good God, she was indomitable. He could see her standing defiant before a horde of sex-starved soldiers, hair escaping its pins and full skirts billowing, brandishing a fiery sword in one hand, shielding a wounded man behind her. Crikey, what an image. More likely, she would use all her knowledge of male anatomy to render each man who dared to approach senseless and sobbing from a well-placed blow to the groin.

July 15, 1918

Dear Sophie,

I apologise for the tone of my last letter. I had no right to suggest you don't know what you're doing or can't decide your affairs for yourself. My only excuse is that I was worried about you, my friend.

We rarely hear much about what's happening in theatres other than our own, but news of the American victory in June at Belleau Wood trickled north to us. A whole mob of Diggers cheered for your Doughboys.

July 24, 1918

Dear Joe,

There's no need to apologize. My parents can't convince me to leave Paris either. They're in England now, managing our family's factory in Birmingham. It manufactures small but vital bits of machinery for transports and motorcars. Most of the men who worked there left to go fight, so Father has taken on a foreman's duty and mother is handling the books. It's a far cry from heading the board, which is his usual job.

Do you remember I told you about an English doctor who visited the hospital? His name is Michael Edwards, and he's in Paris again. This time he brought several photographs of patients to show us. The 'new' faces aren't perfect, far from it, but the doctors are improving techniques, and they learn with every patient. I could see myself doing that kind of nursing after the war is over. There are so many men who will need help. It will be so difficult for them to start over with horrifically disfigured faces. This war can't possibly last forever and I could really make a difference in their lives when it's finally over.

October 3, 1918

Dear Sophie,

I can imagine you doing whatever you want to do after the war is over. Those poor blokes would be lucky to have you.

The allies had a big push in early August, all the Australian divisions plus the Tommies and the Canadians, and we sent Fritz packing about eight miles east. The Battle of Amiens, they're calling it because that city is no longer vulnerable. Thousands of

Kaiser Bill's men surrendered. I think they're even more sick of fighting than we are.

Last month, your fellow Yanks fought with us at a place called Saint Quentin Canal. It's a three-mile-long concrete-reinforced tunnel that the Boche occupied for months. They enjoyed the comfort of a safe, practically indestructible shelter until a few days ago, when we took it back from them. We had a bloody awful time of it, though. Gas (ours) that drifted back to us, tanks (British) that didn't show up in time, plus low clouds and mist (French) meant no Australian air support was possible.

The Yanks fought well under difficult circumstances. Their casualties were high, but without them we couldn't have taken the canal and broken through the Hindenburg Line.

There's talk that the tide has finally turned in our favour, that we might be near the end. I hope to God it's true. I'm ready to forget all this ever happened. I'm past ready to go home.

Home. There it was, in black and white. Home for Joe was halfway around the globe, in another hemisphere. When the war was over, she would never see him again.

Sophie let herself grieve for what could never be. She reread all of Joe's letters and then tied them together with a ribbon and tucked them away in her steamer trunk. There had to be at least one other man in the world like Joe. Perhaps she would find him one day.

October 15, 1918

Dear Joe,

News of those battles has reached us here in Paris. In fact, a nurse here is the sister of a soldier in the American 30th Division. They're from Indiana, I think. He told her at Saint Quentin that so many American officers were killed that they were basically leaderless and lost and couldn't have made it through without the Australians taking them under their wing and finishing the job. He was quite impressed with, and I quote, 'the quality of the Aussie soldiers.'

The 'flu is still an immense problem at the hospitals. Very few recover, and everyone in Paris is wearing masks, not just those of us who work at the hospital.

I have a request. Two, actually. Keep yourself away from anyone who's coughing or sneezing, if you can, and tell your men to do the same. Wash your hands as often as you can. You've made it through so much and you need to stay healthy so you can go home to Annie and Sam. Second, don't you dare leave France without letting me know! I'll come and wave goodbye from the platform or the dock or wherever you are!

TEN
UNTHINKABLE NEWS
NOVEMBER 1918, FRANCE

MELBOURNE NOV 30 1918
TO ACT CAPT JH PARKER 57BTN 15DIV AIF FRANCE
REGRET TO INFORM YOU ANNIE SUCCUMBED TO
INFLUENZA STOP
SAM SAFE WITH ME STOP
LETTER FOLLOWS STOP
MOTHER

ELEVEN

AU REVOIR

Two months after the armistice, Joe strode into the American Hospital. Hours after he received his mother's telegram, he had written to Sophie, a rambling, grief-stricken letter he didn't post, deciding instead that seeing her one last time was one of the few things he had left to look forward to, to live for even.

His mind raced through all the things he wanted to say while he waited his turn to ask for her at the reception desk. Good-bye? Thank you? Come home with me? God no, not that. Only a cad would say something like that so soon after his wife's death.

He concentrated on the pattern of the tiled floor as the battle over what to say raged in his head. A pair of child-sized lace-up boots disrupted the geometric shapes. He looked up a little and saw Jean-Luc staring at him, his small hand held by a woman's gloved hand. His heart thumped in his chest as his eyes traveled up further. To hell with holding back. He was going to kiss her. Just once. Then he would explain.

Jean-Luc pointed to him and cried, "*Maman! C'est Joe!*"

He lifted his eyes. "You're not Sophie."

The woman holding Jean-Luc's hand shook her head. "No, I'm not. Who are you?" She looked down at her child and then again at Joe. Recognition dawned on her features. "You must be Joe! I'm Natalie, Jean-Luc's mother. Sophie told me all about you."

He nodded and listened in stunned silence. "Sophie isn't here," Natalie said. "She married an English doctor."

Oh, Jesus. He was too late. He would never have the chance to tell her anything. "Michael. Michael somebody."

Natalie nodded. "Yes, Michael Edwards. The surgeries he performs fascinated Sophie and she looked forward to working with him as his nurse. They've already left for London. She wrote to tell you. I know because I posted the letter for her. Didn't you receive it?"

He shook his head. Tried to swallow. He couldn't. Natalie was saying something. "Do you have somewhere you need to be? Would you like to come home with us for dinner?"

No. He could not go back to that flat, not if Sophie wasn't there. "Sorry. No. I have a…." He had to get away. "Would you tell Sophie that I…. No. I'll write a note. Could you send it to her for me?"

"Yes, of course. I'd be happy to." Natalie searched his face. "Are you all right?"

"I'm fine, fine. Just a little…." His heart was in his throat. He could barely breathe. "I'll be quick. Just a quick note, so I don't hold you up." He could hardly think or speak. He forced himself to hold his pen and make his fingers work properly.

January 11, 1919

Dear Sophie,

I was sorry to miss you today. I'm in Paris, waiting to be demobbed, and I thought I'd make good on my promise to buy the next ice cream. Jean-Luc's mother has told me your news. I hope you'll be happy in your new life. Your husband is a very lucky man.

I'll always remember the day we met by the Eiffel Tower and the day we went back to your apartment for a meal. Your hair came loose, and I helped you to pin it up. You were threatening to cut it all off. I wonder if you ever did. And then you told me to take off my shirt so you could find the shrapnel splinter in my back. I was shocked at the time, but you were just being a confident, efficient nurse, which I'm sure you'll continue to be.

Thank you for corresponding with me. Every time I received a letter from you, I felt like a candle had been lit in the darkness. I'll never forget your many kindnesses.

Au revoir,
Joe

It was far less than he felt—he wanted her to know how much she meant to him, that she'd given him something real and precious to hold on to, that he would always be a little in love with her—but it was all he could write. He tore the page out of his notebook, folded it, and handed the note to Natalie.

Joe dropped to a crouch in front of Jean-Luc. "Goodbye, little fella. Take care of your mum," he said, so despondent he forgot to wiggle his ears to make the boy smile.

PART TWO

There's the old love wronged ere the new was won, there's the light of long ago;
There's the cruel lie that we suffer for, and the public must not know.
So we go through life with a ghastly mask, and we're doing fairly well,
While they break our hearts, oh, they kill our hearts! do the things we must not tell.

Henry Lawson, "The Things We Dare Not Tell"

TWELVE
ANOTHER MOTHERLESS CHILD
MARCH - MAY 1928

6 March 1928, London

Dear Natalie,

Well, the last of the business of settling Michael's affairs is finished, twelve long months after his death. His patients have all been transferred to other facilities and I've sold the house in Surrey. If I have to accept anyone else's condolences, I will scream. You were right. I loved him, but I didn't know him well enough to have married him.

God, I need a break. I'm in London now, at my family's town-house, and if I have to stay here one more week, I'll go mad. Can I come stay with you and Jean-Luc for a while? I'd arrive in Paris next Thursday—the usual Dover ferry to Le Havre, and then the train from Le Havre to Paris Gare du Nord. I need a change of scenery. I need to speak French again, cuddle Jean-Luc again (even though at 12 he's too big to cuddle) and curl up on the couch with my best friend and chat about whatever we want to chat about.

After that, I just don't know.

Bisous,
Sophie

PARIS 12 APRIL 1928
TO LILY HOLT BIRMINGHAM ENGLAND
NATALIE BADLY INJURED IN MOTORCAR ACCIDENT
STOP
STAYING HERE FOR DURATION STOP
SOPHIE

May 11, 1928, Paris

Dear Mother,

Thank you, again, for coming over for Natalie's funeral. I couldn't have done it all without you.

Jean-Luc and I have decided we're going to go on an adventure. I can't bear the thought of living in England again and he can't bear the thought of staying in Paris. The search for his parents' remaining family turned up no one except an ancient aunt in the throes of dementia. The poor boy has only me, his godmother. Natalie had already entrusted him to me after Louis' death at Verdun—she had the legal papers drawn up while she and I were both in Paris during the war.

So, we bought a Baedeker and a Thomas Cooke railway guide, pulled out all the atlases in the flat, and charted possible paths around the world. He's been studying French explorers in school and learned that the French had sent naturalist exploration expeditions to the Antipodes throughout the 16th, 17th, and

18th centuries. I mentioned that Aunt Flora and Uncle Richard are in Sydney, and something clicked for both of us.

I've spoken to the head man at his school. He thought our plan was terribly irregular but agreed that Jean-Luc's education wouldn't suffer too much if he was out of school for six months or so while we travel. Jean-Luc is an exceptional student, at the head of his classes in biology and English. I'll enroll him in high school wherever we settle. I'm sure the man thinks I'm completely eccentric, but I showed him all the legal documents Natalie had the foresight to update every year, and he agreed to set up a course of study that Jean-Luc can follow as we travel.

I've been in contact with my bankers, and they will make arrangements, so I have access to funds wherever we are, so you don't need to worry yourselves about that. Between the money I inherited from Grandmother, the proceeds from Michael's estate and Natalie's, and the income from my investments, we have more than enough to live comfortably for a good long while.

Could you and Father come to Paris so we can say our good-byes here? Jean-Luc is still trying to decide whether he wants to sail to Australia via the horn of Africa or through the Suez Canal. Either way, we can embark on a ship in Marseille. If he wants to visit North America, we'll sail from Le Havre to New York, travel by rail to San Francisco, and then sail to Sydney. We'll set off when the school term is over in a few weeks. By the time you arrive here, we will have decided our route.

We're both heartbroken and weary of being so sad all the time. We need something to look forward to.

Much love to you and Father,
Sophie

THIRTEEN

ARRIVAL IN AUSTRALIA

SYDNEY 1 NOV 1928
TO LILY HOLT BIRMINGHAM ENGLAND
ARRIVED SAFELY IN SYDNEY STOP
LETTER FOLLOWS STOP
SOPHIE

November 7, 1928, Sydney

Dear Mother,

Good heavens, I've had quite an eventful introduction to life in Sydney!

The first things on Aunt Flora's agenda, once Jean-Luc and I were nicely settled in (the house and grounds are gorgeous, by the way, Uncle Richard is apparently quite successful in the banking business) were to whisk me off to a luncheon so I could meet her friends and their daughters before we attended what is apparently the social event of the pre-Christmas season.

A ball, Mother. An actual ball with an orchestra, more French champagne than I've seen since the end of the war, a seated dinner, and dancing until long past midnight.

I have to say I was enjoying myself immensely. But the evening was entirely eclipsed by the sudden death of one of the women I'd met at the luncheon the previous day!

And that's not all! I saw her husband slip something into her champagne moments before she collapsed. I thought perhaps it might have been medicine of some sort, or a headache powder, but as I watched, he practically forced it down her throat.

Naturally, I imagined the worst and pulled our hostess, one of Flora's friends, aside and told her I thought the death might be suspicious and that she should call the police. She consulted with one of the guests, who turned out to be the police commissioner, and he agreed.

A bevy of officers arrived, and they divvied all of us up between the constables to give our details and relationship to the deceased, etc., etc.—all the things you imagine police must do. It was quite a fascinating thing to be a part of.

But the most incredible part of the evening was the detective who arrived. I only saw him across the ballroom and never had the chance to get any closer, but I was almost certain he was the Australian soldier I knew during the war. You remember, I told you he found Jean-Luc after I lost him by the Eiffel Tower. But the soldier, Joe, was from Melbourne, not Sydney, so it can't possibly be him, could it?

I must appear at the police station tomorrow to give a full statement, so I'll have a chance to discover who the mysterious detective is!

It's either very, very late or very, very early, so I'll sign off for now and have Aunt's staff post this letter to you as soon as possible.

I'm well, Jean-Luc is well. Flora and Richard send their love. I'll write again soon.

Much love to you and Father. Give him a kiss for me.

Sophie

FOURTEEN
REUNION IN SYDNEY
NOVEMBER 8, 1928, SYDNEY

Detective Inspector Joe Parker looked up from the case notes spread over his desk when Sergeant Fred Thompson knocked once and opened the door a few inches.

"Sir?"

"Yes?"

"A Mrs. Edwards is here to speak with you. She says she's here about last night's death."

In the early morning hours, a woman died at a society party. The medical officer's guess was poison, but the report that would pinpoint which poison wouldn't be on his desk until after lunch.

Joe rubbed his bleary eyes. "Remind me, Thompson. Which one was Mrs. Edwards?"

"Rogers interviewed her, sir."

Joe scanned the list of witness names from the night before. Ah. There she was: Mrs. M. Edwards. He must be more tired than he thought because he couldn't place a face to the name. Granted, he had arrived at the scene long past midnight, and there were so many guests and staff he'd delegated initial interviews among several constables. The only person he remembered with any clarity was someone who looked like Sophie. He scanned the witness list again and frowned. No one named Sophie—it hadn't been her.

"Right. Give me a moment and then send her in."

His door clicked closed, but he could hear a muted conversation in the reception room. Something about the woman's voice sounded familiar.

Thompson knocked again. "Sir, I'm to say that Mrs. Edwards is Sophie–"

He pushed past Thompson and rushed out of his office.

Last night he thought he was seeing things when he looked up from a woman's body sprawled on the floor of an elegant home and saw one of his constables speaking with someone who looked like Sophie, but the woman across the room had been swathed in ruby silk instead of a practical navy-blue skirt and a white blouse.

But it was Sophie who was outside his office, eleven years since they'd last seen each other. She had grown up from a pleasant-faced young woman whose hair and hats were constantly at odds. She had made good on her vow to cut her hair short, and soft dark waves framed her face. Her hat seemed secure on her head. Artful application of powder softened the smattering of freckles across the bridge of her nose, and whatever it was women used to enhance their eyelashes did its magic on hers. Her elegant suit hinted at her figure in a more conservative way than the gown she'd worn last night.

He hoped she didn't notice him swallowing hard, as he took in the sight of her. She was stunning. He couldn't think of another word to describe her. Her husband was a very lucky man.

"Detective Inspector?" Sophie was grinning at him. Her dark brown eyes still held the mischievous glint he'd seen the first time they met.

He snapped back to the present moment. "Mrs. Edwards. Thank you for coming into the station." He led her into his office.

"Joe, please. I'm still the Sophie you knew. I'm only Mrs.

Edwards in name now. Michael passed away two years ago."

"I'm so sorry. Is that why you're in.... Why are you in Sydney? I always imagined you'd be living in England. Or America, even."

"We were living in England. When Michael died, I decided I couldn't stay there, so I went back to Paris. Then...," she paused and Joe saw a tiny shake of her head. "Then, my friend Natalie, Jean-Luc's mother, died in a traffic accident. The poor boy had no family left. Since I'm his godmother, and we were both at loose ends, we came to Australia. We only arrived last week."

Her story was almost too much to take in. "Please accept my condolences. Losing your husband and your best friend must have been very difficult." They were still standing, so he pulled out the visitor's chair for her. "Have a seat." He had never seen her legs before, and he tried not to stare as she crossed one slim leg over the other. "Jean-Luc is here? In Sydney?"

Sophie nodded. "He is. We decided we wanted a fresh start. He thought Australia sounded very exciting, and I liked the idea of coming back to the country where I was born. I don't remember if I ever told you I have family here. My mother's sister, my uncle, and their two sons all live here in Sydney. They welcomed us with open arms and, well, here we are."

He listened, entranced. Her voice still held a hint of Continental cadence in the American-English accent.

"Joe?"

Once again, he came back to the present. "Sorry. It's lovely to see you again. It's been a long time, hasn't it?"

"It has. Now I know I'm here for official reasons, but first, tell me all about you! How are Annie and Sam? He must be, let's see, Jean-Luc is thirteen, so Sam is fourteen? Fifteen? Did you and Annie have any other children? And what on earth are *you* doing in Sydney? You're from Melbourne!"

"Ah." He cleared his throat. "Well. Long story short, Annie

died before I returned home from France. Influenza. Sam and I moved from Melbourne to Sydney a year after. We needed a fresh start, too."

Sophie gazed at him for a few moments, shock and sympathy spreading over her features. "I'm so sorry, Joe. I didn't know. You poor things. Sam was so young to lose his mother."

He nodded. "It was a tough time for him. Getting used to me again wasn't easy, either."

"Did you remarry?"

"Erm, no. I'm seeing someone, though. We'll see how it goes." It was his standard response to ward off many of the nosy questions people loved to ask eligible widowers. He stole a glance at Sophie. They had been close, but that was a long time ago. Too long ago to confide that the spark with Alicia Baldwin, a lovely widow who owned a favorite bookstore, seemed to be progressing the way he'd hoped. The future he'd wished for with Annie might be possible with Alicia.

He shifted the subject. "What about Jean-Luc? Where is he in school?"

Sophie brightened. "We're looking at Sydney Boys High School for the new term. He didn't like the grammar schools we visited, and I don't want to send him off to a boarding school."

"That's where Sam is. What are the odds our boys could be in the same school at the same time?"

They both spoke at the same time. "We should.... They should...."

Sophie laughed. "We're right, Joe. They should meet. Jean-Luc needs friends who are his own age. You and Sam must come for dinner as soon as you're able."

She glanced at the piles of paperwork on his desk and remembered the other reason she was in his office. "And we should get down to business because I think you need to know what I saw last night."

FIFTEEN

REKINDLED FRIENDSHIP

Dear Mother,

I've met someone, someone I think is very special. His name is Tony. Tony Ellerbee. The Honorable Antony Ellerbee. The Honorable part isn't important, not to me at least. What's important is that he's wonderful, and he thinks I'm wonderful too. We've seen each other nearly every evening for several weeks. It's far too soon to say where this will go, but I'm enjoying it immensely. I honestly hadn't ever expected to face the possibility of being romantically involved with someone again.

Tony is here to look after the Australian arm of his family's wool business. I've learned more about sheep and wool than I ever thought possible. It seems to be a good, steady business. Perhaps I should include wool in my investments.

My other news is I have a new fundraising project, one that has nothing to do with Jean-Luc's school, the Red Cross, or the local French society. This one is for the New South Wales Police Rowing Club.

Yes. A rowing club, even though I despised that obnoxious acquaintance of Ben's who was captain of the rowing club and who thought he was God's gift to women.

Rowing is so much more pleasant when a friend is involved. The friend is Joe Parker.

Joe and I have become good friends. Sam, Joe's son, is often here because our house is closer to the school than Joe's so the boys often do their homework at my dining table. On the nights when Joe has to work late, Sam stays here until Joe comes by to pick him up. Sam is a sweet boy, and smart too, but he's a little high-spirited and sometimes has a tendency to indulge in the occasional bad idea. Joe says Sam reminds him of his brother who died in the war—he has good brains, but he sometimes forgets to use them.

At any rate, Joe often stays for a late supper, and he told me all about the police rowing club. They have a record they're proud of and they want to build a new boathouse, buy several new sculls, and train more vigorously for the various competitions in Sydney (I had no idea this city had so many rowing clubs!) and around the country. If they're successful enough, they could qualify for the next summer Olympics.

But to do all that, they need money, lots of it, so they asked me to organize a series of fundraisers for them. I attended one of their races (Sunday morning at 7 am! I took a thermos of coffee). Joe made breakfast afterwards while we discussed different things the club could do. I love that Joe and I are good enough friends that a little teasing is perfectly acceptable. You should have seen the look on the poor man's face when I told him they needed to use pictures of the team in their rowing singlets and shorts on the advertisements!

I must run—I hear the telltale thump of a school satchel hitting the floor in the entry hall. That means Jean-Luc is home. He needs to prepare for a school botany trip in a few days. I'm not sure what he'll pursue after graduation, but I know plants of some sort will be involved.

Aunt Flora sends her love, as do I. Kiss Father for me.

Sophie

Sophie had liked some things about rowing very much, especially the sight of Joe chatting with his fellow rowers after the races finished. He was unselfconscious and delicious in his rowing uniform, even with the heavy woolen socks he wore to protect his feet drooping around his ankles. What a difference from the dark three-piece suits and polished brown oxfords she usually saw him dressed in! Did Alicia, the woman he'd been courting, have any idea what she was missing?

She made a concerted effort to keep her eyes on Joe's when he made his way over to her. "Well done," she said gaily.

"Did you enjoy it?"

"Some parts more than others. But on the whole, yes, I did."

"Are you hungry? If you're up for it, let me reward a new fan with breakfast."

"I could devour some Eggs Benedict right about now. Where shall we go?"

"That's far too fancy for after training. I do a great Sunday morning fry-up, though. Come to mine and I'll prove it to you."

"That sounds marvelous. You can tell me what the club needs and we can talk about ways to raise awareness and money."

"Good. I'll shower and get dressed. Won't be long."

He turned away from her and she let her eyes fall, her heart skipping a beat at the sight of the scars on his shoulders. She swallowed the urge to smooth her fingers over them, to check they'd healed properly. All the men on the dock had scars, either from the war or from their profession or both. Yet somehow, despite all the horrors they might have witnessed, they were here on a clear Sydney morning, laughing and cheerfully insulting one another. Were some of them only able to laugh like this when they were together? Or were some of them able to simply put it all behind them?

Seated in Joe's car a few minutes later, she closed her eyes and breathed yet another quiet prayer of thanks that Joe was alive and well.

Joe's voice filtered through her thoughts. "Are you tired? Would you prefer I take you home?"

She shook her head. "No, I rarely get up so early on Sundays, that's all. I'll bring two thermoses of coffee the next time. One wasn't enough."

"You really aren't a morning person, are you?"

"Flattery like that will get you absolutely nowhere."

"I'll do better next time. Especially since we do need your help with ideas for raising funds."

She grinned at him and opened her car door. "See that you do."

Rudy, the family dog, met them enthusiastically when Joe unlocked the front door. "I should go first," he warned, "and save you from being licked to death."

"I don't mind, honestly. Ben and I always had dogs when we were growing up."

"Yes, but Rudy loves ladies, and we don't have many female visitors. He might forget his manners and embarrass both of us."

A couple of stern words to Rudy had him sitting and staying while she took off her jacket and hat. She presented the back of her hand to Rudy for his inspection, and, receiving his approval, passed into the front room without being accosted.

"What can I do to help?"

"Come with me."

She followed Rudy and Joe into the sunny kitchen at the back of the house.

Joe rummaged in a drawer and produced a small pair of scissors. "Why don't you go out the back and cut whatever herbs you'd like on your eggs?"

She passed through the screened back verandah—he and Sam used it as a sleepout on nights when it was too hot to sleep indoors, even with the electric fans going—and down the steps to the grass. She paused to take in the small garden. Bordered beds for vegetables and flowers lined the fences, their neat lines interrupted by a small shed. She could hear muted clucking from chickens somewhere close. She found a basket to carry everything and turned to the flowerbeds to pick some herbs. Bees lolled above the pale-yellow blooms of a wattle tree growing by the laneway behind the garden. She snipped a few stems, thinking they would look lovely gracing the breakfast table.

A cat watched her from his vantage point on the roof of the shed. He hopped from roof to fence to grass and wound around her calves as she inhaled the scent of the wattle and then followed her across the grass to the kitchen garden Joe had planted in the sunniest corner of the yard.

"I have chives and some parsley," she called when she came back into the kitchen. Heavenly aromas of percolating coffee and sizzling bacon greeted her. She stopped short of the table and took in the sight before her: Joe in rolled-up shirtsleeves, cracking eggs into a frying pan.

"I had no idea you were so domesticated!"

Joe shrugged. "I've been feeding myself and Sam for a long time. I've had a lot of practice."

He sounded happy enough when he spoke the words, and she was proud of him for having managed so well, but how had such a nice man been on his own for so long? For at least the third time that morning, she wondered about the relationship he had with Alicia

He glanced at the wattle flowers she still held. "Did you want flowers on your eggs too?"

She burst out laughing. Rowing apparently had a wonderful effect on Joe. He was always polite and pleasant, and he was often amusing, but this morning he was positively, well, fun.

"Silly man, they're for the table. Do you own a vase?"

"Not quite that domesticated, I'm afraid."

"Never mind, a water glass will do the trick. Which cupboard?"

Joe, busy lifting the bacon out of the pan and laying it to drain on a folded newspaper, didn't look up. "To the right of the sink."

"I'll make the toast, shall I?" she asked after filling a glass with water and placing it, full of wattle blooms, in the center of the table.

"When was the last time Mrs. Collins let you in her kitchen?" Mrs. Collins, Sophie's live-in housekeeper, was an excellent cook. She also regarded the kitchen as her personal domain.

"I'll have you know I sneak in on her day off and practice my tea and toast-making skills." She arched a playful brow at him. "Sometimes I even manage a sandwich."

Joe's shoulders shook with laughter as he plated their food.

They didn't speak for the first few minutes beyond asking each other to pass the marmalade or the rack of toast. Rudy, who had behaved himself well in the face of bacon and a lady visitor, received a few bites of Joe's portion placed in his food bowl.

"This is delicious. You should place flyers of the team photo around town and offer to cook breakfast for the fans."

"Where do you propose I seat them all?" Joe deadpanned.

She rolled her eyes at him. "Hilarious. You do it at the boathouse. People could eat in the stands, or you could hire tables and chairs."

"We don't have cooking facilities there."

"Fit up a temporary kitchen, then. Or you could hold an after-noon event and offer tea and cake and sandwiches. Ask everyone to pay whatever they think is fair. People will pay more than you'd think, especially if you all mingle with everyone before you change out of your singlets and shorts."

Joe's brows shot up halfway to his hairline.

"I'm not joking. If you're serious about attracting donors, you'll need to get comfortable using whatever assets you have to further that goal. I've done some research. The other clubs host all kinds of events, like dinners, and dances, too. Of course, the funding you'll need is on a scale that a single event wouldn't bring in, but it would be a start."

"You're saying we should post photographs of the club members, in our rowing uniforms, around the city?"

She resisted the urge to give him an appraising, appreciative once-over, only saying, "Trust me, you all have definite assets. I'd be willing to bet the ladies of Sydney would agree with me. And wouldn't it be nice to give the people you protect a reason to look at you in a new light?"

While Joe digested that bit of innuendo, she took the last bite of her herb-sprinkled eggs. "Oh! I've just remembered something."

He had his own mouthful to deal with, so he could only manage an interrogative "Hmm?"

"I never had the chance to make you an omelet. Do you remember I told you I'd make you one the next time you were in Paris? Tony would never get up that early, but we could invite Alicia to join us. I can't believe she hasn't snapped you up yet."

Joe stilled at her statement. "Ah. Alicia and I are no longer seeing each other."

"Oh, I see. Why not? Sorry. It's none of my business."

"It's fine, really," he said, wiping his mouth and folding his napkin. "We've, erm, we've decided our lives are too different to be compatible. One of us would have to change too much to accommodate the other."

"Oh dear."

"Truth be told, it's been a long time coming. It's nothing tragic. Her daughters are allergic to Rudy so that was a problem too." Hearing his name, Rudy laid his muzzle on his master's thigh. Joe stroked the dog's head. "Don't worry, old boy. I would never give you up." A hint of self-deprecation flitted over his features. "There's nothing like a good dog to get you through dark times."

"I still dream about it all sometimes," she ventured, not wanting to pry but curious how he was coping under his usual unflappable façade. "Do you?"

"Sometimes. I usually know when something's happening that will trigger a bad one. That's when a dog and a book work a treat." He gave Rudy a last pat and rose to clear the table.

"Well, I'm sorry to hear about you and Alicia. Her bookstore is very nice. She has good poetry and literature selections."

"We parted on good terms. I still shop there. What about Tony? What sorts of books does he read?"

She considered his question for a moment. "Honestly, we haven't talked about it. All we ever seem to do is go to parties."

SIXTEEN

ANOTHER MAN'S MISSTEP

The setting was perfect: soft music playing in the background, champagne in their glasses, a full moon setting over Sydney Harbour. Tony's arms around her waist were strong and sure. He had pursued her from the moment they met, and Sophie had a feeling that tonight he was going to offer her everything he thought a woman would want: his heart, his name, his home.

His breath against her neck was warm. "Sophie, I adore you. Make me the happiest man in the world?"

Sophie felt safe, happy, and desired. So desired, in fact, that all she could manage was a hum in response to the lips caressing the curve of her neck.

"If that's a yes, let's leave as soon as I've wrapped up my business. Two weeks, three at the most. If I never have to come back here, it will be too soon."

The spite in his words penetrated the haze of lust his lips had invoked. "What do you mean, never come back?" she murmured.

His lips kept roving. "Just what I said. Never come back. There's nothing here, and no one, except you, to tempt me. This place is a colony. It isn't civilization. Not as we know it."

She pushed away and stared at him. "What are you saying?

Australia is civilized. Sydney is just as civilized as London, or Paris, or New York!"

Tony pulled her back and began a gentle assault on the other side of her neck. She felt his snort of derision before she heard it. "Darling Sophie, you've had your fun, escaping to the ends of the earth. It's time to leave this godforsaken place and go back to the real world. The world that matters. Say you'll come home with me."

She struggled to get free. "My fun? What about Jean-Luc? Our home is here."

"Couldn't he stay with your aunt and uncle? Or your pet police officer? It isn't as though the boy is your own son."

She couldn't believe the same man who had so generously donated one hundred pounds to the French Alliance of Sydney had just suggested that she abandon the child of her dear friend, the child entrusted to her so many years ago, a boy now on the cusp of manhood, whom she had loved and raised as her own.

It was true that Tony and Jean-Luc had never really warmed to each other. But this? She took a step back. "You cannot mean that. Leave Jean-Luc?"

Tony shrugged. "Fine. Let him tag along. Find a boarding school. England is flush with them. You can see him at the holidays if it's that important to you."

"I don't want to see him only on the holidays! I want to see him every day, like I do now! He's my son! I can't believe you're suggesting this!"

"Sophie, he isn't your blood. You need to think about the children you and I will have. We have to secure the line after all." Tony stepped forward and pulled her back to him. "And I for one am keen to begin as soon as possible."

She twisted out of his grasp and prepared to shove him away if he attempted to touch her again. "No!"

The jaw she had once admired fell slack. Tony Ellerbee, eventual Baron and member of the House of Lords, gaped like a fish. "But what about our future? Just think what we could do with your money and my lineage."

"You'll have to find someone else to be your brood mare. And to fund your ridiculous dreams."

Before she stormed away, she fixed him with a withering glare. "You may be an English gentleman, but 'my pet police officer' is more civilized than you will ever be!"

SEVENTEEN

A CIVILIZED MAN

Sophie seethed until she arrived home and followed familiar voices to her dining room.

Jean-Luc, Sam, and Joe, seated at the table, were in the middle of an animated discussion. They must have been at it for a while: Jean-Luc's hair was standing on end the way it did when he grabbed it when he was thinking. Sam sat sprawled in his chair, lips pursed. Joe, in his shirtsleeves, was making a point about something. Open books and papers covered the table.

The boys noticed her standing in the doorway. Was that panic she saw on their faces as they shoved sheets of paper under their books?

Joe jumped up from his chair and scrambled to put his jacket back on. "Sophie!"

"There's no need to get up, Joe. What were you all discussing so intently?"

Joe blinked, almost imperceptibly, and turned to the boys. She was certain both of them were shaking their heads without moving.

Joe turned back to her. "Just a little biology homework."

"Well, don't let me keep you from it. Will it disturb you if I put on some music in the drawing room?"

"We're finished," Joe said, and she was again certain some unspoken conversation was occurring because the boys looked relieved. "They just need to tidy up."

"Join me for a nightcap then?"

Joe followed her to the drawing room, his breath catching at the expanse of bare skin revealed by a backless gown the color of turquoise shallows. To give himself a moment to recover from an unexpected naughty image of Sophie as a mermaid welling up in his head, he said, "I'll join you for a small one. I have an early start tomorrow."

Sophie sank into an armchair, kicked off her shoes, and massaged the ball of one foot. "Ugh."

"How was your evening? We didn't expect you home so early."

"Well, let me put it this way." She hesitated, and then it all came out in a rush. "Tonight, I discovered Tony isn't interested in me, only my bank account and my womb."

He was accustomed to Sophie's straightforward manner, but he had no idea how to respond to that declaration. Luckily, he didn't have to because she was nowhere near finished.

"Don't misunderstand. I enjoy having money. It gives me the freedom to do whatever I want to do. I have a lovely house, which is mine, not the bank's, and I can afford to send Jean-Luc to whatever school is best for him.

"And I don't mind spending or sharing my money, but Tony wanted me to marry him, abandon Jean-Luc with Aunt Flora, or you," she said, widening her eyes at him, "and never come back to Australia."

"It's true," she said, calming down and gazing at him fondly. "I told him you're a better man than he'll ever be."

Had she really said that to Tony? And now to him? Silence seemed like his best option.

"I've been an idiot," she groaned. "I wanted it to work so much." Her eyes ranged around the room, picking out a painting, the mantel, the drinks cart. "I give up. Apparently, a happy marriage isn't in the cards for me."

"You weren't the idiot, he was." An overwhelming urge to throttle Tony Ellerbee for hurting her lent vehemence to his words. "And idiots don't deserve you. Perhaps someone will still sweep you off your feet, if that's what you want."

"Ha! I won't let that happen again. Gosh, that sounds horrible, doesn't it? I mean, I married Michael because I thought I loved him."

"Didn't you?"

"I did at first. It turned out we wanted different things. He didn't want a wife. He wanted an administrator."

He had always assumed Sophie married Michael for love, but this sounded more like a business arrangement. "Why even get married? Why not just hire someone?" She had never fully explained why she married Michael—not that he expected it, or that she owed him an explanation—but she was speaking more candidly about Michael than she ever had before.

"That's just it," Sophie began. "When I think about it, it's not so improbable that we would have chosen each other to begin with." She stared off into space for a moment, shaking her head. "He was doing important work, and I wanted to be part of it. That part never changed. It was what brought us together after all."

She rolled her neck forward to dispel the tension in her shoulders. "The real problem was we weren't friends to begin with and after a while, he stopped talking to me about anything that wasn't related to his patients. And Tony never wanted to talk about anything except elevating his place in the world. Or he never listened to me. Or something. I don't even know any more. Don't ever stop being my friend, Joe. Please?"

She sounded so vulnerable and unhappy that he ached to comfort her. What could he say to assure her things would get better? Their usual banter seemed too trivial in the face of such a momentous request.

Before this evening, aside from offering a hand to help her out of the car or his arm when they were in a crowd, he had barely touched her in all the time they had known each other. She had touched him from the beginning, in Paris all those years ago, first his arm in thanks, his back to find the shrapnel sliver, his cheek when watching Jean-Luc sleep was too much to bear.

The thin straps of her evening gown exposed her shoulders, but he didn't dare offer to massage them for her. Instead, he glanced at the foot she was rubbing and moved his armchair closer to her. He patted his knees. "Let me," he said.

Her eyes widened in surprise, but she gave over her foot when he affirmed his intentions with another pat on his knee.

"God, that feels good." She lifted her other foot to his knee. "Would you?"

For a few minutes, the only sounds in the quiet room were Sophie's soft sighs and the rustle of her skirts as he massaged from her ankles to her pink painted toenails. She was still the cheerful, smart, caring woman she'd been when they first met, but right now she seemed as fragile as the delicate bones his fingers were swirling over.

The effort required to lift her head must have been too much because she spoke through the dark curls veiling her face. "What were you and the boys talking about? It seemed awfully serious."

"Erm...." She needed to know, and that meant he needed to tell her. "Biology. The birds and bees sort of biology."

Sophie's head popped up. "Oh?"

"They asked, and I thought they should have correct information instead of relying on what they'd heard from their friends. I know it was presumptuous of me to speak to Jean-Luc without asking you about it first. I hope you're not upset."

"Good heavens, no. I was dreading having that talk with him. I know I shouldn't have. I was a nurse. I ought to be able to talk to him about sex, and the differences between men's and women's bodies, and how babies are made. And how to prevent making babies, come to that, but—"

"That's the sort of talk his father should have had with him?"

"Exactly. I wasn't sure how I should broach the subject, since he hadn't asked. Thank you for relieving me of my fatherly duties." She laughed a little. "Oh Lord, you should tell me how much you told them."

He felt his ears getting warm.

"Joe! It's me! There's no need to be embarrassed. Knowing you, you covered all the possibilities. You're nothing if not thorough."

He smiled. "There may have been some drawings, too. Badly done, of course, but accurate. Promise me you'll never tell the boys you know about them."

Sophie dissolved into giggles, which made him laugh, and then she laughed until she was wiping tears from the corners of her eyes. He wasn't sure if she was laughing at his words, or because the cognac had made her silly, or because his fingers had tickled her sole, but she was laughing, and that was enough.

She smiled at him, reached for his hand, and squeezed his fingers. "Thank you. I needed that."

As much as he would have loved to gather her in his arms and say that her laugh was the most wonderful sound he had ever heard, and he would do anything he could to deserve her, tonight was not the time. If he ever made a declaration, it wouldn't be on the heels of another man's misstep. Instead, he made an elaborate show of placing her feet on the rug and moving his armchair back in its place.

"In that case, my work here is done."

Sophie laughed again and walked with him to the front door where Sam was waiting.

EIGHTEEN

VOYAGE TO ENGLAND

SEPTEMBER - OCTOBER 1930

LONDON 15 SEP 1930
TO SOPHIE HOLT EDWARDS SYDNEY AUSTRALIA
FATHER HAS SUFFERED HEART ATTACK STOP
PROGNOSIS VERY POOR STOP
COME EARLIEST STOP
MOTHER

SYDNEY 16 SEP 1930
TO LILY HOLT LONDON ENGLAND
ARRANGING FLIGHTS TRAINS SAILINGS STOP
ARRIVING THREE WEEKS STOP
ALL MY LOVE TO BOTH OF YOU STOP
SOPHIE

October 15, 1930, London

Dear Joe,

You can't imagine how touched I was by the beautiful wreath you and your men arranged for Father's funeral. The service was lovely, and the church was packed with his friends and business associates. He was a wonderful man and well-loved. Mother and I felt so comforted by that in the days afterward.

We have a lot to do now with the lawyers and accountants, so I'll have to stay here in London as long as Mother needs my help. Of course, that means I must continue to rely on your help with Jean-Luc for a while longer. I know I'm asking so much, too much probably, but I really don't know what I'd do without you.

All my best,
Sophie

NINETEEN

TU ME MANQUES

NOVEMBER 1930, LONDON

"Post for you, Miss." Jones, the family butler she grew up with, presented her with a small parcel on a silver salver. Recognizing Joe's careful print and the Australian stamps, she reached for it eagerly.

The past few weeks had been long: a rushed voyage by sea, air, and land from Australia to England, trying to work through her own sorrow over the death of her father days after she arrived, plus helping her grief-stricken mother deal with funeral arrangements, solicitors, and accounts. A letter from Joe would be a great distraction, one best savored in the quiet and privacy of her own room.

"I'm going upstairs to rest before dinner," she said to her mother, Lily.

She waited until she was ensconced on the chaise in front of the fireplace to open Joe's parcel. The scent of home wafted from the brown paper-wrapped contents. Joe had slipped a couple of eucalyptus leaves between the pages of a slim volume of Dorothea Mackellar's poems. She snuggled under a cashmere shawl and read the news in his letter first.

Dear Sophie,

You'll manage beautifully, just like you always do. We all miss you, but please, take as much time as you and your mother need. The important thing is that you take care of her and yourself.

Your Aunt and I encountered a few glitches at the beginning, but she raised two boys of her own and I think I might be doing a reasonable job of it with Sam, so between the two of us we've settled into a good routine with school, sports, and all the clubs they're involved in.

Jean-Luc's latest school reports were excellent, as always. His English teacher says he's capable of teaching the class himself, but he's more interested in that extra botany class he's been taking. Sam's marks in French were not excellent, but he did well in mathematics. He must have inherited that from my mother since she was the numbers wizard in my family.

Rudy had yet another biffo with the neighbor's cat. You think he'd have learnt by now that the cat shouldn't be messed with, but he hasn't, and he's sporting a large scratch on his nose.

Thompson and the rest of the lads at the station send their regards. They're looking a little thinner since you haven't been supplying them with treats for their tea breaks. I wonder if that has anything to do with the fact he and his mob have become the eights to beat at the rowing club.

Let me know how you and your mother are coping. I've enclosed a little something to remind you of us in the 'sunburnt country.'

All my best too.
Fondly,
Joe

She opened the book of poetry to the place Joe had marked, breathing in the astringent scent of the leaf, imagining his voice reciting the poem, longing for home. It was late spring in Sydney, warm and sunny, and she was shivering in a damp, cold English autumn. But as much as she missed Jean-Luc, her friends, and her own house, going weeks without Joe's quiet hellos and dry humor and steady presence had become unbearable.

She murmured, "*Tu me manques,*" to the flames in the fireplace, as though the smoke could carry her words, "*you are missing from me,*" up the chimney and across the miles to Joe. Her eyelids grew heavy, and she drifted into a dream where she stood on the dock at the police rowing club, wondering why there were no boats, or rowers, or anyone else around. Golden flowers floating down from wattle trees lining the banks barely disturbed the water's mirrored surface.

In the far distance, a single scull making its way from the harbor became visible. She watched Joe's steady rhythm as he rowed to the dock and then lifted the boat from the water and stashed it in the shed.

She openly drank in the sight of him as he walked toward her, long legs and broad shoulders, the thin fabric of his rowing singlet and shorts hinting at the promise of his body.

He stopped when they were only a few inches apart. "This is a nice surprise. I didn't expect to see you here this morning."

Still gazing at him, she slipped her arms around his waist and breathed in musky, sun-warmed male. His heart thumped under her cheek. He was sturdy and resilient, like a tree that had weathered a hundred storms and still leafed out each spring. He felt like forever. She had always known he would.

"I miss you," she whispered against his chest. "So much. I never want to be away from you again."

Joe gathered her close, cradling her head under his chin. "Come back to me. I'll be here when you come home."

She startled awake when the book of poems dropped to the floor. Her dream had been so vivid that if Joe had been anywhere in the vicinity, she would have declared she was hopelessly in love with him and then ravished him on the spot. Instead, she did the next best thing.

Dear Joe,

Thank you for all the news and the book of poetry. It's such a thoughtful gift. I miss you more than I can say in a letter.

Tell Fred I'll be bringing Mrs. Collins' shortbread again soon. Perhaps that will help give your mob, as you call it, a needed edge!

I don't know if you remember, but I was on a committee to raise funds for the Sydney Observatory. The culmination of our efforts is a gala on New Year's Eve. Would you do me the great honor of accompanying me?

I plan to be home on the 30th—I'll rest up that day, but I can't imagine waiting longer than the next evening to see you again! Please say yes to the gala.

Fondly,
Sophie

TWENTY

RETROUVAILLE

DECEMBER 31, 1930, SYDNEY

Dressing for the gala on New Year's Eve, Joe felt rather daunted by the idea of spending several hours in a crowd of wealthy people he didn't know. Still, it was preferable to staying home. As much as he enjoyed quiet evenings with a good book and a glass of whiskey, the prospect of seeing Sophie for the first time in four months made him feel like a teenager giddy in the throes of his first crush.

For four long months, she had been his last thought before he slept and his first thought when he woke. He had fallen asleep more than once wondering what it would be like to glide his palms up her silk-stockinged legs or trail his fingers down the silky skin on her back. Even more than longing for her physically, he missed her fond smiles, her gentle teasing, and her quick mind challenging him.

As he checked his reflection to make sure his bowtie was straight, he knew this was no mere crush. He was deeply, irrevocably, in love with her.

The only question was how to proceed. How could he gauge her interest and retreat gracefully if it seemed she wasn't interested in a romantic relationship with him? Her last telegram had said something about celebrating the new year, full of things that had never been, He could drop a hint about things that had never been but could be now.

He arrived at the festive, lighted tents surrounding the Observatory, and immediately spotted Sophie making her way to him. The jewels at her throat sparkled. Her dress shimmered. She parted the crowd, radiating like a sunbeam that had burst through the clouds.

When Sophie reached him, he was so surprised by her exuberant hug that he responded in kind. When they finally pulled apart, they held each other's gaze for so long he was certain the friendship and affection that existed between them blossomed into something else entirely.

Moments later, waltzing with her in the prescribed and proper way—his hand skimming her bare back and her hand light on his arm, their fingers curled together—he couldn't imagine anything he would rather do than hold Sophie in his arms. For a blissful moment, everything was possible. Then a man with more money, more connections, more of everything he wasn't, reminded her she'd promised him a dance.

Therein lay the problem. How could he have missed it? He could never afford to give Sophie jewels or dresses like the one she wore tonight. His salary was sufficient for him and Sam to live comfortably, and he had a modest family legacy he tried not to touch except for extraordinary purchases. There would always be a man who could give her far more than he could. He couldn't compete.

He guided Sophie's hand to the waiting gentleman and left the dance floor.

∼

Joe strode away from the lights and laughter in the tents to the edge of the lawn on Observatory Hill. Storm clouds had concealed the sun most of the day, but they had moved on, unveiling a clear sky ablaze with stars. He lifted his face to them and willed himself to breathe normally.

He stood, hands thrust deep in his pockets, wrestling with how he could give up loving her, until an arm slipped around his and Sophie tucked herself close to his side, her face turned upward too.

"When we left Australia for California, Ben and I were so confused by our new house and all the strangers and the funny accents. We'd lie on the grass, look at the sky, and pretend we were navigating by the stars to get back home to Australia. Well, Ben navigated. I just thought the stars were shiny and pretty."

He loved that she often poked fun at herself. "So, your interest in astronomy goes way back," he said and huffed a laugh, relieved that things between them hadn't changed. They could pick up where they left off before she went to England. He wouldn't let her know how he really felt about her. Their friendship was too important for him to spoil it with unrequited feelings.

She squeezed his arm and laughed with him. "I was only five."

"After Annie died, someone told Sam that his mother was watching him from heaven, and he liked to guess which star she was hiding behind. I didn't have a better answer, so we spent hours looking at the stars from the back garden."

"What a lovely thing to do for Sam! I'll bet that's why he likes the stars so much. They remind him of his mother and spending time with you."

Was it any wonder he loved her?

"Ben was certain he could get us back home if he could just find the Southern Cross," Sophie said. "He never had the chance to see it again. When I came back to Australia, and I saw it for the first time in years…."

She rested her head on his shoulder. "On the night Ben died, the stars seemed close enough that I could reach up and run my fingers through them. It was such a gift to see something so beautiful after a day of misery and pain and death. He's the main reason I helped raise money for the Observatory with this gala."

In the silence after she spoke, a tear shimmered and slid down her cheek. He smoothed it away with his thumb.

"In the trenches, we could only see narrow strips of the sky. On clear nights, I was so grateful to see even that small part of it. I realized there was nothing we could do to make the stars go away, even though we were doing our damnedest to wipe humanity off the face of the earth. I often wondered if you were looking up too."

They stayed still, and quiet, and close until Sophie shivered when a slight breeze came upon them.

He detached himself and turned to her. Her gown had no sleeves, only straps that crisscrossed over her back. "We should go back to the tents. You're depriving several gentlemen of the pleasure of your company on the dance floor."

"I don't want to go back."

"Then take my coat." He shed his dinner jacket and held it open for her to slip one arm in, then the other. To his surprise, she caught his hands, turned so she was standing with her back to him and guided his arms around her waist.

When she murmured, "You're the only man I want to dance with," he couldn't have moved away if he tried. Surely she could feel his heart pounding when she leaned against his chest.

He laid his cheek against her head, and let himself fall, jewels and tears and stars forgotten. "Your letters…." He faltered for a moment and then rallied. "I thought about you all the time."

Sophie turned and draped her arms over his shoulders, her

dark eyes luminous in the starlight. "I couldn't wait to see you again."

"I couldn't wait for you to come home." He searched her face until he was certain she understood his hope.

Sophie nodded, and their lips met in the softest of kisses. Then she tightened her arms around him, and the full force of how much he had missed her and how much he loved her tumbled around him. He poured all the love and longing he'd ever felt for her into that kiss.

They were breathless when he rested his forehead against hers. Then she whispered, "Thank goodness. I feel exactly the same way about you." He felt the smile on her lips as they kissed again.

TWENTY-ONE

A NEW LIFE

Joe was smiling at her. Sophie resisted the urge to abandon the letter she was writing and convince him to abandon his. She raised a brow at him, a promise for what was to come later.

Dear Mother,

Do you remember saying I should go home to Sydney and tell Joe how I felt about him? You asked me what was the best that could happen.

It turns out the best that could happen is that I'm going to marry my best friend. With whom I also happen to be head over heels in love.

Joe is smart and funny and careful and loyal and loveable under the strong, silent type exterior. I think he's also very handsome, which isn't nearly as important as all the other things are, but my goodness, it doesn't hurt. What I feel for Joe is completely different from what I felt for Michael or Tony. I feel like we have a truly solid foundation of friendship that I never had with either of them. I'm not sure I can describe it, Mother. It's liberating. I feel like I can be myself with a man I love. Finally.

I'm thirty-six years old and financially independent and well past the age of girlish flights of fancy, but I can't, and don't want to imagine life without Joe. I told him I thought we should get married as soon as possible and he agreed with me!

Aunt Flora told me if I'm happy she would manage the gossips who think wealthy women shouldn't marry men who aren't. We're getting married next month. It will be a registry office ceremony—I'm not religious anymore and Joe isn't either. Jean-Luc, Sam, and Aunt Flora and Uncle Richard will be our witnesses. I think Richard and the boys are more enthused at the prospect of a good, long wedding lunch!

Joe is writing to his mother and Annie's mother in Melbourne to let them know. He and I will travel there a week or so after the wedding for a short honeymoon. I want to see where he grew up and meet his mother.

We found the most wonderful house. It's on a hill, with views of the Pacific Ocean from the front and Sydney Harbour from the back. The previous owners were dreadfully overextended when the markets crashed and they fled to Queensland or Western Australia or somewhere, abandoning their house and leaving a huge number of debts. I managed to grab it at the bank's latest auction. We're going to rent out my house and the house Joe bought when he and Sam first moved here. The real estate market is still down, but people will always need a place to live. You taught me to manage money well, Mother dear. I'll always be grateful for that. My investments are holding steady. Wheat, beer, steel, and timber are always in demand, even though the prices can fluctuate wildly in the short term. I've also invested in wool for the same reasons. My only real indulgence has been travelling with Jean-Luc to all the places he wanted to visit, and Joe's is books and rowing, so all three houses are paid for.

Unfortunately, crime goes up when the economy goes down, but that means Joe's position is secure, especially since his solve rate is high. I worried less about him staying physically safe after I learned how fit and agile he keeps himself. He says he has to be ready for anything, so he works out at the police gymnasium, rows, and runs. Joe insists his constables stay fit as well and he takes good care of them. He knows all their families and their wives and children's names and, well, he's something of a father figure to them. Not an indulgent father, but a fair one.

I'll close for now. We're going to run over to the new house and see how the painters are getting on.

Much love,
Sophie

P.S. I'm enclosing a newspaper clipping with the photo of me and my dashing detective from the New Year's Eve gala at Sydney Observatory. I'll send wedding photos as soon as they're developed.

TWENTY-TWO

THE LINE OF DUTY

FEBRUARY 1939, SYDNEY

Sophie pushed through the phalanx of photographers and reporters crowding the hospital's entrance steps.

"Where is he? Where's Joe?"

Joe's second in command, Fred Thompson, caught her as her shoe snagged the hem of her silk evening gown.

"He's in surgery. He went in as soon as we arrived."

"What happened? He was supposed to meet me at my aunt's party. He never arrived."

"Rogers' wife went into labor. The Inspector told him to go be with his wife, that he'd take his place. We'd planned the raid for weeks. It should have gone without a hitch, but—"

She struggled against Thompson's burly arms still holding her in place. "I need to see him."

"Mrs. Parker, the medics said he should be fine. The bullets passed through his shoulder without hitting anything important. They just need to patch him up."

She had spent enough time nursing wounded men to know anything could happen. Infection, an adverse reaction to the anesthesia, a slip of the scalpel. She could barely conceive of becoming a widow again in the far distant future—becoming one tonight was unthinkable. She fought her panic. Tears could come later. Right now, she needed to be strong. "You can let go of me now, Fred," she said.

Abashed, her husband's senior sergeant dropped his hands. "My apologies. I was only trying to steady you," he said. "Let me take you in and we'll wait for the doctors to finish the surgery."

She turned to the men who had been watching and waiting, their hands full of notebooks and cameras. She knew some of them, but at the moment she could hardly remember their faces, much less their names. "Thank you all for being here. It means everything to me you're so concerned about my husband. I'm sure Sergeant Thompson will keep you apprised of the situation."

February 6, 1939

Dear Mother,

There is so much to say, and so many plans to make, that I don't know quite how or where to begin. Bearing all that in mind, please, do both of us a favor and sit down in your favorite chair by the window in the morning room and read this letter quickly first and then again slowly. You'll understand why after the first read through.

Joe has been injured. Don't worry, he's fine, and recovering. In twenty-six years of police work and two years on the Western Front he managed to escape serious injury until a raid earlier this week at the dockside lair of Sydney's most notorious drug kingpin. Luckily, Joe's men were all unharmed, but he was shot—twice in the left shoulder and a third bullet grazed his left temple. How the kingpin reached such exalted status without being a better shot is beyond my understanding (and Joe's too)! I will be eternally thankful for inept criminals.

Following some very spirited discussions with me and his

superiors, Joe agreed he could put his extensive experience to safer use, and he accepted the Police Commissioner's offer to take over as head of the force's new forensics department.

There was one condition, however, about which I was adamant. Joe is to be allowed an extended leave of not less than four months and probably closer to eight to recuperate fully and transition from everyday policing to an administrative post. I asked the Commissioner if it would be possible for Joe to meet with his counterparts in North America and London to study how each city incorporates the latest forensics techniques in their work. He agreed!

We sail from Sydney to San Francisco in April and from New York to London in early June. We'll return to Sydney in mid-August. I want to take Joe to Paris. He only had a few days there during the war and it will be like a second honeymoon for us. I loved our first honeymoon in Melbourne, but there's no place like Paris, is there? I'm finally ready to go back there and I want to see it all with Joe and he wants to see it with me.

Now I come to the next point of this letter. I would like you to consider the possibility of leaving England and coming back to Australia with us. You have a capable manager in Mr. Burgess, and you could leave the business in his expert hands. With telephones and airmail, it would be easy for him to consult with you if needed and you could plan a visit every couple of years. Or you could even consider selling all or part of the business to him. With Father gone, and me and Aunt Flora living in Sydney, doesn't it make sense to be close to us instead of on the other side of the world?

You can expect a letter from Aunt Flora as well. I've told her my idea, and she's hoping you will live with her. She says her house is far too big and empty with Uncle Richard gone and the boys grown and raising families of their own. I think she thinks the two of you could re-live your glory days and take Sydney by storm!

Think about it. Please?

Joe sends greetings. He has been cross and grumbling about not being able to row while his shoulder heals, but the prospect of finally seeing parts of North America has given him something to look forward to. He spends hours researching what to see and where to go.

I'll send the last details of our journey as soon as I know them, but plan on seeing us in London in June.

Much love,
Sophie

PART THREE

We see but pride in a selfish breast, while a heart is breaking there;
Oh, the world would be such a kindly world if all men's hearts lay bare!
We live and share the living lie, we are doing very well,
While they eat our hearts as the years go by, do the things we dare not tell.

Henry Lawson, "The Things We Dare Not Tell"

TWENTY-THREE

SOJOURN IN PARIS

JULY 14, 1939, PARIS

Joe and Sophie arrived at the Gare du Nord train station in Paris on the morning of Bastille Day.

Joe turned to the left and right, taking it all in. The wrought iron rafters and dusty glass roof spanning a multitude of tracks were the same. The crush of arriving and departing passengers was the same. But brightly dressed women, over-excited children, and linen-suited men swarmed the platform, not khaki-clad soldiers. Sophie was by his side. Frankie, Sid, Davy, and Geordie were nowhere to be seen.

The masses jostling to get the best spot to watch the pomp of the Bastille Day parade on the Champs Elysée were overwhelming. When Sophie tugged his hand, he followed her away from the crowds and toward the River Seine instead.

Music and laughter beckoned from around corners along their way. They found street parties where everyone in the neighborhood was out, dressed in their best. Old couples and young couples and every age in between danced in the street and toasted the day, France, and Paris.

At Sophie's urging, he stuffed a generous number of francs in the barrels placed outside a *pompier* station and they shook hands with the firefighters. They were invited to join another street party, "*Venez, madame! Asseyez-vous, monsieur!*" and share a communal dinner at tables lining the length of the street.

Sophie sang the *Marseillaise*, danced with him and anyone else who asked, and kissed cheeks with complete strangers who put aside their normal reserve on the 150th anniversary of the day the French gained independence from the monarchy in 1789.

Her French was almost as fluent as it had been when she left France in 1918. Joe had studied Latin in school, but he had experience listening to Sophie and Jean-Luc converse, and his wartime French came back in snippets throughout the day.

Once twilight fell and the streetlights flickered on, he was pleasantly full and a little tipsy and he discovered he understood far more French than he thought he did. An ancient veteran, his medals crowded and clicking on his dusty black coat, hobbled over and pumped their hands when he learned they were Australian and American.

He listened with amusement when the old man told Sophie she was *très belle* and asked her for a Bastille Day kiss. She pecked him on both grizzled cheeks and said, "*Et maintenant, mon mari, qui est très beau et qui j'adore, m'attende.*"

"Your husband is very handsome?" Joe asked when she sidled up to him. "And you adore him?"

"*Absolument!*" she exclaimed. She linked her arm with his led him to the Pont Neuf bridge to watch the fireworks over the river.

Reality faded when he heard the staccato of firecrackers. Explosions pounded his ears. Whiffs of cordite drifting on the evening breeze woke long-buried memories. Fromelles, Bullecourt, Polygon Wood, Villers-Bret, Saint Quentin Canal surged into his consciousness.

He reacted instinctively, pulling Sophie close, shielding her body with his, all the while gauging which weapon—knife, pistol, grenade—he could reach to protect her.

Then appreciative oohs and ahhs, not pained groans, filtered through his scrambled thoughts. Dozens of affectionate couples, not dying soldiers, surrounded them on the bridge. Fireworks, not shell bursts, bathed faces lifted to the glowing sky.

Unaware of his lapse, Sophie leaned over the railing to wave at a passing barge crammed with revelers, her movement and scent grounding him firmly in the present and triggering an entirely different set of responses. Again, he reacted instinctively, nuzzling her neck, holding her more closely against his body— things he would never do in public at home.

TWENTY-FOUR
PARCE-QUE JE T'AIME
JULY 15, 1939, PARIS

The next morning, Joe woke feeling rested and refreshed. He tucked a hand behind his head and ran through what had happened the night before. The fireworks had triggered a few bad memories, but that wasn't surprising given this was his first time in France in two decades. He hadn't had a war dream, at least not one he could remember. Then again, he always slept well after making love with Sophie. The results of last night's race to their hotel after several very public, increasingly passionate embraces on the bridge had been...rather spectacular.

Sophie shifted beside him and slipped her arm around his torso. "Mmmm...that was a lovely surprise last night."

He lifted her hand to his lips and kissed her knuckles. "I have another one for you."

"Oh good," she murmured, still drowsy. "We can do that again whenever you like."

"That's not the surprise I had in mind. You'll have to wait until after we get up and get dressed."

She slid her leg over his and snuggled closer. "Then what should we do before we get dressed?"

After a late breakfast, Joe led Sophie through a nondescript passage in the Latin Quarter and into the Arènes de Lutèce, a tiny Roman arena.

"I knew the Romans had colonized France, Spain, England, and even a sliver of Germany," he explained as she twirled around, astonished that she'd never known about this place. "I visited some Roman sites when I went to England for training. But I figured I'd never have a chance to see any sites in France, so being able to see a Roman ruin in Paris was a lucky break."

"You didn't go back to the Eiffel Tower when you were demobbed?"

"I couldn't face going there without you. I had a rotten headache from too much wine after I found out you were married and had already left Paris. Concentrating on the Romans was a way to put everything out of my mind."

He grabbed her hand, eager to show off his find. "C'mon," he said. "Let's climb to the top."

After visiting the arena, they headed past the Bois de Boulogne to Suresnes, the American cemetery where those who had died at the American Hospital during the war were buried. Sophie had several patients buried there. Ben's grave was there too.

They stopped at a flower shop on the way and purchased several bunches of flowers. Joe stayed close while she wandered the rows, placing a few blooms at markers where she recognized a name. When they reached Ben's headstone, she sank to the ground and ran her fingers over his name engraved on the marble cross. She still missed him and their easy friendship. Ben had

been less than two years older than her, and they had been insepa-
rable when they were children.

"You would have liked him," she said eventually. She squared
her shoulders, took a deep breath, and rose from the grass.

"I wish I'd known him," Joe said. "Your brother was a brave
man." He touched the top of Ben's headstone, smoothing his
fingers over the cool marble as they turned from the grave.

The cemetery was on a hill to the west of Paris. When they
exited the gold tipped, black wrought-iron gates and looked to the
east, they could see the entire city below them.

Joe held her hand until she could speak. "Thank you for
coming with me."

"Of course I was going to come with you." He pulled her
close and laid his cheek against the top of her head. "I'd rather be
anywhere with you than anywhere by myself."

They made their way to the Eiffel Tower and stood beneath it,
Joe looking up and she looking at him, marveling that they had
found each other to begin with, had found each other again in
Sydney, and that they were here now.

"To think this is where it all started," Joe began. Before he
could finish, she shifted from his side and kissed him, a long, soft,
sweet, slow kiss.

His eyes fluttered open, wide and wondering, when she pulled
back. His hands played at her waist. "What was that for?"

"For being such a good man, Joe Parker. Then and now. *Et
parce-que je t'aime*."

His expression of triumph when he puzzled out the French
words was so silly and so endearing that her mood lifted. "I don't
know what *parce-que* means, and I don't know how to say also,
but I love you too."

In the remaining days in Paris they felt, as well as heard, the reverberations and echoes of an organ concert at Saint Sulpice and strolled through a kaleidoscope of colors from light streaming through the stained glass at Sainte-Chappelle. They marveled at the ability of humans to create beauty from bellows and strings, sand and fire, paint and marble. They watched the world go by from sidewalk cafés, dined by candlelight in tiny restaurants, and crossed the bridges over the Seine hand-in-hand. Even with the poignant moments, their sojourn in Paris was as romantic and memorable as sojourns in Paris should be.

TWENTY-FIVE

FROM PARIS TO THE PAST

JULY 21, 1939, VILLERS-BRETONNEUX

Since Villers-Bretonneux was less than a four-hour drive to the east, they took their time leaving Paris a week later. They woke as the bells of a nearby church tolled seven times. His rumbled murmurs and Sophie's soft sighs mingled with the pigeons cooing above their open windows. When the bells tolled eight, he untangled his legs from hers and called for coffee, croissants, and newspapers to be sent up to their room. They breakfasted and read and then Sophie bathed while he shaved and dressed.

As far as Joe was concerned, the Australian national memorial would be little more than a monument to pomp and circumstance that was the least his king and country owed its loyal subjects. No speech, anthem, or wreath could bring Robbie back or save Stanley from the German's knife. When they left Villers-Bret, Sophie and he would resume their life just as they left it before they stepped onto the memorial grounds.

When they left the hotel, Joe was satisfied he had a grasp of how the next day would unfold, and he relaxed while Sophie navigated to the outskirts of Paris and beyond. She enjoyed driving, and was good at it, even if she drove faster than he would have liked. In Paris, she was in her element, maneuvering the car through the crowded streets with an *élan* that the Parisian motorists appreciated. She deserved the admiring looks she received. He knew he deserved the envious looks he received.

That attitude served him well for the first hour outside Paris. The luxurious car they were in was far more comfortable than the troop trains he had relied on for transportation when he was here during the war. The trains, with their haze of cigarette smoke and fug of sweaty, uniformed bodies, had always been noisy with songs and jokes on the journeys away from the front and slurred stories and snoring on the train's return.

Joe had heard time and time again that Villers-Bret had been the greatest Australian victory of the war, that it was one of the decisive Allied victories that had halted the German army less than two hours from Paris. Having just spent a glorious week there with Sophie, the idea of an occupied and defeated Paris was inconceivable.

When he left this country behind twenty years ago, it was a frigid, grey winter and the land was fallow. Now, in late July, it was warm, sunny, and vibrant. The fields were fertile. The air was fragrant. Lulled by the quiet rumble of the engine and the scents of soil and green things warmed by the sun, he dozed.

Sophie pulled off the road and gazed fondly at her husband.

"Joe? Darling?"

He turned his face into the warm hand cupping his jaw. "Hmm?"

"We need to look at the map."

He stretched and sat straighter in his seat. "Sorry about that. Just having a bit of a kip. Are we there yet?"

"Not quite. And it's perfectly understandable. We had a very busy week and a lot more wine than usual.

"And less sleep than usual. Not that I'm complaining, mind you."

"Less sleep than usual is one way of putting it," she teased, patting his thigh. In Paris, they'd made love far more often than usual. Unfettered by the daily demands of work, telephones, and society, they'd indulged so often that Joe had joked they were having their second, third, and fourth honeymoons all at once. Then there were the times they woke during the night, caressing each other with the urgency of newlyweds or parted lovers reunited after a long separation.

She handed Joe the book of maps they'd purchased in Paris. "Let's get out and stretch our legs and figure out where we are."

She waited quietly while he flipped through the pages of the Michelin Guide and then opened the map against the hood of the car. Knowing exactly where they were, she had purposely stopped here so Joe could acclimate himself to the reality that he was once again very close to the former front lines and the towns where he'd fought. On the surface, he had been remarkably sanguine about visiting the memorial, but she remembered the tight line of his jaw when they discussed the invitation in London. This was his first return to France since the war and she believed treading lightly was the best approach.

She had needed time to adjust the first time she returned to France in 1919 for the dedication of the Suresnes American Cemetery, where Ben and many other patients from the American Hospital in Paris were buried. Her parents and Michael had been there, too. The day had been solemn, but it was also joyful because she saw so many old friends and acquaintances. The experience had comforted her, and she hoped Joe would feel the same way at the memorial.

She laid a gentle hand on his back and silently ticked off names while he continued to take it all in: Amiens, Villers-Bretonneux, and Saint Quentin, towns in the heart of the Somme valley where he'd spent the final months of the war, were all within fifty miles. Fromelles, where he fought when he first arrived in France, was less than a day away. Bullecourt, where he'd been wounded and his brother Robbie had gone missing, was only slightly further afield.

She waited a few moments before pointing to the map. "We're here." She indicated two branches of the road. "I'm wondering whether it's better to stay on the road we're on toward Amiens or take these smaller roads toward Corbie and then go west to Villers-Bretonneux. Both ways will get us there."

Joe's eyes darted over points on the map. To the far north lay Ypres and Zonnebeke, known to English-speaking soldiers as Wipers and Polygon Wood. To the east lay Verdun with its fortress. Forests—Argonne, Ardennes, and rivers—Marne, Meuse, Somme, bore names that figured just as large as town names.

His heart beat faster as he registered the staggering number of military cemeteries, memorials, and lost villages in France and Belgium. Polygon Wood in Belgium had been as bloody a battle as Fromelles had been. There were no trench lines, division markers, or headquarters symbols on the map, but all 450 miles of the Western Front, from the English Channel to Switzerland, appeared before them. They were on the westernmost edge of the front, a place he had never dreamed he would return to, but he was here on a peaceful mission to find his brother's name on a wall, not to fight.

That knowledge calmed his racing thoughts. He checked his watch. "It's almost four. Why don't we take the smaller roads to Villers-Bret? Let's find the memorial and get the lay of the land."

When Sophie agreed, he refolded the map and they set off

again. On the way, he told her how the Romans built many of the roads and bridges throughout Europe, including the straight road which would take them from Villers-Bretonneux to Amiens.

Talking about something else had distracted him and helped soothe his nerves, but where they were heading became a worrying reality when the town marker for Villers-Bretonneux appeared. The Roman road was still there—of course it would be —it had been there for centuries and would be for centuries more. The Red Chateau, a manor house owned by the local gentry, was there too, but barely. It was ruined, but its façade was still standing, its once gracious windows now framing sky and clouds.

Most of the other structures in the town had been rebuilt. The returning townsfolk must have recovered all the undamaged brick, timber, and roof tiles and set to recreating their homes and businesses. He supposed the street names were the same too, but Rue de Melbourne? Melbourne Street? When had that happened? If not for the Red Chateau and the Roman road, he wouldn't recognize this place. The last time he was here, piles of smoking rubble blocked most of the streets. Australian flags hadn't been flying from the lampposts and windows either.

The memorial's great tower that rose above the plains was visible long before they arrived at the gates. Sophie drove past the far wall and stopped on the side of the road.

He got out of the car and swivelled slowly to take it all in. The surrounding countryside was lush, with fields of grain and grass in every direction. He had forgotten how wide the horizons were here, how morning mists filled the hollows and evening sunsets saturated the sky with color. It was quiet now, but that night had been quiet too, at first, before his and two other Australian battalions crossed the broad, gently rolling plain and fought their way from the north to the town.

"If the Germans had held on here, then Amiens and the channel ports would have been next, wouldn't they?"

Her question startled him out of his memories. "Yes." He cleared his throat to mask the tremor building in his voice. "The war would have been over, or close to it."

He could control his voice, but not the cold sweat pricking his skin. Smoke from a neighboring farm caught in his nostrils. Bullets flew. Bodies dropped. Blood dripped from a knife's edge down to his cheek. He barely heard Sophie's next words.

"France could have fallen if you'd failed," she murmured. "And then England. We would be living in a different world."

TWENTY-SIX
NIGHT TERRORS

Joe stared at the ceiling while Sophie slept, dreading what might happen if he fell asleep. He couldn't row or run until exhaustion set in, so instead he slipped out of bed and did push-ups until his shoulder ached, and knee bends until his legs were like jelly. He lay on the floor rolling and massaging his shoulder, flexing his feet, rotating his ankles. Sit-ups until his stomach muscles quivered would be next.

He could do this. He had stayed awake through many a stake-out, many a night watch. Everything would be fine if he could get through the night.

TWENTY-SEVEN

IT WAS JUST A DREAM
JULY 22, 1939, VILLERS-BRETONNEUX

Joe's shout was primal. Savage. Terrifying.

Sophie woke, gasping and panicking. In all the years of their marriage, she'd never heard anything like this.

Joe leapt up, rejecting her efforts to help him calm down before she even said anything. "It was just a dream. I'm fine. I'm fine."

He paced their hotel room as restlessly as a caged animal, looking out the window now and then, scraping fingers through his hair. It took all her willpower to leave him be.

When he headed to the bathroom, she pulled his pillow close and waited anxiously until a waft of clean, masculine scents comforted her. Joe had washed, shaved, and tamed all his wayward waves. Normally, when she was awake at the same hour he was, she thoroughly enjoyed the sight of her husband sauntering in from his morning ablutions and would do her best to tease him back to bed for whatever delights he had time for.

Not this morning.

When he turned to reach for his clothes, he was holding his body differently than other mornings. Today there was a rigid set to his shoulders and jaw. His movements were measured, with none of the usual lithe animation that made her sense his limbs were thrumming with life and his mind sparking with anticipation for whatever the day held.

He turned and his face in profile appeared drawn and pale. He stood stock still for a moment and she had an extraordinary sense she'd seen him in marble somewhere. The *Borghese Gladiator* at the Louvre perhaps, every muscle tensed and ready to absorb a blow, or the *Discobolus*, poised to let his discus fly, in the sculpture gallery at that country house in Derbyshire.

She hugged her knees to her chest and watched the play of muscles when Joe stooped and stretched to pull on his undershorts. He pulled a singlet over his head, covering the scars across his back that had faded to faint silver, then pushed one arm, then the other, into a starched shirt. All his physical scars—knife, shrapnel, bullet—disappeared, hidden under snowy-white cotton.

She liked him best in the blue suit that made his eyes even bluer, but today he reached for the dark grey. His movements as he did up his shirt buttons and slid his braces over his shoulders were deft and automatic. A tiny furrow appeared between his brows as he maneuvered his watch around his wrist, but his eyes and thoughts seemed to be elsewhere.

Joe told her once that there was nothing special about him, that he was only one of an entire generation of survivors who honored their fallen comrades by getting on with the business of living useful, upright, uncomplaining lives. Her heart had broken a little at his words, that such a steadfast, honorable man seemed not to understand how special he was to her, to Sam, whom he'd raised to be respectful of everyone he met, and to Jean-Luc, whom he treated as his son. The police officers who served with him knew him to be tough but fair and willing to put in the time and effort required to get to the truth of whatever they were investigating

She had never known Joe's father and brother, but he'd hinted they were both brash and could be quick to lose their temper. Joe was the opposite, keeping his thoughts and feelings close. If her stomach was roiling while she kept her feelings to herself, how must he feel?

Joe let her slip the tie from his fingers. She fastened his collar button and slid the knot of silk up to his throat. Still silent, she fastened the buttons on his waistcoat and then held his suit jacket for him, like a page dressing her knight before battle. She wanted to be a part of this ritual moment so when he remembered it, he would also remember she had been there with him.

She rested her palm on his chest. The enormity of how fragile their lives were loomed in the rhythm of his heartbeat. She closed her eyes and willed him to understand *you're a good man, I love you, you're too far away from me, please come back*.

"I need to get some air," he said.

He turned abruptly and left the room. She let him go without protesting. Some men drank, or gambled, or became violent when they couldn't cope. Joe disappeared into himself, reemerging only when he felt sufficiently recovered to present an imperturbable face to the world. If she pressed him for an explanation, he would withdraw even further. He would tell her when he was ready to tell her, and not a moment before. Sometimes it took only a few minutes. Sometimes it took hours. She had no idea how long it would take today.

TWENTY-EIGHT

WE WILL REMEMBER THEM

Sophie found Joe pacing outside their hotel. He barely spoke during breakfast and progressed to complete silence on the drive to the memorial site where the names of all the Australians whose bodies had never been found were carved on high stone walls. The reflected heat and glare of the sun off the walls made it even warmer in the visitor center that housed photographs of the memorial's construction and dedication.

A newsreel, projected on a pale stone wall, played a continuous loop of hundreds of troops, mostly Australian but some French too, who were gathered outside the memorial to watch the unveiling a year ago today. Throngs of dignitaries and invited guests were inside the site. Most of the women wore dressy, summery frocks, but the Queen, in feather-trimmed white brocade, and one of her ladies-in-waiting in a fur-trimmed suit, must have been roasting. The thought of fur or feathers against her neck on a day as hot as this one made her doubly glad she'd chosen to wear a broad-brimmed hat and a lightweight linen suit.

She stood shoulder to shoulder with Joe while they watched the flickering dedication ceremony, through all the speeches and prayers and music. Tension radiated from his body as they listened to a speaker proclaim it was impossible for those who did not serve to imagine how great the carnage had been, or how terrible the conflict.

The bugler played the first plaintive notes of the *Last Post,* and she stole a glance at Joe. His lashes fluttered and his eyes squeezed shut. The muscles of his jaw worked furiously beneath his lean cheek throughout the exhortation that followed. His lips formed the response, "We will remember them," but his voice made no sound.

When the drum roll signaling the ceremonial minute of silence began, she moved closer to him so she could brush his hand with hers. When the *Reveille* ended, he slipped his forefinger under her gloved little finger. He breathed deeply. She nearly staggered with relief at his touch.

After King George laid a wreath, and Queen Elizabeth placed a posy of poppies on top of it, the crowds rose from their places. The memorial grounds hummed with conversation and movement as masses of men in suits, morning dress, and uniforms shifted to the lines where their majesties would greet them. The newsreel ended with dignitaries and a color guard escorting the King and Queen to waiting limousines.

Still silent, she and Joe made their way to the Bullecourt panel of the wall and found Robbie's name. It felt strange to recognize the name of a man she'd never met, a man who was a huge part of her husband's life, who had helped to shape him into the man he'd become. Even though Joe was the elder brother, he'd always been the smaller, slighter one in the photos she'd seen of the two of them. Joe was the quiet, careful, cerebral brother. Robbie was the opposite.

"Sam reminds me of him," Joe had said more than once, usually when Sam came in laughing and loud after a cricket match or an afternoon at the beach. He would sprawl on the couch, relating his activities to anyone who would listen, his belongings scattered across the entry hall where he dropped them when he came home. But Sam had a broad streak of sweetness in him. Joe had never described Robbie as sweet.

Joe fidgeted with the brim of his hat as he looked up at his brother's name. Then he nodded as though he'd found some sort of closure. "At least Robbie's name is here. That's something."

He didn't seem to recognize any of the other men on the Bullecourt panel, but his eyes lingered as if he could honor the fallen simply by reading their names. She was loath to leave him, but she was parched, so she went back to the car to fetch the thermos of cold water after Joe assured her he would be fine on his own. Once she had cups and the thermos in hand, the few other people on the grounds had entered the tower, leaving Joe almost alone on the expansive lawn.

He held his hat in his hand so he could look up at the wall without it falling off. Occasionally, he rubbed the back of his neck. She stopped and watched as another man approached him. Joe remained aloof when the man began talking. He was waiting until the other person felt the need to fill the silence, which she knew was a typical police technique.

The contrast between the two men was striking. Joe, in his dark suit, white shirt, and a somber tie, had re-donned his hat. The man who approached him was taller, with a bulkier build than Joe's. He wore an Australian army uniform. He held his slouch hat in one hand and the slight breeze ruffled his sandy hair. He stood relaxed, as if he was at ease with talking to strangers. Joe looked like a coiled cat, wary and watchful, ready to spring, as he did earlier when she watched him dress.

TWENTY-NINE

BROTHERS IN ARMS

Joe had sensed the person approaching him wasn't Sophie. He had turned, tamping down his irritation at the intrusion and took in the man's appearance: the uniform, the insignia, the Anzac rosette, the rank chevrons and long-service bars. The regimental patches on the man's shoulders weren't the same as his, but he could have been looking at any of hundreds of men in his battalion.

The man spoke. "Sorry, I didn't mean to disturb you."

He shook his head. "No, no. You surprised me, that's all." He hesitated, gathering his thoughts. "It's so odd...to see that uniform...in France...after so many years."

The man nodded. "Is there someone you're looking for?"

"Was. I've found him."

"Looking for other names you might recognize?"

"I suppose so. But there are so many."

"Yes. Almost eleven thousand. It can overwhelm, I know." The uniformed man held out his hand. "I'm Will Ryan. 4th Battalion, then the 56th. I work here."

He shook the proffered hand. "Joe Parker. 57th."

"Ah, a Melbourne man," Will replied. "Let me think. You

arrived here in June of '16 and were unlucky enough to cut your teeth at Fromelles in July."

"Yes, that's right."

"By all accounts the 57th had a supporting role and fewer casualties than the other battalions, but you still had a hell of a hard time of it," Will said. "You survived the battle, so they probably promoted you as soon as possible. How many wounded diggers did you carry out of No Man's Land afterward?"

"To second lieutenant the first time and captain before it was over. And I lost count." He stared at a spot on the grass. "How do you know all this? Wait. You're 56th. You were at Fromelles too."

"I was. Rotten show." Will paused and scanned the nearly empty memorial grounds. "You fought here as well." He turned back at Joe. "Are you here with anyone? Sometimes it's tougher to be here with someone who doesn't know how it was."

He glanced at Will. "My wife. She knows we took the town back from the Germans." He fell silent as his nightmare crowded back into his thoughts. That's all he had ever wanted Sophie to know. If she knew what he'd done afterward when they rounded up Germans in the town, she would never look at him the same way again.

"I ask because I often have to tone down the war talk when wives or mothers are present," Will said.

"It's fine. Sophie understands. She was a nurse at the American Hospital in Paris." He turned and pointed to the Bullecourt panel. "We're here for my brother." A wisp of memory. Climbing the forbidden Moreton Bay fig tree at Carlton Gardens and the sickening feeling in the pit of his stomach when Robbie fell and broke his arm. Their father had thrashed him for letting Robbie climb the tree. As if he could ever stop Robbie from doing anything. He learned from that experience that he had to convince Robbie to do something less stupid instead of trying to restrain him physically. That approach had worked so well he used it years later when he became a police officer. It also meant no more thrashings. "Robert Parker, 14th. His name is just there."

"Right." Will closed his eyes. "Robert Harold Parker, born 1884, Carlton, Victoria. Arrived at Anzac Cove on 25 April 1914. Survived Hill 971 and Hill 60 at Gallipoli and the gas at Pozières here in France. Went missing on 11 April 1917 at the first battle of Bullecourt." He opened his eyes and look at Joe. "They never found his body."

Joe's jaw fell. An incredulous "How?" was all he could manage.

Will shrugged. "I work here. When the war ended, I volunteered for the Graves Detachment to help with the burying. Seemed like the right thing to do since so many of my mates wouldn't be going home. I had no family to go home to, so I stayed here and made myself useful. I've been in France ever since."

Will spread his arms to the surrounding area. "I've worked in all the Australian cemeteries here and in Belgium, but this memorial is my patch now. I know every name on the walls and headstones. It's the least I can do." He paused a moment before speaking again. "We're still looking for all the lads who are missing."

"That's good to know. I did everything I could to find out what happened. Letters to his commanding officers. To his mates who made it home. The Red Cross group that helped families. Our mother did the same thing until the day she died. Sometimes I still think he'll knock on my door. But that won't happen. It's been over twenty years."

"We won't stop looking," Will assured him. "When was the last time you saw him?"

"In Vignacourt. He was on rest after Pozières. How we ended up in the same place at the same time is still a mystery. I was walking down a street and heard someone calling my name. The next thing I knew, my brother was slapping me on the back and dragging me into a *café*." Joe's thought back to the last time he saw his brother, who seemed to be on the edge of exhaustion and shock. Robbie was even brasher than usual, too loud, too generous with the wine, too rough as he grabbed the madam of the house and pulled her to his lap. "The plonk was bloody awful, but there was plenty of it. It gets very fuzzy after that."

Will nodded. "Yeah, there were lots of fuzzy mornings in Vignacourt." He pursed his lips and scrutinized Joe's face. "You know, I met a lot of diggers from the 14th when I was in Mena. I reckon I could have even met your brother. If he's who I think he was, he was a hell of a poker player."

He huffed a laugh. "God yes. That he was. How much did he take you for?"

Will shook his head and chuckled. "Too much, that's for sure."

"When we were lads, he taught me to play. First, he won all my marbles. Then he won my slingshot. And he wouldn't let me try to win them back, the bastard. The only other thing I had that he wanted was my bicycle, and I wasn't going to lose that too."

Will chuckled again. "It's always something with brothers, isn't it? Listen, what are you and your missus doing for dinner tonight? You should come to mine."

Joe knew he should do the polite thing and decline, but in reality he hoped Will would repeat the offer. It would be nice to relax for a bit, somewhere that wasn't a restaurant or a hotel dining room and speak about nothing and everything with someone who sounded like home. "Thanks for the offer. Let me check with my wife. She's around here somewhere."

Sophie stood by the car and watched her husband speak with the man in the Australian uniform. The tight coil of Joe's body slowly unwound as they chatted. The man laughed at something, and Joe laughed with him. She beat down a tiny jealous part of her that questioned how a stranger could be more helpful than she'd been. Anyone who could make Joe laugh, after the nightmare he'd had, deserved her thanks and appreciation.

She approached them, calling out in the most carefree voice she could manage. "There you are! You two look like old friends. I thought I should come investigate!"

The man in the uniform stuck out his hand at the same time Joe introduced her.

"Sophie, this is Corporal Will Ryan. He works here. Corporal Ryan, my wife."

She looked at her hands, full of the cups and thermos, then Will's hand, and laughed. "Sorry, I can't."

"It's nice to meet you, Mrs. Parker. I was just asking your husband if you'd like to come for dinner tonight."

She liked Will immediately. His friendly, open manner was so typically Australian. She poured a cup of water for Joe and offered one to Will. An invitation like this was far more important than her being thirsty. "That's very kind of you, but—"

Will grinned. "It's no trouble at all. My wife is used to me bringing home unexpected guests. She'd wonder what I was up to if I stopped doing it."

She heard Joe chuckling. He was chuckling! She didn't know what sort of magic this man possessed, but she was determined to take advantage of the offer if Joe was willing.

She turned to him. "I think we should help Corporal Ryan stay out of trouble," she said. "Don't you?"

"I do," Joe said.

"Righto. That's sorted," Will said. "Why don't I show you the view from the tower before we leave?"

THIRTY
DINNER WITH NEW FRIENDS

Joe pulled the bell cord by Will's front door. A dog barked somewhere within the house. Moments later, a young woman who bore
a striking resemblance to Will opened the door.

"You are Monsieur and Madame Parker, *n'est-ce pas? Entrez,
s'il vous plaît.*"

He nodded and gestured for Sophie to enter the house ahead
of him. An older woman, dark-haired, smiling, bustled in. "Come
in, please! We are so happy you have come!" Her English was
spoken with a heavy French accent. She dried her hands on her
apron before she held out a hand. "I am Hélène, Will's wife."

He shook Hélène's hand and introduced himself and Sophie.

Hélène introduced the young woman who had answered the
door. "This is our daughter, Marianne. And this one," she patted
the grey-muzzled dog standing at her side, "is Rex, the laziest dog
in the Somme valley. Let him sniff your hand so he can go back to
sleep and pretend he has done his job guarding the house. Marianne, take their coats and hats, please, *chérie.*" She turned from
her daughter back to her guests. "Will is in the garden. We eat
outdoors tonight since it is such a beautiful evening. Come, come
this way."

Aromas of roasting chicken set his mouth watering as Hélène guided them from the entry hall through a comfortably furnished room filled with books and flowers and on through French doors that opened on to a large stone patio. Beyond that, a stretch of grass bordered by vegetable and flower gardens led to the banks of the river. He eyed the little rowboat bobbing under a willow tree longingly. The last time he'd been out in his scull was months ago, before the raid when he'd been shot. It felt like a lifetime ago. He rubbed the softening callouses on his fingers. He had weeks of blisters to look forward to once he was home and rowing again.

Will manhandled a long table into position on the tree-shaded patio while a young man arranged the chairs.

A delighted grin spread across Will's face when he saw them. He left the business of furniture moving to come shake their hands. "Captain, Mrs. Parker, welcome! Glad you could make it!"

"Please call me Joe. I resigned my commission a long time ago."

"And you must call me Sophie," Sophie said as Will enveloped her hand in his huge one.

"Righto. Welcome Joe and welcome Sophie." Will motioned for the young man to come forward. "This is my son Chris." Chris was dark-haired like his mother, but with Will's height.

At the sound of his master speaking, the old dog, sprawled on the edge of the patio, thumped his tail on the stone. Clearly, Rex was used to visitors. The ginger cat seated on a retaining wall took one imperious glance at the newcomers and then ignored them.

"Thank you so much for inviting us," Sophie said. "It's very kind of you to welcome us into your home."

Will smiled back at her and pulled out chairs for them. "It's our pleasure. Please take a seat. Would you like a glass of wine?"

With perfect timing, Hélène arrived carrying a tray with

glasses, a bottle of white wine, and a pitcher of water, and set it all on the table. Will picked up the bottle and Sophie nodded yes. "Joe? Wine for you?" Will asked. "Or would you prefer a beer or pastis?"

"Wine, please, Will. I never developed a taste for pastis. I had a bad bout after too many licorice allsorts once."

Marianne placed plates, napkins, and cutlery for everyone, hesitating before she laid the last setting. "*Papa, Edmund arrive ce soir ou non?*"

"He isn't coming tonight, love," Will said. "He'll be here tomorrow."

Will turned to his guests. "Edmund's a friend of ours, an American freelance journalist. Last year he wrote about the Villers-Bret dedication. He's in Berlin at the moment."

"Does he also cover American stories?" Sophie asked.

"American, European, Commonwealth," Will said. "A bit of everything, really. He writes special interest stories, sells them to the American newspapers and magazines. Ed's an interesting fellow. He fought with us at Saint Quentin Canal, Joe."

Sophie turned to Joe. "The last letter I received from you was just after that battle."

He let out a huff of breath. "It was at the end of September. It took another six weeks for the Germans to call for an armistice."

He turned back to Will. "Edmund was in that part of the American army that didn't fight under Pershing?"

"Yes. The 27th and 30th Divisions fought with the Brits and us. Edmund was in the 27th. He wrote about the dedication of the American memorial at Bellicourt too. The Yanks built their memorial right by the canal."

"The Americans lost a lot of men there. They were as inexperienced as I was at Fromelles." He paused for a moment, trying to picture where the Americans had been positioned, but he couldn't recall. "Did you know him then?"

"No, we met in—"

Hélène and Marianne brought food to the table and Hélène cut in gently. "Will, *s'il te plaît*. We talk about Edmund after. We eat dinner now." She raised her glass. "*Santé. Et merci pour les Australiens.*"

THIRTY-ONE
MERCI POUR LES AUSTRALIENS

Dinner was casual and lighthearted with Sophie asking the Ryans about their life and the Ryans happy to provide details.

Chris and Marianne had attended the local school that was partly funded by donations from school children in Melbourne and the state of Victoria. The local citizenry had christened the school *École Victoria*.

"You should see inside," Chris said. "*N'oublions jamais l'Australie* is painted on the wall of every classroom."

"The same thing in English, *Do not forget Australia*, is also painted outside on the playground," Marianne said. "But I cannot forget what I have not seen."

Sophie turned to the young woman. "You've never been to Australia?"

"No, madame. I want to go but Papa says I am too young to travel so far by myself."

"Ah. May I ask how old you are?"

"I will be twenty-two on my next birthday." Marianne stole a look at her father deep in conversation with Joe, and lowered her voice so only Sophie could hear. "I work for a dressmaker in Amiens, and I have almost saved enough for my passage. My friends from school are all married and have babies, which I do not want to do. I want to see the world. I could work as a seamstress as I travel. Or a lady's companion. Anything."

Goodness, Sophie thought. Marianne seems sensible and enterprising. "I hope you get the chance to do what you want. If you're ever in Sydney, my Aunt Flora and I could help you find a position." Then, sensing they could stray into territory that might not be appreciated at the dinner table, much less in front of guests, she changed course.

"And how old are you, Chris?" He was tall, like his father, and had almost outgrown the coltish, awkward stage. "Eighteen? Nineteen?"

Chris blushed. "No, madame. I am seventeen."

"You're a few years younger than Jean-Luc and Sam."

Hélène's puzzled look prompted her to explain. "My godson, Jean-Luc, his parents were very dear friends of mine. His father died in the war, and his mother died in a motorcar accident after the war. I was Jean-Luc's godmother and since neither of his parents had a family who could care for him, I raised him as my own. My husband had died, so we decided to escape our troubles and go on an adventure to Australia. We never left."

She looked at Joe to tell his story. "Sam's mother died a few months before I arrived back in Melbourne after the war," Joe said. "Influenza. There was a rash of civilian deaths once the troopships starting arriving home. Sam and I moved to Sydney a couple of years later. We needed a fresh start."

When Will invited Joe to stroll to the river, Sophie got up to help Hélène clear the table. After they set the plates in the kitchen sink, she impulsively squeezed Hélène's arm. "Thank you so much for this evening. I can tell Joe is enjoying himself. Will has a way of putting people at ease, doesn't he?"

"He knows what the people who come to the cemeteries and memorials need," Hélène said. "The mothers, the wives, they are grieving, and they need comfort. Will walks with them to the grave or to the wall. He explains the ways the men are honored."

Hélène gestured to the kitchen window where they could see Joe and Will walking across the lawn to the river bank. "Will likes to take a guest to the river so they can talk privately. The men who fought, well, they might not say it, but they are also grieving. Sometimes they are angry too. They need to talk and remember with someone who understands."

"Yes, you're right. Joe and I corresponded during the war, but I could hardly believe it when Will took us to the top of the tower at the memorial and I saw beautiful fields that were once bloody battlefields." She looked away, wanting to say more, wanting to ask if Will still had nightmares, but the question seemed too intrusive and personal. "If I was that emotional about seeing where Joe fought, I can't imagine how he must have felt."

"Does your husband…Joe…does he have, I am sorry, but I cannot remember the word in English. In French it is *cauchemar*. Do you know it? Bad dreams?"

She saw only understanding in Hélène's expression. "Joe rarely remembers his dreams, at least that I know about. Normally I wouldn't say this to someone I've just met, but accompanying Joe on this trip and watching his tension grow every mile we got closer, without really knowing what he went through, made me feel helpless. But last night, God, it must have been awful. I felt like I was back in the hospital, surrounded by men who had just come off the front lines. Some of them were completely silent until they slept, and they would wake the ward with their screaming and shouting. In their dreams they were back in battle."

She blinked back the tears stinging her eyes. "It was different for me since I wasn't fighting, but—"

"Will told me you were a nurse. What you did was very hard. It was just different."

"My brother was driving ambulances, and I decided I had to come over to France to help too. I can't knit socks to save my life. And you, you and your mother and sister made them food that reminded them of home. Something that wasn't heated in its tin over a paraffin fire in the trenches."

"We all did what we could, according to our gifts. You are good at taking care of people. I am good at cooking."

This time, Hélène squeezed her arm. "We are very lucky to be here now, together."

"Yes, yes, we are," Sophie agreed. As Hélène and she walked outside with dessert plates and an apple tart, they heard laughter mingled with birdsong.

"It is good they are laughing and talking," Hélène said. "For Will, it lets him think about the war and his work without going too far to a dark place. I hope it will be the same for your husband."

THIRTY-TWO
A PROMISE OF RESPITE

Sophie and Hélène returned to the table as the men were walking back from the riverbank. Their jackets were removed, ties loosened, sleeves rolled up. Rex ambled between them and the ginger cat led the way. She caught the last snippets of Joe telling his story about some of his men appropriating ladies' silk underpants to avoid lice, which had plagued them all by burrowing into the seams of their uniforms and Will started in on a story about a group of Canadian soldiers who had donned ladies' white nightgowns to spook some Germans.

Sophie sat back and watched the men enjoy themselves. She hadn't ever seen Joe so at ease with new acquaintances so quickly. Being among these friendly, welcoming people was having an obvious, soothing effect on his rattled psyche. Thank goodness. She couldn't bear thinking he might have another nightmare like the one he had last night.

"I'd like to hear more about these clothes you all absconded with," she said. If they insisted on talking about the war, perhaps they could stick to the lighter moments. "Any stories about wearing feathered hats or high-heeled shoes?"

They shook their heads, grinned at each other, and gave her

their most innocent looks. Clearly, they wouldn't say more with ladies present.

Sophie rolled her eyes at the men. "Hélène, since they won't tell us more, you must tell me how you and Will met."

"Hélène took a shine to me from the very first," Will interjected. "She made me the best scrambled eggs I'd ever eaten."

The story was slightly different when Hélène told it—Will had taken a shine to *her* from the very beginning—and she'd made him not only the best, but also the first omelet he had ever eaten. "My mother, sisters, and I ran an *éstaminet*, a little café, in a neighboring village," she explained. "We cooked eggs and chips for homesick Diggers and Tommies.

"I wanted to come back here to raise my children. War had badly damaged the town during the war, but it still existed. Not like some that disappeared because of so many bombs. Will was apprenticed to a furniture maker before the war. His carpentry skills were much in demand after the war was over."

Will blushed at his wife's compliments. "I hated furniture making at first. I'd moved to Sydney from the Blue Mountains because I didn't want to work in the mines. Furniture apprentice was the only work I could find. Being near the ocean was nice, but I missed climbing in the Blueys something awful."

"You must miss them still," Joe said. "Here there's nothing much higher here than a church steeple."

Hélène caught her eye. "And you Sophie? I am thinking there must be a very interesting story behind how the police officer and the lady met. Am I right?"

"The first time we met was in Paris, during the war. I was a nurse at the American Hospital there. Joe was on rest, and I found him by the Eiffel Tower."

"I found Jean Luc by the Eiffel Tower. Then we found you," Joe corrected.

"I turned my back and Jean-Luc had disappeared. At any rate, I bought Joe an ice cream."

"That was my reward for finding Jean-Luc."

"We met years later in Sydney when a case of a cheating husband turned into a murder investigation."

"Murder?" Hélène's brows shot up. "It is not the most romantic reunion, but it is interesting."

"Someone murdered an acquaintance of mine at a party I was attending. I didn't know Joe had moved to Sydney, so you can imagine how surprised I was that he was the officer who came to the scene to investigate. He thought I shouldn't interfere with serious police business."

"And Sophie thought I was a befuddled police officer with no imagination."

They grinned at each other again. "We're joking, of course," she said. "Joe was amazingly receptive to discussing the case with me."

"Well, you knew almost everyone at that party," he reminded her. "The evidence in the investigation made it look like the servant had done it. If it hadn't been for Sophie's eyewitness account, and her ability to get information from the woman's society friends, we would have arrested the wrong person."

Marianne spoke for the first time since the whispered conversation. "It sounds very exciting. And you, monsieur, you do not mind that your wife does these things?"

"She's often in the right place at the right time, but her insights are invaluable. Sophie would be an excellent investigator. She has a good mind and clever interrogation techniques. Believe me, I've been on the receiving end of them. It's almost impossible to keep a secre—birthday surprise from her."

Joe had barely hesitated, but Sophie caught it and the sudden, distant cast in his eyes before he recovered. Perhaps his conversation with Will had included something that had happened at

Villers-Bret. She wished she knew more. "It's amazing what we can accomplish together," she managed.

While Hélène served the coffee, Will poured liqueur into tiny glasses and passed them to everyone.

Will tilted his glass toward the bottle. "This is Génépi. It's a liqueur from Chamonix, in the French Alps. The American journalist friend I mentioned earlier, Edmund, and I met in Chamonix in 1917 and we climbed Mont Blanc together."

Even Joe, who had years of practice controlling his expressions, looked impressed. "You climbed the highest mountain in Europe? While the war was going on?"

"Yes," Will said. "Edmund and a university friend of his plus me and my mate."

"How did you get leave to travel so far?" Joe asked. "That seems like a pretty fair distance from the front."

"My mate was a supply sergeant," Will said. "He told the quartermaster he'd found a supplier of fresh cheese or lamb or something and convinced him to give him a truck for a few days. I didn't know how far Chamonix was. I just knew I was sick to death of flat land. I didn't realise how much I missed mountains. I asked to come along."

She had never met anyone who had just gone off to climb a mountain on a whim. "How long did it take?"

"Less time than you might think," Will said. "You don't climb from the valley floor, although you could, if you wanted to. We caught the cog train that goes up to the first refuge.

"Hiker's huts," he explained, when he saw her confusion. "The first one is Nid d'Aigle—the Eagle's Nest. It's where you can get kitted out and find a guide and porters to climb with. That's where the four of us met. We hiked up to the next refuge, spent the night there, and made the ascent the next day. We had such a good time we agreed to stay in touch and try it again one day if we all survived the war." Will raised his glass skyward in a silent toast. "Only Ed and I made it through."

She glanced at Joe, who was listening intently to Will's tale. Good. Perhaps she could keep this conversation in a neutral place. "But don't you need to be experienced?" Joe asked. "Or is this route an easy one? Relatively easy, of course. I can't imagine anything about climbing a mountain being easy."

"Oh, Georges and Vanni climb with us. They're the professionals."

Before she could ask, Hélène explained. "Georges and Vanni are friends of this crazy man."

"Sorry. Georges and Vanni. Where to start." Will leaned forward in his chair with the businesslike air of a man whose job it was to remember myriad names, dates, and relationships. "Georges was in the *Chasseur Alpins*, the French Alpine troops, when the war began."

So much for changing the subject from the war. She would have to wait until Will finished talking and try again. She glanced over at Joe. He was ticking his fingers as Will spoke. Joe was also adept at processing this type of information, and she had relied on his prodigious memory for people and places more than once. They probably wouldn't need this information at any point in the future, but since he was paying attention, she didn't have to. Good. A bit of distraction for him.

She caught the last of Will's explanation. "Vanni's from Courmayer, which is on the Italian side of Mont Blanc. He was *Alpini*, that's the Italian Alpine force. He spent the war fighting the Germans and the Austrians in the Dolomites."

"I knew they were fighting at the borders," Joe said, "but it never occurred to me to add mountains to the equation."

Will nodded. "They called it the war on snow and ice. You

should see the pictures of the Italians hoisting cannons up mountains."

"Was there fighting in the French Alps?" Joe asked.

Will shook his head. "No. The Germans never came near them. The Chasseurs Alpins fought all over the Western Front, though. Georges was at Lorraine and the Yser and Verdun. He met his wife Monique at the hospital after he was wounded at Fort Douaumont. Ended up losing part of his left leg. Below the knee, though. He has a beautiful wooden leg and foot. Gets around like nothing ever happened."

Sophie shuddered. The French had ultimately been victorious after months of fighting at Verdun, France's most important fortress, but they had lost over three hundred thousand men to death and wounds. She had nursed her share of the combatants, most with horrific injuries. She nudged the conversation away from the war again, this time to tamp down her memories. "We traveled through the Rockies on the train, but part of that was at night. I've never seen the Alps. How high is Mont Blanc?"

"Fifteen thousand seven hundred and seventy-seven feet," Will said. "It's the highest mountain in Europe."

"And you've climbed it," Joe said. She heard admiration in his voice. "Well done."

"Oh, we climb it every summer. Edmund and I head down to Chamonix, meet up with Georges and Vanni, and spend a few days climbing and hiking. Vanni usually takes a day or two to cheer on the Italians riding in the Tour de France when they pass through one of the nearby towns." He paused. "When do you have to be in Marseille? Ed and I are driving down to Chamonix in a couple of days. You should join us."

"Well…we've planned a leisurely tour of Provence, complete with Roman ruins and rosé. We're starting in Lyon."

"If you can spare the time, come along for a few days," Will said. "There's plenty to do that doesn't involve crampons and ice axes. It's the best way I know to get the world's problems out of my head. Mountains, glaciers, alpine meadows. It's one of the most beautiful places I've ever seen."

Sophie pondered the invitation. A brief stay with friends in Chamonix might be a perfect opportunity for Joe to decompress and finally tell her why Villers-Bret had affected him so badly. "It sounds amazing," she said. "I'd love to see it."

"I could call Georges and Monique in the morning," Will offered. "They'll have a room ready for you by the afternoon."

"Georges and Monique run a lovely hotel in Chamonix," Hélène added. "It has a beautiful terrace facing Mont Blanc and bathtubs big enough to swim in."

"It sounds marvelous!" She turned to Joe. "Darling, what do you think?"

"Why don't we take a look at the map tonight," he said, "and we'll let Will know in the morning."

THIRTY-THREE
DEMARCATION

Joe was willing to consider changing their travel plans after hearing Will's enthusiastic recommendation of Chamonix. It could be a great way to get Villers-Bret out of his head so Sophie and he could get back to having a relaxed holiday.

During the drive back to their hotel, his unexpected, "What was that?" startled Sophie so much that she nearly ran the car off the road. Roman or not, the road had only two narrow lanes and very little room to maneuver.

"What?" she cried, braking and pulling to a stop on the grassy shoulder. "What's wrong?"

He pointed to a waist-high grey stone at the side of the road. "That."

Sophie peered at in the fading twilight. "It must be a demarcation stone. After the war, the French wanted to place them at every kilometer to mark the extent of the German advance." Her brows knit as she tried to remember. "There was a subscription to pay for them. I don't know whether they raised enough money for however many they needed though."

Joe opened his car door before she asked if he wanted to get out and look at it. The waist-high stone was topped with a French helmet and a laurel wreath. Villers-Bretonneux was carved in the granite. As he examined the demarcation stone, realization dawned that his efforts had helped to draw this line. The people they'd spent the evening with had a chance at a good life because of it. He finally had the chance to experience this part of France the way it should be experienced, sharing food and wine with friends under a glorious sunset. Peace was worth what he'd done here, wasn't it?

Joe changed into his pajama bottoms and brushed his teeth while Sophie opened the map on the bed in their hotel room.

"Chamonix is only a couple of hours east of Lyon," she called to him. "It's right at the border of France, Switzerland, and Italy."

He turned off the bathroom light and sat on the bed next to her. "Show me."

She moved the map to their laps so they could both see it. "You wouldn't mind if we take a few days from Provence? Or would you rather visit the other Australian memorials instead of going to Chamonix? We could even go to Ypres and see the Menin Gate."

God no. The Menin Gate memorial included the names of 55,000 British and Commonwealth war dead whose bodies had never been found. Earlier today he had seen enough names like that to last a lifetime. "I don't want to spend the time or the money going to Belgium. This trip is already costing a fortune."

Sophie stiffened, and he knew she was thinking *this again*? They'd solved the money issue years ago. She had a knack for handling the legacies and gifts from her family, and from an accounting point of view, she was worth far more than he ever would be. When she asked him if he'd want to marry her if the situation was reversed, he'd said of course he would.

Still, he'd balked at the cost of the trip, especially traveling first-class, which she'd insisted would be less taxing on his healing shoulder. He stopped resisting when she reminded him it was unlikely they would travel around the world again in the foreseeable future, and they should seize the chance. She had even dusted off her schoolgirl Latin: *Carpe diem*, she'd declared.

"Sorry," he said, lifting his chin at the map. "If you want to go to Chamonix, let's figure out how we can fit it in before we go to Provence."

She folded the map so only the route through Provence was visible. "I finally understood why you were so intent on luring me to Provence for the Roman ruins when you took me to the arena in Paris."

He glanced over at Sophie now. She was studying the folded map, running a finger down the length of it. She gave him the map and tucked herself under his arm. "Show me again where you want to go."

While he traced a route from Lyon through Orange, Aix-en-Provence, and Nîmes, and on to Marseille, Sophie tangled her fingers in the hair on his chest and slid a leg between his, a sure sign she was feeling affectionate "So, we could spend two days in Chamonix? Maybe three?"

"That sounds about right. I suppose we'll know more once we arrive and figure out what we want to do there."

When they turned off their lamps a few minutes later, he believed an impromptu side trip to Chamonix would be just the thing to distract him from the memories Villers-Bretonneux brought back. They wouldn't have a chance like this again, and they still had time for the places he wanted to see in Provence. He swept broad strokes over Sophie's back and bottom, and she shifted, inviting him to continue to her breast and belly. Then she tugged the tie on his pajama bottoms, and mountains and memorials vanished from his thoughts.

~

Sophie lay awake for a long time afterward, her head on Joe's shoulder, and her hand on his chest rising and falling with his deep, even breaths. He still hadn't said a word about his nightmare, but he seemed to be in a much better frame of mind, despite their exchange about visiting other memorials. They had some sad moments in Paris, but they'd recovered quickly and had a wonderful time there.

She was drifting off in their bed in Amiens when Joe mumbled something in his sleep and twisted away from her. She held her breath and prayed there wouldn't be any shouting tonight.

THIRTY-FOUR
AVE ATAQUE VALE

In his dream, Joe surveyed the Roman road that led from Amiens, through Villers-Bretonneux, to Saint Quentin. Centuries of repaving and four years of war would never alter its course. It was still as arrow straight as it had been when the Romans built it almost two thousand years earlier.

He hefted his rucksack and checked his mental list. Notebook, photos, and compass were tucked in jacket pockets. Helmet was strapped on his rucksack. Grenades and ammunition were stowed in bandoliers. Gas mask hung around his neck. His sidearm was holstered and his knife was sheathed.

The luminous hands of his wristwatch showed one minute to go.

He saw a match flare, a face illuminated, a glowing cigarette end pass between mates. He heard a joke, a cough, a muttered curse.

He checked his watch again. Three seconds…two…one….

The bugle sounded.

"Fall in!"

The men settled and waited for the next order.

"Quick march!"

Several dozen pairs of hobnailed boots sparked on the dry pavement of the Roman road until the men slowed to a stop when they reached the Villers-Bretonneux demarcation stone. They squinted at the inscription in the moonlight.

Ici fut repoussé l'envahisseur.

"What's that mean?"

"Dunno, cobber."

"Oi, somebody wrote it in English on this side."

"What's it say, then?"

"From here the invader was pushed back."

"What's *that* mean?"

"It means we pushed the Boche out of Villers-Bret!"

"My bloody oath, we did it!"

The men entered the town, their orderly columns forgotten as they peered in windows and down the side streets.

"Where're we billeted?"

"Billeted, hell. Where's the grog? And don't tell me napoo grog!"

"These are nice lookin' houses. They're not even shelled. All the roofs are still on 'em."

"It isn't raining. We don't need a roof."

"We could kip here tonight. Reckon there's plonk in the cellars? Or did Fritz drink it all?"

"Why aren't we stopping?"

They passed through the town and entered the memorial grounds.

Someone recited the words on the stone of remembrance. "Their name liveth forevermore."

"Whose name?" someone else asked. "Why're we in a cemetery?"

"What's goin' on here?"

"Captain?"

He took in the sight of the men gathered around him, meeting their eyes, answering their questions with a single response. "You've all done a damned fine job," he said. "This is your last stop. Go find your names on the walls."

The men fanned out across the grass, peering up at the tower and around at the walls carved with battles and dates and more names than they could take in at a single glance.

Robbie stayed behind. He looked his older brother up and down, settling on the insignia on his uniform. "Captain, huh?"

"Hmm. Not sure why."

"You're not coming with us?"

"Not this time."

"Did you make it home, Joey?"

His breath hitched at the use of his childhood nickname. Robbie had always thought it funny to call him by the name of a baby kangaroo. "I did."

Robbie nodded once, acknowledging his meaning, and strode toward the Bullecourt panel.

His duty done, Joe walked away, not looking back until he reached the road. The great lawn was deserted. The memorial glowed in the moonlight.

He saluted the fallen.

"*Ave atque vale*," he said.

THIRTY-FIVE
ARRIVAL IN THE ALPS
JULY 23, 1939, CHAMONIX

"How did you sleep?" Sophie asked while they dressed the next morning. "You mumbled something that sounded Latin, and then something else that sounded like hail and farewell." She leaned closer to the mirror and checked her lipstick, smoothing her top and bottom lips together.

Joe, standing behind her at the mirror, parted his hair and began combing. "Latin?" He checked the results of his efforts. "Must've been all that talk of Roman roads and ruins." He shrugged. "I'm fine. Are you ready to leave?"

Yesterday morning before they left Paris for Villers-Bretonneux, Joe had looked as though he didn't recognize her. This morning there was a tilt of his head and upward tick of his lips as he gazed back at her in the mirror. She couldn't tell if he had dreamed and couldn't remember, or if he remembered, but wasn't bothered by it. Either way, the vast improvement in his demeanor this morning compared to yesterday morning was very welcome.

Joe always tells me when something is bothering him, she reminded herself as they left Amiens and turned south toward Chamonix. He'll tell me about the nightmare. Eventually.

Sophie spent much of the drive listening to Joe describing the history of the Roman sites they would visit after Chamonix. There was a note of pleasure, joy even, in his voice that he would finally see the places in France he wished to visit. The amphitheater in Lyon, which was the capital of Roman France, was the largest in Gaul. The arena in Arles was used for bullfights, but in Provence, the bulls weren't killed like they were in Spain, he assured her. There was a theater in Arles too, but the theater at Orange was one of the best-preserved Roman theaters anywhere. And there were ongoing archeological excavations in Orange that they might be able to see. The Pont du Gard in Nîmes was the highest aqueduct the Romans had ever built. Plumbing came from the Latin word for lead, which the Romans used for water pipes, and….

Joe was far more interested in the Romans than she was, but she enjoyed listening to him ramble when the subject was something that fascinated him so much. What more could she ask for? He was happy and she could tell Jean-Luc, who loved growing grapes and making wine, about the fabled Châteauneuf-du-Pape wine country. Visiting Cézanne's workshop in Aix would be a bonus.

She was so engrossed in thinking about what they would do that when she steered the Peugeot around a curve, Joe's gasp made her jump. Then she saw them too. After hours of driving, the French Alps were finally visible.

She slowed and pulled to the side of the road as far as she could and stopped the engine. They scrambled out of the car, stiff limbs, perspiring backs, and Roman ruins forgotten. Mountains filled half the sky.

"Where did those come from? We drove for miles and miles through hills, but they weren't all that high."

Joe craned his head to take in the peaks. Some were jagged, spiked rock slabs turned nearly vertical. Others were softer and rounded, smooth under snowcaps. "It looks like they were just set down in the middle of nowhere."

She craned her head too. "They're not as high as the Rockies, but we could see those ahead of us from miles away. This is—"

"A huge surprise."

"Let's look at the map. I think we have another half an hour of driving but let's see where we are."

Joe pointed to a town on the map called Saint-Gervais-les-Bains. "We should be almost here."

"Isn't that where Will said he and Edmund caught the train to Mont Blanc? We're closer than I thought, then. Where is Mont Blanc anyhow? We should be able to see it, shouldn't we?"

He peered at the map, rolling the unfamiliar town names over his tongue as he spoke, looking at the mountains and going back to the map. "I think we're still a little too far south to see it. See how the road curves to the north a few miles from Chamonix? Once we enter the valley, it should be," he pointed in the general vicinity to their right, "there. Your guess is as good as mine, though."

"So, by the time we reach this place called Servoz, the road should lead straight towards the mountain all the way to Les Houches."

Joe nodded. "Would you like me to take another turn at the driving so you can look at the mountains?"

"I've gotten us this far," she began.

"And you've done a fine job. But I know how much you like shiny things."

She fixed him with a mock glare that softened to a grin. She did like shiny things. Precious stones set in platinum were always nice, but she usually limited herself to more prosaic interpretations of shiny such as gift-wrapping paper and Christmas tree ornaments. Shiny things in their family also meant intriguing or interesting things, like legendary mountain ranges. But more importantly, Joe teased her when he was happy and relaxed.

"Fine. You drive the rest of the way." She would stay quiet for several minutes to let him settle into the driving. Joe's willingness to put in the effort required to do a task properly was one of the things she loved most about him. She curled around his side and kissed his cheek. "That leaves me free to admire the scenery." She waited until he nodded to add, "And the mountains, of course."

Joe gave Sophie a quick hug and handed the map to her so she could fold it. She smiled at him when she got into the passenger seat. "Onward!" she exclaimed.

Driving on the right wasn't something he'd done often, so for the first few miles he drove carefully, getting reacquainted with the clutch, gas, and break pedals, and steering wheel opposite to where he was used to them. Sophie was much more practiced at it, but the rest of the route was straightforward.

He was right about Mont Blanc coming into view when the road curved around, and they passed through Les Houches, and entered a deep, U-shaped valley. He thought the mountains they first saw were huge, and they were, but Mont Blanc's height and breadth dwarfed everything else. Its summit was smooth and rounded, covered with snow that was blinding in the bright sunlight.

Since the road was parallel to the mountains, and the mountains were so high, he couldn't see the tops from Sophie's window. She had to tilt her head at an angle that threatened the ability of her hat to stay on her head. By the time they arrived in Chamonix, his neck was stiff, and Sophie had tossed her hat onto the back seat of the car.

Many signposts pointed the way to the town's hotels and sporting venues, and he found their hotel easily. It was just as Will and Hélène had described it: a cream-colored building of five stories with wrought-iron balconies and dark green shutters at the windows.

He slowed and turned onto the hotel's gravel drive, drove through the gates past a shaded lawn dotted with lounge chairs and up to the level of the reception entrance. The terrace, running the width of the building, had plenty of room for tables and chairs. Masses of pink geraniums topped the stone balustrade overlooking the drive and the lawn.

As soon as the car came to a stop, Sophie flung her door open, ran to the edge of the terrace, and called to him, "Joe! Come look!"

He set the emergency brake before he got out of the car to join her. They had an unobstructed view of Mont Blanc and the surrounding mountains.

Sophie wrapped her arms around his waist and did a little wiggle at his side. "It's magnificent, isn't it? I'm so happy we're here!"

"We are also so happy you are here!" They turned around to see a smiling, dark-haired woman walking toward them. "You are Monsieur and Madame Parker, yes?"

The woman held out a hand first to him and then to Sophie. "I am Monique Pascal. You made good time. Will thought you would arrive in the early evening."

"Will and Hélène told us how beautiful it is here!" Sophie was practically babbling with delight. "They convinced us to come."

Monique nodded patiently. "Yes, Will said when he telephoned this morning. He told me you have never seen our Alps and to give you one of our special rooms."

"Special rooms?"

"Monsieur, you and madame will love it, I am certain. It is a big corner room with views of the mountains on this side."

Monique gestured to the front doors of the hotel, propped open by multiple pots of more geraniums so the breeze could filter into the building. The windows of the ground-floor rooms were open too, their sheer curtains fluttering here and there, offering glimpses of the public rooms for guests. "Come, let us get you registered."

He and Sophie followed Monique into the hotel, where she introduced a teenaged boy waiting beside the reception desk. "This is my son, Nick. If you will give him your car keys, he will take your bags up to your room and park your car behind the hotel."

Joe handed the keys to Nick and their passports to Monique, who noted their information in the guest register.

As she wrote, she kept up a running commentary about when breakfast was served in the mornings and asked if they were planning to dine at the hotel this evening. Even if they dined elsewhere, Monique added, the hotel had a custom of serving aperitifs on the terrace between six and seven every evening. "If you would like to dine here, I should tell you on nice evenings we serve dinner on the terrace. It seems a shame to waste wonderful weather by eating indoors. However, it is as you like. Some people don't like to eat outdoors."

Joe checked his watch. "It's just gone five, Sophie. Why don't we unpack, change, and decide what to do then?"

"Yes, I understand." Monique handed him their room key, walked around to the lift, and opened the door. "Your room is on the fifth floor. Ring me at reception if there is anything you need. *Bienvenue à Chamonix!*"

Joe unlocked the door to their room on the fifth floor and gestured for Sophie to proceed him. An enormous bed made up with a down comforter and down pillows faced two sets of French doors that led to a wrought iron-edged balcony. The far wall of the bedroom had another set of French doors and a balcony.

The windows were open, and the sheer curtains billowed into the room. Sophie went from window to window, exclaiming about the views of the mountains and the town. He followed behind her, checking the safety of the room, an ingrained habit after years as a police officer.

Satisfied, he took off his jacket and loosened his tie. Sophie was already running a bath and unpacking her toiletries on the dresser in the bathroom, leaving the shelf between the sink and the mirror for him to use for his shaving things and for their cups and toothbrushes.

She opened her suitcase and rummaged through it. When she found her dressing gown, she shed her traveling clothes as quickly as possible.

Joe unpacked and when he turned from the wardrobe, Sophie was flitting across the room in her tap pants and bra, grabbing her dressing gown in one hand and heading into the bathroom. She poured bath salts into the water, raised a come-hither brow to him, and dispensed with her undergarments.

She turned off the taps, stepped into the tub, and slid into the water with an audible sigh of relief.

A knock sounded at the door while he was laying Sophie's discarded stockings on the dressing table bench. He opened the door to see Monique holding a tray with two glasses of chilled white wine

"This wine is Aprémont, from the Savoie region just south-west of here," Monique said, placing the glasses on the table just beside the door. "It is light and refreshing, especially after a long drive."

He thanked Monique and closed the door. Sophie called to him at that moment, asking him to open the bathroom window. She oohed and ahhed over the view of Mont Blanc through the window. "It isn't much higher than the peaks surrounding it. It's just so wide and solid looking compared to them. What were they called on the map? Aiguilles?"

While Sophie kept up her running commentary of the view, he undressed, picked up the two glasses of wine, and padded back into the bathroom.

"Oh my goodness," she said when she saw him, wiggling her shoulders in the way that promised a highly enjoyable interlude. "The scenery here really is wonderful."

Her enthusiastic reaction made the long drive and the change in plans more than worth it. *Carpe diem* indeed, he thought as he handed her a glass of wine.

THIRTY-SIX

STARRY NIGHT

Bathed, relaxed, and dressed for dinner, Joe followed Sophie through the hotel's lobby and out to the terrace for what Monique called 'the *apéritif* hour.' Several guests were in attendance already, some leaning against the balustrade, admiring the mountain views, others seated at the small tables that dotted the terrace. Nick carried a tray with little bowls of olives and peanuts, which he served to each table.

Monique bustled out to greet them. "You must meet my husband Georges, who is great friends with Will, and also their friend Giovanni. Come, come this way." She led them to a table nearby where two men were studying a newspaper.

"Georges, Vanni, put the paper away. You can talk cycling later," Monique scolded. "This is Monsieur and Madame Parker, our new guests."

The two men rose from their chairs and delighted smiles crossed their faces. "Welcome, welcome," Georges said, as he and Vanni shook their hands. "We are so happy you have come. When Will telephoned this morning, I was afraid he would say he could not come because the memorial needed him for some special task. But instead, he tells me new friends are coming to stay with us."

"I'm not sure Will could stay away from this place for any other reason," Sophie replied. "He spoke so highly of the town, and the mountains, and you and Monique, and you too, Signor," she said, tilting her head at Vanni.

"Signora, you must call me Vanni," the Italian insisted. "We are all friends for a long time. If Will says you are friends of his, then you are friends of ours."

"Please, sit. Share the table with us." Georges pulled out a chair for Sophie, who gave him a dazzling smile.

Joe waited until she sat, and Vanni indicated the chair next to him. "I couldn't help but overhear you talking about cycling. The Tour de France?"

"*Si.* Yes. An Italian, Gino Bartali, is my cycling idol. He won last year but he cannot ride this year." Vanni's eyes fell as he spoke. "They permit no Italians this year."

"No Germans or Spanish, either, I gather. We read about the smaller field in the Paris newspapers. Well, Sophie read it and translated for me. My ability to read French is very limited, I'm afraid."

"Like my ability to read English," Vanni confided.

"You speak English beautifully," Sophie said. "All of you do."

Monique placed two wine glasses on the table. "We have many English tourists in Chamonix. They come in winter for skiing and in summer for hiking and climbing. We have to learn to speak English."

She held a bottle of Aprémont and a bottle of a dark liqueur. "This wine is the same as you had earlier. Did you like it?"

Sophie hummed her appreciation. "It was wonderful. Thank you for making such a lovely gesture."

"Would you like to try it as an *apéritif?* We add some *mûre* first," Monique said. "*Mûre* is blackberry. Just a little, and then the wine." As she poured, the slightly effervescent wine mixed with the liqueur. "Try it and tell me if you like it."

Joe raised his glass and grinned at Sophie. "*Salut.*" He loved surprising her with his few tidbits of French when she least expected it.

Sophie smiled at him, took a sip and nodded her approval to Monique. "Oh, that's nice."

"Monsieur? What do you think? You can be honest! And if you would prefer something else, I can bring it for you."

"It's good, Monique," Joe said. "I think I prefer the wine by itself, but it's good."

"*Bon.* I am pleased you like our invention. Now I must ask because the cook needs to know. Will you join us here at the hotel tonight or will you dine elsewhere? We have a simple family dinner planned, *tartiflette avec sa salade verte* and fresh fruit for dessert. Or I can recommend some restaurants if you prefer."

He mentally reviewed the dishes they'd had in Paris. Green salad was easy, but he didn't recognize the rest of it. "What's *tartiflette?*"

"Potatoes with *lardons*, bacon in English, and onions, with Reblochon cheese melted on top. Very hearty and very good," Georges said.

"Sounds delicious. Sophie, what do you want to do?"

"Darling, I think we should dine here and enjoy this lovely terrace. We have a magnificent view and the promise of what sounds like a divine meal." She gave him a flirty smile and nudged his calf under the table. "What more could we ask for?"

"Two for dinner," he said to Monique, and just to surprise Sophie again, he added, "*s'il vous plaît, madame.*"

"*Très bien, monsieur.*" Monique turned and hurried inside to give the cook the count for dinner.

There was a lull for a moment or two while Sophie and he sipped their aperitifs, and he took stock of their new acquaintances. Georges was dark-haired and solidly built. Vanni was also dark-haired, but wiry, with a slighter frame. Both men's faces and arms were tanned, and both sported mustaches. Vanni's was wispy. Georges' was thick, edging over his top lip.

Vanni folded the newspaper he and Georges had been reading earlier. "I must cheer for France this year, but that is fine. My mother was French."

"Are you a cyclist also?" Joe asked.

"Not to compete. I ride to clear my mind. It is different from what I do for my job, helping people climb mountains. When I cycle, it is just for me."

"I understand. I do the same sort of thing."

"You cycle too?"

"I row. I run too, but the police force has a rowing club, so I train with them."

"Police force? Are you a police officer, Signor?"

"Yes. I was a detective for many years. Now I'm moving to a new position in the forensics department."

"I can see where sports are good for you. You are always using your brains all day. When you exercise your body, your brain can rest."

"I used to compete," Joe said, "but not anymore. Now I get out early on Sunday mornings before anyone is awake."

"Early is right," Sophie interjected. "The criminals are in bed or in jail at that hour."

Georges said, "I remember a great Australian cyclist. We French called him Sir Oppy. He wore a beret when he cycled in the 1928 Tour."

"Hubert Opperman. In the early twenties he rode in the Warrny."

Baffled, Georges asked, "Excuse me, what is this warrny?"

"It's an annual road race from a town called Warrnambool to Melbourne. It's about 300 miles in one day."

"Monsieur, do you know of the *Circuit de Champs de Bataille*?"

"*Champs de Bataille?*" He cast his mind back to his wartime French. "Is it something to do with battlefields?"

"Exactly right. In 1919, the Cycling Union had a race from Strasbourg to Luxembourg to Brussels to Paris and then back to Strasbourg through the Vosges Mountains."

"But that's impossible. In 1919 there were hardly any roads left in those areas."

"And, monsieur, even though the race took place in late April and early May, it was freezing that year. Sleet and snow the entire time during the race."

"The conditions must have been appalling. And dangerous." Joe shook his head. "Whose idea was this race?"

"A newspaper called *Le Petit Journal*," Georges answered. "They said it was to reinvigorate cycling after the war, but I think they just wanted to sell more newspapers."

"It's hard to believe anyone would be so callous to route a race through those areas. That was only a few months after the war ended. There were unrecovered bodies and unexploded ordnance everywhere." His face fell, dismayed at the images of devastation running through his mind. "It will take years, decades even, to find everything."

Sophie rushed to shift the subject when Joe's expression changed so abruptly. "Tell us all about Chamonix, please, Georges. What sorts of exciting things happen here?"

Georges wagged his head back and forth in a Gallic move that she loved. "Many things happen here, madame. Since we hosted the first Winter Olympics in 1924, Chamonix has become a destination for many sports and many tourists. And where there are tourists, there are some people who like to take advantage of them."

"Makes sense," Joe said. "Tourists are easy marks."

"So, we should behave the same as we would in any tourist location."

"*Oui, c'est ça*, madame," George replied, his head bobbing in agreement. "And do not worry; it is only little crimes we experience. The occasional pickpocket. Sometimes things go missing, not from this hotel, but others have reported these things."

"The usual petty thieves?" Joe asked.

"Not precisely, monsieur. Every season there is a new face or two that the police investigate. Some people say this year he is a brunet, some say he is a blond. Others swear it is a woman dressed as a man. This summer the restaurants are reporting problems. Someone is stealing food. Someone is stealing hiking gear too. Ropes, axes, maps. Things have gone missing from hiker's huts."

Georges shrugged. "Chamonix is a small town. We have a small police force. They cannot be everywhere at once. Just keep your wits about you if you are in a crowd and you will have no problems."

She stole a glance at Joe. As a Detective Inspector, he'd handled murders and assigned his less experienced men to less serious crimes. But she could see the wheels in his head turning as he pondered something that reminded him of his work.

Good. If Joe was thinking about work, he wasn't thinking about war. Then the mouth-watering aromas of cheese and potatoes wafting from the *tartiflette* Monique placed on the table replaced her worries about the war.

Sophie scooped up the last bite of *tartiflette* on her plate, dabbed at her lips with her napkin, and sat back in her chair, replete. "Monique, that was wonderful."

"Did you save room for dessert? Tonight, is figs with *sabayon au Génépi*. And coffee and *digestifs* after if you like." Monique gestured to Nick, who looked up from his book and came over to clear their plates.

"We had Génépi at Will and Hélène's home, didn't we, Joe?"

Georges chuckled. "Will says it is aviation fuel flavored with alpine wildflowers."

"I will be happy to see Will and Edmund tomorrow," Vanni said. "I hope the weather is good so we can do all of our climbing."

"Will told us you and Georges met when the Olympics were held in Chamonix," Sophie said. "You were both on your country's mountain patrol teams? That's a combination of cross-country skiing and rifle shooting, isn't it?"

"If you are wondering how a man with a wooden leg could compete in the Olympics," Monique interjected, "let me tell you why. It is because he is stubborn. If you tell him he cannot do something, he will do whatever it takes to prove you wrong." She glanced at her husband, who had opened his mouth to protest. "You know I'm right, Georges."

"Of course, you are *chérie*." Georges turned to Sophie. "Let me assure you, madame, I am not the only stubborn one in our family. Monique was the reason I had to try it."

His wife gazed at him fondly. "Perhaps I gave you a little push."

"I needed a push," Georges admitted. "I had been feeling very sorry for myself." He crossed himself. "*Dieu merci,* I was not blinded. I would be weaving baskets instead."

"You Australians and New Zealanders were such a long way from home," Vanni commented. "But if not for you and the Canadians and Americans, we might not have won the war."

"Do not forget the Africans and the Indians," Georges added.

"Whether or not you like it, having colonies gave the French and British many sources of men to fight."

The party was quiet for a few moments, the men staring at their drinks, until Vanni raised his glass. "To all of them, and to us. I am very much afraid we will do that again." He shook his head and downed his drink.

Sophie opened her mouth to say something, anything, to move away from the subject of war. Monique seemed to have the same idea because she rose from the table and motioned them to the balustrade. "Come and look at the sunset. It is one of our favorite things."

They walked to the edge of the terrace. Georges pointed to the mountains on the west side of the valley. "The sun is setting there. Now watch the colors on Mont Blanc."

The bright snow on the top of the mountain became tinged with pale pink and then deepened to rose. When the sun dipped behind the mountains, the snow glowed with the faintest hint of blue.

"I love to see that," Georges said. "It is *magnifique*."

"Madame," Monique said, turning to Sophie, "we have a beautiful evening, and the weather report says tonight will be *une nuit bien etoilée*."

"A starry night?"

"Yes. Lots of stars. If you like to see them, there is a good place by the *mairie*, the town hall. It is an open plaza with no tall buildings to block the sky."

"A walk would be nice after all that driving," Joe said. "What do you think, love? Shall we take a stroll?"

"To see the pale stars rising?" she asked, referring to her favorite Rilke poem.

He offered her his arm, trying to remember the next line, but only managing to paraphrase. "Come with me."

THIRTY-SEVEN
DARKNESS AND DAWN

Joe and Sophie found the town hall tucked in a quiet little plaza away from the lights and bustle of the touristy streets. Sophie leaned against him, her back to his chest, and pulled his arms around her waist as she looked up.

The sky deepened from violet blue to the deepest, velvety black, dotted with stars and constellations they could recognize without having to recollect the atlas of the northern sky she bought when they docked in Honolulu.

When they sailed from New York to London, they repeated the ritual they'd begun on the voyage across the Pacific: if the sky was clear and the seas weren't too rough, they settled into deck chairs away from the noise and lights of the ship's ballroom and watched the wheel of the Milky Way rolling above them.

The Chamonix sky was drastically different than the vast bowl of the sky at sea. Here the tremendous height of the mountains, so steep that no one lived on their slopes, revealed only a slice of sky. The black void from the valley floor to the top of the mountains brought on an unnerving sense of looking up from a trench that was deeper and more intractable than any he'd ever been in.

Sophie turned in his arms. "You know darling, I'll always be glad I invited you to that gala."

The first time they met, she had been like the dawn, lighting up his darkness. She still was. He drew her close and focused all his attention on her. "I'll always be glad I offered you my coat," he murmured, and he felt her smile against his lips.

THIRTY-EIGHT

MOUNTAIN WILDFLOWERS

JULY 24, 1939, CHAMONIX

I lifted my rucksack onto my shoulders and stepped off the train. I pressed through the crowds of arriving and departing passengers. When I reached the station exit, I looked around for the signpost marked Chamonix-Mont Blanc.

I found a cheap hostel on the outskirts of the town and paid for one night. Tomorrow I will get local maps of all the trails and find a place where I can camp. I need to save my money for food and the journey home. I should have taken more money from the tin.

No matter. I am here and those stupid boys are at home playing with wooden rifles in the village square, pretending to be soldiers while they sing Deutschland Über Alles.

To prove I was here, I will carve an edelweiss along the trails I explore and mark each trail on the map with an edelweiss.

For luck, I touched the silver edelweiss hidden in my pocket.

The next morning, Sophie sat with Joe at a table in the hotel's wood-paneled breakfast room. Posters of Chamonix winter and summer sports adorned the walls and relieved the expanses of knotty pine. Monique poured Sophie's coffee. "Did you sleep well?"

"Blissfully well." Sophie glanced at Joe, who was valiantly trying to ignore her hand wandering on his knee. "Our bed is so comfortable we didn't want to get up this morning, did we, Joe?"

Monique nodded her approval and poured a cup for Joe. "May I ask what your plans are for the day?"

"We thought we'd explore the town in the daylight," Joe answered, "and see what we missed last night."

"Perhaps an easy hike to get your bearings? We can make you a picnic lunch and I will give you a map of a good trail that is gentle and not too far from here."

A little while later, Sophie stood in the lobby with Joe. Nick held a rucksack for him to carry on his shoulders.

It was such an unexpected sight, seeing Joe slip first one arm, then the other, through the straps and squirm to settle it against his back, as if he was still a soldier preparing to march somewhere.

Still fiddling with the rucksack straps, Joe glanced at her, looking more than a little self-conscious.

"Darling, is your shoulder all right?"

"It's nothing. I'm fine, fine," he said.

Joe's odd moment with the rucksack had been unsettling enough that she kept an eye on him for any further signs of discomfort until they stood on a wide bridge with the River Arve roiling several feet below them.

"I expected a clear, babbling mountain stream," she said, raising her voice to be heard over the rushing river. "Not a murky, raging torrent." She flipped through the little brochure Monique had given them. "The source of the Arve is a glacier. In the winter, the river runs clear and slow. In the summer, melting snow and ice combines with soil. That's why it's so muddy."

"That must be why the air temperature is so much cooler, too," Joe remarked.

They found the trail marker, with a little flower carved next to the arrow, and set upon the path. The well-maintained trail rose steadily through a forest of firs and ferns. Her legs were more tired than she expected when they stopped to get their bearings after an hour of hiking.

"It's so quiet," she whispered. The only sounds were birdsong, a slight breeze ruffling the needles of the trees and water trickling somewhere close by. They had made a gradual, but steady ascent, and they could see the rooftops of Chamonix and the muddy river churning its way through the town.

Joe had a drink of water from the canteen and then offered it to her. "I'll trade you for the field glasses." She slid them off her shoulder and passed them to him. He fished the map out of his jacket pocket and unfolded it.

She stood beside him so she could study the map, too. "That must be Le Brévent," he said, pointing to the mountain across the valley from them. "Switzerland is to our right, Italy is behind us, and Mont Blanc is to our left. It's funny that it dominates the entire valley, but where we are right now, we can't see it for all the trees."

She flitted around the trail for a few minutes, admiring the views and breathing in the scent of the firs. "I wonder if there's a waterfall close by. Let's go look."

They wandered for a few moments and found a tiny waterfall, its source the barest crack in a craggy rock formation far above them. The wet stones glistened in the dappled sunlight. She dipped her fingers in the water. "Oh! It's freezing!"

Joe availed himself of a stump from a fallen tree and pulled off the rucksack he was wearing. "Since we've found a source of water to refill our canteen, I suggest we eat our lunch and rest up."

They delved in and found a cloth to spread on the ground, ham and cheese sandwiches made with fresh baguettes, two apples, and a package of chocolate. "Perfect!" she said. Joe, who had already tucked into a sandwich, nodded in agreement.

She took a bite of her sandwich and turned so she could use his shoulder as a headrest and hummed contentedly. "This is beautiful. What luck we had meeting Will and him suggesting we come here. I'm so glad we did."

They ate in silence for a few moments. Joe finished his sandwich and started polishing an apple with his handkerchief. "When I pointed out Robbie's name, Will knew where he fought and when he went missing. I'd be willing to bet he could tell you the same about any of the names on those walls." He bit into his apple and chewed. "He has a remarkable memory."

"Perhaps he's just made it his mission to know. Hélène told me he meets the visitors and walks with them through the memorial."

"I wish my mother could have visited the place. Other mothers received a photograph of their son's grave. You know, a wooden cross, painted white. It might have helped her to accept that Robbie really was dead."

She waited a few minutes, comparing Ben's neatly tended grave at Suresnes with what Joe had said long ago about burying bodies on battlefields, and wondering whether he might say more about Robbie or even the nightmare he had before visiting Villers-Bret. When Joe said nothing else, she stood and dusted off the seat of her trousers. At least he'd started talking. Perhaps he would say more soon. As concerned as she was about the nightmare, she couldn't push him, but she could subtly prod. She stood and stretched. "I know I'll sleep well tonight after all this exercise and fresh air," she hinted.

Joe didn't take the bait. "If you'll fill our canteen, I'll pack everything up," he replied.

He was wrapping the apple cores in the sandwich papers and folding the cloth when she cried out. Joe came and crouched beside her at the little waterfall. "What is it?"

"Look how much more water is coming down now. I was holding the canteen in the water and I heard a noise above me, and some small rocks tumbled down. One of them hit my hand."

"Are you all right?" He examined a tiny gash on the back of her left hand.

"I'm not hurt. I was just startled. I thought someone was watching me. A boy or a young man."

"What did he look like?"

"He had blond hair." Without warning, she thrust the canteen into Joe's hand and scrambled across the wet rocks.

"Aha!" She plucked something out of the water and hurried back to him. She held a metal flower about an inch and a half wide, with nine silver petals and seven gold dots in the center. "It looks like the carving on the trail marker."

"Huh," Joe commented as she turned it over.

"There's no maker's mark on the back. And it's heavy for its size. It must be costume jewelry, not silver."

"You know jewelry isn't my forte."

"I didn't notice this before." She showed him a rock the size of a golf ball with a thick crystalline vein running through it. "This is the rock that tumbled down and hit my hand. It looks different from the ones in the—"

Joe touched her arm and looked up. She heard it too. Someone, or something, was moving above them, close to the source of the waterfall.

She watched Joe shift into detective mode, listening and observing, trying to determine if someone was up there, or whether it was an animal or simply the day's warmth causing the rocks above them to expand and shift.

After a few minutes, he shrugged, satisfied there was nothing to be concerned about. He pulled his handkerchief out of his pocket and held it so she could deposit the metal flower and the rock in his palm. He closed his fingers over the items and pushed the lot into his trouser pocket.

She, however, was not ready to dismiss the odd experience. The slope was too steep to climb up or down. The person she'd seen might catch up with them at the trailhead or the bridge and she could give the flower back. "Darling," she began. "Since I've filled the canteen, shall we head back? I'd love to do some souvenir shopping."

She despised souvenir knick-knacks, and Joe knew it. He rolled his eyes and bit back an indulgent smile.

His smile faded to a grimace as he settled the rucksack on his shoulders. She saw that too but said nothing.

When they reached the bridge, she walked to the middle of it and turned to watch the river. "Let's stop for a minute. It's turned out to be a very warm day, and this spot is surprisingly cool."

Adopting her best carefree tourist pose—face lifted to the sun, eyes hidden behind dark sunglasses—she scanned the people walking on the trail side of the river.

She walked over to the other side of the bridge, looking around for several minutes. But nothing unusual happened. No blond boys came limping off the trail, so she sauntered back over to Joe's side and linked her arm through his. "Know where we are, darling?"

Joe, also in dark glasses, had pulled out the map and was studying their surroundings. "Of course, I know where we are," he answered, barely keeping the laughter out of his voice when he murmured, "No one on my side either."

She smirked and bumped his shoulder with hers. "I wanted to

see if the blond boy I saw would come to find us. Shall we head back to the hotel?"

He folded the map and quirked a brow. "What about those souvenirs you wanted?"

"I planned to window shop along the way."

"Right. Get an idea of who has the best merchandise." He held out his elbow for her to take his arm and they set off toward the shops across the street.

A quarter of an hour spent peering at shop windows full of local liqueurs, Mont Blanc snow globes, and mountaineering gear, and scanning the reflected passers-by, netted nothing.

No one caught her eye except Joe, fidgeting with the straps of his rucksack.

"Have you seen enough? Because I'd like to get this thing off."

No wonder he seemed impatient. "Your shoulder! You shouldn't have carried it for so long. Take it off and give it to me."

"My shoulder is fine. The rucksack isn't heavy, it's just hot. I'd forgotten how hot they can get. I never guessed that it would be so warm in the mountains."

"Then let's get back to the hotel and have a cool drink and try to figure out what I found."

Their arrival on the hotel's terrace coincided with another, much noisier, arrival. Sophie heard Will's Australian voice booming a greeting to Georges and a less booming American voice greeting Monique. Then the two newcomers switched partners. Will was swinging a laughing Monique around and when he put her down, she kissed him soundly on both cheeks. Will's son Chris dutifully accepted Monique's hug, Nick shook hands with Will and

Edmund, and then both boys loped down the hotel drive in search of whatever seventeen-year-old boys are in search of.

"And now, beer," Georges said, and he trotted into the hotel.

Will greeted Joe and Sophie warmly, although Will refrained from swinging her as he'd done with Monique. Then he introduced his friend Edmund Stone, bespectacled and rumpled from the long drive.

Sophie watched over the top of her sunglasses as Joe slid the rucksack off and rolled his shoulders several times. He caught her looking at him. "You're hovering, love. There's nothing wrong with my shoulder," he insisted as he pulled out a chair in the shade for her.

She kept an eagle eye on him, nonetheless, watching as he pulled off his linen jacket and then his hat and ran his fingers through his hair to smooth it. He sat, grimaced, and rose and took the handkerchief holding the silver flower and the rock from his pocket. "Much better," he said as he sat again.

When she was satisfied Joe was fine, or at least fine enough he wasn't grimacing anymore, she took off her sunglasses, unpinned her hat, and shook out her short waves, lifting them from her neck and forehead. She searched in Joe's jacket pockets for the map and used it to fan herself to dry the damp tendrils at her nape and temples.

Will lifted his glass to her and grinned. "G'day, Sophie. So how do you like it here? Are Georges and Monique treating you right?"

"It's wonderful here, Will, and they're marvelous, as you well know."

He took in her trousers, sturdy shoes, and the rucksack hanging off the back of Joe's chair. "Been hiking?"

"We have. We wanted to get our bearings and Monique pointed us to an easy trail and packed us a lunch."

"Good for you," Will replied. "Hélène likes the trail that starts by the Balmat statue. She says Mont Blanc and the Aiguille du Midi get all the attention and the shorter mountains deserve some too."

"That's the one. It was lovely. We saw waterfalls, and it was so quiet and cool in the forest. And something rather odd happened."

"Odd?" Georges asked.

"Show them, Joe," she urged, and he opened his handkerchief on the table. "We found a waterfall, just a trickle along the rocks, before we had our picnic. Then, after we ate, I went over to fill our canteen and some rocks came tumbling down. One of them hit my hand. Oh, it's nothing," she assured Monique, who wanted to see. "That's when I saw this silver flower in the water. It wasn't there before. I have a very good eye for shiny things."

"She does," Joe agreed, nodding.

"I thought I saw someone high above me before the rocks fell. I kept the rock that hit my hand. I thought it was unusual, with this vein of crystal in it." She passed the rock to Georges and the flower to Monique. "It's pretty, isn't it? I should put up a lost and found notice," she said as Monique examined the silver flower. "The owner must miss this."

"I have never seen a brooch like this," Monique said. "I think it is a wildflower that is common high in the mountains. Georges? Do you know?"

THIRTY-NINE
SOUVENIR FROM CHAMONIX

Earlier today I tripped and hurt my left knee. The rocks underfoot shifted. I slid down a vertical slope, scrambling and grabbing for tree trunks and low-lying branches to slow my descent. I uttered an anguished cry as my silver edelweiss arced through the air and disappeared with a final glint. I got a firm hold and pulled myself along a branch to a point at which it was strong enough to support my weight. I held on for dear life, my heart pounding and my palms stinging from the rough bark. Blood from my knee made a slow trail down my calf.

I could hear voices far below. I didn't dare move. The descent could be noisy, and I didn't want to draw any attention to myself. I listened carefully to the voices. The woman's was as clear as a bell. The man's was low and quiet, like the air after the ringing stopped, but the vibrations still thrummed in the ears. I have never heard accents like theirs before. They sounded English, but not English.

My left knee throbbed from the rock I'd fallen against before the slide. But the tears stinging my eyes were not for the physical pain. They were for losing my precious edelweiss, my talisman. I remembered how it had looked and felt in my palm, the weight of it, the dull silver and shiny gold. I must find those people and get my edelweiss back.

～

Georges, intent on examining the rock, gave the silver flower a cursory glance. "Madame, we call it *Étoile des Alpes*, Star of the Alps. In German it is *edelweiss*. They grow in the high alpine meadows throughout Europe. They are white, with yellow centers. The coat of arms for Chamonix has five of them."

"I hope no one claims it, then." Sophie shot a mischievous look at Joe. "It would be a perfect souvenir from Chamonix, don't you think, Joe?"

"Better than a snow globe?"

"Infinitely. And even if someone does claim it, I'll still have the rock as a memento of our hike."

Georges placed the rock on the table. "That is quartz in your rock, madame. It is common, but you have found a nice specimen."

"Thank you, Georges. I'll treasure it." She turned to Will. "Hélène didn't come with you?"

"She and Marianne will be here in few days. Marianne is doing some extra work to help her boss finish a trousseau for a young lady who's getting married next month. That's one of the perks of working," he joked, "you're always at someone else's beck and call. Edmund offered to drive us so I could leave our car with the ladies."

"I'll be glad to see them again."

"Marianne told me that if Chris got to learn to drive when he turned thirteen, then she deserved to learn too since she was fifteen. I found I couldn't argue with her when she put it that way."

"So, you're raising a modern young woman," she teased. "It takes a special kind of father to do that."

Will looked so pleased at the compliment that Edmund let out a snort of laughter. He leaned toward her and uttered in a stage whisper, "Will's a special kind of father, all right. He wanted her to learn to cook. Unlike her mother, Marianne hates cooking."

"When you have kids of your own, you can talk," Will said.

Georges placed several more bottles of beer on their table. "We have an unexpected guest who will arrive soon," Georges said. "I must help Monique prepare his room."

"Thanks for the beer," Will said. "Don't worry about us. We'll entertain ourselves."

"It may be a while," Georges replied. "Madame, is there something I can get for you?"

"No, thank you, Georges. I'm perfectly comfortable here in the shade with this charming company," Sophie said, her eyes darting between Will and Edmund. "Will didn't explain how he met two Americans climbing French mountains in 1917."

"My friend and I left university to come over and drive ambulances," Edmund began.

"That's exactly what my brother Ben did." A fresh twinge of grief rolled over her: waving goodbye to Ben as he drove a shiny new ambulance into the unknown, and racing to meet the dusty, battered ambulance that brought him back to Paris for the last time. "How did we not know you in Paris?"

"We were only there for a couple of days. When we arrived, the French needed truck drivers more than ambulance drivers, so they assigned us to the *camions* instead. We went to Chamonix on a whim. We used to hike and ski during term breaks at a place called Lake Placid in upstate New York."

"That's the sort of fellow he was," Will interjected good naturedly. "Footloose college boy."

Edmund shrugged. "We were young and dumb, and we figured we should see the French Alps while we had the chance."

She took a sip of her beer, hoping to steer the conversation away from the war. "Will told us you're a journalist. What are you working on now? I'd love to read it."

"I just finished a piece about the Hitler Youth. It's compulsory for all German children now." He rubbed his forehead and blew out a dejected breath. "Kindergartners saluting and shouting *Heil Hitler* is more than I can stomach. It's so much worse there than it has been. It was bad enough last year when Hitler used Heckmair, the first man to climb the Eiger, to glorify the Third Reich. And before that, he used the summer Olympic Games in '36 as a vehicle for Nazi propaganda.

"You're right," Joe said. "I remember our team saying that stadium was packed with spectators every day of the games. They also said Berlin and the stadium were blanketed with Nazi banners."

Edmund and Will turned to him at the same time. "Your team?" Will asked.

"The Australian eights rowing team was made up of members from the New South Wales police force rowing club. All of us rowers helped the team train for the games."

Edmund poured a new beer into his glass, waited for the foamy top to dissipate, and drank thirstily before he turned to Joe again. "Will told me a bit of your story on the drive here. Australian soldier and American nurse reunited years after the war. What brought you back to France? If you don't mind me asking, of course."

"I don't mind. I was wounded in a drug raid several months ago, and Sophie and my commissioner convinced me to take over the forensics department. The current head is retiring."

"But you're here instead of there?"

"In the process of convincing me I've worked too long to still be getting shot at, they gave me the opportunity to meet with the police departments in Vancouver and Toronto to study the forensics methods they use. Then I met with Scotland Yard in London while Sophie helped her mother get her affairs in order before she leaves England."

She picked up their story when Joe paused to finish his beer. "My mother is moving to Sydney to be near us and her sister. We sail home from Marseille on August fourth."

"You've been away from home a long time," Edmund said.

"It's been the trip of a lifetime," Joe said, "but I'll be glad to get started on the new job. While we're sailing, I plan to write a report on how all the cities we visited use forensic techniques and try to figure out how we can best use them in Sydney."

"I could write about you two," Edmund said. "I've been casting about for something less serious. People tire of reading too much doom and gloom and I get tired of writing it. What do you think? I don't remember whether Will said you have children," he hinted.

"Joe has Sam. He's twenty-five. I adopted my French godson, Jean-Luc, when he was twelve. He's twenty-four now."

"Sam's a pilot," Joe said, twisting his glass in his fingers. "He loves the stars, and he loves flying, so he's learning to navigate by the stars. Frankly, the thought of him flying at night scares the hell out of me. He swears he knows what he's doing, though."

"Celestial navigation, like the sailors of old," Edmund mused, "only his ship is in the sky rather than the sea."

Sophie smiled at Edmund. "That's a romantic way of looking at it. We'll have to remember to tell him that."

"What can I say, it's the writer in me. What does Jean-Luc do?"

"Jean-Luc loves wine. He's been working at vineyards, learning everything about the business. I'm supposed to report back to him about the wines Joe and I try while we're here in France."

"Makes sense, given he's French," Edmund mused.

"It also makes sense because he's lived the past ten years in Australia. We have a lot of vineyards throughout the country."

Edmund beamed at her. "I didn't know that. Can you tell me more? You may have given me another idea for a new—"

Sophie was more than willing to brainstorm new article ideas with Edmund, but an old Citroën 7CV struggling up the drive in the wrong gear drowned out the rest of his response. The car made it up to the level of the hotel reception, but the engine rattled after the driver turned off the ignition.

Will, who had been dozing unobtrusively, startled awake. "The new arrival," he said, smothering a yawn. "Remind me never to run a hotel."

An old man emerged from the car, smoothing his bushy white mustache and pushing his glasses up the bridge of his nose as he shuffled his way to their table.

Will unfolded himself from his chair and shook the old man's hand. "Will Ryan. Georges and Monique are making up your room. I'll take you to find them."

"I am sorry to disturb you with my noisy automobile. I am broken in third gear."

The old man's voice trailed off as he stared, expressionless, at the silver flower on the table. Then he smiled at her. "That is a nice edelweiss. Do you know it is the national flower of my country, Switzerland? It is said that giving this flower is a promise of dedication to a loved one."

"I didn't know," she said, picking it up and admiring it considering this new information. "What a lovely thought."

Joe checked his watch and then looked over at her. "What do you want to do about dinner tonight? Do you want to go out, or…?

"If you like, join me and Will here at the hotel," Edmund offered. "He and I talked about some places we could take you before we go for our big climb. We can compare plans over dinner and help you make the most of your time here."

"That's very kind of you, Edmund." Hélène's comment about the benefits of laughing and talking for men like Joe, who had freshly opened wounds from the war, bubbled up in her mind. The idea of another casual evening with friends was appealing. She looked at Joe, who nodded.

"Sounds lovely," she said. "We'll meet you back down here."

She could think of another advantage to dining at the hotel. They had more time to enjoy their lovely bathtub that was almost, but not quite, big enough to swim in. Coming here was indeed taking Joe's mind off Villers-Bretonneux.

Dinner was as lively as it had been at Will and Hélène's home, with the added entertainment of watching Chris help Nick wait tables. Chris struggled to balance a tray full of plates. Nick nearly dropped his tray when he smirked at his friend and promptly tripped over his own feet.

"Chris has to earn his keep when he comes on these trips with us," Will confided. "He helps here, and then he and Nick have a couple of days to do whatever they want to do. Hike. Go camping. Flirt with the girls in town." He tilted his head in the general direction of the two boys, still fumbling with the trays, and shook his head. "Probably best not to think about it too much."

"I'm so glad you convinced us to come here," Sophie said.

"It's wonderful to see you again." She winked at Edmund and added, "And to meet a fellow Yank, too."

"Will told us you were at Saint Quentin Canal," Joe said. "We were glad to have you Americans there with us."

"Your General Monash did a fine job cobbling together a successful attack with armies from three different countries," Edmund said, "even though we had a hell of a time understanding what the Brits and you Australians were saying. Although I understood 'Digger' the first time I had to dig to do trench work."

"I hate to admit it, but I still don't know what Doughboy means," Joe said.

Edmund nodded and took a sip of wine. "That one's easy. Do you remember when it was dry, and we'd get covered in chalky dust? Well, when the Americans were fighting the Mexicans, they'd get covered in the local white adobe dust and people thought they looked like bakers. Hence the name doughboy."

Joe jumped into the fray when Will and Edmund launched into a litany of Australian, British, and American slang phrases that had bewildered them, chuckling at each new phrase, until Edmund stopped and said in mock seriousness, "What stumps me is how you Aussies change words or add an O to the end. *Smoko* for a smoke? How on earth do you come up with these things?"

"It's our rule," Will joked. "Words with one syllable must have at least one syllable added. Words with more than one syllable must be shortened."

"What about *brekkie* for breakfast?" Edmund countered. "It's still two syllables."

"I have an even better one, Edmund. *She'll be apples.*" She looked expectantly at Joe and Will. "Let's hear them explain that one."

Will let out a hoot of laughter. Smiling, Joe shook his head. "I admit I've no idea how that phrase came to mean you'll be right."

Still laughing, they discussed plans for their stay over coffee and Génépi. Edmund, Will and Georges talked over each other with different suggestions.

"What about going to the *Mer de Glace* tomorrow?" Edmund said at the same moment Will proposed, "How about coming as far as the first refuge with us?" and Georges suggested visiting a vineyard or two.

In a gesture Sophie knew well, Joe held up his hands to calm the chatter. "Sophie and I are happy to put ourselves in your capable hands. We're only here for a short time, and it's your holiday as well. How can we best accommodate everyone's plans?"

The group was quiet for a few moments until Edmund piped up, "Will and I could do a quick climb tomorrow. Mrs. Parker, you and Mr. Parker could—"

"Edmund, you must call us Sophie and Joe."

"Yes ma'am." Edmund suggested an itinerary where Joe and Sophie would do a vineyard tour and then visit the *Mer de Glace* glacier. "If you can stay one more day, we could also take you to the refuge on Mount Blanc."

"It all sounds marvelous," Sophie said. She looked at the cloudy sky. "I'm afraid we can't stargaze again tonight. What else can we do in the evenings?"

"There is a casino, if you like to play cards," Monique said. "If the Englishwoman is there, she will give you a good show. She wins so often the casino suspects she counts cards, but they haven't been able to prove it."

"Sometimes I think the Englishwoman is the ringleader of the summer thieves," Georges said. "Something always happens when she is in Chamonix. Last year it was a big fight in the casino."

"No, Georges." Monique shook her head. "That was the year before. Last summer was the argument at the market."

Georges was undaunted. "No. It is her companion who is the

ringleader. She is so drab and quiet no one would ever suspect her."

His look of delight didn't abate when Monique rolled her eyes at him.

Oh, this might be a fun diversion. Sophie quirked a brow at Joe. "I'd like to visit the casino, darling. Since we're doing the vineyard tour tomorrow, we won't have to get up early in the morning."

FORTY

EVENING AT THE CASINO

Joe knew that look very well. Sophie had been in a Paris sort of mood, merry and mischievous, when they stood on the bridge and she played detective after their hike. Their time in Paris, exploring the city and making new memories together, had been carefree and enjoyable. Villers-Bret had taken that away from them. If Sophie playing detective in Chamonix was a chance for them to get back to the fun they were having before the memorial, he wouldn't object.

"What are you expecting to find?" he asked while they strolled the short distance from the hotel to the casino.

"I'm not sure. But Monique and Georges made it sound like the casino is a web of intrigue."

"And you suspect you'll solve the mystery of the English-woman, and the Chamonix summer thieves?"

Sophie squeezed his arm when they stepped through the casino's front door. "Let's see what happens."

He swept practiced eyes around the room. The casino wasn't a big place, but it was busy with tourists and locals. A lively craps table took up the center of the room. Poker, blackjack, and baccarat tables were in three corners of the room, with a bar tucked in the fourth corner. "There's a woman at the blackjack table," he murmured, "and a mousy-looking woman sitting behind her."

Sophie was far less subtle, but he admired her delivery. "Oh! There's a blackjack table," she exclaimed, and then dropped her voice to a whisper "Do you want to play or shall I?"

"You do the honors. I'll watch for a few minutes and then start walking around. If I see anything unusual, I'll come over and pretend to check on you."

"Good plan. Keep an eye on that companion of hers too."

"I will. Would you like a glass of champagne to complete the illusion?"

"You read my mind," Sophie answered.

He chuckled quietly when she added a little more sway than usual to her step and a flirty glance over her shoulder as she walked away from him. Apparently, she had decided to play *femme fatale* as well as detective. He indulged himself for a moment, enjoying the view as she sauntered to the cashier to buy chips.

He waited to get drinks until Sophie reached the blackjack table, placed her first bet, and began to play. She was an excellent blackjack player. He preferred poker, despite Robbie's rough introduction to the game, but his playing was within the bounds of friendly games with colleagues once a month, and for far lower stakes than he was seeing at the poker table here in the casino.

He collected a whiskey for himself and champagne for Sophie and delivered it to her. Her small pile of chips had already grown. He wasn't sure what her plan was for playing, but she would adjust it as she observed how others at the table played.

"Thank you, darling. This is so exciting," she enthused, staying in character of an excited tourist. "I've already won ten francs!"

The woman's companion was sitting in a chair against the

wall behind her mistress. At first glance, it appeared she was staying out of the way and waiting within earshot until her employer needed her, although for what remained to be seen. She caught Joe's eye, smiled, and looked away at once. He nodded, acknowledging her presence, but not enough to draw attention to himself or to her. Then he walked to the baccarat corner and positioned himself to observe the activity at the blackjack table.

The companion fetched another drink for her mistress, but nothing out of the ordinary was happening, so he moved to the next corner and repeated the process. It was harder to see the Englishwoman from this angle, but he thought her movements might be growing careless. Her toss of chips was a little shaky and her speech, what he could hear of it, sounded somewhat slurred. It looked like she was losing, judging from the diminished stack of chips in front of her.

He'd had a beer in the afternoon and wine with dinner, so Joe nursed his whiskey to keep his full faculties about him. As he walked over to the craps table in the center of the room, a commotion began at the blackjack table. The Englishwoman's voice rose, and she stood up, knocking her drink over. Joe couldn't see everything because several others at the table stood up also and blocked his view.

He hurried over to the table. Sophie was wiping her arm with a tiny lace-trimmed hanky, and he offered her his larger handkerchief when he reached her.

In the confusion, the companion was trying to help her mistress. "Just stop it," the woman muttered, sweeping her chips into her bag and thrusting it into the younger woman's hands. "Cash these in. I'll be at the car." She stormed out with her companion bringing up the rear.

The other players had mopped up and stacked their chips, eager to play again. "Let me excuse myself and we'll get out of here," Sophie said.

They exited the building just as the Englishwoman's car roared out of the casino's circular drive.

"What happened?" he asked.

"Two of the men sitting at the table palmed each other's chips in the confusion."

"So, there's cheating in the casino."

"Joe, what if one of them is Chamonix's summer thief? Or what if she is? Georges said the thief could be a woman."

"Perhaps. But it seems a stretch to go from petty theft during the day to drawing attention to oneself at the casino, doesn't it?"

"Hmm." She thought for a moment and then brightened. "Causing a disturbance would be the perfect foil."

Sophie was enjoying herself far too much for him to stop playing along. "Possibly. What about the woman? Was she drunk?"

"I don't know. She seemed fine when I began playing. In fact, at the beginning, I thought she might be counting cards. But then I began winning, and she began losing. That's when her drink spilled. It seemed like she was sober one minute and not sober the next. Maybe she was just angry about losing. It was very odd."

He tucked Sophie's hand around his elbow. "Let's head back to the hotel. You can ask Monique about it in the morning. Maybe she knows something."

FORTY-ONE

PLAYING DETECTIVE

Loitering in the alleys and laneways behind the restaurants and hotels proved to be a fruitful use of my time. I realized there was a great deal of free food to be had when they set out the rubbish after meals.

Why spend my meager funds on food when I don't have to?

Monique shook her head as she poured their coffee the next morning. "Every summer it is the same. The Englishwoman comes to Chamonix for a few days, makes a scene somewhere, and then she and her companion leave and go someplace else."

"What about the two men stealing chips?"

"Ah. Those two men are brothers. The casino knows about them but does nothing."

"You're joking."

"I am not, madame," Monique replied. "Unless they fight, the casino leaves them alone. They only steal from each other, not other players. And, it is not because of the Englishwoman, no matter what Georges said. They do the same thing every time."

Joe shook his head. Sophie knew that after years as a police officer, little surprised him anymore. "Any idea why all this happens?"

Monique shrugged. "Because they are brothers? They own a vineyard, and they cannot agree to make their wine with a grape that is better but harder to grow or to mix it with cheaper Chardonnay grapes. They argue about it constantly."

The old man who had arrived the previous afternoon shuffled out to the terrace.

"Good morning," he called to them and lifted a hand in greeting.

"Good morning," Sophie replied.

"I do not mean to disturb you. I wish to apologize for my noisy automobile yesterday," he explained. "Pardon me, where are my manners? I am Erich Bauer," he said, and held out his hand.

Joe introduced themselves and he and Sophie shook his hand. Bauer executed a little half-bow at the same time. "You are from England?" he asked.

"No, Australia," Sophie said.

Bauer's lips formed a surprised O. "You are very far from home. Not like me."

"No," Sophie agreed. "And you, Mr. Bauer? Where in Switzerland do you call home?"

"I am from Bern. I am near to home." He chuckled, as if pleased with his comparison.

"What brings you to Chamonix?"

"I come to France to see the Swiss ride in the Tour de France. But this year they are not so very good. So now, I should return home. Only I fear my car will not get me there."

Bauer's eyeglasses were so thick she didn't know how he could see to drive, much less pick out individual cyclists, so she took refuge in a platitude. "The Tour is such a big event, isn't it?"

Monique appeared, bearing a large tray with their breakfast. "Here you are."

"I am pleased to make your acquaintance," Erich Bauer said. "I will leave you to your breakfast." He turned to Monique. "Madame? Where would you like me to sit? Here on the terrace or inside, in the breakfast room?"

Joe picked up the French newspaper and snapped it open. Monique turned back to them. "If you are still interested in visiting vineyards today, here is some information. There is one in Switzerland, quite close, that may be of interest because of your son. I can answer questions you have."

Sophie took the brochures Monique offered. "Oh good. Thank you. We'll look at them after breakfast, if that's all right."

"Of course, of course. Breakfast first." Monique poured them fresh cups of coffee. "I will leave this pot with you."

Joe handed over the French newspaper a few minutes later. "I give up. Nouns are hard enough, but written French uses verb tenses I can't recognize. Trade me?"

She gave him the English newspaper and skimmed the French headlines, her eyes alighting on a short column entitled Police Reports. "Joe, listen to this. The Chamonix thief has struck again. 'Vendors at yesterday's market reported missing two baguettes, three apples, and a small wheel of cheese. A pair of English tourists buying provisions for a long hike reported the theft of their rucksacks, which were later found in a bin at the market. The thief stole some crampons and several lengths of rope, plus an unspecified amount of cash that was in an interior pocket of one rucksacks.'"

She closed the newspaper. These petty thefts were still a perfect way to keep Joe's mind off Villers-Bret. "Joe, let's go to the market. Maybe we can spot the thief while I'm shopping for a souvenir. Maybe the thief is the blond boy I saw yesterday!"

Joe took one look at Sophie's shining eyes and knew she hadn't finished detecting. "We have vineyards to visit and wine to taste, remember?"

"We can do both," she declared. "We have all day to do whatever we like."

He drove, since Sophie's ability to read the French guide to the vineyards was so much better than his. Despite reminding himself that it was the job of the Chamonix police to investigate whatever thefts were occurring, he stopped at the market on their way to the vineyards. His reward was another excited smile.

From what he could tell, Sophie thoroughly enjoyed pretending to shop while she watched for anyone who might be a thief. She put on a good show of speaking with merchants, casually moving from stall to stall and asking questions about their wares. If he hadn't known what she was up to, he would have guessed she was simply an enthusiastic tourist practicing her French conversational skills.

The merchants loved her if the sample tastes of fruits and breads and cheeses they offered her were any sign. She shared with him, taking the first bite for herself and offering him the second bite with a mischievous little smile playing on her lips.

Sophie ended up buying a souvenir, but he waited until they pulled onto the main road out of Chamonix to ask about it. "Sophie?"

She was examining her purchase. "Hmm?"

"Why do we need a cowbell? You spent a lot of time talking with that man. Please tell me we don't own a cow now too." Even though he had been by her side, the entire conversation had been in French, and the man's accent had been too thick for him to understand.

"No darling, we don't. But the man who makes the bells does."

He knew that nonchalant attitude. He had to tease the information out of her. "Ah."

"The man who makes the cowbells has cows." She tilted the bell back and forth so she could hear its tone. "Which he pastures up in the high meadows during the summer."

"And?" He played his role in the game and waited for her to reveal her news.

"And he has to hike up to the meadows to check on his cows. He has goats too. That's why he had two sizes of bells."

"Makes perfect sense."

"He was so forthcoming about seeing people he didn't know hiking on the same trail he takes that I bought a bell to keep him talking." She turned to arch a brow at him. "I thought it was only fair to spend more and get the bigger one."

He bit back a juvenile joke about size. "Could one of these people be a young blond man he's never seen before this summer?"

Sophie's answer was a full-throated laugh. "Full points, inspector!"

"Right. We'll just file that information away for future reference, shall we? Speaking of reference, would you check the guide and tell me where I'm supposed to turn? I've been driving with no idea where I'm going."

"Let's see…it says to take the next left for Martigny. That will take us to the area where they produce wine. I'd like to get a case to take home for Jean-Luc and one for Will and Hélène as a thank you for dinner. She fed us a wonderful meal with almost no advance notice."

"Good idea. I'd been wondering what we could do. I thought a bottle of Génépi for Will."

"We can do that too. I'm so pleased that we made their acquaintance. They're a lovely couple."

Joe felt confident enough driving on the right that he turned to smile at his wife. Sophie was the most thoughtful person he'd ever known, genuinely interested in everyone she met. He thought they complemented each other well, his reserve balanced by her exuberance. She was also the most desirable woman he'd ever known, and he squirmed at the memory of her daintily licking her fingers after feeding him a juicy morsel of melon. She charmed him regularly. It was no wonder the merchants at the market had fallen under her spell.

"When we finish, we can head back toward Chamonix and stop for lunch," Sophie said. "Monique suggested Vallorcines."

"Which town is that in?"

"Vallorcines is the town. We passed through it before we crossed into Switzerland. Didn't you see the signpost?"

"I've been on the lookout for wineries," he said, downshifting and slowing the car in front of several signs posted on the side of the road. "Pick which vineyard you want to visit first."

FORTY-TWO
FLASH OF LIGHT

When they returned to the hotel, Joe opened the back of the car to take out the wine they'd purchased, while Sophie sprinted for the lavatory.

Monique rushed over to the car. "*Non*, monsieur, you must not lift those crates of wine. Not with that shoulder of yours."

He fixed her with his best detective inspector gaze. "Monique, how do you know about my shoulder? Did Sophie tell you? Or was it Will?"

She returned his gaze with one of her own. "You will never make me confess," she teased, and burst out laughing at the silly grin that crossed his face.

"Fine. I'll let it go this time," he teased back.

"Nick! Chris!" She motioned for the two boys to come over. "Take this wine out of the car and put it in the larder."

"In a moment, *Maman,*" Nick protested.

"Now, young man. It will take you only two minutes." She went back inside, calling over her shoulder to the boys. "Put the crates off to the side, by themselves. They are not for the hotel."

He walked over to the balustrade of the terrace and gazed out at the mountains. The weather hadn't changed during the afternoon. The sky and air were so clear he could see movement through the trees across the way.

He picked up his field glasses and focused. A flash of reflected light. What was that? Or who was it? Someone with blond hair. Sophie needed to see this for herself. She would love this development. And, if he was honest, he was becoming intrigued too.

Sophie was nowhere in sight, though. Chris and Nick were flipping a coin to decide who would lift and who would park the car. He shrugged and picked up a crate of wine. The weight was manageable, but the crate was more cumbersome than he expected it to be. He was glad Sophie wasn't around to see him grimace when a wooden corner jammed into his left shoulder, right where he'd been shot, starting a throbbing ache.

He would find her after he carried the wine inside.

FORTY-THREE
I DON'T NEED YOU TO SAVE ME

Sophie was wandering the public rooms of the hotel. She and Joe had been so busy she hadn't a chance to explore, and she had a few minutes before it was time to bathe and dress for dinner.

The spacious lounge room at the front of the hotel was furnished with two big sofas and several comfortable armchairs. She could picture this as a cheery place on a winter's evening, the room lit by lamps and with a fire roaring in the fireplace and a view of the snow-covered terrace. At this time of day, with the windows and the drapes wide open, the room was pleasant, airy, and mellowed by late afternoon light.

She peered at the prints adorning the walls, idly wondering if she had time to track down anything similar to take home. She enjoyed collecting those sorts of souvenirs. Should she go with a mountain scene or botanical prints of alpine wildflowers? Where would she hang them? The landings of the staircases, perhaps? Then there was that difficult spot in the telephone nook.

She continued through the double doors that led to the library. It was darker than the lounge room since trees lining the street behind the hotel shaded it. Bookcases covered one wall and dark wood paneling covered the other walls. There were armchairs in here too, and a big writing desk.

"There are books to borrow during your stay," Monique had said. "You are welcome to take one with you when you leave, even if you don't leave one in its place." Sophie thought it was a charming idea. She read Dorothy Sayers' *Gaudy Night* on the trip across the Pacific, finished it in New York, and devoured *Busman's Honeymoon* in London. She liked Miss Sayers' Peter Wimsey and Harriet Vane characters immensely. They reminded her of herself and Joe: intelligent people with complicated pasts who had found each other against all odds and made a life together. Their sleuthing had whetted her appetite for detective stories. She searched the shelves. Aha! An Agatha Christie. Now she could tease Joe that she could be a lady detective like Miss Marple.

She didn't want to be a detective. As much as she enjoyed letting Joe use her as a sounding board and helping him with society tidbits, she had plenty of interests and projects at home in Sydney that kept her busy. He seemed to be taking a passing interest in the summer thief, though. Perhaps he'd decided indulging her was fun. It didn't matter as long as it allowed him to work through whatever had brought on his nightmare.

Satisfied she'd found a book to read, she turned her attention to the prints on the wall in this room. Some were of soldiers wearing large, dark blue berets. As she read the captions, she learned they were *Chasseurs Alpins*, the French Alpine troops. There were other photographs of *Alpini*, the Italian Alpine troops, on a snowy mountainside hoisting cannon up with a complicated set of ropes. Vanni must have taken these photos.

Next were two pictures of men on skis, one captioned French Mountain Patrol team, Chamonix, Olympics 1924, and the other captioned Italian Mountain Patrol team. She looked closer and recognized Georges in one photo and Vanni in the other.

The last two photos were the biggest surprise. The first was of two Australian soldiers in uniform, wearing their emu-plumed slouch hats: Will and his army mate on the *Mer de Glace* glacier. The second photo was of four men with their guide and porters. The label said it was Will and his army mate, plus Edmund and his university friend on Mont Blanc, although the men all wore goggles, hats, and scarves, so she couldn't tell who was who.

Sophie glanced through a far window, spied Joe carrying a crate of wine into the hotel, and her enjoyment of the rooms evaporated. She knew the gunshot wounds to his shoulder had healed. She knew the risk of reinjury was minimal. But she had been on edge for months, terrified when she learned he'd been shot. Injury and death, constants during the war, had faded to unpleasant memories and occasional dreams until she saw Joe lying as pale and still as marble after surgery. Now there was the interrupted sleep when he dreamt, the nerve-wracking wondering whether he would have another nightmare, and worrying about how long it would take him to recover afterwards. And the most terrifying question of all: what if he didn't recover?

The urge to run outside and ask Joe what he thought he was doing hit her like a punch to the gut. She nearly ran into him as he entered the library.

"Sophie, I saw—"

"What were you thinking carrying that crate of wine?" she hissed, struggling to keep her voice down and her emotions under control.

The excitement on his face faded. "The boys were busy," he countered,

"I don't care. You know you're not supposed to be lifting anything heavy!"

"I wasn't supposed to lift anything three months ago. I'm fine now. Please, stop worrying and hovering. It doesn't help."

Hovering? They'd had a wonderful, carefree day that Joe had spoiled by doing something foolish and he had the nerve to say she was hovering? The effort to calm down before she spoke was too much.

"I know you're a grown man and you're perfectly capable of determining your limits. But I can tell this trip has been hard for you." Once the first words were out, the rest followed in a torrent, all hope of keeping her composure long gone. "You've been tossing and turning in your sleep ever since we arrived in Paris. They're different dreams than the ones you have at home."

"You mean before the memorial?" Joe took a step back. "I'm fine. It was just a dream."

There it was again, that phrase. "If you tell me 'I'm fine' one more time, I will scream. That wasn't just a dream, it was a nightmare! You were thumping on the floor and shouting at the top of your lungs when you woke up! You've never done anything like that! How can you be fine?"

Joe took another step back. "Why can't you believe there isn't anything I need to talk about?"

He was also running a hand up and down the back of his head, a sure sign he was becoming annoyed, which irked her even more. Damn it, he was acting like they hadn't been through years of war and friendship and marriage together. Years when something horrific in his work sent him into a funk that could last days, or when one of the boys did something stupid—because teenaged boys believed they were immortal—that sent her into a panic. They'd learned they needed to share the burdens that simply being alive often laid at their feet. And now Joe seemed to be tossing all of that aside, as if it was nothing.

"Why can't I believe you? Because you wouldn't talk to me afterward. You could barely look at me for hours. You bury your feelings and pretend they don't exist! You don't have to shield me or hide things from me, Joe! I'm not Annie. I'm not some shrinking violet who can't help you with whatever demons you're dealing with."

"Annie was not a shrinking violet," he shot back. "And I'm not Michael. I don't need you to save me."

This had not gone the way she meant it to. How could Joe throw aside her concern for his welfare? "I'm going to go bathe and dress for dinner." She left the library without another word.

When she slid into the tub, Sophie had already allowed herself the release of tears and was trying to figure out why things with Joe seemed to be unraveling after the heightened intimacy they had enjoyed in Paris.

She hated fighting with Joe. They had had some unexpectedly nasty arguments when they first married, back when she thought they knew each other well enough that they would share everything. She couldn't have been more wrong. On the days when a particularly brutal case weighed him down, he would become so absorbed in his thoughts it was like she wasn't even there. Then she would get irritated because he wouldn't engage with her, and he would snap back, and they would retreat to opposite corners of the house until her high emotions and his deep funk started to dissipate. Only then would they approach each other again, hesitantly, to assess the other's mood.

Sometimes they assessed too soon, or too glibly, or reacted to the other's approach too defensively, and the retreat-approach-assess cycle repeated until their equilibrium was restored.

Her marriage to Michael, who had proposed the day the armistice was signed, had followed much the same pattern. She and Michael had started out with so much hope, but it had all gone wrong over the next few years. Skin grafting techniques were still in their infancy. Infections were rampant. Michael rarely had a patient improve, not because he was a poor doctor, but because the nature of his work was so experimental.

The deaths of patients became harder and harder for him to bear. He grew miserable, burdened with guilt over what he felt could have happened compared to what had happened. Then money troubles led to staffing troubles. She had to spend all her time on administrative tasks instead of nursing. He had taken to drinking heavily. Sometimes he was an obnoxious, mean drunk, jibing at her or accusing her of doing something wrong. Other times he was morose and depressed, hinting he couldn't see a way forward.

Then there were the days that everything went well. Michael would be brilliant. Caring. Compassionate. He did so much good, and Sophie loved this about him. She loved it so much that most days it was enough. He would wrap his arm around her shoulders and draw her close. "You were wonderful today," she would say, and he would respond, "I couldn't do it without you, my love. You're my strength, my anchor." The kiss he always pressed to her forehead felt like a benediction and all the previous unpleasantness would retreat. She was useful. She was needed. She was making a difference.

But the cycle repeated again and again and again until she was dizzy with the constant swings of his moods and utterly exhausted trying to keep up with them. The thought of spending the rest of her days in this pattern was more demoralizing than she could bear.

It was corrosive too. In the final year of their marriage, spurred on by Michael's angry outbursts and spiteful words, she had begun to believe all their problems were her fault. She had been shattered by his death, but even more devastated at the possibility that it was her fault he had taken his own life.

Joe had never said anything unkind like Michael had, and she truly believed that she had recovered from the psychic wounds Michael had inflicted, but it had taken months for her and Joe to adapt to each other's moods and motivations. She finally admitted that when he went silent and moody, she watched him for signs he would behave like Michael had. Her revelation had stopped Joe in his tracks. He had no idea his silences had been affecting her so adversely. Then he admitted he hadn't had to answer to anyone at home for years and had simply kept on that path and couldn't understand why she seemed to constantly need to know what was bothering him. Hovering, he'd called it, which she hadn't liked at the time, and still didn't, but it was an apt description if she considered it from his point of view. Even though they had shared so much during the war, his reasoning was simply that the war had been a long time ago and home wasn't war.

They had hardly argued at all after they finally agreed that he would try to be more forthcoming, and she would give him time and space to recover from whatever had happened with work.

But when Joe said he wasn't Michael, and he didn't need her to save him…. He had said the most hurtful thing he could, and it cut her to the bone. Why had he reacted like that? Oh God, what if being back in France was somehow causing him to feel the same way Michael had?

No, that couldn't be it, could it? There was an inner strength in Joe that Michael hadn't had. Joe's strength led to him being chosen to command men both as a police officer and as an Army officer. Michael's lack of it caused him to suffer deep disappointments and feelings of failure.

But if she and Joe couldn't work through this, they would have a cloud hanging over their marriage for the rest of their lives. She would always wonder, and Joe would know she was wondering, and the weight of it would crush them until their relationship was in ruins.

She had lived like that with Michael. She loved Joe with all her heart, but she would not live like that again.

Their argument had opened a rift between them she'd never imagined could be possible. Why had she ever thought visiting the memorial was a good idea? Joe wasn't telling her about something terrible that happened at Villers-Bretonneux. She was sure of it now.

PART FOUR

We bow us down to a dusty shrine, or a temple in the East,
Or we stand and drink to the world-old creed, with the coffins at
the feast;
We fight it down, and we live it down, or we bear it bravely well,
But the best men die of a broken heart for the things they cannot
tell.

"The Things We Dare Not Tell" Henry Lawson

FORTY-FOUR

NOT FINE AT ALL

Joe left the library and went back out to the terrace. He stared at the fir trees across the way and fumed.

All he had wanted from this trip to France was to visit Paris with Sophie, lay the memory of his brother to rest, and see a few Roman ruins. Going back to Villers-Bret had blindsided him. He hated that damned nightmare—he hadn't had it in years—but he had brushed off the guilt of Villers-Bret so often it had become second nature to simply ignore it, and the omission had become a lie too great to tell.

But Sophie had hit his most sensitive nerve, and when she exclaimed that she wasn't Annie in the heat of their argument he had thrown her fear that she had somehow failed Michael into the mix.

It was a rotten thing to do. Yes, Sophie watched over him, sometimes hovering to the point that it was annoying, but that was to be expected from a woman who had served in a wartime hospital and had been married to a doctor who worked with severely wounded soldiers and was now dead, perhaps even by his own hand. She had barely let him out of her sight after he was shot in the raid in Sydney—she had haunted the hospital halls and would have slept in the chair by his bed until he was discharged if the doctors and nurses hadn't ordered her to go home and rest.

She did it because she loved him. It was as simple as that. Instead of recognizing that Sophie must have been worried past the point of reason when she brought up Annie, he had lashed out at the one person who didn't deserve it. He had been a damned fool. He should have explained that it was just a dream he used to have a long time ago and being back in France had revived some unpleasant memories.

During dinner, he was still berating himself, but he hid it, affecting an amused expression when Sophie told everyone she'd seen photographs in the library of people who looked a lot like Georges and Vanni, only younger.

He was too troubled to be amused when Vanni and Georges pretended to be confused about how long they'd known each other, but the absurdity of Edmund and Will playing along, shaking their heads and declaring they had no idea who these men were and why were they sitting at the same table, prompted a chuckle despite his mood.

Sophie tilted her head and held out her hand to him, her usual gesture when she wanted to be friends again after an argument. When he didn't react immediately the corners of her mouth turned down; she would interpret his lack of response as continuing the fight—which he didn't want to do—he just needed her to drop the subject of his nightmare.

He responded with a small smile and twined his fingers with hers before she could withdraw them.

After dessert, he turned to Edmund, who was squinting at the day's newspaper. "What's the latest?"

Edmund folded the paper and tossed it on the table in disgust. "Just checking whether Hitler or Mussolini has done anything else that's horrifying." He poured himself a glass of water from the carafe. "I'm afraid it's no longer whether, but when they'll declare war on someone. Poland probably, and then Britain and France will have to declare war."

Vanni and Georges exchanged an unhappy glance.

"What are you two thinking?" Will asked.

"Nothing good," Georges replied. "You know the *Col de la Seigne*?"

"Yeah, it's a pass between France and Italy," Will answered. "It's about twenty miles south of here, isn't it?"

Georges nodded. "Italy is allied with Germany now. There will be nothing except the mountains and the *Chasseurs Alpins* to stop them trying to occupy this valley." Georges stroked his mustache while he gazed at nothing for a few moments. Then his jaw fell slack, and he turned to Sophie. "Madame, do you have the silver flower you found yesterday?"

Sophie pulled it from her pocket and passed it to him.

Georges handed it to Vanni, who dropped the flower on the table as if it had burned his fingers.

"What is it?" she asked, bewildered. "Have you seen it before? Do you know who it belongs to? I'd be happy to return it to the rightful owner."

"This flower, signora," Vanni said, "is not for a lady. It is an edelweiss badge, worn by the *Alpenkorps* in the war."

Joe remembered enough German to guess what the word meant, but he had to be sure. "What is *Alpenkorps*?"

"German mountain troops." Vanni spat out the words. "I fought them in the Dolomites. I know this edelweiss too well."

Sophie's spirits had been sinking steadily while Vanni spoke. "But the war ended twenty years ago," she protested. "What on earth was a German army insignia doing in a waterfall in Chamonix? How did it get there?"

Joe leaned forward, staring at nothing, bouncing his fingertips together. She had seen him like this dozens of times, usually when he was working through all the details of a case. "What if the thieves are Germans posing as tourists, but they're reconnoitering the area? What if the thefts are a diversion for why they're really here? Not all the thefts, of course. There will always be petty criminal activity when large groups of people aren't paying as much attention to their belongings as they should be."

"But why go to all that trouble?" Will asked. "I'd just pretend to be a hiker or a mountaineer."

"Fair point," Joe said. "How would they travel here? What are the routes from Germany?"

Will leaned back in his chair and considered the question. "By train or car from Geneva. There are so many trails in these mountains, I reckon you could hike in from Italy or Switzerland at many points."

"What about language?" Joe was in full investigative mode, asking questions, gathering information. She should have been happy he was distracted from the first war, but her stomach was in knots at the thought of a second one. "Wouldn't their lack of French or English give them away?"

"Plenty of German students learn English in school," Edmund said. "If it was me, I'd say I was Swiss, from one of the German-speaking cantons. That would explain German-accented English like Bauer's or even lapsing into German."

Joe frowned. Sophie could almost see the wheels turning as he sifted through the possibilities.

"Since Germany is allied with Italy," Edmund continued, "the Alps would definitely be in their line of sight."

Vanni rubbed his temples and let loose a rumble of muttered Italian. He switched to English when he saw the puzzled looks on his friends' faces. "The Nazis will want to poke that nasty swastika into the top of *Monte Bianco*. We cannot let them do that. I will never fight for Mussolini and the *Fascisti*."

What had Bauer said about the edelweiss as a promise of dedication? The contrast between the flower as a symbol of war and as a symbol of love was too much to process. She'd used so much energy in the last few days trying to get Joe past the last war, and now it seemed certain there would be another one. The implications were too terrifying to contemplate. Even though Joe had resigned his commission, he could be called up. He would go, of course he would, and so would their sons, and there would be nothing she could do to keep them safe.

Sophie was so immersed in her misery that she didn't notice Erich Bauer return to the terrace or hear him mention to no one in particular that it was a very nice evening for an after-dinner stroll.

As soon as he and Sophie were back in their room, Joe gathered his courage, but Sophie spoke first.

"I'm sorry for what I said about Annie. I was so angry that I wanted to shout at you. I wanted to lash out. Now that I've thought about it, it scares me. I haven't felt that way since Michael, I suppose."

"I'm sorry for what I said about Michael. I had no right to say it. What happened to him was not your fault."

She pulled away and looked up at him. "Joe, you do know you can talk with me about anything that's bothering you, don't you?"

That must be it. She was afraid he would end up like Michael. No wonder she was worried sick after that nightmare. He had to convince her he was all right.

"I'm not Michael," he reminded her, gently this time. "It was only a dream. I haven't had it in years. Going back to Villers-Bret brought back some unpleasant memories. I'm not going to do myself in, or—"

"Joe let's leave in the morning. We could be back in England in two days and sail home from Southampton instead of Marseille."

"Sophie, I'm fi–" Her brow shot up, stopping him mid-word. He tried a different tack. "I thought you wanted to be here."

"I did, but it isn't worth you being unhappy and us arguing."

He smoothed a wisp of hair from her cheek. "We have a glacier to see tomorrow and whatever else Will and Edmund dream up for us after that. And I wanted to see Roman ruins, remember?"

He drew her close with an arm around her shoulders. She snuggled into his side and wrapped her arms around his waist.

"All these hints of another war terrify me," she admitted. "Between the Germans and the Italians threatening France here in Europe, and Japan and Germany are allies now, if there's another war, it could spread to our part of the world."

"We'll deal with it if we have to. Let's not go looking for trouble." They had enough to deal with already, no sense in adding to it. He kissed the top of Sophie's head. "It was nice of you to make all of us laugh so much earlier."

She sighed against his shoulder. "I didn't do it to be nice. I did it because I was still upset with you, and I was trying to hide it."

"Well, you're a wonderful actress," he said. "Let's get in bed. We have a big day ahead of us."

She fell asleep while he rubbed gentle circles on her back.

Rubbing Sophie's back had lulled her to sleep, but Joe was wide awake. Because no matter how often he said it, he was not fine. At all.

Everything to do with returning to Villers-Bret had been a struggle.

When he returned to Melbourne and the police force after the war, he devoted himself to finding ways to prevent crime and minimize conflict.

It hadn't been easy. Many police officers were apt to bash heads first and ask questions later. He was often tempted to fall into that habit, especially when faced with particularly vicious criminals or senseless crimes. Drinking half the night away became his preferred method of coping when demons escaped his rigid self-control. Then his mother, who often kept Sam overnight, gave him an ultimatum: Stop drowning your sorrows or face losing Sam. Joe turned to physical activity to force everything out of his mind: running along the banks of the Yarra River until his leg muscles felt like jelly, or going so many rounds with the punching bag in the police gym that his hands and arms twitched for hours afterward. On those days, he didn't require whiskey to fall asleep.

In 1922, after he and Sam left Melbourne for Sydney, Joe took up rowing with his colleagues on Sunday mornings, both for the physical outlet and to become part of the larger police community. Sam, on the cusp of what promised to be an unruly adolescence, had needed an outlet, too. They spent Sunday afternoons exploring the bays and beaches that outlined their new city, chasing breakers at Bronte and Bondi and swimming races in the calm waters of Parsley Bay. They found a bedraggled puppy someone had tried to drown, named him Rudy, and Joe healed a little more when Rudy came to him after Sam had gone to bed each night.

Instead of drinking when silence descended on their little bungalow, Joe read anything he could get his hands on—the classics, histories, natural sciences, biographies, even poetry and plays.

Between work, physical activity, and a voracious literary appetite, he kept his memories of war buried so deeply they rarely saw the light of day. When they bubbled up, he acknowledged their existence, renewed his vow to not be the man who had created those memories, and pushed them down again. By the time Sophie came back into his life, his waking thoughts were no longer of mud and misery but of what the day might hold in store: work, a bright sky, getting Sam ready for school.

Now his coping techniques, carefully constructed over two decades, were collapsing faster than he could shore them up.

Then there was this place. Will had said Chamonix was the best place to escape the pressures of the present, and he had taken it on faith that the same would apply to him. He couldn't have been more wrong.

Joe had never been in deep mountains like these before, and his initial awe of them was long gone. The mountains were so steep that during the day he felt horribly claustrophobic, like the sheer weight of all the granite surrounding them was closing in on him. At night, the black void between the valley floor and the sky turned into a terrifying abyss. Concentrating on the lights of the town or craning his neck to look at the stars didn't ease the feeling he was entombed and suffocating in a miles-deep trench.

No, he most definitely was not fine. But he had agreed to this trip, all of it, and he would stick with it. In the morning, he would tell Sophie about seeing the boy in the trees across from the hotel terrace. He could use her interests in the blond boy and the summer thief to keep himself on an even keel until it was time to leave this place.

FORTY-FIVE

SEA OF ICE

JULY 26, 1939, CHAMONIX

Last night I walked through the town and passed several hotels. It was below the terrace of one of them that I recognized the accents —English but not English—of the man and woman whose voices I'd heard on the trail. They were with others, friends from the sound of it, everyone speaking English tinged with other accents. Then someone said the word edelweiss.

I crept as close as I dared and listened.

Late the next morning Sophie was the first of their group to board the train at the Montenvers station that served the *Mer de Glace* glacier, followed by Joe and Georges.

Next came Will and Edmund, both wearing rucksacks and carrying hiking poles. A few other passengers were already in the car, among them several teenage boys. Nick and Chris exchanged greetings with the boys and moved away from the adults to sit with their friends.

A blond boy, who no one seemed to know, glanced up while

the other boys were greeting each other. Then he turned his attention to something outside the car.

Joe leaned close to Sophie and whispered so only she could hear. "See that blond boy? Yesterday, I saw him moving through the trees across from the hotel. That's what I came to tell you in the library before we argued."

"He could have been the person I saw on the rocks above me when I found the edelweiss."

"I couldn't be sure, but I thought he was watching the terrace."

"Why would he do that?" she asked, puzzled by this new bit of information.

"I don't know. It was just a feeling I had that he was waiting for someone to appear."

"Let's keep an eye on him. Maybe he was casing the hotel. Maybe he's the summer thief."

"I'll do it. Switch seats with me."

Erich Bauer boarded at the last moment, but other than nodding hello to the men and executing his curious little half-bow to her, he said nothing, seating himself on a bench apart from everyone.

Within a minute, the master of the tiny station took out his pocket watch, nodded to the conductor, and blew his whistle. The train came to life seconds later and began its slow ascent up to the glacier. The tracks were steep and hugged the side of the mountain.

"It's very noisy for such a small train," Sophie said.

"This is a cog train," Georges explained over the clacking of the wheels on the track. "We rise at a very steep angle. The cogs help the train climb up the tracks and prevent it from sliding down."

Having relinquished watching the blond boy to Joe's scrutiny,

Sophie was free to concentrate on the scenery and to page through a guidebook borrowed from the hotel library. "This is interesting. In the 1740s, two Englishmen discovered Chamonix and named the glacier the *Mer de Glace*." She raised a brow at Georges. "Georges, you let the English discover your town and name your glacier?" she teased.

Georges shrugged. "*Les Anglais*. The English need to name everything as if no one had ever seen it before. We called it the *Glacier des Bois* because it descended to a place called *Les Bois*."

"And listen to this," she continued, for anyone who was listening, "Alexander Dumas and Chateaubriand visited in 1801 and described it as a polar sea. *Mer de Glace* means Sea of Ice, does it not, Georges?"

Georges grinned at her, happy to continue her game. "That is correct, madame. It only took the French sixty years to agree with the English."

Edmund, sitting in the row ahead, twisted around. "Loads of famous people visited the alps in the previous century and wrote about them. Samuel Coleridge, William Wordsworth, even Percy and Mary Shelley. Mary came up with the idea for Frankenstein during an alpine thunderstorm. Turner drew a picture of the glacier back in the early 1800s. I think it's at the British Museum in London. It's titled with the old name of the river and the town."

"Yes, the Arve river was called the Arveron back then," Georges said. "And Chamonix was spelled differently too. We French did that on our own.

The train leveled out and came to a stop. "We are here," Georges announced. The town and the length of the valley were visible through ferns, wildflowers, and tall conifers.

Will and Edmund pulled their rucksacks on and gathered their belongings. Both men wore sturdy hiking boots with thick woolen socks, floppy brimmed hats, and goggle-like sunglasses.

"You all look ready for a serious expedition," she quipped.

"Three trails start here," Will explained. "We're going to hike the highest one up to a place called Signal Forbes. It's a tough climb that will take us several hours. Georges will take you and Joe down to the glacier and then on a lower trail to hike parallel to the valley. We'll meet you back at the hotel later."

"Georges, there's no need for you to miss hiking with them," she protested. "Joe and I can find plenty to do. We can even get back to Chamonix by ourselves."

"Madame, it is not a problem," Georges said. "I hike the high trail when they are not here. If I stay with you and monsieur, I can show off my knowledge of the glacier and the mountains and lead you on a very nice hike. Come see the glacier."

"It looks like a huge white river!" she exclaimed when they reached the railing overlooking the glacier. Sharp granite peaks rose on either side of the glacier. The same range of peaks filled the horizon and beyond, becoming blue in the near distance and blurring and becoming lighter blue in the far distance.

"We call those peaks *Les Drus*," Georges said, pointing as he spoke. "That one is the *Aiguille d'Argentière*, and then the *Dent du Géant*, and that one, the highest one, is the *Aiguille Verte*."

"What's on the other side?" Joe asked. "Italy or Switzerland?"

"Italy," Georges said.

Sophie looked around. Joe, Georges, and she were the only members of their group who were still in sight. "Where did the boys go? And Mr. Bauer?"

"Nick and Chris left as soon as we got here," Georges said. "They are on the same trail as the men. As for Mr. Bauer, I have not seen him since we arrived."

"What about the blond boy?"

"I think he headed toward the middle trail as soon as he got off the train," Joe said. He didn't seem overly concerned, so she turned her attention back to the immense glacier below them.

As they picked their way over rocks and to the edge of the packed snow, Georges explained how glaciers form and how they moved, albeit exceedingly slowly, the tremendous weight of the densely packed ice and snow causing friction and melting the bottommost layer of the ice so that it scoured everything in its path as it moved over the rock. He pointed out fissures and crevasses that glowed blue in the ice and explained that the glacier was one source of the River Arve that ran through the valley. "The towns in the valley are having discussions about excavating a cave in the ice so people can go inside the glacier."

Joe saw Sophie's eyes sparkle at the prospect. "I want to do that!"

Despite his newly acquired aversion to being surrounded by miles-high mountains, he couldn't help smiling at her excitement. "If that isn't a reason to come back someday, I don't know what is," he replied.

They turned from the glacier and Georges led them to a marker with arrows pointing the way to three trails. "There are three trails—expert, advanced, and beginner. We will take the lowest of the three. This is new," the Frenchman said, running his finger over a nine-petalled flower carved into the wood by the middle arrow. "I don't remember seeing this before."

Sophie peered around Georges' shoulder. "The same carving was on the marker for the trail we hiked yesterday. It looks like the *Alpenkorps* insignia I found."

Georges frowned as he surveyed the ground around them. "I hope this carving is only someone marking good trails for wild-flowers."

He led them along a trail that was as cool, shaded, and quiet as the one they hiked on their first day, only much higher.

When they stopped to take in the view and have a sip of water,

Joe got the field glasses out of the case Sophie was carrying. There was a break in the trees, with one tree laying on the ground. He clambered around it to get a better look up.

Joe motioned for Sophie and Georges to come over to him. "Up there." He handed the glasses to Georges. "It's the young man from the train. The one sitting by himself. Yesterday evening I saw him through the trees across from the terrace, and Sophie saw him above her when she found the edelweiss."

Georges' response to this information was to put his finger to his lips to signal they should be quiet. When he and Sophie both nodded their understanding, the Frenchman produced a map from one of his many pockets and unfolded it.

"We are here." Georges traced a line on the map. "The boy is on the trail between us and the highest trail Will and the others are on. I know this mountain. Do you want to go off the trail and see what we see?"

Joe considered the possibilities. He had no reason to assume the three of them were in any danger—he had assessed the boy's appearance while they were on the train and had concluded the boy, slight, mid-height, wasn't a physical threat. Sophie was nodding at him. He winked at her and nodded to Georges. They set off with Georges leading the way.

Only the occasional snap of a twig on the trail above them indicated the boy's presence.

When they heard nothing, not even birdsong, for several more minutes, it seemed their quarry had vanished. Joe jerked his head in the direction they had come from, wordlessly asking if they were ready to return to the glacier.

Both Georges and Sophie were signaling their agreement when something came thudding down the steep slope above them. It hit a tree trunk and landed at their feet.

Sophie jumped.

Georges called, "*Allo? Ça va?* Are you all right?"

Erich Bauer's reedy voice sounded through the trees high above them. "My rucksack fell. Do you see it?"

Bauer was up there too? Sophie and Georges looked just as surprised as Joe felt. "Mr. Bauer!" he called. "The slope is too steep for me to climb up to you. Meet us at the train station and we will return it to you there."

"Yes, yes, I will do that," Bauer replied, moving along the trail, noisily this time. "Thank you."

Joe's instinct told him something wasn't right. First, Sophie finding the edelweiss insignia and the boy above her, then the boy watching the hotel terrace, the edelweiss carvings, and now discovering Bauer had been on the same trail as the blond boy and the two of them creeping so silently. He motioned for Sophie and Georges to come close and shield him while he opened Bauer's rucksack, all the while asking what kinds of ferns grew along the trail.

Georges' mouth dropped open, but Sophie caught on as he hoped she would. Without missing a beat, she asked Georges a question about alpine flora.

Rifling through the contents, Joe found an apple, a half-eaten sandwich wrapped in paper, a pair of socks, and a notebook. He flipped through the pages. Journal entries in German. His fingers hit something hard and metallic at the bottom of the rucksack. He extracted it warily.

All three of them gasped. He was holding a trench knife, a weapon used during the war for killing in close quarters with a single thrust. The knives were silent, deadly, and so well suited to their purpose that every country adopted the idea.

Seeing a trench knife in a peaceful forest glade in the French Alps brought a chill to Joe's blood. He examined it quickly Someone had kept it clean and sharp.

"Not a word to Monique, please," Georges murmured. "I do not want her to worry. The edelweiss plus this…."

Without hesitating, Joe stashed the knife in his own rucksack. "Sophie and I will figure out what to do with it," he assured Georges.

FORTY-SIX

PIECES OF THE PUZZLE

Back at the train station, Sophie returned Bauer's rucksack to him. "One of the buckles was undone, and everything went flying as it tumbled down," she fibbed. "I hope we found it all."

He pushed his glasses up his nose and peered at her, but she couldn't tell if he believed her or not. "Thank you, madame. I was not looking where I was walking, and I tripped over a root or a rock."

"You're lucky you didn't fall all the way down to our trail! You could have been badly injured. Are you sure you're all right?"

"It is nothing," he assured her, but he winced and limped when he boarded the train for the return trip to Chamonix.

She stayed close to Bauer on the ride back, suggesting he put his foot up on the seat facing him, and trying to come up with a way of asking if he had seen the blond boy.

"You'll need to rest your ankle for a day or two," she said. "We thought we saw someone on the same trail as you. It's too bad they didn't help you get back to the station."

"There was no one else on the trail, madame."

She shot an incredulous glance at Joe. His barely perceptible flick of an eyebrow confirmed he'd heard Bauer's lie, too.

They disembarked from the cog train and walked past the main Chamonix train station. Sophie caught sight of the town's war memorial, with its life-sized bronze *poilu*, a French infantryman from the Great War, standing atop a tall base of granite.

"How did we miss seeing this earlier?" Sophie took several steps toward the memorial before she remembered her plan to keep things in the present. She and Joe should stay with Bauer, too, after the knife incident. She turned back to the old man. "Oh! I'm so sorry. We need to help you get back to the hotel and rest that ankle."

"You and monsieur look at the statue, madame," Georges said. "I can help Monsieur Bauer to the hotel. Monique and I will take care of him. Do you know how to get back?"

"We can manage, Georges, thanks," Joe said. He turned to Sophie. "I'd like to see it."

She welcomed his agreement. She was practically bursting to speak about the knife with hm. What was Bauer going to do when he discovered it was missing? Would he suspect they'd taken it or was her excuse good enough? What were they going to do with the thing?

A sense of solemnity replaced her excitement as they walked the few steps to stand in front of the memorial to the sons of Chamonix who fell in the war. *Chamonix a ses enfants morts pour la France 1914–1918* was carved in the granite above a bronze plaque of names. She recognized several surnames from shops and hotels in the town.

"So many for such a small town," Joe murmured. "And so many are from the same families."

"I hope they never have to use the other three sides." She

picked off the most faded flowers from the wreaths the townsfolk had placed at the base of the memorial on Bastille Day.

"Come with me," she said, tugging him to the shops on the corner. They returned with an enormous bunch of flowers tied with blue, red, and white ribbons. She looked up to the *poilu*, whispered, "*Merci pour votre service,*" and placed the flowers at the base of the memorial.

She moved back to stand beside Joe. He reached for her hand, and they stood in silence for several minutes, fingers entwined.

"Sophie?"

"Hmm?"

"Could we have an early dinner somewhere else tonight?"

"Do you mean a restaurant instead of the hotel?

"Yes. Just the two of us."

"Of course, we can, darling. Do you have somewhere in mind? Or shall we wander until we find someplace that looks appealing?"

≈

"Let's wander," Joe said.

Sophie tucked her hand around his arm and gave his bicep a gentle squeeze. "Do you want me all to yourself this evening, is that it?"

The longer he thought about it, the more the mix of the knife, edelweiss insignia, Bauer, and the blond boy bothered him. "I want to run a few thoughts by you and get your opinion."

"Good. I have a few ideas of my own. Where shall we talk?"

"It can wait until we've found a restaurant."

They reached the first intersection from the *poilu* memorial and paused at the flower box-laden bridge over the river. The sky had changed dramatically since they left the glacier a couple of hours earlier. Clouds obscured the top of Mont Blanc and most of the mountains on the eastern side of the valley. A stiff breeze pushed storm clouds from east to west, which parted now and then to uncover a peak. At one point, only the summit of Mont Blanc was visible, brilliant white contrasting against the deepening grey of the clouds. To the west, sunlight streamed through a mountain pass, casting an eerie yellow glow below the grey cloud cover.

He eyed the sky. "Georges said there can be evening thunderstorms during the summer. It looks like we'll be caught in one soon."

Sophie faced the long street lined with shops, cafés, and restaurants. "There are lots of places where we can take refuge. Why don't we turn here and follow the river? If we don't find something appealing on this side, we can try the other side."

"And if we find nothing on either side, we'll raid the larder at the hotel. I can make eggs and toast." He meant it as a joke, and he bit back the grin that began as Sophie's eyes widened in response.

"Hilarious. Just for that I'll order *escargot* and make you sample them." The wicked little smile that signaled he was in for some serious teasing tugged at her lips. "Or I'll order *rognons*."

The one time he ordered *rognons* in Paris, he hadn't known they were kidneys. Their housekeeper's steak and kidney pie was delicious, but a plate of kidneys without luscious chunks of steak and flaky pastry was another thing entirely. He had vowed never to make that mistake again.

"I'm sure we'll be able to find someplace to eat dinner," he countered. "Isn't there a fish place somewhere on this street?"

She grinned at him and took his arm again. "I think you're right."

They found the fish restaurant, cozy, with tiny, candlelit tables for two, at the end of the street. Sophie ordered a big bowl of mussels to share and a bottle of Rousette that the waiter recommended. She chuckled when she recognized the wine was from the winery of the arguing brothers.

"I have to know." She picked up the bottle and read the back of label. "No, it doesn't say Chardonnay grapes were used to make this wine."

He relaxed a little. Sophie seemed content to wait a while before they discussed finding the trench knife. "Well, one brother is happy, at least. They make excellent wine, despite the arguing."

The waiter removed the mussels bowl after they soaked up all the broth in the bottom with crusty bread and then served trout *Meunière* for Joe and langoustines on a bed of homemade pasta for Sophie.

Sophie curled her ankles around his under the table as she leaned forward to offer him a bite, and he relaxed a little more. The waiter had to clear his throat several times to get their attention when it came time to remove their empty plates and tell them what was on offer for dessert.

She waited until the waiter served her chocolate mousse and his lemon tart and left them to themselves again. "This was a lovely idea you had," she began, "dinner, with just the two of us. It's been very romantic." She paused a moment before continuing. "But you wanted to talk about something."

He took a bite of his dessert, ordering his thoughts as he chewed and swallowed. "I feel uneasy, like something is about to happen or has already happened and we don't know it yet."

"You've always said you have to trust your instincts."

"I'm not sure what it is. Maybe it's the mountains. I can't see the far horizons. I feel claustrophobic here." He shook his head and waited, wondering if she would pounce on his admission.

But no. She was listening intently, no sign of judgment on her face. Before he was wounded in the raid, her willingness to listen without rushing to solve a problem for him was one of her traits he appreciated most. During his recovery, they had fallen into a less equal relationship, with him becoming more and more frustrated by her worrying and the limits the injury placed on him. Perhaps this conversation could help them regain their balance.

"I had an odd feeling about Bauer before the business with the knife," he continued. "He kept looking at the blond boy on the ride to the glacier."

"So blond his hair was almost white," Sophie said. "Pale blue eyes. He's seventeen or eighteen. I wanted to memorize his face so I can recognize him again if I need to."

"You're very observant. He stared out the window the entire trip up the mountain."

"Is Bauer a homosexual, perhaps?"

"I don't think so." He stared off in the distance, remembering what he'd seen. "It was more like he recognized him from somewhere. The boy ignored everyone. That's hard to do when someone keeps looking at you."

Sophie glanced around the restaurant. There wasn't anyone sitting close to them, but she lowered her voice anyway. "And then there's the trench knife. I thought the handle looked German. The Americans had things to slide over their knuckles and the French had…. I can't remember. A curl or curve at the end of the handle?"

"How do you know so much about weapons?" he asked, astonished.

"Joe. Please," she scoffed. "I had to undress hundreds of soldiers. They had weapons hidden everywhere. I was always grateful to find knives instead of grenades."

He had seen enough of them himself to be sure, including one he would never forget. "I'm certain it's German." He fell silent for a moment. "The real question is why are we finding German items from the war? First the insignia for German mountain troops and now the knife. And why did Bauer lie about no one else being on the trail with him?"

Sophie was quiet for a few moments while she pondered Joe's questions. "There's something Edmund mentioned that's been bothering me," she said. "I don't know what Swiss regional accents sound like, and this might be far-fetched, but what if Bauer is German and not Swiss? Would that explain anything?"

"It could. I think we should let the police deal with the knife and the insignia. The items are unusual enough that someone should be missing them. Shall we stop at the police station on the way back to the hotel?"

Sophie nodded, and he leaned back in his chair and gazed at her. She had reacted just the way he'd hoped she would, helping him work through the puzzle, filling in blanks, and adding pieces he didn't know were missing.

Seeing their discussion was at a pause, the waiter hurried over and told them the storm was worsening. The three of them peered out the front windows of the restaurant. The clouds had dropped so low that the top half of the mountains were no longer visible.

"I suggest we skip the coffee," Joe said, and when Sophie agreed, he asked for their bill. "The police will have to wait. Let's make a run for it as soon as we pay."

The first crack of lightning lit the valley seconds after the first rumble of thunder. The temperature dropped and fat raindrops became sheets of rain. Even with an umbrella borrowed from the restaurant, they were drenched long before they arrived at the hotel.

FORTY-SEVEN

ALPINE THUNDERSTORM

Monique took one look at them, shivering and dripping on the tiles of her reception floor, and took charge. "Come with me, please."

She led them into a large laundry room at the back of the hotel and traded each of them a towel for a jacket. "I will hang these in here. If you go to your room and get out of those wet clothes, I will be up in five minutes to collect them."

"Oh Monique, that's not necessary," Sophie protested. "One of us can bring our things down and hang them in here."

"As you wish, madame."

Monique shook her head as the thunder rumbled and lightning illuminated the street behind the hotel. "Will and Edmund have already gone to bed. The hiking today wore them out. I hope they can sleep through this."

They turned to leave the laundry room, but Monique stopped them. "Shoes too," she called, "give them to me as well. I will stuff them with newspapers so they will dry faster."

Feeling very much like a chick fussed over by a mother hen, Joe slipped out of his shoes and handed them to Monique.

"Is your rucksack wet, monsieur?"

"It is, but I'd prefer to keep it." He didn't intend to let it out of his sight. Monique raised an eyebrow and handed him another towel. "I won't set it on the furniture," he said. "I'll keep it in the bathroom."

They padded to their room in stocking feet and peeled off their wet clothes as soon as the door closed. Sophie pulled on her dressing gown and tucked her feet into her slippers.

"I'll take our clothes downstairs. I'm sure Monique won't mind if I make us something hot to drink, too. Do you want tea or cocoa?"

Joe had already carried his rucksack into the bathroom. "Whatever you want is fine with me," he called, unfastening the buckles and pulling out the contents.

Sophie lit the stove to start the kettle and rummaged through the cupboards for a teapot and two cups. She spooned loose tea from the canister into the pot and looked around the big hotel kitchen while she waited for the water to boil.

Rain streaming against the windows obscured the view outside, until intense lightning strikes illuminated the street. Low, swirling grey clouds veiled the mountains behind the hotel. Rumbling thunder echoed through the valley, rattling the windows and the neat stacks of crockery and cutlery laid out for breakfast.

The cycle of lightning and thunder came faster and faster, so bright that she had to blink away afterimages and so loud that she had to press her ears to relieve the pressure on her eardrums. They had seen tremendous storms as they crossed North America, the endless plains lit by lightning to the far horizons. They experienced tremendous summer storms at home too, thick, dark clouds roiling across the open water, enveloping Sydney in pounding rain.

At home, though, and on the plains, the sound dissipated over flat landscapes. Here in Chamonix, the narrow, deep valley trapped the thunder, where it reverberated against miles of solid granite. She couldn't recall ever experiencing a storm as loud as this one. She hoped the electricity didn't go out—the thought of carrying a fully laden tea tray up five flights of stairs in the dark was daunting.

The storm lulled for a few moments. Rain splashed on the pavement and gurgled through the downspouts, but other sounds caught her attention. She closed her eyes and concentrated.

Voices. She was hearing voices. Male, but she couldn't make out any words, only the tone. It sounded like an argument, but the inflections didn't sound French, and the cadence didn't sound English. *"Ich habe es nicht!"* sounded German, and angry German at that.

She craned her neck to see to the corner of the hotel. The streetlamps were far enough apart to create pools of light on the pavement with larger swaths of darkness in between the light. Two men stood in the dark corner, pressed against the building to stay out of the rain.

She drew away from the window, so if they looked in, they wouldn't see her. There was no way she could open the window to hear better without alerting the men outside to her presence, so she squatted down and shuffled back to crouch beneath the window.

The last thing she heard before the kettle whistled was *"das verdammte Messer nicht!"* and she had the oddest feeling that the raised voice was Erich Bauer's, only without the usual tremulousness of the old man's voice.

The voices stopped, and Sophie scuttled away from the window so if anyone looked into the kitchen from outside it would appear that she was only now coming in to turn off the stove and make tea.

She filled the teapot and piled spoons, sugar, and a small pitcher of milk onto a tray as quickly as possible. Rushing to the lift, she pushed the button with her elbow. She had to tell Joe about this.

"Hurry, hurry, hurry." She pushed the button again, willing the lift to move back down to the ground floor, despite knowing lifts cannot be hurried.

While she waited, the front doors of the hotel opened, and a rain-soaked Erich Bauer stepped into the reception area.

Bauer stared at her. She was certain he was just as startled to see her as she was to see him. A chilly wind rushing through the open doors swept over her.

The lift arrived, and she struggled to look casual and competent as she balanced the tray on her hip. "Good evening, Mr. Bauer," she called, trying to sound like her usual cheerful self. She pushed the wrought iron sliding door closed and pressed the button as quickly as she could. "We were soaked too when we came in! Go past the reception desk and hang your wet clothes in the laundry room with ours. That's what Monique told us to do."

The bedside lamps in their room were off, but light shone beneath the bathroom door. Sophie rapped lightly. "Joe?" He didn't answer, so she pushed the door open. The bathroom was empty. Joe's open rucksack lay on the edge of the sink.

"Joe? Where are you?" she called, trying to tamp down the panic rising in her chest.

A bolt of lightning illuminated the room, and a gust of wind blew a curtain back. Joe stood at the threshold of the far balcony door.

She rushed over to him, ready to ask what on earth was he doing standing in the cold in just his pajama bottoms, but he was staring out the window, trembling but otherwise so still it frightened her.

"Joe?" she whispered, not wanting to startle him. Another bolt of lightning cracked through the clouds hiding the mountains just opposite their windows. The sky glowed. The largest roll of thunder yet reverberated through the valley. Joe gasped and grabbed her. He twisted his body over her and shouted. "Get down!"

She struggled to get free, but comprehension dawned when another crack of lightning and roll of thunder sounded and Joe bent further, holding her tighter, pushing her to the floor. She had never seen Joe have a flashback, but dozens of men experienced them when she worked at the hospital. Whatever Joe was imagining, they weren't in Chamonix, and this wasn't just a terrible thunderstorm. She stopped resisting and let him protect her.

She stared at the rug and wondered whether she should insist they leave France as soon as possible—poor man, first that nightmare and now this—until there were only sporadic rumbles and flashes as the storm moved off to the west.

"Darling, it's over, it's finished," she murmured again and again, until his hold loosened, and he let her up.

She closed the windows and turned to face him. His heart was pounding under the hand she pressed to his chest.

"It's over, darling," she repeated as she led him to sit on the side of the bed and turned on his bedside lamp. Then she poured a cup of tea, added sugar, and stirred. Hot, sweet tea was a time-honored remedy for shock. "Drink this. I know you don't like your tea sweet, but this will help, I promise."

She stood by his side while he drank. He still hadn't said a word, but he did as she asked when she gestured for him to drink all of it.

When he finished, she took the cup from him and plumped the

pillows on his side of the bed. "Scoot back and get under the covers."

She got into bed next to him, positioning herself so she could put an arm around his shoulders and hold him close.

"We're safe, darling," she whispered and ran her fingers through his hair, repeating the words and motions until her familiar scent and voice worked themselves into his consciousness and he believed he was in the present and not somewhere in the past.

She knew he was back when he gasped, "Sophie?" and sat up so he could see her face.

She gave his hair a final smooth. "I'm here, darling. How are you feeling?"

He shook his head. "One minute I was looking out the window, watching the storm, and the next minute.... I don't remember." He fell silent, looking baffled.

"The next minute, you were somewhere else. It's perfectly understandable," she insisted. "It was a terrific storm, but it's over now, thank heavens."

"Hmm," was all he said, and his body relaxed, his regular breaths puffing against her skin. She lay awake for a long while, trying to guess what Joe experienced during his flashback. Eventually, her eyelids grew heavy, and her last thought before she fell asleep was that she hadn't told Joe about the conversation she'd overheard while she was in the kitchen making their tea. There was something else, the merest wisp of an idea, but the more she tried to concentrate on it, the more elusive it became. She gave up trying and slept, her head pillowed on her husband's shoulder and her hand over his heart.

FORTY-EIGHT

THE INVESTIGATION BEGINS

A crazy old man on today's trail startled me while I rested for a moment. I ran to hide from him, but I forgot my rucksack on the ground. As soon as the old man was gone, I realized my rucksack was gone too. My knee was still bothering me, but I ran down the trail back into town and waited by the train station for him to arrive back from the glacier. I slipped into a shadowy doorway and watched the old man and the French man make their way down the street.

I was waiting and dozing, huddled against the rain, when the old man came back alone. He had my rucksack! I grabbed his collar and dragged him to a dark corner. I didn't bother asking him who he was or why he had been following me. I felt for my knife in the rucksack, but it was not there. I grabbed him again and demanded to know where my knife was.

I hadn't spoken to anyone in days. It felt so strange to speak again.

He shouted he didn't have my knife, so I pushed him away and ran off to think.

After the rain stopped, the forest was dark, and I could not get to my campsite and my cache of provisions. At least I got my ruck-

sack back from the old man, so I have my map and my notebook.
Those English-not-English people have my edelweiss. They must
have my knife also.

It was still dark outside when the light from Joe's bedside lamp woke her. She grunted and shielded her eyes from the light. "What time is it?"

The bedcovers pulled tight when he twisted to reach for his watch on the nightstand. "It's just past two."

"Why are you awake?" she groaned. "Were you dreaming?"

"No, I've been thinking. While you were downstairs, I examined the knife more carefully. It's German, as we thought, not American or French or British. I suppose that was part of what brought on the.... I suppose it was a flashback I had. I don't remember any of it."

Sophie blinked several times to focus before she opened her eyes fully. If Joe was going to talk about what had happened, she would give him her full attention, regardless of the ungodly hour.

"So, holding a trench knife again plus the thunderstorm...and you said earlier the mountains were making you claustrophobic. Can you tell me where you were?"

"I don't know. Nowhere in particular. We have thunderstorms at home. We've had them on this journey. They haven't bothered me in years. But after that first rumble of thunder, I couldn't see anything across the way except a black wall and low clouds that looked like smoke. I thought I was at the bottom of a trench. The thunder sounded like the big guns firing over and over, like we were being bombarded."

"You shouted get down and then you wrapped yourself around me and pushed me to the floor."

He shrugged and walked over to the table and poured a glass

of water. "I don't remember doing that, but it sounds about right. You train and drill to keep your men safe. You push down your worries about what might happen and deal with what's in front of you."

She reached out to touch him. That was a reasonable explanation. It also fitted with Joe's habit of disappearing into himself while he processed whatever was bothering him. At least he'd admitted to burying memories. "Like being a police officer?"

"Exactly."

She gave Joe a long look, which he returned so calmly she was tempted to believe he really was all right. "Well, whatever you were shielding me from, thank you. I always feel safe when I'm with you. You're very good at your job and taking care of your men," she added. "I'm sure you were an excellent army officer too."

"I tried to be. But I've had a lot more experience being a police officer."

"Are you feeling like your police officer self again? Is that why you're awake?"

"It's what I do. I get to work. I try to figure out the puzzle." A surprising hint of mischief sparked in Joe's eyes. "Since you're awake, I could use your help. I've told so many people what a talented investigator you are that I'm beginning to believe it."

She smiled at his gentle teasing and marshalled her thoughts, remembering her vow to keep things in the present instead of the past. Using his work as a distraction was the best course of action at this point. "Good, because I have a lot to tell you."

She patted the bed for him to join her and told him about the arguing voices she'd heard while she was in the kitchen making tea. "One of them sounded like Mr. Bauer, but different. Not just louder, but younger. You know how his normal voice has a reedy or tremulous quality that people can get as they age? How old do you think he is? Sixty-five? Seventy?"

"That sounds right. His moustache and eyebrows are white. His skin isn't so wrinkled, but he stoops and shuffles like an older person."

"What I heard was," she closed her eyes, concentrated, and then recited: "*Ich habe es nicht.* And then I heard *verdammte Messer nicht.* Do you know what that means?"

Joe repeated the phrase, recalling snatches of German he'd learned as a soldier, translating each word. His eyebrows shot up. "*Messer* is knife. *Nicht* is not. *Verdammte* is…it means I don't have the damn knife."

"When I saw Bauer coming in from the rain while I waited for the lift, I just wanted to get away from him as quickly as—" She stopped short, her lips forming a silent oh. "There's something I was trying to remember before I fell asleep. Only the more I tried, the less I could. I know what it was now. I don't think Bauer had a rucksack when we were on the train going up to the glacier and he didn't have one when I saw him downstairs earlier."

Joe turned to her. "Great observation!" He rubbed his eyes as he tried to remember. "Did you see him get off the train when we arrived at the glacier?"

"No, I didn't. I was taking it all in. The glacier, the mountains. I wasn't watching the boy. But Bauer had a bench to himself on the train and I don't recall seeing a rucksack on the seat next to him."

Understanding dawned on Joe's face. "So, it's possible the rucksack that fell from the trail isn't Bauer's."

"And if the rucksack isn't Bauer's, then the knife isn't his."

Joe slowly nodded. "So, the rucksack and knife belong to the blond boy."

"Yes, I think so." She stretched and shifted to tuck her cold toes under Joe's leg. "The boy wasn't on the return train. Where did he go?"

"Right. Well." Joe ran a hand through his hair. "First thing in the morning, we ask everyone who they saw. And we'll ask if anyone knows who the blond kid is."

"Where's the knife now?"

"I put it on top of the wardrobe. It seemed like the safest place for it." He got up, rummaged in his suitcase, and found a small notebook and a pen. "Let's make a note of everything you can remember."

"Good thinking, Inspector."

They worked well together, making notes of everything they could remember about the train journey, who was where and when, their hike with Georges, the contents of the rucksack, and what she'd seen and heard downstairs, including Erich Bauer's arrival at the hotel afterward.

Joe summarized what they knew about the silver edelweiss, including where and when they found it. "I also wrote up that conversation we had about the possibility of German soldiers disguising themselves as tourists," he said as he placed the notebook and pen on his nightstand. "I don't like the sound of this. Will you promise me you won't do anything rash?"

"Now who's hovering?"

He huffed a breath. "We don't know what we're getting into with Bauer and this blond boy. I don't know what they're involved in, but it worries me."

FORTY-NINE

THE INVESTIGATION CONTINUES

Morning came much sooner than Sophie would have liked. A knock on their door and the bounce of the mattress as Joe rose from bed roused her. Julie, the girl who helped in the kitchen and around the hotel, had a note for them.

Joe squinted to decipher the message. "It's from Will. He says they're thinking of delaying their Mont Blanc climb because the snow might be too slushy after the storm. They'll wait on the terrace for us so we can decide what to do today. Or they can leave us to our own devices, and they'll meet up with us whenever they get back." He reached over and tucked a strand of hair behind her ear. "What do you want to do?"

She groaned and returned his questioning gaze with heavy-lidded eyes. She wanted to snuggle into the warm cocoon of sheets and covers and go back to sleep, but they needed to ask questions before everyone went their separate ways. "Let's get dressed and talk with them now."

"I agree," Joe said. He asked the girl to tell their friends they would be downstairs as soon as possible.

"Monique is a mind-reader," Sophie commented as she surveyed the terrace. Their table was so laden with coffee things that the top's lacy ironwork was hardly visible.

"She's used to over-tired tourists," Will said. Both he and Edmund looked bleary-eyed.

"I am an expert at tourists of all sorts." Monique smiled at them as she moved cups and saucers to fit pots of jam and a basket of croissants on the table. "Let me know if you want muesli or eggs or toast."

Sophie poured coffee for herself and Joe and then passed the pot to Edmund, who refilled his cup before he moved to the balustrade. She was trying to stifle an enormous yawn when Monique sidled over to her.

"You and monsieur are all right?" Monique murmured. "It was a horrible storm last night."

"We're fine now," she admitted quietly. "Is Georges upset by thunderstorms?"

Monique looked over at Georges reading the paper and shook her head. "*Un peu*," she answered, just as quietly. "A little. Perhaps in another twenty years he won't be."

Then Monique glanced over at the balustrade and raised a brow. Sophie followed her gaze to Edmund, standing with his head bowed. Monique's eyes were soft with concern. The silent conversation between them continued for a moment longer and ended with Sophie rising from her chair and turning to the balustrade. Monique approved her intention with a slight nod.

Sophie walked over to Edmund and stood beside him. The sky was so clear the mountains looked like they were resting against a blue glass. The only sign of the storm was masses of pink geranium petals strewn on the terrace by the balustrade. "It's so beautiful this morning that it's hard to believe we had such a dreadful storm last night," she said.

"Do you remember what I told you about Mary Shelley writing the Frankenstein novel during an Alpine thunderstorm?"

His response was not what she expected, but it was a start. "Gothic horror isn't my preferred genre. After last night, that novel makes a lot of sense."

Several minutes passed. She was about to leave Edmund to his thoughts when he took a deep breath. "If Joe ever needs to know, the rest of us understand."

She didn't want to embarrass Joe, but Edmund's comment sounded heartfelt. "You heard?"

Edmund nodded, his eyes never leaving the mountain. "I'm in the room just below you. Monique came to check on me after the storm passed."

Monique, bless her, had known he needed checking on. Sophie didn't know whether to look at Edmund or the scenery. She opted for the lawn below the terrace. "We talked afterward. I think it helps." She stole a peek at Edmund. He was still gazing at Mont Blanc.

"Does it? Sometimes I don't believe it does," he said. "It won't bring hi- them back."

The dejected man speaking with her now seemed at odds with the confident man she'd come to know. "No, it won't bring them back," she agreed. "But it can help us remember the good things. It can help us cope with the pain of missing them."

"It was his idea to leave university and volunteer in France. And then to climb Mont Blanc in the middle of the war. I was just a footloose college boy, like Will told you, but I would have followed him anywhere."

"He's the one in the picture in the library?" Edmund nodded. "I'm so sorry. You must miss him terribly." The thought that he must feel so alone at times was heartbreaking.

"I returned to the States after the war, but only to finish my degree. My family doesn't understand why I stay in Europe. He's the reason I write. Trying to make sense of everything that happened then and what's happening now…how it will affect…all of us."

Dishes clattered on the terrace tables. Edmund turned to her. "Normally I'm fine. Lots of time has passed after all." He scrubbed his face and managed the ghost of a smile. "But you're right. Talking helps a little. Let's have breakfast. Monique is a firm believer in the restorative powers of good food."

As she let Monique's excellent coffee work its magic, Sophie surveyed the quiet terrace. Erich Bauer hadn't made an appearance. The hotel must have far fewer guests in the middle of the week, or perhaps some of them were sleeping late or had an earlier start. Whatever the reason, the terrace was empty except for their group.

She waited until Joe finished the last bite of his croissant and took a sip of his coffee before she asked no one in particular. "Has anyone seen Mr. Bauer this morning?"

"He did not eat dinner here," Monique said. "I have not seen him since yesterday morning."

No one else had, not even Georges, who was always the first one downstairs in the mornings.

"I wanted to check his ankle after his tumble yesterday."

"He seemed fine when we returned from the train station," Georges said. "He left me at the gate and said he was going to…. I cannot remember where he was going. The pharmacy? The book shop?"

She tilted her head at Joe and rose from the table. "Excuse us for a moment," she said. Joe rose and followed her across the terrace and around the back of the hotel.

Bauer's car was still parked in the street. Joe scanned the area. "Where were the men standing when you overheard them?"

"Here, at this corner." She walked along the back of the hotel, peering in the windows until she found what she was looking for. "This is the kitchen window."

He gauged the distance from where she was standing to the corner of the hotel. "That's a good ten or fifteen feet. What else?"

"The streetlight at the corner wasn't lit," she recalled. "I saw them during a lightning flash. I couldn't make out any details. And I didn't want them looking into the kitchen so I moved away from the window, crouched down, and crawled back under it so I could hear what they were saying."

He nodded and jotted something in his notebook. "What happened next?"

"The kettle started whistling right after the knife comment. I crawled to the door and stood up so if they heard the whistling and looked in the window it would seem like I'd just come into the kitchen to turn off the stove."

"Then you gathered everything up and went back upstairs?"

"Yes. I wanted you to see them."

"All right. I should diagram this. Can you pace off the distance between the window and the corner? And then between those three streetlights?"

She had just called out five paces when Monique poked her head out of the kitchen window. "There you are! We are making omelets for Will and Edmund. Would you like one too?"

"Yes, please," Joe replied.

"Not for me, thank you," she said.

"I checked your clothes and shoes this morning, madame. They are dry. The boiler keeps the room warm."

"Oh good. We'll collect them after breakfast."

Joe closed the notebook and tucked it in a pocket. "Why don't you handle the boys," he said as they made their way back to the terrace.

Georges eyed them when they took their places at the table again. "What is it?"

"We'll tell you later," Joe replied in a low voice. He leaned back in his chair as Nick and Chris set omelets on the table.

She nudged Joe's knee under the table. "Did you boys have a good hike yesterday?" She pretended to be fascinated by pulling a croissant apart and brushing the buttery crumbs from her fingers.

Chris grinned at his father. "We beat Papa and Edmund going up and coming back."

"That's because you're always in a hurry to beat me," Will grumbled. "Next time we start together."

"It's nice that you boys met up with friends on the train." She gave the croissant another pull. "Do you often hike with them?"

"Sometimes," Nick said. "They live in the next town, so it depends when we see each other."

"And the other boy?"

"What other boy?" Nick asked.

"The other boy on the train. The one with blond hair. Isn't he one of your friends too?" She abandoned the unraveled croissant and casually nabbed a forkful of Joe's eggs, hoping his reaction would distract the boys from wondering why she was asking so many questions.

"No, madame," Nick said, grinning at Joe's half-aggrieved, half-comical reaction to the loss of part of his breakfast. "I have seen him hiking, and in the town, too. But I don't know who he is."

"Oh." She shrugged and smiled at Joe. "Thank you, darling. I hope you don't mind. Your omelet smelled delicious, and I couldn't resist."

$\approx$

The plan for the day was to meet Vanni at the first hiker's hut on Mont Blanc. Will, Edmund, and Georges needed to discuss the state of the mountain and the snow with him and the other mountain guides.

Joe looked at his empty plate and then at Sophie. "Since you've finished my breakfast, why don't we run that errand on our way to the train station?" Assuming they could deliver the knife and edelweiss to the police, they could update their friends during the train ride to the refuge. Then everyone would know the situation, which would be a relief.

"Oh, you mean the errand we discussed earlier?"

She sounded so casual and guileless that he reckoned she could have had a career on the stage. "That's the one."

When they arrived at the Chamonix police station, it was full of tourists complaining about a pickpocket who'd been active the day before. Joe took one look at the crowd and the two harassed-looking officers behind the desk and shook his head. "We won't get the attention we need," he said. "Let's try again this afternoon."

Sophie reached for his wrist and checked his watch. "We don't have time to take the knife back to the hotel and get to the train in time. We're going to walk around with a trench knife in your rucksack all day," she muttered.

She sounded just as frustrated as he felt. "I don't have a better idea. Do you?"

FIFTY

NOT A COINCIDENCE

They made it to the station in Saint Gervais in time to meet Georges, Will, and Edmund on the platform. As the train traveled up to the first hiker's hut, Sophie told them what she had heard during the storm. After that came a discussion about what Bauer and the boy might be up to, whether one or both of them were merely a summer thief, or whether they were spies reconnoitering Chamonix for Germany.

Their friends, grim-faced, headed off to find Vanni.

"The Eagle's Nest is an appropriate name, don't you think?" Joe asked while they trudged through slushy snow to the panoramic viewpoint at the hut.

"It's the highest we've been since we got here." Sophie put a coin in the telescope and began a visual sweep of the valley and the mountains. "Joe! Come look at this," she called a few minutes later. She moved back so he could look through the eyepiece. She had it pointed to the rough trail that hugged Mont Blanc's lower slopes.

"That's Bauer following the blond boy," he said.

"How is he keeping up after he hurt his ankle yesterday? Is it possible he faked the injury?"

"What the devil is going on with those two?"

He kept his eyes on Bauer and the boy until Will's voice sounded behind him. He turned and saw Will, along with Georges, Vanni, and Edmund, standing together.

"Why do you think it's so important to turn the knife over to the police?" Will asked.

"We know it's a German trench knife. We know the edelweiss is a German army insignia. If you all are right, and another war is coming, I think we should turn the items over to someone in authority as soon as possible. Even if someone local owns them as souvenirs from the last war, the knife passed into our possession under what could be suspicious circumstances. If everything is perfectly innocent, doesn't it make sense that the rightful owner would go to the police and report their missing items? But if everything isn't innocent, finding both items with the same people involved is more than a coincidence."

Georges was frowning and shaking his head. "I do not believe the circumstances are innocent. Look at what Germany has done, annexing the Sudetenland, Kristallnacht, trapping Jews in ghettos. Germany and Italy are allied now. If they make war on France it would be easy to invade through the Alps here in Chamonix. If Bauer and the boy are German, I am afraid they may wish to cause us harm. I cannot allow that to happen, monsieur. We must do what we can to stop them. We cannot wait for the police."

"We're not climbing the mountain today," Will said, stepping forward from the group. "We don't like the sound of what you told us. If those two are German spies, we need to do something. Edmund and Vanni will follow them. Georges and I will go back to the trail Bauer and the boy were on yesterday and see if they left anything there."

Joe opened his mouth to object to their plan, but Will spoke again.

"It makes sense," Will said. "We know these mountains and

trails, you don't. We need you to keep an eye on Monique and the boys, plus Hélène and Marianne are arriving this afternoon. But you're the detective. So far, you've found a trench knife, an *Alpenkorps* insignia, and a journal in German. Tell us how we should proceed. What do you want us to do if we find anything that looks suspicious?"

He considered their proposal. All four men were former soldiers and presumably capable of handling themselves in risky situations, but Georges' words verged on vigilantism, just the sort of thing a police officer tried to keep from happening. He had no authority over them, but they had come to him for direction, so he used that to corral any instincts they might have to take things too far. If he couldn't stop them, he had to keep them as safe as possible.

"Right. Edmund and Vanni, if you see Bauer and the boy just observe. If you must engage with them, say you couldn't do the Mont Blanc climb because of the weather, so you decided to do something else instead. Will, if you and Georges find anything suspicious on the trail, don't touch it if you can avoid it. Do you have something to write with? Good. Make a note of whatever you find and where you found it."

He felt Sophie fidgeting beside him as he spoke. Despite the gravity of the situation, he nearly smiled at the steely gaze she had fixed on Will and Georges. She did the same thing to Sam and Jean-Luc when they proposed an idea that she thought wasn't particularly sensible.

"Isn't Monique going to wonder why you're not climbing the mountain today?" she asked.

"*Non*, madame," Georges answered. "We often change our plans. We will return in time for dinner."

"When we found the knife, you asked us not to tell Monique. Have you told her?"

To his credit, Georges didn't flinch. "I have not told her. She might be angry with me for not telling her, but she will understand this is important for me to do."

Sophie turned to Will, and he could have sworn Will's eyes glinted in amusement before he drew himself to his full height and towered a head above her. She must have seen the glint too, because she graced Will with the same unwavering gaze she'd trained on Georges.

"What shall we tell Hélène and Marianne?"

"I've always found it best to tell Hélène the truth," Will replied.

She turned to Edmund and Vanni. "What about you two?"

"We'll be back when we know something or if we lose them," Edmund said. "It could be this afternoon or late tonight." He and Vanni adjusted the straps on their rucksacks. "It could even be tomorrow. If we can, we'll call and let Joe know our status."

Joe was relieved that Sophie and he didn't have to handle this on their own anymore, but uneasy because their friends were involved now and could be in harm's way. He shook hands with each man. "Be careful, please. Sophie and I will keep trying to get the attention of the police. We'll see you back at the hotel."

FIFTY-ONE

WOMEN AND WAR

Today I woke at first light, determined to perform one of the tasks I set for myself before I arrived in this place. I let the steady rhythm of walking and climbing take over until I reached the glacier by Mont Blanc. I trekked across snow slushy from last night's rain and soft enough to slow me down. But that was a good thing. I needed to know everything about this place so I can make a faithful report. All was quiet until I heard a man calling me by my name. Rolf. No one here knows my name. How does he know my name?

I panicked and ran, angling down to the tree line, evading my follower. I was certain it was the old man, and he ran so fast he almost caught me.

Back at the hotel, Joe spent a few minutes telling Monique everything that had transpired at the refuge.

Monique took the news in stride. "They are excellent climbers," she said. "They will be careful."

"You're not angry with Georges for not telling you about the knife?" Sophie asked.

"Madame, please believe I mean no disrespect," Monique replied, "but Australia is very far from here. You and Monsieur Parker do not live close to where so many wars have been fought. We are much more aware of things that could happen with Germany and Italy. I trust Georges. If he believes he must try to protect us, then I cannot be angry with him. Will and the others must feel the same."

She turned back to Joe. "Now, monsieur. What do you need me to do here at the hotel?"

"I'd like you to go about your normal, everyday routine," he said, thankful that Monique was reacting so calmly and dismayed she took the possibility of another war for granted. Whatever respect he'd felt for her before doubled in the face of her strength of character. These people would not go down without a fight if the Germans invaded.

"At the moment, Bauer and the boy aren't a threat to any of us here at the hotel, but they could be back at any time. Where are Nick and Chris? I want them to stay as close as possible."

"They are cleaning out the cellar," Monique said.

"Is there something they can do outdoors instead? Or on the ground floor? I'd like them to stay within shouting distance."

"Certainly. They could trim the bushes below the terrace. Then they could watch the street and the drive."

"Good idea, Monique. Do you have any idea when Hélène and Marianne will arrive?

"They left home early, so they should arrive here in the middle of the afternoon."

"All right. What about other guests? Are you expecting anyone to arrive today?"

"No, monsieur."

Joe took a moment to think everything through—spies in their midst, another war imminent, the probability that all their sons would fight—he needed time to process everything. "It sounds like we'll have a quiet afternoon. Even if Edmund and Vanni don't get back until late, after Georges and Will arrive, we'll have nearly a full complement to look after things this evening. I'd like to use the desk in the library. I can keep watch over the back of the hotel while I read and organize the work I was doing in London."

Sophie had been watching him and Monique talk, her eyes darting back and forth between the two of them. She was practically bouncing in her chair. "Darling, what do you want me to do?"

"Can you cover the terrace and the lawn?"

Sophie nodded. "I'll take my book down to the lawn and read in one of those comfy-looking lounge chairs."

Before she settled down with her book, Sophie stood by Joe when he called the police, in case he needed her French-speaking skills.

He replaced the handset with exaggerated care after he rang off, a sure sign he was frustrated with the person he'd been speaking with. "The constable who answered spoke English fairly well," he said. "But he doesn't know when someone will be available to meet with us. The chief is away at some sort of training. The sergeant is out because his wife has gone into labor two weeks earlier than expected, and the other constables are out on their usual patrols through the town."

"If they're that short-handed, we wouldn't have gained anything by going to the police station again," she said. "We'll just have to wait it out. I'm glad you took the knife upstairs and put it back on top of the wardrobe, though. If it takes until tomorrow for the police to get back to us, we don't want the maid to find it when she cleans the room."

"I don't like what Georges and the others are doing. So many things could go wrong."

"You know as well as I do you couldn't stop them, Joe."

Joe grunted and rubbed the back of his head, still annoyed by the phone call. The worries she had about him not coping well with memories from the war seemed like they'd happened in the distant past instead of hours ago. At least he was too busy now to be bothered by them. Since there was nothing else she could say or do to help, she grabbed her book and headed to the lawn.

A couple of hours later, she checked on Joe to tell him that Hélène and Marianne had arrived. "Monique and I told them what's happening."

"How'd they take it?"

"Almost as calmly as Monique did. I must admit, it shocked me they spoke so openly about expecting more trouble with the Germans, even the possibility of another war. I suppose Monique was right. They've become accustomed to it and don't worry about it all the time. At any rate, we're going to have tea. Would you like some?"

When she returned with a tea tray, it was impossible to put the tray on the desk. Joe had papers spread across its surface. He liked to see everything in front of him and he would move pages around like puzzle pieces.

"It's why I like police work," he'd said the first time she saw his desk covered with files. "Each case is a puzzle. I just have to figure out which pieces go where." If she woke during the night and he wasn't beside her, she usually found him in his study, pajama-clad and tousle-haired, pouring over pages on his desk.

"No, you don't need to move anything," she said when he peered up at her. "I'll use this side table instead." She poured him a cup and left him to his work.

Joe emerged from the library after another hour, looking so pleased with the progress he'd made that she suggested they take a stroll around the hotel's perimeter to stretch their legs. "I received a telegram from my mother. There's a problem with her plan to sail home with us, and I'd like to hear what you think of an idea I've had to deal with it."

"Let's review," Joe said after Sophie finished relating the news from her mother. "Your mother may not meet us in Marseille as planned because Edwina, her companion, doesn't want to leave England."

Sophie nodded. "The man Edwina has been stepping out with decided he didn't want to live without her. He proposed, and she accepted."

"Could your mother travel without a companion?" He wasn't sure he understood the vagaries of wealthy women and their personal servants, but he was certain he didn't want to inadvertently step on any toes. He had liked his mother-in-law immensely when they finally met in London and Lily seemed to like him. He preferred to keep it that way.

"Yes, she can. But Edwina was also a personal secretary, and they were close, friends even. Consequently, Mother's at a loss. Edwina's been with her for so long she knows she'll miss the companionship, but she doesn't want to impose on us."

He had an inkling of where this conversation was headed—their plans would change yet again—he just didn't know how yet. "Tell me how your idea fits into all of this?"

"When Hélène and Marianne arrived, it was obvious they had been...not arguing, but I could see neither one was happy with the other."

He grimaced. He didn't relish the possibility of witnessing a family disagreement on top of everything else that was happening.

"The night we had dinner at their house, Marianne told me she's determined to find a way to go to Australia. She's almost twenty-two but Will doesn't want her to travel so far by herself."

He considered the situation. If he had a daughter, he would feel the same way. Any journey where an attractive young woman traveled alone could be fraught with peril, regardless of whether the distance was twelve or twelve thousand miles. However, he limited himself to a simple, "And?"

"Marianne could take Edwina's place."

He paused mid-step and faced Sophie. He'd been right. Their plans were changing again.

"Don't look at me like that, Joe. I didn't interfere or meddle or anything like what you're thinking."

"I'm not thinking anything. I'm listening."

"Hmm. Anyhow, I was having tea with Hélène, Marianne, and Monique when Mother's telegram arrived. I read it right away in case something was wrong. Apparently, I looked so worried at first, and then so relieved, that everyone asked if everything was all right. So, I told them Mother's news. Then we all started talking and Marianne asked if she could take Edwina's place. Hélène pulled her aside and, well, the upshot is Marianne has her mother's blessing if Will agrees."

"But what about your mother? Doesn't she have a say in all this?"

"Of course she does. I wrote out a note asking her to consider it and respond by tomorrow morning before we leave. The girl who helps in the kitchen took it to the post office and sent a telegram for me."

"What if your mother says no? What will Marianne do then?"

"I don't think she'll say no. Mother wants to live in Australia, so she's close to Aunt Flora and us. Edwina's change of plans is just a bump in the road, so to speak."

He took a deep breath. He remembered Marianne as a charming young woman, but having a third person accompany them through Provence wouldn't be particularly relaxing. "How will Marianne get to Marseille?"

"Hélène and Will or Chris will get her there by car or train, so she arrives in time to board the ship."

"It sounds like Hélène is in favor of this."

Sophie nodded. "She is, Joe. I spoke privately with her. She doesn't want Marianne in France if…when…war breaks out again." She stopped and seemed to be working through something that was just occurring to her. "It's 1939. Marianne is almost twenty-two."

"And?"

Sophie quirked a brow at him. "Think about it. That means she was born in 1917. Will had a family here in France before the war ended."

"When we first met Will, told me he didn't have any family to return to in Australia."

"Pregnant and unmarried during a war." Sophie winced. "Hélène must have been terrified something would happen to the baby or to Will. She's probably worried history could repeat itself."

"When will they talk with Will?"

"Tonight, most likely. I'm sure Hélène will choose a time she thinks best."

He shoved his hands in his pockets and worked through the possibilities. "Hélène's right. If Marianne was our daughter, we'd want her as far away from France as possible. I'd be willing to bet her father will agree."

"The boys won't have the same chance, will they?" Sophie asked.

Discouraged, he massaged his temples with one hand. Boys. If there was another war, they'd become men, whether or not they were ready to be. Nick would be conscripted into the French army. And Chris? Was he a French citizen, or did he have dual citizenship? Australia had voted down conscription twice in the last war. What would Sam and Jean-Luc do? Volunteer? He scrubbed a hand over his chin. He couldn't think about that now. The present situation took priority over worrying about the future. He shook his head. "No. If it's war again, Chris and Nick will be in it, I'm afraid. They all will, God help them."

Joe and Sophie met Georges and Will coming up the drive with the news they had found nothing on the trail Bauer and the boy had taken from the Mer de Glace yesterday. They compared notes and filled each other in over a dinner of ham, sausages, and cheese, plus salad and bread. When Joe relayed the reasons the police still didn't have the knife and edelweiss, Georges smacked himself on the forehead.

"The chief, he is new in Chamonix. I have heard he is a member of the high mountain troops. They are training at Col de la Seigne. That is why you could not speak with him."

Edmund and Vanni called during dessert to say they had followed Bauer and the boy to Les Houches and were staying overnight there. Joe considered that new information and planned what everyone would do tomorrow.

When he finally drifted off to sleep, Joe's dreams were a jumble of Bauer tramping across glaciers and through woods after the blond boy.

Then his dream shifted, and Sophie was young as she had been when they first met in Paris. She was alone in a room where all the beds were empty except for one. She carefully wrapped a boy's body in a clean sheet. As he watched, she smoothed his blond hair before she pulled the sheet over his head.

FIFTY-TWO

DON'T TEMPT ME

The next morning, a police constable returned Joe's call before breakfast. The police chief had been in contact with the station and had requested that Sophie and Joe keep the items until he returned from training tomorrow.

Joe didn't refrain from letting his frustration show when he relayed the latest news to Sophie. "Damn it, we're stuck here and there's nothing we can do about it. We'll have to stay at least one more day."

"I don't suppose we could forget what the constable said, drop everything at the police station, and leave as soon as I get Mother's telegram. We could be in Lyon by lunchtime."

"Don't tempt me. As much as I'd like to leave right now, I don't want to get summoned back by the French authorities. At least Georges and Will have returned. They can keep watch over the hotel and their families for a few hours. Let's find something to do to pass the time."

He was flipping through the Chamonix guidebook he found in the hotel's library. The thought occurred to him that being up higher might feel less oppressive than staying in the valley. He didn't dare suggest they head out of the valley—he might not turn the car around to return to Chamonix, despite what he'd said to Sophie. He stopped at the description of Le Brévent, a mountain in the lower range on the west side of the valley.

"What about going up to the top of Le Brévent? I've never ridden in a gondola." He studied the map of trails from the summit, tracing the line on the plan that led to Lac du Brévent. "There's a trail that takes two-and-a-half hours to make the circuit around the lake. What do you think? Some physical activity after all the sitting we did yesterday afternoon?"

The gondola to the mid-point was steep, but the sight of the valley below them growing smaller and smaller as they glided up the mountainside fascinated Joe. The second gondola to the top was another story. The cables operated on the same principle—one long loop of steel cable pulled by powerful motors at either end. But being suspended thousands of feet in mid-air, with the wind whistling through the cabin and causing the gondola to sway, was so frightening that Joe wasn't sure he actually breathed during the ascent. Sophie clenched his hand all the way across and didn't let go until they stepped onto solid land.

He flexed his fingers to get the circulation going again while he looked around in awe at endless Alps on the eastern side of the valley. "This is incredible. It looks like they go on forever." He turned west. Grey granite slopes descended to green hills that flattened to the farmlands of central France. It wasn't anything like the view from their house at home, where he could see all of Sydney from the harbor side of the hill and the Pacific from the ocean side, but he could see far horizons again instead of the suffocating trench of the valley. He took a deep, calming breath.

"What's amazing is we're at the top of this mountain and yet we're only a little higher than we were at the Eagle's Nest yesterday," Sophie said. "And there's no snow on this side, except patches that must be in deep shade all the time. It's completely different looking at the mountains from up here."

They found a perfect spot in the alpine meadow overlooking the lake to catch their breath and eat their picnic lunch. He lay on his side, propped on one elbow, taking in the horizons and watching birds of prey soaring on the air currents.

After a group of hikers passed by them, Sophie stretched beside him and rested her head on his shoulder. He trailed his fingers up and down her arm for a few minutes before he spoke. "So much has happened that I haven't had a chance to thank you."

"Whatever for?"

"For knowing what to do the other night after the thunderstorm." His fingers began their gentle trail again.

"There's no need to thank me, darling. You may have to do the same for me one day."

"You're the strongest person I've ever known. I doubt I'll ever have to do the same for you." He paused, gathering his thoughts. "There was something you said the other day about shrinking violets. It wasn't Annie's fault. I decided early on I couldn't tell her what was really happening. How can anyone who wasn't there understand?"

∼

Joe rarely talked about his relationship with Annie, but he was opening up, even if obliquely. Sophie pushed for more. "You know, we're lucky," she began.

"I know I am," Joe said before she could finish.

"I'm serious. We experienced different things, but they were alike enough that we had an idea of what the other went through. Most people at home didn't have that shared experience." Now would be a good time for him to tell her what he'd been dreaming about. She waited, hopeful.

"Hmm," was his only response and, if not for the warm fingers tightening and pulling her close, she would have guessed he'd fallen asleep. He turned onto his side, tipped his hat back from his forehead, and kissed her at length in the open air and the warm sun.

Even though he had been remarkably demonstrative in Paris, public displays of unbridled affection were not in Joe's usual repertoire, especially not in full view of hikers who had rounded the lake. She giggled at their clapping. Joe's ears turned pink.

As soon as the hikers disappeared from the trail, she checked that no one else was coming before she kissed him, just as thoroughly. If Joe was going to try to distract her, she would return the favor. Only this time, they were in full view of a pair of mountain goats who cared nothing about what humans did in public.

FIFTY-THREE
THE MISSING EDELWEISS

Yesterday, I climbed a tree and waited until the old man and the two men who were following were gone. Today, I returned to Chamonix before dawn and hid in the shrubbery until I could hear conversations on the hotel terrace. They were going to a mountain called Le Brévent. That meant their room would be empty for several hours. The man and woman I nicknamed English, not English, passed so close that I could smell her perfume.

I worked my way around to the side entrance and crept up the service stairs until I found the floor, and then the door, where her scent was strongest. The door was locked, so I waited at the end of the corridor until the girl who cleans came to their room. She left the door open to go fetch clean towels, so I sneaked in and hid under the bed until she finished cleaning.

I found my edelweiss and knife in the room!

Tomorrow I will hike the last trail and then I can go home.

~

When they returned to the hotel to freshen up after their afternoon at Le Brévent, Sophie went to fetch a clean handkerchief from the dressing table drawer. "It's missing!" she cried. "The edelweiss is missing!" She removed the drawer and dumped the contents on the bed. The silver flower wasn't tucked into the stack of hankies where she left it or mixed among the loose coins deposited in the drawer.

Whatever peace Joe had found during their hike vanished. "When did you last see it?"

"This morning. I saw it when I was putting on my hat before we left for Le Brévent. Don't you remember? I asked you to make sure the knife was still on top of the wardrobe."

He checked his watch and jotted everything down in his notebook. "Someone stole it in the last three or four hours."

"Is the knife there?"

He stood on the dressing table chair and felt for the knife. "Bloody hell! They took the knife, too. Why didn't I ask Monique if the hotel has a safe? How the hell did this happen?"

Sophie threw up her hands. "Bauer and the boy must have been watching the hotel somehow."

"They must have," he agreed. "When we arrived, Monique said Will and Georges had gone to the Col de la Seigne to talk with Georges' friends in the mountain troops. Edmund and Vanni left with Marianne and the boys to patrol through the town. Where did she say Hélène was?"

"Joe, this isn't Hélène's or Monique's fault. They were on the terrace talking and catching up on each other's news. They're friends, for heaven's sake."

"I'm not trying to find fault, Sophie. I'm trying to figure out how this could have happened! Bauer or the boy must have entered through a side door. They'd see from the reception board which room is ours and run upstairs without being seen."

He shoved his notebook and pencil into his jacket pocket.

"That does it. One kid and one old man outsmarted all of us. We're going to do the police's job instead of waiting for them to come to us. Come on."

They headed down the stairs and around to the street behind the hotel where Bauer's car was parked under the trees.

He pulled the notebook and pen from his pocket. "Read the license number, please." He had just finished making a note of the car's physical description and had handed his handkerchief to Sophie when Monique leaned out of the kitchen window.

"Is there a problem? Why are you—" She stopped talking and watched Sophie cover the door handle with the handkerchief so she could open it and examine inside the car.

"There's nothing here, Joe. No registration papers, no maps. Monique, we'll explain in a minute," she said and nodded when Joe pointed his pen at the back of the car.

Using the handkerchief to cover the latch, Sophie opened the trunk and peered in. "Nothing here either."

"Monique," he called, "do you know what year this car is?"

"No, monsieur. I am not an expert, but this one is not new."

"And Bauer said he was having troubles with the clutch. Sophie, do you remember if he said where?"

"It was Saint-Gervais-les-Bains," Monique said.

"Right. Good. Thank you, Monique." He made a note and peered at the license plate on the back of the car. "Are we certain this is a Swiss plate?"

Monique nodded. "Yes. The white cross on red is for Switzerland. And the black bear is the crest for Bern."

He pocketed his notebook. "The police can contact the Swiss authorities and have them trace the license number."

"Swiss authorities?" Monique's eyes narrowed. "Monsieur, what has happened?"

"Someone has stolen the knife and the edelweiss from our room. Sophie, you're the only one who has seen Bauer here at the hotel in nearly forty-eight hours. We need to search his room. Will you show it to us, Monique?"

Joe saw her hesitate, as if considering the hotel's reputation and what the consequences could mean to her business, before she agreed. "Yes, of course. His room is on the first floor. I will get the key and meet you at the stairs."

There was nothing of interest in Bauer's room. His belongings were gone. The maid had already vacuumed, dusted, and changed the towels and bed linens.

Sophie and he searched everywhere, but they found no sign of the silver edelweiss or the trench knife. Neither item had been hidden under the mattress, or taped to the bottom of a drawer, or tossed on top of the wardrobe.

"Now that the edelweiss and the knife have been taken, maybe the police will pay attention," Joe said after Monique locked the door to Bauer's room and all of them returned to the reception desk.

Shouts from the terrace stopped them in their tracks. Chris sprinted into the hotel and skidded to a stop in front of them, panting and sweating.

"Inspector! You must come! Quickly! Monsieur Bauer and the blond boy are on the bridge by the Balmat statue. They are shouting at each other in German."

FIFTY-FOUR

BATTLE ON THE BRIDGE

Joe took control and issued orders. "Monique, please call the police and tell them to get to the bridge immediately. Sophie and Chris, come with me."

They ran the half mile to the bridge and pushed through the crowd that had gathered. Nick rushed over to them. "The boy threw something in the river before they started fighting."

Joe moved closer and saw Bauer and the blond boy wrestling for control of something. The boy twisted and slipped from Bauer's grasp. The boy held the trench knife and looked like he was ready to lunge at Bauer, who had backed up against the bridge railing. Neither Bauer nor the boy appeared to be injured. Yet.

The bridge was crammed with gaping locals and tourists. No police yet, damn it! He had no authority here, but he was possibly the only person with the experience to take control of the situation. He would have to take charge.

Without taking his eyes off Bauer and the boy, he raised his hands, motioned to the crowd. "Move back! Everyone! Get back!"

A chill swept over him when he remembered the German words he needed without thinking. "*Halt! Hände hoch!*"

The boy stopped and shot him an incredulous look.

Joe shouted at the boy again. "*Hände hoch!* Stop! Hands up! Mr. Bauer, move away!"

"Drop the knife! *Drop das Messer*!" he roared when the boy did nothing.

Joe watched as the boy crouched, the hand holding the knife nearing the pavement as though he would drop it. The boy looked around frantically, and Joe knew he was trying to regain an advantage.

Someone gasped, distracting him. The instant Joe looked to see who it was, the boy pivoted and ran toward Sophie, who was a few feet behind him and to the side.

Joe saw the blade of the knife as a blinding flash racing toward Sophie. He ran to her, as did Bauer, who moved faster than Joe believed possible. In two steps, Bauer was close enough to lunge at the boy, shoving him away from Sophie before he landed heavily on the ground. The boy swiveled to kick Bauer in the head. Bauer rolled away, groaning.

Joe grabbed the boy and hurled him against the bridge railing. What the boy lacked in fighting skills he made up for with sheer desperation, thrashing against him, one fist flying and the knife in his other hand flashing dangerously close to his head. Joe took the blows from the fist, desperate to get the knife. He wrapped one hand firmly around the boy's throat, and the other around the wrist with the knife and pounded the boy's forearm on the rail.

The boy screamed in pain.

The knife clattered to the ground.

Joe loosened his grip on the boy's throat. They both scrabbled for the knife. Joe got it first and tossed it over the bridge.

The boy twisted over the railing in a futile attempt to catch the knife.

Joe grabbed the boy's ankle, but he didn't have enough leverage to hold on to the kicking, struggling boy.

He gaped, horrified, as the boy slipped from his grasp and plunged onto the jagged rocks lining the edges of the freezing, rushing river.

Damn, damn, damn! Joe willed his lungs to fill with air. He turned back and forth looking for Sophie. She ran up to him and threw her arms around him. "Thank God you're safe! But your eye—"

Still breathless from the struggle, he gently extracted himself from her embrace. "I'm fine. Go check on Bauer."

He reverted to police officer mode, issuing curt orders. "Nick!" The boy came running to his side. "Call for an ambulance."

That left Chris unaccounted for. "Chris?" he shouted. "Where are you?"

"I'm on the rocks, Inspector." Chris yelled. "I don't know if I can reach him."

He leaned over the railing. Chris was picking his way over the rocks, trying to edge his way down to the boy.

"Don't try!" He was damned if he was going to see another boy get hurt on those rocks. "Stop where you are. Just tell me what you see. Is the boy alive?"

Chris looked at the boy lying face down on the rocks, then back to Joe. He shook his head. "I..., I don't know!"

"Get off the rocks. There's nothing you can do. The police will be here soon."

The Chamonix police, medics, and rescue personnel arrived while Sophie tended to Bauer. One medic stayed on the bridge with her, and the others ran down to the rocks. Joe knew the worst had happened when a medic shook his head while feeling for a pulse. Many in the crowd crossed themselves when the medics carried the boy's covered body to the waiting ambulance.

The police officer in charge instructed his men to fan out and take statements from the witnesses. He approached Sophie and him, and with a simple, *"S'il vous plaît, m'sieur, madame,"* led them to a police car, and drove them to the police station.

FIFTY-FIVE

WITNESSES

It was past midnight before Sophie and Joe got back to the hotel after making their statements to the police.

The crunch of wheels on the gravel drive alerted their friends to their return. They came running out of the hotel's front door and pulled up short when they saw them exiting a police car.

"Monique, we need to go straight to our room. We aren't under arrest," he added when Monique started sputtering, "but we're witnesses, and the police need to verify our identities. The officers will explain."

Sophie pulled her hat off her head and pressed the lift button. Joe had asked for silence during the drive, but they were at the hotel now, and she assumed he had worked through what had happened.

"How's your eye?" she asked as soon as he closed the door to their room. "Let me look."

"There's nothing wrong with my eye," he snapped. "Why on earth did I let you get involved with this? I got distracted, and you nearly got killed."

"I did not nearly get killed! If Bauer hadn't pushed the boy away from me, I was going to stomp on his foot or go limp and drop just like you taught me."

"If you hadn't…. If anything had gone wrong, he could have killed you!" He rubbed his temples in frustration. "We're incredibly lucky nothing worse happened to either of us. We can't rely on luck!"

Sophie scowled, and he had the distinct impression she was resisting the urge to stomp on his foot. "I didn't rely on luck, Joe! I—"

"Sophie. Please, could we have some quiet for a little while? I need to think through everything that happened. I'm directly involved in a death in a country where I have no authority."

"I was there too!" she protested. "Everyone saw what happened. It was a horrible accident, but it wasn't your fault that the boy went over the railing."

"You weren't…." He fought to keep his voice from rising to a level he didn't want to use with his wife. "You weren't the one with your hand wrapped around someone's throat! Please. Just let me be."

He moved past Sophie to the far balcony and stared into the black void of the mountains. His mind raced. Instinct and experience had governed his actions on the bridge. How else could he have handled the boy? How the hell had he lost control of the situation? Or were circumstances beyond that?

Part of his brain registered the sounds of Sophie preparing for bed. He heard water running in the bathroom. She came to the door of the balcony, her shadow elongated across the tiled floor. He heard her whisper his name and sigh when he didn't turn to her. He heard the rustle of linen as she got into bed.

She wouldn't like the rules he was going to set, but in his opinion, they needed to be very formal when they met with the police chief in the morning. Sophie and he weren't suspects, but they were unknown quantities in an unusual death. The police sergeant had informed him they would send an urgent wire asking for confirmation of their identities. In return for letting them spend the night at their hotel, and not as guests of the Republic of France, the police had kept their passports and his warrant card.

Intellectually, he knew he would have done the same thing if the situation had been reversed. He would have stationed officers at the hotel just as the Chamonix police had done.

Emotionally, he was close to panicking. He had only received a punch below his eye in the struggle, but the fear that Sophie could have been injured, and the boy struggling while his hands were around his throat, had transported him back to that dark house in Villers-Bret. He had always known that neither the trauma of strangling the German soldier nor the self-loathing for what he was capable of would ever leave him, but he had been able to suppress it. Not anymore.

He could handle the authorities. He could shore up his coping walls again, but Sophie was already putting pieces together. She would somehow discover his deepest secret, would never look at him the same way again. How could he endure if his marriage to Sophie was broken forever?

FIFTY-SIX

GROUND RULES

Joe crept through the house in Villers-Bretonneux, stopping short when a shadow on the stairs moved. "Grenade!" he yelled. "Get down!"

For the second time in a week, he woke, thrashing, with Sophie in a panic beside him. For the second time in a week, he paced their hotel room like a caged animal.

He should have told Sophie he didn't want to go to the memorial. Robbie was dead, for Christ's sake, had been for over twenty years. Robbie would never know he and Sophie had gone to the damned memorial to find his name on the wall. He should have never agreed to this side trip to Chamonix. He cursed the blond boy and Erich Bauer for possibly being German spies and for putting Sophie and him in danger.

If they'd kept to their original plan—Paris, then Provence, then home—he wouldn't have been dragged back into his morass of memories. Now he was drowning in them when he needed all his wits about him. And this time Sophie would not sit by quietly. She was already out of bed and tugging his arm.

"What happened?" she cried. "Tell me. Please tell me."

Jesus, she was frantic. She had grabbed both his arms and was trying to force him to face her. He wrenched an arm free, picked up his watch, and held it so she could see the time. "It's six o'clock. We have to be at the police station at eight. I need to shave and shower. You need to do whatever it is you do. We need to eat breakfast. We don't have time to talk about a ridiculous dream I had."

"Joe, whatever that was, it wasn't just a dream and it wasn't ridiculous!"

"We have more important things to do. I need to clear up the mess I'm in, and we need to get as far away from this place as we can."

"*We're* in this mess, Joe. Not just you. *We*. We have to get through this together."

Sophie wasn't going to like his response. "Since I'm the only one of us who's a law enforcement officer, I'll answer the questions unless a question is directed specifically to you. Keep your answers as concise as possible. Don't offer any extra information."

He was right. She didn't like it. She stalked to the bathroom and shut the door far harder than was necessary.

FIFTY-SEVEN

MONSIEUR LE CHEF

Sophie and Joe arrived at the police station at eight o'clock. The young constable who drove them from the hotel to the station ushered them into the chief's office and closed the door behind him.

The police chief of Chamonix, tanned, fit, and about the same age as Joe nodded his greeting. "Senior Detective Inspector Parker. Madame Parker. Thank you for being prompt." He shook their hands and gestured to the guest chairs. "Please, sit. Would you like a coffee while we go over the events of yesterday?"

"Nothing for me, thank you," Sophie replied.

"Nor for me," Joe added.

He saw the chief studying him first, then Sophie, his glance lingering over the bruise under his eye and the careful makeup hiding the evidence of Sophie's earlier tears.

"Very well." The chief opened the file on his desk and extracted several items which he handed to Joe. "Here are your passports and your police identification."

He examined everything briefly before tucking their passports and his warrant card inside his jacket. Who in Sydney did he need to thank for moving heaven and earth to respond so quickly? The Commissioner's secretary, most likely.

"Since the authorities in Australia have confirmed you are who you say you are, Senior Detective Inspector Parker, and Madame Parker," the chief did a sort of seated half-bow in Sophie's direction, "I am free to discuss this case with you as I see fit."

Joe nodded. He would have allowed himself the same autonomy. What was more interesting was that the chief had returned their documents early on, subtly letting him know that Sophie and he weren't suspected of any serious wrongdoing. "I understand. Thank you, Monsieur le Chef. Is Mister Bauer all right? He may have saved my wife's life."

"Mr. Bauer was disoriented after the blow to his head, so he spent the night in hospital. The nurses say he was mumbling Madame Parker's name during the night. I will question him as soon as the doctors allow it. As for the young man, the coroner will be here this afternoon to determine the official cause of death." The chief emptied the contents of a large envelope and the trench knife tumbled onto the desk.

"Unless I am mistaken," the chief continued, "this is a *Nahkampfmesser*, a German trench knife. I saw many of these weapons during the war but none since then until this one was recovered with the young man's body."

The chief sat back in his chair and looked at him. "Did you fight in the war, Senior Detective Inspector?"

"Yes. In the Somme, and in Belgium." If he had to provide specific battles, he would, but he hoped his answer would suffice. "And my wife was a nurse at the American Hospital in Paris."

"Then you would have seen weapons like this. You would have had a similar weapon of British or Australian manufacture, yes?

"Yes. Monsieur le Chef, if it is the knife I think it is, someone took it from our hotel room sometime yesterday."

The chief's eyebrows shot up. "Excuse me? Why would you have such a weapon while you are on holiday in France? Is it a souvenir you acquired?"

"No, it isn't a souvenir. It isn't even mine. I don't know who it belongs to. Perhaps Bauer. Perhaps the young man."

The chief nudged the knife on his desk with his pen. "This is a formidable weapon and I do not like it being in my police station, much less in my town."

"I don't like seeing one again, either," Joe said. "Since our friends are certain the edelweiss is an *Alpenkorps* insignia, and we're certain the knife is German, the possibility exists that either Erich Bauer or the boy are German spies. Why else would they bring those items to France?"

"Before you and madame found the edelweiss and the knife, we had no reason to think Germans might be active in this area. Truthfully, we have been more concerned about the Italians than the Germans."

He moved to a large map of Europe on one wall and ran a finger over the border between France and Italy, through the mountains and south to Nice on the Mediterranean coast as he spoke. "We are vulnerable at several points in the Chamonix valley. However, we are more vulnerable at other points further south where the Alps are not as high. You may not know that the southeastern part of France belonged to Italy not so long ago. And Italy is allied with Germany now, so many people may have mixed loyalties. It worries me that our mountain borders with Italy are open and unguarded."

Joe heard Sophie, who had been silent so far, utter a soft "Oh no."

"Perhaps, Detective Inspector Parker, we should start at the beginning, and you tell me how this knife came to be in your possession."

Joe reached for the notebook he had in his pocket. "Do you mind if I refer to our notes?"

The chief shook his head. "No, not at all. Last night I spoke, at length, with Madame Pascal. She not only told me why you and Madame Parker are here in Chamonix, she also, what is the expression in English? She gave me an earful for not believing who you said you are and for stationing police officers outside her hotel." The chief smiled. "I must tell you her husband, Georges, did the same thing. Contacting the Australian authorities was a formality I had to perform."

Despite the gravity of the situation, Joe smiled too. At breakfast earlier, Monique mentioned she'd spoken with the chief. She hadn't shared what they talked about, but her righteous indignation when they left the hotel had been remarkable to behold. He hadn't understood most of what she said to the constable at the front door of the hotel, but he was certain she told him he'd better not harm a single piece of gravel on her driveway, or she would have his head.

"So. Please retrieve your notebook and tell me the entire story. And madame, please contribute any thoughts you may have." Sophie's brow lifted. "I believe women see things differently than men," the chief said, "and you may have insights that your husband and I do not. And Madame Pascal gave me another earful that I should treat you with as much professional courtesy as your husband. She was very impressed at how you helped your husband search Bauer's car. Now, if you please, Senior Detective Inspector. Begin."

FIFTY-EIGHT

COLLEAGUES

At home, they often discussed whatever it was Joe was working on, usually over dinner or in his study, but Sophie had never spent so much time observing Joe and a fellow officer going through the details of a case. Watching Joe and the chief work together was so fascinating that she forgot she was still angry with him for refusing to tell her about his most recent nightmare.

In the beginning, the two men continued to get the measure of the other, addressing each other by their formal titles—Monsieur le Chef, Senior Detective Inspector—until Joe asked to use the chief's chalkboard to write out a timeline. By that point, the chief's office was already very warm, the mid-morning sun streaming through the windows. They had dressed formally for this meeting and Sophie was wilting in the same linen outfit she'd worn to the memorial. Sweat glistened on Joe's forehead. He must be roasting in his dark suit.

The chief mopped his face with his handkerchief and removed his uniform jacket, inviting Joe to remove his suit jacket too.

Joe took off his jacket and rolled up his sleeves. The chief joined him at the chalkboard and from that moment, the two men were colleagues—Chief and Inspector—bouncing ideas off each other, correcting each other, sharing tidbits of previous cases each had solved.

She became a colleague too when the chief asked her a question about the merchant who had seen the blond boy on the trail to the meadow where he summered his cows and goats. She took off her jacket, picked up a piece of chalk, and took her place beside the two men.

Church bells tolled noon when they finished telling the chief everything that had happened since they arrived in Chamonix. Coffee cups, water glasses, and opened files littered the chief's desk. Diagrams and notes covered the chalkboard. At some point, Joe and the chief had loosened their ties. Her perfume mingled with the scents of petunias and alyssum wafting inside from the window boxes that hung below every window in Chamonix.

The chief looked back and forth between her and Joe. "May I say, Inspector, and Madame Parker, I am very impressed by your investigation. I feel I must ask…." He hesitated, as if reluctant to say what he was thinking. "You said you have become friends with Vanni, the Italian friend of Georges and Monique. Is there any chance that he could be working for the enemy?"

Her jaw dropped as she tried to comprehend the implications. The word enemy was so fraught. Not Vanni. Georges and the others would be devastated by such a betrayal.

"No. I don't see it." Joe's emphatic words and firm shake of his head reassured her. "Vanni's reaction to the edelweiss was visceral. He's still angry, twenty years after fighting the Germans. Disgusted, even. And he was itching to go after Bauer and the boy when we were at the Eagle's Nest. As I said earlier, I didn't want any of them to go off on their own, but I told them what to do to keep safe."

"Very well," the chief said. "And now, Inspector, until the coroner has finished examining the body, I am certain you and Madame Parker will be more comfortable at your hotel. I will have someone take you there. I am going to the hospital see Monsieur Bauer. I hope he will feel well enough to answer some questions."

Good, Sophie thought on the drive back to the hotel. We made it through the interview. Joe was right. Getting through this investigation is our most important priority. But when it's over, he and I are going to have a serious discussion about his nightmares.

∾

"Ugh!" Sophie said as she paced from the door of the library at the hotel to the window for what seemed to Joe like the millionth time.

They had eaten lunch there. Monique had carried in a tray of ham sandwiches and fruit, fretting because the chief had requested they stay indoors at the hotel.

"I would do the same thing your chief is doing, Monique," Joe had assured her as she plumped pillows and opened the windows. "We're perfectly comfortable."

Sophie frowned at him. "Would you really have confined us to the hotel, the way the chief has? I feel like we're under house arrest!"

He stifled a heavy sigh. "We are not under house arrest. You heard what the chief said. We have no way of knowing if there's anyone else involved in this...I'm not even sure what to call it... this business with Bauer and the boy. But, until we know, the chief is doing everything he can to keep us safe and get through this investigation as quickly as—"

"Who else could be involved? We haven't seen anyone else who—"

"Just because you and I haven't seen anyone else who could be involved doesn't mean there isn't someone," he reminded her tersely. "So yes, I would do the same thing the chief is doing. I'm just glad we're here in the relative cool of the library and not in a hot, stuffy room at the station. Would you prefer a hard chair in an interview room over a comfortable armchair here at our hotel?"

He checked his watch two hours later. He had been alternating between trying to read a book from the hotel's collection and running through what had happened on the bridge. The German soldier in the house in Villers-Bretonneux kept pushing into his mind.

The difference between how the boy and the soldier died was intent. He had been furious the boy on the bridge might have injured Sophie, but Joe knew he hadn't strangled the boy. He'd been very careful, only pressing on the artery and vein hard enough to cause the boy to lose consciousness momentarily so he could get the knife out of his hand. But the boy had thrashed so wildly that his plan hadn't worked. He had a bruised eye as proof. Thank God the police chief was competent and broad-minded. And he'd said he knew Joe wasn't responsible for the boy's death, which eased his mind, because it meant they could apply their energy to helping to solve this case instead of finding a solicitor.

Relieved or not, Sophie's pacing had become intolerable. He closed the book and rubbed his eyes.

"Sophie, please. Stop. You're wearing a thin spot on the floor."

She frowned at him. "I can't stand being cooped up in here!"

"You could always go up to our room."

She dropped into an armchair and leaned her head against the back of the chair. "I'd rather stay downstairs with you. But I still feel trapped." She glanced out the window and jumped up from the chair. "Joe, come look! The police are collecting Bauer's car."

They walked to the window and listened to the rapid conversation. The same young constable who had ushered them into the library had been joined by a second, even younger, constable. A mechanic peered into the engine compartment and then lay on the pavement to examine the undercarriage.

"What are they looking for? They're speaking so quickly I can only pick out a word or two."

"They keep saying *embrayage*, whatever that is. My French doesn't extend to automotive vocabulary. Maybe it's the clutch. Remember when Bauer arrived? He said there was something wrong with it."

Joe walked over to the bookcase, scanned the shelves, and chose a book. He raised his brows at her, walked back to the window, and handed her a French-English dictionary. "*Voilà.* Perhaps you can guess at the spelling?"

"*Em, embray, embrayage*," she murmured as she flipped through the pages. "Aha! *Embrayage* means clutch."

"Good. Can you understand what else they're saying about the car?"

"I'm not certain, but it sounds like there's something wrong with it."

They watched through the window as the mechanic rose from the pavement and dusted off his coveralls. He attached the car to the truck with chains and tested the connection, nodding to the two young police officers who had been watching. The tow truck and car eased away from the curb.

Sophie leaned out of the window. "*Bon jour!*" she called and continued in French. He recognized *embrayage* for clutch and *voiture* for car, so he assumed she was asking if there was something wrong with the clutch. "Do you know what is wrong with the car? Did someone tamper with the clutch?"

Joe watched the two young officers, mentally betting what their reactions would be to an attractive woman talking to them about anything, much less about something automotive. He mentally collected his winnings when they didn't think twice about answering her questions.

Sophie pulled her head back into the room. "They say it's just an old car that hasn't been well-cared for. It doesn't look like someone did anything to it."

"So Bauer was telling the truth when he said something went wrong with the car."

"I wonder if he'll tell the truth about anything else," she replied.

He was about to apologize to Sophie for being so curt before they went to the police station, but the youngster—he couldn't think of him in any other way after he'd fallen under Sophie's thrall at her friendly *bon jour*—knocked and opened the library doors wide. "Monsieur? It is time to depart."

Joe pulled on his suit jacket. "Hopefully I'll know soon," he said.

Sophie grabbed her jacket too. "I'm coming with you."

He glanced at the young copper and back to her. "I don't think you're invited."

"Nonsense," Sophie declared. "We're in this together, remember?"

Joe knew there was only one way to settle this without an argument. "We'll let the chief decide, shall we?"

FIFTY-NINE

LET US LEARN WHAT WE WILL LEARN

Joe eyed the street signs when the police car stopped for a group of tourists crossing the street. Something wasn't right. He didn't recognize this intersection. "This isn't the way to the police station."

"No, inspector." The driver caught his eye in the rear-view mirror. "We are going to the hospital. Monsieur le Chef said he was certain you would want to see the body."

Sophie gave him a quick look of approval at this turn of events. "The chief is amazingly broad-minded."

"He is, madame," the driver said. "Very different from the chief before him."

The chief was waiting outside when the police car pulled up in front of the hospital. He walked down the steps and opened the door for Sophie.

"Madame Parker, this is a surprise," the chief said as he offered his hand to assist her.

"Yes, I imagine it is," Sophie replied. "I realize you probably won't let me any further than the hospital reception."

"Alas, this is true, madame. Despite you being a nurse during the war, our coroner forbids civilians who are not relations in his domain."

He turned to Joe. "However, he will not object to a police officer. Inspector, am I correct you would like to see the body?"

"I make a practice of it at home. Our coroner is very thorough, just as I'm sure yours is. But I often learn more from seeing for myself than simply reading the report."

"That is what I thought you would say," the chief replied. "And I am the same. I want to see things for myself."

The chief ushered them into the hospital, directed Sophie to a chair to wait, and led Joe to a remote part of the hospital and into a cool, tiled room. "Let us learn what we will learn, Inspector."

The familiar, cloying smells of formaldehyde with an undertone of decay assaulted Joe's nostrils. How many times in his long career had he entered a morgue, pulled back a sheet, and examined a body—either to confirm what he already knew or to glean clues to what he didn't know? Too many to count, but he always learned something. This time would probably be no different.

The coroner, an older man with salt-and-pepper hair, looked up from the covered body on the table and greeted his colleague. The chief introduced him to the coroner, who then pulled the sheet back to the boy's shoulders.

White-blond hair matted the boy's skull. A deep, ragged gash marred his left temple. Rigor mortis had not yet dissipated, but Joe knew if he could lift the boy's eyelids the light blue irises that had flashed in desperation while they fought on the bridge would now stare at nothing. The same reaction he had every time he examined a young body rose in his mind: what a waste of a life.

He gazed at the boy for several moments. "Would you move the sheet so we can see his legs and torso?" The coroner did as he asked. The boy was thin and underfed, his ribs visible under pale skin. Compared to Chris and Nick, who were well cared for, this boy, whose beard had barely come in, looked more like a child. When was the last time the boy had smiled or been happy? What demons had he been chasing that made him attack an old man with a trench knife?

Joe only half-heard the chief asking questions while he examined the faint bruising his fingers had left when he grasped the boy's neck. Broader, darker bruises from the bridge railing marked his right forearm.

The fall onto the jagged rocks lining the riverbank had battered the boy's torso. Half-healed cuts and yellowed bruises speckled his shins. His left kneecap was heavily bruised, swollen, and scraped. The boy must have fallen hard, at some point. Joe pointed at the boy's knee. "Do you have any idea when this could have happened?"

"Sometime within the past few days," the coroner said.

"He could have fallen during our first hike," Joe said to the chief. "That could explain why the edelweiss fell to the spot where we were eating our lunch."

"Was there any water in his lungs?"

"No, Monsieur le Chef," the coroner said. "He did not drown in the river."

The chief pulled the sheet back up to the boy's chest. "Did you find any papers or identification?"

The coroner shook his head. "No identification. Only a map of the valley showing all the major trails and a notebook which was soaked through."

"These are his clothes and shoes?" the chief asked, pointing to a table a few feet away. When the coroner nodded, he examined the clothes the boy was wearing when he fell into the river. "There are no labels and nothing in any of the pockets." He frowned and handed the clothes to Joe, who did another check.

"No laundry labels either," he said. "What about his boots?"

The chief had already loosened the laces and was examining the boots under the lamp on the coroner's desk. "The insoles are so worn I can't see the maker. All I can read is the size stamped into the leather."

They went back to the boy's body. "How old do you think he was?" Joe asked the coroner.

The coroner glanced at his notes. "Possibly as young as seventeen."

The chief turned to the coroner. "Would you tell us your conclusions?"

"The wounds on his chest would have occurred when he fell on the rocks," he began. "There is not enough bruising on his neck to do any damage. The bruises on his right forearm and wrist are consistent with being hit against the bridge railing."

The coroner covered the boy's body. "The cause of death was blood loss from the wound to the head."

Unlike the other young German in the Villers-Bret house all those years ago, Joe hadn't caused this boy's death. Nevertheless, he had played a part and been a witness to it. He silently asked for the boy to find peace in death that he hadn't found in life. Then he came back to the present, lifting his head and pulling in a big breath. His shoulders snapped to their usual square. "Now we need to know who this boy was and why he and Erich Bauer were fighting on the bridge," he said.

SIXTY

THE INTERROGATION

Joe followed the chief out to the hospital lobby. The woman at the reception desk called to the chief. "Monsieur le Chef?"

Sophie rushed up to him from the opposite end of the lobby. "Joe? What was the cause of death?"

"Blood loss resulting from a blow to his head when he fell on the rocks," he said. He shoved his hands in his pockets. "Christ, Sophie, he was only seventeen or so and skinny as a rake."

When the chief returned to them, he explained. "The station telephoned while we were examining the body. Monsieur Bauer has been released from hospital and is now at the police station. He has requested that you and Madame Parker are also present when I interview him."

"That's very unusual," Joe said. "Guests aren't normally allowed at interviews."

"No, they are not," the chief said, "but this is an unusual situation. As you know, I spoke with Mister Bauer while you were at your hotel. I do not believe he is a spy, and I am satisfied he did not intend to harm you or your wife or the boy, but I do not think we know the whole story yet. What do you think, Inspector Parker? Will you work with me to interview him?"

"I would be happy to," Joe said.

"And you, Madame Parker, am I correct that you would like to attend as well?"

Sophie flashed him an appreciative glance. "Monsieur le Chef," she began, "I've been thinking. Joe and I know Mister Bauer in different circumstances than you. I believe I have a bit of rapport with him, and his actions on the bridge probably saved me from injury. What would you think if I start by asking him how his head feels? It could be a way to get him to lower his guard before you and Joe question him."

Joe turned to his colleague. "That approach might work. Or Bauer could decide you're foolish for letting her speak."

The chief regarded Sophie. "What Bauer thinks of me is not important. I am more interested in learning what happened and why. Madame, if you are willing, I welcome your help. However, if at any point I believe you should not be present I will ask you to leave the room. Are we agreed?"

∾

Erich Bauer sat with his back to the door of the interview room. Sophie walked around the table and sat across from him. Bauer rose from his chair and executed his usual little half bow. The chief sat beside Sophie.

Joe remained standing, taking up a position where he could see everyone's faces, even if only in profile.

Sophie cleared her throat and leaned forward. "Mister Bauer, you've suffered a terrible shock and injury. Are you feeling all right? Were you injured except for the bump on your head? Is there anything you need? A glass of water, perhaps? A headache powder?"

"You are still taking care of patients, madame," Bauer said, his voice less tremulous than usual, but he looked tired and drawn, nothing like the cheerful old man Sophie and he met only a few days ago. He touched the large bandage on his head and winced. "My head is still sore, but there is nothing I need.

"Thank you for agreeing to speak to me like this," Bauer continued. "Madame, you and Monsieur Parker have been involved from the start and I would like you to hear my story too." He sat straighter in his chair. "I have a solemn task to perform, and I cannot fulfill it from a police interview room in Chamonix."

Joe looked over at the chief. Did he want to take over now after Bauer's surprising statement? No. The chief gestured for Sophie to continue, and she leaned forward and regarded the man sitting across from her. "What task is that Mister Bauer?" she asked.

"It is complicated. But I must inform my sister of the death of her son, the boy who died yesterday," he answered, and returned her gaze.

The chief shifted in his chair. Joe moved around the table so he could watch Bauer's face. His nephew? This no longer sounded like possible spy craft, but a family drama gone terribly wrong.

The chief finally spoke. "Then it is time to tell us why you and the boy were here in Chamonix."

SIXTY-ONE

FATHERLESS BOY

"Yes," Bauer replied. "It is time." He paused as if to gather his thoughts. "I must go back a little further than the recent past, so you will understand. I am forty-seven years old. In April 1918, I was badly wounded, and was sent to Switzerland to recover. I chose not to return to the war afterward. I have lived in Switzerland ever since."

Wounded in 1918? Joe knew that meant Bauer was....

"I am German," Bauer said. "I fought in the Dolomites, at Verdun, and in Romania. I wish it had not been so. But the *Alpenkorps* fought in many places."

"*Alpenkorps*!" Sophie exclaimed. "So, the edelweiss insignia is yours?"

"It is. The knife is mine also."

The chief shifted in his chair again and glared at Bauer.

"Monsieur le Chef, I did not bring the knife or the edelweiss to Chamonix, I promise you. My nephew brought them here. He took them from a trunk of my things in his mother's home. His mother is my sister." Bauer sighed. "I have not seen her in over twenty years. I never saw her son, Rolf, my nephew, until a few days ago."

"Why have you not seen her?" the chief asked.

Bauer's shoulders sagged. "I cannot go back to Germany. My countrymen would not receive me well."

Joe saw Sophie raise her eyebrows. The chief shifted in his chair beside her. They had to be thinking the same thing he was.

"Mister Bauer, did you desert?" Joe asked.

Bauer bowed his head and closed his eyes. "Yes," he whispered.

The chief gave him a nod, which Joe interpreted as permission to continue. "How did you know we found the edelweiss and the knife?"

"I guessed. I listened to your conversations. The first time I saw my edelweiss on your table at the hotel, I worried you might be in danger." The shock must have been plain on Joe's face, because Bauer hastened to explain. "I feared my nephew would do something foolish or harm you if he knew you had it. When my sister wrote to me, she told me the boy was enthralled with Hitler and everything about the Reich.

"But the Hitler Youth organization dismissed him. He missed too many meetings because he was hiking in the mountains. She told me he was determined to prove his worth to the Nazis. He came to Chamonix to scout. To learn about the mountains here. To gain some knowledge the Nazis would be grateful to have. It is all in his notebook. He planned to go back home, find someone to give his findings to, and try to regain his place in the Hitler Youth."

Bauer paused, and the chief gestured for him to continue.

"The boy never knew his father, and he grew up thinking I had died for the glory of Germany. He wanted to be *Alpenkorps* like I was. Why, I do not know. Perhaps my sister kept the photograph of me in uniform. Perhaps he made up stories to tell the other boys.

"He found the trunk with my things and left without telling

my sister anything except he was going to go exploring in Chamonix. My sister wrote all of this to me. She included a photograph of the boy so I would recognize him."

Bauer had admitted to desertion, but some details still weren't clear to Joe. "Why didn't you go back to Germany? Why did your sister have your knife and insignia?"

"My wife and child died before the end of the war," Bauer said. "They were ill and starving. Because of the British blockade of Germany, there was no food, no medicine in Germany."

Silence descended on the stuffy little interview room. Joe's breath hitched. Losing Annie had been devastating. He couldn't imagine losing Sam, too.

"I'm so sorry," Sophie said.

Bauer, head bowed, stared at his hands on the table. "I thought I had nothing left to live for when I learned they were dead." His voice thickened with emotion. "I became despondent. I jumped off the train to escape returning to the front. Only I did not roll down a mountain and die in the fall as I hoped I would." He shook his head. "I broke my shoulder and my ankle. They have troubled me ever since.

"I sent my things and a letter to my sister to tell her I could not return to Germany. I told her she must say I was dead if anyone ever asked." Bauer continued. "But I devised a way for her to contact me if she ever needed to. Her recent letter was the first one I received in many years. She asked me to come to Chamonix to look for her son."

"When was the first time you saw your nephew?" the chief asked.

"On the train to the Mer de Glace glacier. Monsieur and Madame Parker and all their friends were on the same train. I followed my nephew on a trail, and I startled him. He ran off. I grabbed his rucksack, but it rolled down to the trail below."

"So, you knew we had the knife too," Joe said.

"Yes," Bauer said. "And I was happy you did. I hoped you would keep it hidden or safe or even give it to the police. Anything to keep it from the boy. I saw him several times loitering around the hotel. But during our argument on the night of the thunderstorm, I told him I did not have the knife. He would not believe me. He grabbed his rucksack from me and ran away.

"I saw him creeping out of the hotel yesterday. He must have stolen the edelweiss and the knife then. Today I followed him to the bridge. When I found him by the statue, I approached him. I told him my true identity, and that I had not died in the war."

"Is that when you struggled with him on the bridge?"

Bauer's fist landed on the table with a thud, surprising them all. "I tried to convince him to stop what he was doing and come to Switzerland with me. He would not listen. He held up the edelweiss and shouted that I had disgraced it. He had my knife and tried to stab me with it. He did not know how to fight, but I was so shocked I did not have my wits about me. You know what happened next."

Yes, Joe thought, he knew what happened next. It was the whys that riveted him. Bauer had revealed so many surprises, moving back and forth between his story of loss and desertion and the story of a fatherless boy who needed to prove himself worthy of what? Serving his country? Avenging his country's defeat? Filling the empty places in his life? There was such a fine line between patriotism and fanaticism. And what about Bauer? What were the penalties for desertion twenty years afterward? Life imprisonment? Execution? Now that they knew his secret, Bauer must wonder if he and the chief were feeling vengeful toward someone who once was their enemy.

Sophie's voice filtered through his swirling thoughts. "Where is the edelweiss now, Mister Bauer?"

"It is at the bottom of the Arve River, madame."

SIXTY-TWO
THE BLOND BOY'S NOTEBOOK

The chief rose from his chair. "Excuse us for a moment, Monsieur Bauer." He gestured for Joe and Sophie to follow, and the three of them walked down the corridor to his office.

"*Mon Dieu,* what a story! What is your opinion, inspector? Is Bauer telling the truth?"

What was his opinion? Understanding and compassion? Or something else? Joe didn't hate Bauer because he was a former enemy or wish him ill. He just wanted to put all of this behind him and leave Chamonix. The best way to achieve that goal was through solid police techniques. There were only a few details left to verify Bauer's story.

"I'm inclined to believe him. He showed no obvious signs of lying. Do you suspect him of being more than a German who deserted a few months before the end of the war?"

"I don't." The chief blew out a breath. "Of course I have contacted the authorities in Bern to confirm his residency."

"Will you hold him here at the station until you get answers?"

"Yes, even though without charge I should release him. Madame? What is your opinion?"

Sophie must have been thinking rather than listening during

their exchange because her response wasn't an answer to the chief's question. "What about the boy's notebook, Monsieur le Chef? Has someone translated it yet?"

The chief shook his head. "No, madame. No one on my staff reads or speaks German. I will have to go through official channels and send it to the prefecture at Annecy. That will take several days. I would prefer not to have rumors about possible German spies in Chamonix on top of the summer thief problems we already have. I love my town but depending on tourists can make life difficult."

"What about unofficial channels?" she asked. "Could you ask Bauer to translate it? We could sit with him while he reads it aloud. I could even act as scribe if you prefer to keep this as quiet as possible."

Joe laughed for what felt like the first time in days. "Are you implying that police officers are gossips?"

"Of course not, darling. I'm just trying to find a discreet way to resolve this case quickly." She turned to the chief. "If one of your men can confirm Bauer lives in Bern…."

The chief nodded. "We will have a better idea of whether Bauer is telling the truth about himself and the boy."

"And we may wrap this up before the day is over," Joe said. The sooner they could put this behind them, the better.

Erich Bauer gazed at the damp, standard-issue school notebook the chief placed on the table. The pages rippled between cardboard covers swollen from being wet.

"Whenever you are ready," the chief said. "Read each entry and translate it for us aloud. Madame Parker has offered to write everything you say."

Bauer nodded once, opened the cover, and began reading.

14 July 1939

I would rather climb and hike in the hills than pretend to be a soldier. I was reprimanded, privately at first, then publicly when it happened again. The leader stripped me of my badges and said lazy vermin like me couldn't possibly do any job the Fatherland required. He said I was an imbecile, weak, worthless.

What does he know? On my birthday, when I am 18, I will enlist. I will be a real mountain soldier like father and Uncle Erich. Until then, I will prepare myself.

"Am I reading too fast, madame?"

"No, you're doing fine," she said.

Bauer shook his head. "The *Alpenkorps* would never accept him after being dismissed from the Hitler Youth."

16 July 1939

I spent several days thinking and wondering what I could do that would make a difference. I feel small and insignificant compared to such brave men who came before me. It is a tragedy Germany was not victorious. Surely, there is something I can do to prove my worth and my loyalty to the Führer. I studied maps and read whatever I could find that described events and engagements and battles in the war. I devoured the current news. I began carrying a pencil and a little notebook and updated it whenever I read something of interest or had an idea that might be useful. I had never been much of a reader. Now I became one.

Then today I made a grand discovery. I found a trunk full of

Uncle's things hidden under the rafters. I lifted out one item after another. A photograph of a young woman and a baby. A long-bladed knife. His uniform jacket with a silver edelweiss pinned to the collar.

As I gazed at these things, a fierce sense of pride filled my heart. Father's lungs were so damaged by gas that he died when I was still a child. Uncle died of wounds in Switzerland. I am the only man left in the family. I must find a way to avenge them.

"*Mein Gott*," Bauer said. "Poor little man."

19 July 1939

The idea came today while I was hiking on the highest trail above the village. I went back up to the attic and opened Uncle's trunk. I gazed at the silver edelweiss and the fierce pride filled my heart again. Father and Uncle were Alpenkorps. One day I will wear a uniform like this one.

I returned everything except Uncle's knife and edelweiss to its proper place and packed my things. Mother keeps the house-keeping money in a tin in the kitchen. I took some of it and wrote her a note to tell her where I was going. Perhaps I should have tried to explain why I had to come here, but she would not have understood. Everyone will be proud of me when I come back home so she will not be angry about the money.

I put the knife in my rucksack and the edelweiss in my pocket. It will be my good luck charm.

"My sister wrote to me the next day," Bauer explained.

24 July 1939

I lifted my rucksack onto my shoulders and stepped off the train. I pressed through the crowds of arriving and departing passengers. When I reached the station exit, I looked around for the signpost marked Chamonix-Mont Blanc.

"The boy arrived in Chamonix the day after we did," Joe said. "And you arrived the next day."

SIXTY-THREE

THINGS HE CANNOT TELL

Joe was silent during the drive back to the hotel. The interview with Bauer, all of his secrets laid bare, had been so emotionally charged that he was completely wrung out. At least Bauer had an empathetic audience. Once the man had begun telling his tale, and the police chief knew he wasn't facing a nest of German spies in Chamonix, he let Bauer speak freely, instead of demanding answers.

Monique eyed Sophie and Joe expectantly as they got out of the police car. "Well? What has happened?"

"Sophie and I are free to leave Chamonix. The chief asked us to wait until he receives one last bit of information before we say anything. He hopes to know something by morning."

Their ride in the lift to their room was silent, too. Once inside their room, they quickly shed their jackets. Sophie tossed her purse on the bed, then kicked off her shoes and removed her stockings, as if peeling the layers of the day away. He followed suit, removing his waistcoat and tie. Cufflinks came next, and he rolled up his sleeves.

He poured two whiskeys, handed one to Sophie, then went outside on the balcony.

On the terrace below, a full complement of newcomers was experiencing the hotel's *apértif* hour. Monique flitted from guest to guest. Glasses and bottles clinked on the drinks cart as Nick wheeled it across the paving stones. Chris maneuvered his way around the little iron tables with a tray of *amuses bouches*. Georges and Vanni pored over their newspaper. Snatches of laughter and conversations in English and French drifted upwards.

Everything was completely, utterly, normal. Life on the terrace continued as if nothing had happened, as if a boy hadn't died, as if Bauer's final anguished words had never been spoken. *The boy needed someone to take the place of his father and all he found was Hitler.* He had bowed his head and lifted a hand to wipe his eyes. *I was a coward. I should have gone back to Germany. I should never have stayed away from him.*

That poor bastard. Badly wounded, losing his wife and child, feeling so devastated that he deserted and never returned home, and then having to keep everything secret until the death of his nephew compelled him to tell his truths.

Joe knew how much energy it took to keep secrets. He didn't have the energy anymore. He had to tell Sophie what had happened that night in Villers-Bretonneux. He had no idea how their story would unfold afterward, but she deserved to know the truth.

Sophie thought Joe looked exhausted. Aside from answering Monique's question, he hadn't said a word since they left the police station. Even though the afternoon had ended with Bauer sobbing over his nephew's notebook, she thought the German looked unburdened after his confessions in the interview room. She hoped they could go forward with that same spirit. If he would tell her what he had been keeping hidden for so long, then perhaps they could leave that burden behind them.

She had tried everything she could think of to give Joe time to tell her about what had caused his nightmares: distracting him with silly attempts at investigating the Chamonix summer thief, diverting conversations away from the war, engaging him in the Bauer-blond boy puzzle. None of her efforts had borne fruit.

Picking up the drink Joe had poured for her, she followed him to the balcony. She had to try one last time, but she had no idea what to do, and hoped against hope that simply being near to him might do the trick.

Across the valley, a snow-capped Mont Blanc glittered against a deeply blue sky. Joe stared at the mountain as if mesmerized.

He was still staring at Mont Blanc when he finally spoke.

"My dream," he began. "The dreams I've had…they're about Villers-Bret."

She held her glass with both hands to keep it steady.

Joe emptied his glass in one long swallow. "It's one of those things that happens and you wish to God it never had." He stared out across the valley and was silent.

Don't hover. Don't make eye contact. Just be matter of fact. "So, you bury it and try desperately to never think of it again?"

He nodded but said nothing.

"I've always thought…." Her voice hitched. She swallowed and began again. "I've always thought wondering and worrying was worse than the knowing or the telling. I keep thinking about the first argument we had. You didn't want to tell me about the child who was killed in that gang brawl, and you clammed up for days. I told you if your solution to problems was to go silent and moody that I couldn't live with that."

Joe turned to her, his brows drawn in concern.

"It's obvious something happened that affected you badly, and it's still affecting you. Do you remember the Lawson poem? *We fight it down, and we live it down, or we bear it bravely well…."*

She pressed her head against his shoulder. "You're the best man I've ever known. All I want is for you to tell me what's bothering you. I'll understand if you can't tell me all the details, but please, please, don't shut me out anymore. Please tell me why you woke up shouting. Please trust me enough to tell me what happened."

SIXTY-FOUR

THE BEST MEN DIE OF A BROKEN HEART

...but the best men die of a broken heart for the things they cannot tell. Joe had always thought he understood the poem, but until this moment, he hadn't realized how perfectly it described him.

He nodded, his heart already breaking at the thought he was about to lose the love and respect of the woman he loved.

Sophie blinked, and a tear splashed on her cheek. "The first nightmare you had. Was it the same one you had last night?"

"No. The first one was about the battle. Christ. It was a slaughter, more than a battle. Only we were the ones doing the slaughtering. Last night was about clearing the town afterward."

He reached out to stroke the tear from her cheek but stopped short. He couldn't bring himself to touch her. How could she forgive the fact that he'd killed a mere boy with his bare hands? "I'll understand if you can't forgive me."

"Tell me. Please."

He couldn't look at her while he spoke—he barely felt brave enough to tell her what he'd done, much less anticipate her reacting in horrified disgust while he described the brutal, berserker rage of the battle. The swish of machine gun bullets flying over his head. The slide of his bayonet slicing through wool and flesh. The solid thunk of his rifle butt hitting a skull in just the right place. The grenades in the house afterward. The German pulling the knife from Stanley's belly and lunging at him. Fighting frantically for the knife. Losing control and not caring. Squeezing his hands around the soldier's neck and forcing the life from his body.

"Joe." Sophie moved to face him. "It's all ri—"

He took a step back. She was too calm. She still didn't understand what he had done. "No," he countered, shaking his head in short, sharp bursts. "It isn't all right. It's one thing to kill your enemy in battle. It's quick and impersonal when you're shooting someone fifty yards away or you're shoving your bayonet into their guts before they can shove their blade into you. It's another thing entirely to force the life from someone with your hands. Do you have any idea how hard it is? Or how long it takes? Your hands are the most primitive weapon you have. Don't you see? Whatever veneer of civilization you were clinging to disappears at that moment. You can never get it back. Ever."

He stepped into the room, dropped to the foot of the bed, and waited for Sophie to realize the man she'd married didn't deserve her love, that he wasn't the good man she thought he was, that they were finished.

For several moments, Sophie was silent. Then, to his utter amazement, all she said was, "What happened afterward?"

He huffed and ran a hand through his hair, thinking back. "I was summoned to the major's office the next morning. He wanted to know what had happened and how many men I'd lost that night. I said all thirty in my command had survived the battle. Of the six men I took into town, only Stanley didn't make it. I told him about the house and the grenade. Stanley. The German.

"I told him I couldn't justify my actions, but he stopped me. He said our objective had been to recapture the town from the Germans. He looked me straight in the eye when he said that, as if he was telling me it didn't matter *how* we'd done any of it, just that we'd done what had to be done.

"Then he informed me I'd been promoted to acting captain, effective immediately. He said we didn't have time for anything more official, and a field promotion would have to do.

"I really wasn't surprised. They'd promoted me after every damned battle I fought in. Why should this one be any different?

"I started to say I didn't deserve a promotion, that I'd just done my job, but he cut me off. He said he'd been told I was always cool under fire, and he needed officers like that. There was nothing I could do, short of being insubordinate. I saluted and turned to leave but he called me back and ordered me to get some sleep before I wrote to Stanley's family." His shoulders slumped even further. "I didn't sleep at all that night."

Sophie refilled their glasses. He drained his and set it on the floor. "I was never seriously wounded. I didn't catch whatever disease was making its way through the ranks. I survived when so many other men I served with lost their lives. I have no idea why I was lucky."

He could trust Sophie not to say something inane like he was meant for great things or something equally ridiculous. The gunshot wounds he'd suffered during the drug raid in Sydney had been serious, but not life threatening. He had been lucky during the war and lucky in his profession, too.

"What I experienced was nothing compared to most. I wasn't sucked into the mud at Passchendaele. I wasn't gassed at Pozières. I didn't...I didn't have any of my limbs blown off. I have all of my faculties. What right did I have...," his voice broke, but he soldiered on, his hands curling into fists at his sides. "What right do I still have to that kind of luck?"

He flexed his fingers, still horrified by his actions in that dark house.

"I lost control. I killed a man with my bare hands. Christ, he wasn't even a man. When we pulled him out of the house, we saw he was just a boy. He was big and strong, but he couldn't have been any older than the boy on the bridge. I should have stopped, but I didn't. I didn't want to stop. I wanted to kill him more than I'd ever wanted anything."

~

Sophie took a moment to consider the best way to respond to Joe's confession.

"Thank you for telling me," she said, staying calm and hoping to counterbalance his raw emotional state. "I know you like to push past distractions and concentrate on the task at hand, but you're not the sort of man who can just brush things aside and forget about them. You care about doing the right thing too much to do that."

She ran her hands down Joe's arms. He was clenching his fists, so she held on to his wrists. "Are you worried you're capable of doing the same thing again?"

Joe's chin dropped to his chest. He let out a long, shuddering sigh. "I did something that night I never dreamed I could do. When it looked like the boy was going to attack you, I had to force myself not to do it again."

She squeezed his wrists gently. Joe solved puzzles every day in his work, but he hadn't been able to solve this one by himself. She had to help him see how all the pieces fit together. "A German soldier killed Stanley and then attacked you. You fought for your life. Your actions may have saved some of your men. No one would have reacted differently."

He swiped his eyes with the backs of his hands. "I've taught myself how to cope with it, but what happened in that house is a part of me that won't just go away. I should have told you long ago. You should have had the chance to change your mind before we got married. I know you can't forgive me for not telling you."

Oh my God. That's the second time he's said I can't forgive him. We've both been terrified this would break us. She took a deep breath. "I knew. Not about this, specifically, but I'm not naïve, Joe. I was always aware that the men I nursed might have done something horrific when they were desperately trying to stay alive. It stands to reason that something similar happened to you."

Joe's fists were still clenched, but she prized them open enough to lace her fingers with his, tethering him to her. "What happened is a part of you, but it doesn't define you. You could have taken that experience as an excuse to be a rotten father or abuse your position as an officer of the law. You didn't do any of those things. You raised a fine son. You helped raise another man's son. Your police officers look up to you because you treat them and the people you serve with respect."

Joe crumpled and put his head in his hands, shattered and shaking. She knelt beside him, pulling his head to her shoulder, running her hands through his hair and over his battered back until his sobs ceased.

She pressed a kiss to his temple. "Darling, there's nothing for me to forgive. Yes, a terrible thing happened. I understand why you never wanted anyone to know. Not Annie, not me, not anyone else. I understand why you buried it. But you don't have to be alone in this," she whispered, her lips still close. "We have to keep going forward. Together."

SIXTY-FIVE

LOCAL EXPERTS

The next morning, Joe stood before their friends and explained how the case had been resolved. As he spoke, everyone on the terrace listened to the tale in open-mouthed silence.

Georges was the first to respond. He frowned and grumbled, "Why is Bauer not in jail?"

"He didn't commit a crime. At least, not in Chamonix."

"But he is German," Vanni protested. "He is *Alpenkorps*."

"He *was Alpenkorps*. Bauer deserted. The chief contacted the city officials in Bern, and they confirmed Bauer has been living there and working as an orderly in a clinic for the last twenty years. He escorted Bauer to the Swiss border instead of turning him over to the German authorities. They would probably court-martial him and then he'd be executed. What good would that do?"

Vanni pursed his lips and looked away, clearly unsatisfied with the arrangement.

"What of the boy?" Monique asked. "And his poor mother? It is such a waste of a young life."

"They will send his body back to his mother," Joe said. "The police chief will send a note of condolence for her son's accident."

"Mr. Bauer said he hoped his sister would find some peace knowing her son died of an accident before he had the chance to do anyone any harm," Sophie added. "She has worried for a long time about her son's stability. Apparently, he took the propaganda of the Nazis very much to heart."

Joe picked up the story. "The chief asked Bauer to translate the boy's journal, and Sophie transcribed as he read. Rolf—the boy—seemed to be a misguided loner. He was expelled from the Hitler Youth, so he hatched a plan to restore his honor. When they were fighting on the bridge, he told Bauer the Germans should invade France here, in the French Alps, since they hadn't done so in the first war. He was here to scout and gather information. He planned to present it all to someone in authority when he returned to Germany."

Georges frowned again. "What is this information the boy was going to give to the Nazis?"

Joe shrugged. "The only things the police found in the boy's clothes were the notebook and a map showing the major trails in the area. It explains why we kept seeing him on trails." He glanced at Georges, who looked ready to say something. "It's only the map from the Tourist Information office."

"Then, monsieur, how are we supposed to know…?" Georges leaned back in his chair, defeated. "…anything? Are we in danger because of this boy's actions?"

"The chief doesn't think so. The boy was acting on his own. He may have left caches for himself on some of the trails. It may even explain some thefts of hiking gear."

He pulled a map from his jacket pocket and unfolded it on the table. "The police have the original, but they copied the locations to this new one. Since the chief doesn't have enough men to search all the trails, he hopes to enlist the help of local experts to search for any items the boy might have hidden."

Joe slid the map across the table so the four men could see it. His part in this case was over. Sophie and he could leave this place, and, if he was lucky, he could leave his nightmares behind too.

While Joe and the local experts poured over the map, Sophie motioned Monique aside. She handed the French woman an envelope. "Mr. Bauer asked me to give this to you to pay for his room and meals since he couldn't give it to you himself."

"Thank you, madame." Monique blinked back the tears that brimmed. "My heart breaks for the boy's mother."

She hugged Monique. "I'm so glad we had the chance to meet you and Georges."

"Perhaps we will meet again someday," Monique sniffed. "I hope we do. Will you write and tell me about your travels back to Australia?"

"I will. And will you write to tell me about what's happening here?"

She turned to Hélène and Marianne and the three women kissed cheeks. "You have our contact information in Marseille. Marianne, just let us know if you change your mind. Otherwise, we'll see you there."

She walked over to Joe, who was still looking at the map, and laid a gentle hand on his back to get his attention. "Darling, it's time to say our goodbyes. If we leave now, we'll arrive in Lyon by lunchtime."

Will rose and shook Joe's hand. Then he gathered her into a farewell hug. "Here I thought I was inviting you to Chamonix to relax, but you end up investigating something that was going on right under our noses. Well done."

"Thank you, Will." She smiled up to him. "It was definitely an adventure."

"You folks realize you must let me write a story about this," Edmund said as he took his turn shaking Joe's hand and hugging Sophie goodbye. "Writing about the sex appeal between you two is a little outside my usual range, but—"

"The sex…what?" she sputtered. Will let out a hoot of laughter at her reaction that had Monique forgetting her tears and Joe's ears turning pink.

"Please madame," Monique scoffed, "there is a constant frisson between you and your husband, even when you are searching a hotel room for clues."

"But it has everything else," Edmund persisted, undeterred. "Intrigue, war, peace, an unexpected death, scenery—"

"And monsieur, it is obvious that you adore your wife," Monique continued. "We do not have to be detectives to see it."

SIXTY-SIX

ROMAN RUINS

As Joe steered the car away from the Chamonix valley, the bands of shame and self-loathing that had been wrapped around his psyche began to shatter and fall away. The shards and splinters would litter the roadside, he mused, the debris growing smaller and smaller in the rearview mirror.

As he drove, the mountains diminished to hills and then to rolling plains. The rushing river by the side of the road slowed to a meandering stream. A final bend in the road and the wide expanse of central France lay ahead of them.

He breathed deeply and glanced at Sophie. She was trailing one hand out her window, catching the rushing air in her palm and twisting her wrist to release it. Her other hand lay loose on her lap. He reached for it and laced his fingers with hers. Sophie smiled as he lifted her hand to his lips and pressed a kiss on her knuckles.

"How long until we reach Lyon?" he asked.

Her brows rose. Her dark eyes sparkled. "Three hours if you keep driving ten miles below the speed limit."

"Let's see if we can make it two-and-a-half." He disentangled his fingers from hers, grasped the steering wheel in both hands, and pressed down on the accelerator.

Fertile fields in every shade of green flew by. Cows and sheep grazed contentedly. Long, ordered rows of vines bordered many of the fields, the leaves sheltering clusters of miniature grapes that would swell and sweeten over the next months until the skins could barely contain the riches within.

A farmer in his cart began to cross the road ahead of them. The horse ambled.

Joe slowed to a stop. The farmer fixed him with a baleful eye, daring him to challenge his right to progress at a leisurely pace.

Having wished his burdens good riddance many miles ago, he felt no compunction to hurry the old man.

Sophie leaned her head out of her window and waved. *"Bon jour, monsieur!"*

The farmer's expression softened. He flicked the end of his cigarette to the ground and lifted his battered straw hat. "*Bon jour, 'dame, 'sieur,*" he called back. He clicked his tongue, but the horse had no intention of hurrying. The farmer shrugged an apology.

"*Ça ne fait rien,*" Sophie called.

Ça ne fait rien, Joe thought. It doesn't matter. I fought in this country for the right of all old men to amble across the road. Waiting for this old man is nothing in the scheme of things.

When the cart was off the road, he began again, edging the speedometer up to where it had been before, the warm wind whipping into the car.

Sophie's curls tumbled around her cheeks, but she only smiled at him, her arm stretched along the back of the seat and her hand resting on his shoulder until they arrived at the outskirts of Lyon.

She had the map and navigated him into town, over the Rhône River, past buildings constructed in 19th-century neoclassical style with shops and cafés at street level and five or six stories of apartments above. They passed the enormous square of Place Bellecour and turned into the surrounding warren of streets to their hotel.

After a quick check-in, they decided not to take the small lift but to walk up the spiraling stone staircase to their room where tall windows overlooked the baroque Théâtre des Célestins and a little tree-lined square. After a quick wash up, they walked back down the stairs, fitting their feet into the depressions worn by thousands of feet before theirs, and out into blindingly bright noonday sun.

～

They exited the funicular high above the city and walked to the lookout point at Fourvière Hill. Sophie opened their guidebook to the Lyon chapter.

"You will see Old Lyon below you," she read, "then the Saône River, then Presque'île, and then the Rhône River. On a clear day, you can see the French Alps and snowcapped Mont Blanc, the highest peak in Europe, on the horizon."

The horizon was hazy, hiding the mountains in the distance. Joe turned from it and gazed instead at the amphitheater hewn into the side of the hill by the Romans.

They spent the afternoon talking and walking hand-in-hand in the amphitheater. Only squawking birds and a few fellow tourists interrupted their conversation.

Joe helped Sophie find a smooth spot to sit. "I wonder if it's easier for the people who live there."

She bumped his shoulder with hers. "Who live where, darling?"

"In the towns and villages where we fought." He looked around them, taking a moment to order his thoughts. "Take Villers-Bret, for example. If you gave the place a casual glance, you'd never know what happened there. The people who live there picked up the pieces and rebuilt their homes and their lives. They could see the progress they made. When I left, everything was still in ruins. That's all I knew of it. Only the worst and none of the best."

"Whereas you returned home, and nothing had changed there? No piles of unexploded ordnance by the side of the roads, or trenches that needed to be filled in?"

"Or ghosts peering around corners. The people who stayed at home had no idea what it was like."

"Couldn't you talk about it at the RSL club on Anzac Day?"

"There's as much drinking and playing two-up as there is talking. I didn't know anyone well enough to talk to them. Almost all my friends were dead before I even arrived in France. After Annie died, it was all I could do to keep Sam and myself afloat, even with Mum's help. I had to get away from Melbourne."

"Like I had to get away from England and Europe after Michael and Natalie died, so I escaped to the furthest place I could."

He reached for her hand. "I'm so sorry you had to."

She leaned against his shoulder. "I am too. But if I hadn't, you and I wouldn't be here today."

SIXTY-SEVEN

FAIR WINDS AND FOLLOWING SEAS
AUGUST 4, 1939, MARSEILLE

Their conversation continued in fits and starts as they made their way south through Provence. "Joe," Sophie began, on their last afternoon in France while they wandered the beach in Marseille. "We're intelligent and—"

"Why do I sense there's a 'but' coming?" he interjected, but his tone was mild.

"And I think you tried to manage everything with Annie the same way I tried to manage everything with Michael."

She waited for him to interrupt again. When he didn't, she continued.

"You and I have a different sort of relationship than we had in our first marriages, don't we? Can we go forward with that in mind? Could you be more forthcoming? Sooner rather than later, so I don't start to worry and wonder?"

She looked up at Joe, studying his face, looking for signs of tension or upset. She found neither. He looked so calm and contented when he nodded his agreement that she felt the weight of the world lifting from her shoulders. The sheer joy of it bubbled up and suffused her with a mad desire to sing or dance or do handstands on the sand.

Then she remembered she hadn't ever been able to do handstands, even with Ben's help when they were children, so she combed her fingers through Joe's wind-tousled hair and grinned at him instead. "Your nose and cheeks are pink!"

The fine lines at the corners of his eyes crinkled as he returned her grin. "It isn't surprising," he said, sliding his arms around her waist and pulling her close. "I've been in the sun while you were under that parasol."

"You'll turn brown and I'll just get more freckles," she reminded him.

"I like your freckles." He tucked a curl behind her ear and nudged her nose with his. "They're like flecks of gold dust on your skin."

"That was rather poetic. They're tolerable when you describe them like that." She snuggled around him and let out a contented sigh. "I'm hungry, but as much as I enjoy the sight of you in evening clothes, I'm not ready to run the gauntlet of formal dining. Are you?"

Joe pulled a face. "No, I'm not ready to run that gauntlet yet, either. Let's save it for our first night at sea tomorrow. C'mon," he said, "let's find somewhere to have dinner that isn't an ocean liner."

They climbed the steps that led up to the corniche and wandered until they found a little restaurant in the Vieux-Port, the old part of Marseille where all the fishing boats came in to sell their catch, and they ate their fill of *bouillabaisse*, bumping knees under a tiny table. She smirked at Joe, all covered up like a toddler with his napkin tucked into his shirt collar until a chunk of fish slipped off her spoon and splashed broth everywhere. She received an answering smirk from Joe when she tucked her own napkin into her blouse and tried again.

"Delicious but messy," she commented as they moved their

napkins back to their laps when they finished. "We can go back to looking like grown-ups now."

Joe tipped the last of the rosé into their wine glasses after the waiter removed their bowls and brushed all the baguette crumbs off the table.

Sophie reached across the table and threaded her fingers through Joe's. "I'll miss the friends we made, but I'll be happy to get back to our own house, our own bed, and our normal life."

"Well, as normal as it can be with your mother, Marianne, and my new position added to the mix." He studied their linked hands. "You lived in so many places before Sydney. Were you feeling a little restless when you planned our trip?"

"Maybe a little, darling, but our home is my favorite place in the world."

"Assuming we have fair winds and following seas, we'll be there in four weeks."

She raised her glass to her husband. "To going home," she said.

He nodded and touched his glass to hers. "And to going forward."

AFTERWORD

Almost every country in the world took part in the Great War, which came to be known as World War One. Australia, as part of the British Empire, was in the war as soon as Britain declared war on Germany. Over 250,000 young Australians volunteered and fought in Turkey, Egypt, Belgium, and France. Despite Gallipoli being better known, the battle of Fromelles, on July 19–20, 1916, caused the greatest loss of life in Australian military history. The remains of 250 Australian soldiers who were reported missing, presumed killed, after that battle were not found until 2008. They are now buried at Pheasant Wood Cemetery in France.

Joe's battalion was the 57th Australian Infantry Battalion, 15th Brigade, 5th Australian Division. Drawn from volunteers in suburban Melbourne in January 1916, the 57th was formed in Egypt in February 1916 to bolster the numbers of the Australian Imperial Force after the devastating losses at Gallipoli the previous year.

The United States remained neutral until April 1917. After the US entered the war, General John J. "Blackjack" Pershing allowed two divisions, the 27th from New York and the 30th from Indiana, to augment British troop numbers. The Australians helped to teach the Americans how to fight, and Australian General John Monash chose Le Hamel on July 4, 1918 as the first time Australians fought with their American counterparts. The battle lasted 93 minutes, and the Germans were defeated. Americans and Australians fought together again at Saint Quentin Canal in late September 1918. American casualties were high, but the Australians helped them pull through. The defeat of the Germans at the canal broke Germany's Hindenburg Line and marked the beginning of the end of the war.

German and Austrian mountain troops fought together in the Dolomite Mountains against Italian mountain troops. The Austrians bestowed their edelweiss insignia on the German mountain troops to honor their efforts in the 'War on Snow and Ice.'

Thousands of Americans volunteered as ambulance drivers, truck drivers, nurses, and pilots for the French long before the United States entered the war in April 1917. The American Field Service ran hundreds of ambulances to and from battles. The American Hospital in Paris became a military hospital in 1914 when its board of governors offered the facility and staff to the French government. The American Red Cross supplied many of the nurses who staffed the hospital. Other nurses, like Sophie, trained at the hospital.

French-Swiss artist Eugène Burnand, who completed 106 pastel portraits of Allied military, medical, and support personnel who served in WWI, was my inspiration for Sophie's neighbor in Paris. His goal was to record all the races and countries from around the world who served in the first global conflict. The portraits are on display at the Legion of Honor Museum in Paris.

Two American students from Harvard University and two Australian soldiers climbed Mont Blanc in September 1916; they were my inspiration for Edmund and Will. The two photographs that Sophie sees in the hotel's library can be seen on the Australian War Memorial's website. Just type Chamonix in the site's Search field.

Switzerland remained neutral throughout the war, and when its tourism industry came to a grinding halt, enterprising Swiss hoteliers offered the use of their establishments as rehabilitation hospitals to the French, British, and German armies.

WWI ended on November 11, 1918, after Germany called for an armistice to end four years of fighting.

Chamonix hosted the first Winter Olympic Games in 1924. Among the competitions was Mountain Patrol, a combination of cross-country skiing and rifle shooting. The French and Italian teams were my inspiration for Georges and Vanni.

The New South Wales Police force sent its eight-man rowing team to the 1936 Summer Olympic Games in Berlin. These games are famous for several reasons, not the least of which were African-American Jesse Owens winning gold in the 100-meter dash, which upended Hitler's contention that the Aryan race was superior to all others, and the American eights rowing team winning gold, defeating the highly favored German team, another embarrassment for Hitler. The 1936 Summer Games were also the first to feature the Olympic torch being carried into the Olympic stadium and lighting the flame that burned for the duration of the Games. This tradition has been continued in every Olympic Games ever since.

King George VI dedicated the Australian National Memorial at Villers-Bretonneux on July 23, 1938. The names of 10,773 soldiers of the Australian Imperial Force with no known grave who were killed between 1916 and the end of the war are carved on three high stone walls.

The Suresnes American Cemetery and Memorial outside of Paris is the resting place of 1,541 American civilians and soldiers who died during World War I and 24 unknown dead from World War II. Bronze tablets on the walls of the chapel record the names of 974 World War I missing. The cemetery was dedicated by US President Woodrow Wilson on Memorial Day, 1919 with additions dedicated in 1937. It is the only American military cemetery not located at a battlefield site.

World War II began when Germany invaded Poland on September 1, 1939, and Britain and France declared war on Germany two days later. By June 1940, less than one year after Sophie and Joe visited, the Germans had occupied Paris.

Italy and Japan were allies with Germany against Britain and France.

During World War II, Italian cyclist Gino Bartali, who won the 1938 Tour de France, secretly worked for the Italian Resistance, pretending to train for cycling competitions to glorify Italy and Mussolini when he was really working through the Catholic Church to deliver documents for Jews hidden in Italy.

When German-occupied Italy surrendered to the Allies in September 1943, Germany turned its sights to the French Alps.

The German garrison at Chamonix numbered about 360 soldiers, officials, and secret police. The Germans also occupied towns in and around the Chamonix valley, including Annecy and le Fayet.

The French Resistance, numbering 80 men from Chamonix, plus volunteer corps from every town, liberated the valley on August 17, 1944.

The Germans were still in the mountains, though. The Resistance set up machine gun positions on both sides of the *Mer de Glace* glacier. On October 2, 1944, the Mont Blanc Battalion, made up of resistance fighters and aspiring mountain guides, fought a bloody battle on the glacier against the German *Jaegers* (Mountain Soldiers) who were guided by Anderl Heckmair, the German mountaineer famous for the first ascent of the Eiger's North Face in July 1938.

Fighting continued in the French Alps until February 1945.

For the first two years of World War II, Australians fought in the Middle East and North Africa, leaving Australia only lightly defended against the Japanese forces making their way through southeast Asia. When the Japanese attacked the US Naval Base at Pearl Harbor, Hawaii, on December 7, 1941, the United States declared war and Australia and the United States, plus New Zealand, became fast and firm allies in the fight against Japan. US General Douglas MacArthur, Supreme Allied Commander in the Pacific theater, had his headquarters first in Melbourne and then in Brisbane, Australia. Hundreds of thousands of US service men and women passed through Australian and New Zealand cities, causing much the same disturbance to local life as they did in England: the Yanks were 'overpaid, oversexed, and over here'.

World War II affected Sophie and Joe in all the ways you might think, and some you might not expect, and Sam and Jean-Luc were in the thick of it, just as their parents feared they would be. But that's another story.

ACKNOWLEDGEMENTS

It's often said that writing is a solitary endeavor, and it is, but that doesn't take into account the sheer numbers of friends and family who patiently listened to me talking about writing, characters, locations, scenes, plot points, plot problems, and everything else I bent their ears about. If they think about it, they know who they are, but in case they've forgotten I'd like to remind them.

My husband, Gary, who for months wondered when I would actually finish, but gave me the time and space to read, research, and write, willingly accompanied me on a tour of the Somme battlefields even though WWI isn't his "thing", and who now suggests trips for WWII research.

My dearest friend in Australia, Lyn Raffan, who has been with me from the very start of this adventure, and who read early chapters, critiqued, suggested, and praised—*and*—copyedited Dare Not Tell. It's because of Lyn that every word and sentence in Dare Not Tell is as perfect as it can be.

My dearest friend in the US, Cass Hall, who has also been with me from the very start of this adventure, and who also read early chapters, critiqued, suggested, and praised. There are at least two phrases in Dare Not Tell that she told me never to lose, and I didn't because I love them too.

My mother, Beth Aucoin, an archaeologist, and published author in her own right, read two versions of the book and jumped at the chance to do the final proofread. Joe mistakenly ordering the *rognons* (kidneys) in Dare Not Tell is something that happened to her. How could I not work that into the story?

My late father, Pat Aucoin, a mathematician who rarely read fiction, provided me with perhaps the funniest feedback I'll ever receive: "This book made me hungry!"

My fellow authors Renée, Penny, Sarah, and Rae, who beta read and provided feedback, thank you for the gift of your time, which is especially precious because you're juggling your own writing, careers, and families.

My friends, Hilary, Nannie, Amy, and Ulla, whose time is equally precious, who beta read and provided feedback.

Friends, fellow authors, and family who weren't subjected to early beta reads, but who have been overwhelmingly supportive and enthusiastic—Pam, Anne, James, Doug, Ana-Maria, Sylvie, Sophie, Anita, Suzanne, Bruce, Irma, Jenny, Jeffrey, Jessica, Lise, Teri, Bijoux, Bill, Deborah, Diane, Carla, Caroline, Carolyn, Cehlena, Ella, Karen, Emily, and Alex.

Book coach Deb Lieberman, who guided me from a dreadful first draft to a much better second draft.

The two brilliant, creative women, Suzanne Minae and Jenny Quinlan, who made my interior formatting and cover dreams come true.

Finally, you, dear reader. Thank you for reading Dare Not Tell. It's my greatest hope that Sophie and Joe's journey of love and loss, and secrets and redemption, touched your heart because I wrote it from mine.

All my best to each and every one of you,

Elaine

P.S. If you enjoyed this book and you have a minute or two, I would be very grateful if you would review Dare Not Tell on Amazon. Reviews are a way to help other readers find this book. All it takes is a few minutes and a few words. Thank you!

ABOUT THE AUTHOR

I'm a long-time technical writer who devoured historical fiction and historical mysteries on nights and weekends as a way to escape from writing about computer software during the workday. Then, as the old joke goes, a miracle occurred, and I began wondering if I could write the same sorts of books I enjoy reading. The early answer was no, I couldn't. I had to learn how to write, plot, refine storylines, and dig more deeply than I thought possible into character psyches. Five years and innumerable drafts later, Dare Not Tell has been released into the world.

I grew up in Houston, Texas and southern California, and attended high schools in Algiers, Algeria, Northwood, England, Clear Lake City, Texas, Beirut, Lebanon, and Kingston-upon-Thames, England. For many years I've lived in Bellaire, Texas. My husband and I raised our son here. Now we have three rescue cocker spaniels underfoot and travel as often as we can convince our son to come and look after the dogs for us.

I'm writing the next chapter in Sophie and Joe's story; it's set in Australia and the South West Pacific Area during WWII. There may also be a story in the works about the Acadians who were expelled from Nova Scotia by the British in the mid-1700s. Or I may go back to WWI—Sophie and Joe brought that era to life for me and now it's deeply entrenched in my heart and mind.

Website: www.elaineschroller.com
Email: elaine@elaineschroller.com

Instagram: elaineschroller
Facebook: Elaine Aucoin Schroller
Pinterest: Elaine Schroller
Goodreads: Elaine Schroller

Printed in Great Britain
by Amazon